NOT QUITE FAKING IT

JUST AD LOVE SERIES

BOOK FOUR

AMY LARK

CHAPTER 1

"Do you even have eyes?" The loud and exasperated words carried through the bar.

Logan O'Connell smiled as his best friend, Claire, stood and threw a towel at the TV hanging over their bar table at Legend's. Typical Sunday night football.

"Hey," the bartender yelled to be heard over the crowd, "don't make me throw you out again."

"Come on, Brick. This ref is a complete putz." Claire morphed from angry football fan to sexpot as she smiled at the bartender. She lowered her voice and practically batted her eyelashes. She even gave him a little pout. "It wasn't a hot wing this time. Besides what harm is a towel going to do?"

Brick blushed, rubbing the back of his neck. "Just don't do it again."

Claire spun back to the table and picked up a buffalo wing with a smirk. This was why Logan had become best friends with Claire. She had so many different facets to her personality and knew when to use them to get any job done. She shook her wing at the offending preseason game.

"Are you fucking kidding me? Pass the fucking ball. For

fuck's sake. A blind guy could see Matthews was open. You're a fucking joke!" Claire's mouth was why they'd stayed friends.

She finally resumed her seat and ate her wing. After she downed half of her beer, a loud belch came from her beautiful mouth. She swiped her jersey sleeve across her lips and grinned at Logan.

Shaking his head, Logan relaxed against the back of his bar seat. A couple of guys at the bar turned to watch Claire. Their interest obvious. He couldn't blame them.

Claire was undeniably hot. Long, dark hair. Dark brown, almost black eyes. When she dressed to go out, she smoked all the other women in the club. Her body had curves in all the right places. Breasts that made men weep. Legs that made men stumble. Even at work, she wore high heels and pencil skirts to the detriment of any single, straight male trying to concentrate on work.

Claire Lake was completely and totally fuckable.

Normally.

But on game day, Claire might as well be a big, hulking dude. At least to Logan. Sure, she was still gorgeous with her dark hair pulled up into a ponytail. The jerseys she wore engulfed her whole body over jeans with questionable stains on them. Her game day jeans never got washed. Ever. Oh, she put them in the freezer so they wouldn't smell, but yeah. . . .

Her usual work heels, which gave her an additional three to five inches, were replaced by sneakers with grass stains on them. And the sophisticated city woman turned into a foul-mouthed, boozing, loud, practically abusive fan with no fucks to give. Her makeup vanished to be replaced with face paint. Not a lot, but she had a thing for a player with the number twenty-four and always painted his number on her cheek.

Granted, she still attracted attention, but her sports

personality helped to keep Logan firmly in the friend zone. After all, he didn't want her to become one of the women that he fucked and forgot. They hung out, talked about sports, and if seeing her belch helped cool any wayward attraction, all the better.

The TV cut to commercial, and Claire resumed her seat, filling her plate from the multiple dishes of essential game day foods. All greasy appetizers that Work Claire would turn her nose up at.

They'd met at work and he totally would have tapped that, but they morphed quickly into the friend zone. He didn't usually have women as friends, but Claire wasn't a normal chick and they got along great. She had everything: sex appeal which made her an excellent wing-woman, confidence, a love of sports. And she was completely off limits except as a friend.

"They're playing stupid today." She held out a wing and used it as a speaking aid. "I swear if they don't start shaping up, I'm trading half my roster in fantasy football. That would show them."

"Yeah, right, like they care if they're on your team." Logan tipped back and checked out the chick who had been giving him the eye all night. Sitting with a group of friends, she was pretty, young, built like a fucking brick house, and had legs for days. Blonde, blue-eyed with a cute smile, she gave this little finger wave when she noticed him checking her out.

"Are you done eye fucking that chick yet?" Claire's eyebrow raised as she smirked at him.

Rule number one of game day, no hookups, which meant the hottie at the bar would have to wait for another time.

Claire took a bite of wing and at least covered her full mouth when she said, "What happened to Kelly? Weren't you still hooking up with her last week?"

Logan sucked in a breath. "Fuck, no. I shut that down. I'm

lucky she hasn't shown up here yet. She shows up everywhere else I go these days. Biggest cockblock of my life."

Sure, Kelly gave excellent head and had the flexibility of a Yoga master, but something had been a little off about her. Logan hadn't picked up on it until he'd already had his dick in her a few times. Now, she was practically stalking him, especially since he stopped answering her texts.

Claire snickered. "You so deserve that one."

"I admit I should have recognized the crazy, but man, she's crazy good in bed." Logan drank some of his beer. Her crazy was a problem because she had started to think they were more than fuck buddies.

"You should probably stop texting her 'u up' every night you're alone."

"You know how it is." Logan smiled at her. "When you find talent like that, you just figure one more time won't hurt."

"Until she's standing over your bed holding a knife." Claire's laugh filled the whole bar. "I don't think any dick could make me that fucking dumb."

Claire had him pegged. Not that she was innocent in the game. She had a few fuck boys on speed dial. She was probably right. He hadn't called Kelly since last weekend, so hopefully she was over whatever spell he'd cast on her.

"What about that built guy you left the club with on Saturday?"

Claire chuckled. "He was a dumbass and on the small side." Frowning dramatically, she held up her pinkie finger.

Logan laughed. "Did he at least know how to use it?"

She leaned forward across the table and gestured for him to join her for secret time. He leaned in. His eyes dropped to her cleavage revealed by the V-neck of her jersey, and he swallowed hard.

"You know that one move that makes a woman's toes

curl?" She glanced over her shoulder like she was worried someone might overhear, but most likely she was fucking with him.

"Which one?" He gave her a cocky grin.

Claire's phone rang right as the game came back on. "Fuck. It's my mom."

They both sat up straight.

She sucked the wing sauce off her fingers before using a napkin to wipe them off. Even as dude-like as Claire could get on game day, she still oozed a sexuality Logan wasn't immune to. She was still unintentionally sexy and he wasn't blind. And when she did shit like that, his traitorous body reacted. He shifted in his seat to get more comfortable and looked up at the screen to focus on the game and not on Claire's pouty lips.

Claire had it all, and if thinking she was a dude on game days helped him not fuck up their friendship that was what he'd do. After all, she was his best friend.

"Hi, Mom," Claire said into her phone after fumbling to answer it.

Logan leaned forward across the bar table and yelled, "Hi, Mom."

"Oh, are you on a date with Logan, sweetie? Tell him I said hi." Her mother's voice was saccharin when it came to Logan O'Connell. Yup, Claire had let her mother believe Logan and her were an item and not just besties on the prowl together.

It kept her mother from sending her pics of her best friend's sister's boyfriend's brother. Besides, the harmless lie made her mother happy.

Claire met Logan's dark eyes. "Mom says hi."

Logan didn't know about her lie though. He puckered up his full lips and smacked them like he gave her mother a kiss. Then he winked at Claire. Insatiable flirt.

"Logan sends his love," Claire told her mother, rolling her eyes.

"I'm so happy you two are still together. Betty was saying girls your age couldn't afford to be picky, but I told her to wait until she sees the hunk you've got on the line."

First off, her age? Really? She was twenty-six not forty-six.

Second off, Logan would be a catch. On paper, her mom would think he's perfect. He was fun, confident, into sports. If he were actually available, but he never would be, no matter what he said. He went through women like they were a disposable commodity, and they flocked to him like pigeons to spilled popcorn in the park.

She couldn't blame the women for being dumb when it came to Logan. He kept his dark hair shaved short in a crew cut like dark velvet. It was so black it tinted blue in some lights. His eyes drew girls with their almost dark honey shade of brown. She'd actually heard one girl claim they made him look sensitive. Claire had barely managed not to laugh out loud at that particular comment. Honestly, he had the face of a fucking model, which got him a lot of play when they went out. And even when he shaved in the morning, he always had some dark scruff on his defined jawline, which just led to dirty thoughts.

He kept claiming O'Connells were built for relationships, but he'd never been in one she knew of. And didn't seem to want to settle down anytime soon. He was still enjoying his "bachelor" years. Not that she wanted to settle down either.

"Yeah, sure, Mom." Claire only half listened to her mother going on about what Betty Miller, her mother's best friend from their lake house, said. The bar got a little rowdier and she turned back to watch the game. Their team was down seven to ten and lining up to kick a field goal.

"Labor Day weekend is coming up and I told everyone you would bring your boyfriend so they didn't need to worry about bringing guys for you. You two have been together long enough for him to meet your family and not go running."

The kicker lined up the shot. As soon as the ball was snapped to the holder, the defensive line broke through, heading straight for the kicker. Her chest pounded as a big-ass lineman raced toward the kicker. *Kick the fucking ball.*

"He will be able to come, right?" Her mother's voice was in one ear while she focused on the game. "Or if he's not ready to commit, I have a nice young man who came to fix the toilet yesterday. I'm sure you two would get along famously. He's really sweet and looking for a gal. He seems really settled. Has his own business."

The kicker got to the ball. It flew over the lineman's head through the posts to even up the score. The whole bar went crazy around Claire. Logan held up his hand and Claire gave him a high five.

"Do you remember Alan Thomson from school? Betty's son Matthew's best friend. Betty said he would be joining them up at their lake cabin, so if Logan can't make it, you could always hang out with Alan. He's a doctor now. His long-term girlfriend just broke his heart. Called it quits when he was practically days from proposing. Poor guy. Betty said he's just now ready to date again."

"Alan who?" Shit. She should really pay attention to her mother. She covered her other ear to block out the noises of the bar.

"Thomson, from school. I think he's a couple years older than you. But I told Betty you and Logan are inseparable and there might be wedding bells in the future."

A burning sensation filled Claire's chest. Married? Yeah, no. She'd have to fake breakup with Logan so her mother didn't start sending bridal magazines. Her gaze flicked over to Logan whose eyes were back on the blonde at the girly girl table. Claire almost laughed but knew her mother wouldn't understand. Logan wasn't looking to settle down anymore than she was. "I don't think we're quite to that point yet, Mom."

Like he knew her eyes were on him, Logan turned to her, raised an eyebrow and mouthed, *what?* Claire shook her head. Like she could explain the machinations of her mother to Logan while on the phone with her mother.

"Oh, then maybe you shouldn't bring Logan and give Alan a chance. Did you hear me say he's a doctor? He's probably ready to stop playing the field since he's older. He'd be married if that girl hadn't stomped on his poor heart. I mean, how long have you and Logan been going out? It seems like forever, and if he's not ready to settle down, maybe you should be looking at greener pastures."

Three months. Her fake relationship should have lasted longer before her mother pushed them to move to the next step or move on. She and Logan had been friends, though, for over a year, so maybe Mom included that. Claire took a deep breath and counted backwards from ten. *Focus.* She needed her mom off the topic of guys and setting her up. "Labor Day weekend at the cabin?"

"Yes, sweetie. Bring that hunky boyfriend Logan with you, or don't and we'll make sure you have someone to snuggle with by the fire." Her mother was so flippant sometimes, but also so very persistent.

Claire squeezed her eyes shut and rubbed at her temple. "Don't worry. I'll convince my boyfriend to come with me."

"All right, sweetie, let me know when your flight gets in." The line clicked off.

Claire put her phone down and opened her eyes to see Logan staring at her with a quizzical brow.

"Boyfriend?" He smirked when he said the word. "When did you get a boyfriend? Is it little Willy?"

He held up his pinkie finger and raised an eyebrow. Then he picked up a wing and ate it as she collected herself. She glanced at the TV screen and saw it had gone to commercial again.

"You're going to think I'm crazy." She rubbed her forehead and met his eyes.

"Probably." Logan shrugged and grinned.

At least he was easygoing. He'd probably just laugh and say sure why not. It was just a weekend after all. Long weekends they usually spent clubbing and getting laid, but they could still have fun at her family's lake cabin. The other option was to go alone and have her mom thrusting the plumber and poor Alan Thomson her way. If only it were that simple.

She took a deep breath. "We're friends, right?"

"The best." Logan gave her a questioning smile.

She tried to give him her most winning return smile, but she knew it had cracks around it. "I have to go home for Labor Day weekend. My family owns a cabin at this lake, and we all get together to celebrate the holiday with our neighbors. I haven't gone in the past few years, but my mom wants me to come this year."

"Okay, but when did you get a boyfriend?"

"I'm getting to that part." She held up her hand. "My mom is constantly nagging me to date, but you and I both know neither of us are really built for long-term dating."

Well, at least not with the guys she went out with. Sure, she wouldn't mind someone steady, but the guys who were confident enough to handle her when she dressed up usually balked when they saw her on game days when she dressed down. She'd given up on finding a guy who would accept all of her. Besides, she could compromise in a few years. She wasn't in a hurry.

Logan nodded, still paying attention.

"When she calls, you and I have been together. So when she thought you and I were *together* together, I didn't disabuse her of it." Claire flinched and bit her lip.

"Your mom thinks we're a couple?" His hand waved back and forth between him and Claire.

Claire nodded.

Logan looked thoughtful. "So I'm your boyfriend?"

"Yeah, mom is expecting me to bring you on Labor Day weekend to the cabin." Claire shrugged.

"How long have we been dating?" Logan got a twinkle in his eyes and rested his elbow on the bar table and propped his chin on his hand. He had on that player look he got when he spotted a woman he wanted to get with. Not because he actually wanted to get with Claire, but because he was messing with her because of this stupid situation. That ship had sailed long ago. They never actually tried being anything more than friends to each other. They fell into the friend zone quickly, because neither of them would be good for the other. Too much of a good thing. They never discussed it, but instead slipped easily into being friends.

Claire pressed her fingers against her temples. "About three months."

"That's a pretty long time to be dating." Logan tapped a finger against his lips. "I assume we're exclusive and neither of us cheats on the other?"

"Look, I'm not proud of lying to my mom, but you have to understand how persistent she can be." Claire straightened. "On that phone call, she mentioned two eligible guys she wants me to meet but has called off the neighbors from finding more since I'm supposed to bring you."

"We must not be that serious if she wants to set you up with other guys." Logan smirked and his tone was teasing.

"You don't understand the lengths my mom will go to. There have been. . . incidents." Claire looked away. Anytime she was home, her mother always had something brewing. "Last Christmas she set up mistletoe traps everywhere." She cringed, remembering the one above the bathroom door. "She always made sure she introduced me to a guy right under one and insisted we keep up the kissing tradition."

"That's not so bad."

"Two Thanksgivings ago, she trapped me in the bathroom with Patrick Roberts for forty-five minutes, saying the doorknob fell off." Once Claire told Patrick she wasn't interested, he had spent the entire time reading on his phone.

"How did she manage to get you both in the bathroom?" Logan leaned forward.

"Witchcraft? I don't know, but she's one tricky woman."

Logan chuckled.

"You think it's funny, but she has a single doctor to throw at me this time. I wouldn't be surprised if she figured out a way to lock us naked somewhere together with a bucket full of condoms." Claire tightened her ponytail and blew out a breath. She met Logan's eyes, hoping he could read the pleading in hers. "What do you say? Pretend to be my boyfriend for Labor Day weekend and I'll owe you."

Logan tipped back and his eyes drifted to the blonde at the bar again. "I don't know. It's a long weekend where I'd have to be on my best behavior. I'd miss out on prime hookup days. So what's in it for me?"

She should have seen this coming. The thing was she didn't have a lot to offer him. A vacation where he wouldn't be able to get any action over a weekend when he normally had a rotating door of all the chicks he drew in. She'd have to figure out what offer could be enticing enough to make him come with her.

Logan popped the last bite of his mozzarella stick into his mouth and continued to watch her. She didn't think the friend card would work this time. The only thing guaranteed to get his full attention was sex. That wouldn't be happening, so she needed to come up with an alternative and quick.

CHAPTER 2

By Tuesday morning, Claire still hadn't figured out what she could give Logan to make him accompany her. A favor to be named later hadn't received much enthusiasm. She tried offering simple things like cleaning his apartment or picking up the bar tab for a while, but it hadn't worked. She had football season tickets, but she definitely wasn't willing to give those up. They were like gold for dates.

Guys either liked that she was into sports or they were intimidated by her when she knew more than them. Finding a happy balance between being wanted sexually and being wanted for who she was had always been an issue. But most guys liked to go to a game and she could control her normal exuberance at games to get laid if she wanted to.

Lacy walked into the break room and grabbed a coffee mug. Lacy was sweet and cute and until last year, she'd crushed on Logan hardcore. As she filled her mug, she asked, "How are you this morning?"

"Peachy." Claire forced a smile. She'd been sitting at the break room table alone, trying to figure out what would tempt Logan. A hot girl would tempt him, but that kind of defeated the purpose of him coming with her and pretending to be her boyfriend. She didn't think her mom would believe they were a thruple.

Besides, finding a woman who could hold Logan's interest for a long weekend would be difficult enough. She, at least, kind of dated the guys she slept with, sometimes.

Jonah came in and wrapped his arms around Lacy, pulling her back into his front for a hug. Lacy rested against Jonah as she sipped her coffee. He rested his chin on her head. His eyes landed on Claire. "Hey, Claire."

Claire lifted her hand and tipped her lips into what she hoped was a convincing smile. It seemed like the whole office had coupled up over the past year. Morgan and Drew had been a couple when they started the business. They hired Jonah, and he and Lacy got together. Then Aiden started and he and Phoebe got together. On more than one occasion Logan and Claire had been paired off at happy hours or a charity thing once, but not as lovers, just friends.

She didn't mind. She and Logan hung out a lot. He was fun and they had a good time together. A bit of a manwhore who tended to ditch her when a cute skirt caught his eyes, but a great wingman at bars. They worked well together, but they were definitely friends.

Maybe she should be looking for more. More than just sex for a few nights. Maybe a date or two. Maybe she should be looking for something like what Jonah and Lacy had. It wasn't like Claire had completely given up on finding a true boyfriend, but her prospects weren't really good long-term choices. She'd meet a guy. They'd date. Sleep together. And as soon as she thought they might be something, she'd drop her guard and let them see all of her.

Or as Logan called it, Game Day Claire. But fuck, if a guy couldn't handle her being herself, she didn't want him. Being a sports fan was a major part of who she was. Okay, maybe it was a little more than a sports fan. Her whole family had gotten into game days, growing up. Her dad, her older brother, younger brother, and she went to the games or watched them in the living room while Mom brought out snack after snack.

Unfortunately the guys who were confident enough to ask her out didn't want a buddy on game day. They wanted a sexy date to show off to their pals. And guys who liked Game Day Claire wanted her to tone down her club wardrobe and hide that part of her.

It was definitely a lose-lose situation. Which was why Claire was happy to just play the field with Logan at her side. If she didn't invest any time in a guy, he wouldn't let her down.

Jonah pressed his lips to Lacy's hair and she gave a little content sigh. Maybe it might be worth toning down for something like Jonah and Lacy had. But what guy would be worth that effort?

Logan walked in and gave an exasperated sigh. "Is this really going to be an every morning thing? We should have a cuddle-free workplace. Besides, it feels like you're rubbing salt on the wound."

Logan pressed his hand over his heart dramatically. Lacy chuckled and turned a little red.

"We've been over this before." Claire rolled her eyes and drank some of her coffee. "You were only interested in her because she was unavailable."

It wasn't like Logan slowed down because he liked Lacy for a hot minute. He still went home with whatever chick struck his fancy for the night. And never promised monogamy.

"For Lace, I would have given up all other women," Logan declared.

Claire laughed and Logan sent her a grin.

Jonah chuckled and tightened his arms around Lacy. She tipped her head back on his shoulder to look up at him. Even Claire could see the love in their eyes as they looked at each other.

"You didn't stand a chance." Jonah shrugged. "Maybe if you'd pulled your head out of your ass before I got here."

Logan just shook his head. "Nah, once you entered the picture, any crush Lacy had on me was gone."

"On that note," Lacy said, extracting herself from Jonah's arms, "I'm getting back to work."

Lacy headed out into the office with Jonah following.

"That could have been me," Logan said, fake wistfully.

Claire smirked. "You would have either dropped her by now or cheated on her."

Logan held up his finger. "I'll have you know I've never cheated on anyone in my life. I've also never officially dated anyone, but semantics. I'm straightforward with everyone I get with. And if I'm ever committed to a woman—" he paused to shudder as if the thought alone freaked him out— "then she'll be all I need."

Claire rolled her eyes. She'd been privy to his talk on more than one occasion. He didn't settle for one woman ever. How dumb did a girl have to be to fall for his "I'm just not ready to settle down" line? He must have some moves because they always came back for seconds. She shook her head and drank her coffee.

"We've got the Noble Brewers account to work on." Logan poured himself some coffee and gestured with his head toward the door. "How about we actually do some work today?"

Claire stood, ran her hands over her skirt and lifted her head to follow Logan. His gaze lingered on her legs. She glanced down, looking to see if something had splattered on her. "Do I have something on my legs?"

Logan cleared his throat. "Nope."

Her eyebrows drew together, but she followed him out into the office. Still checking her legs for whatever he saw.

Emily cleared her throat loudly from reception.

Logan turned and Claire followed his line of sight to crazy Kelly sitting in the waiting area. She flipped through a magazine while her crossed leg swung.

Claire moved closer to Logan and whispered, "Were you expecting her?"

"No. Fuck." Logan blew out a breath. He turned his body into Claire's. He held up one finger to Emily.

Emily nodded. Logan grabbed Claire's arm and tugged her back into the break room.

"Did you call her last night?" Claire asked as soon as the door closed. She barely kept the smirk off her lips. The number of women Logan ghosted was astronomical, but to have his booty call show up at work. . . . That shit was hilarious.

"No, but she texted me last night." Logan ran a hand over his hair. "I didn't answer her though."

"Just tell her you aren't into her." Claire leaned back on the counter and set her coffee mug down.

"I have." Logan looked at the floor before lifting his eyes to her, a devious glint in them. "You gotta help me."

She let out a bark of a laugh. "What am I supposed to do?"

"You want me to go to your cabin and act like your boyfriend?" He gestured at the door. "Go out there and act like my girlfriend and I'll do it."

Claire didn't waste anytime thinking it over. She needed him there to ward off her mother's matchmaking attempts.

"Deal." Claire held out her hand. That was easier than she thought it would be. One crazy stalker and she had Logan's undivided attention for a weekend. They shook on it. She poked her finger into his chest. "I'll book the tickets. We leave Friday. No backing out."

"Fine." Logan took a deep breath. "Okay, how are we going to play this?"

Claire grinned and rubbed her hands together. "Watch the master at work."

Leaving the break room with Logan hot on her heels, she made her way to the front. Kelly straightened and looked at her and then smiled at Logan.

"Hey, baby," she purred as she stood.

"Excuse me?" Claire stepped into Kelly's space. She had a few inches on Kelly. "What did you just call my man?"

"*Your* man?" Kelly glanced uneasily at Logan. "But we. . . ."

"You what? You fucked him? You think that makes you special?" Claire crossed her arms over her chest and continued to glare at Kelly. "You and about fifty other women, but you know what? When he's done slumming it, he comes home to me. So unless you want a restraining order against you or if you want to take this outside—"

Claire reached for her earrings like she was going to take them off to get ready for a fight. Pretty sure Kelly wasn't that crazy though, but Claire could hold her own. Growing up with two brothers would do that to a gal. Of course, she didn't want to ruin her outfit.

"No." Kelly backed away a step and held her hands up. "I didn't—he didn't—I'm sorry."

Claire almost felt sorry for the chick. After all, she just wanted something like Jonah and Lacy had. Too bad she tried to find it with Logan. Wrong dude, my chick.

Kelly glanced at Logan. A little bit of fire lingered in her eyes. "You shouldn't cheat. It only hurts everyone involved. Lose my number."

She took a deep breath and met Claire's eyes. "I really am

sorry. I didn't know or I wouldn't have— You deserve better. You know?"

Claire smiled softly. "What can I say? I'm possessive when it comes to Logan."

Logan stepped behind Claire and rested his chin on her shoulder. It was easy for him when she wore heels. His hands hovered above her hips. It looked like he was touching her, though he really wasn't, but she could feel his heat surrounding her. She didn't hate the feeling.

"I'll do better, Claire Bear." Logan kissed her shoulder though her blouse.

Claire Bear? She almost gave him a what-the-fuck expression. Kelly's lips tightened and she shot him a fierce look before she turned and left the office. The elevator doors opened and she disappeared.

"Definitely block her number." Claire stepped forward away from Logan and turned to face him.

Logan swept her into a hug. "You were amazing."

Emily's mouth had hung open during that whole exchange.

Claire could feel her cheeks warming as Logan didn't let her go. His whole body pressed against hers. His warmth felt a little too nice. But this wasn't how they were friends. "Okay, that's enough, Logan."

He released her and stepped back with a grin. "I should use you to get rid of all the clingers."

Claire scoffed and turned to Emily. "Sorry for the theatrics. Apparently, Logan sucks at setting boundaries for women."

Emily looked down to hide her smile and then back at both of them. "You guys make a pretty convincing couple."

"Which reminds me" —Claire tapped his shoulder— "I have some plane tickets to buy."

~

"CLAIRE, I know enough about you to fake being your boyfriend." Logan held up the sheet of paper Claire had given him after they boarded the plane. A list of all things Claire. It was almost insulting to him. "I've spent more time with you than anyone else this past year."

"Just because we're friends, doesn't mean we know everything about each other." Claire shook her head and tapped the paper. "Do you even know what side of the bed I sleep on?"

"Ha, that's a trick question." Logan smiled, because he knew he was right. He had this one down. "You sleep on the side farthest from the door. And you rarely let anyone actually sleep with you, so you generally just take the middle of the bed."

Claire's mouth dropped open.

"Drunk Claire likes to talk when I drop her off." Logan tapped her nose with his index finger. "I've also had to help Drunk Claire into bed a couple of times."

Claire's cheeks deepened to a dark pink. "We just need to make sure we aren't telling people different stories."

"As long as we stay as close to the truth as possible that shouldn't be an issue." Logan leaned back in his chair. As the flight attendant went by, his gaze dropped to her ass. She had this wiggle in her walk.

"That's going to be an issue," Claire muttered.

"What?" Logan smirked. "Just because we hitched up doesn't mean I don't still have eyes."

"My mom notices everything. If she thinks I'm 'losing' you, she'll push guys on me. Defeating the entire purpose of you coming along." Claire rolled her eyes. "You need to be hopelessly devoted to only me or this won't work. If we get away with this, I can probably get a reprieve over the holidays when you break my heart."

"Aw, Claire Bear, I would never break your heart."

Claire gave him a glare that would shrivel a lesser man. "No, on the nickname."

"But, Claire Bea—"

Her hand slammed over his mouth and she lowered her head a little like a fierce bull. "No."

He smiled and licked her hand.

"Ew." She wiped her hand on her jeans.

"I like it when you get feisty. Add that to the notes." He gestured to the sheet of paper he'd given back to her. "Feisty Claire, two enthusiastic thumbs up."

"Fine, we'll keep it simple. We met at the office. Started hanging out together and then started a relationship—"

"Does that mean we have sex?" Logan raised his eyebrows, but the last portion of the question he almost whispered like it was too naughty to be said out loud. Claire seemed wound so tight about this whole thing. The truth was they were hot enough to convince pretty much anyone they were dating.

Claire didn't talk about her family much, but it shouldn't be difficult to convince them.

Claire's eyebrows came together in the middle. She sounded disgruntled when she said, "I suppose."

Logan shook his head slowly, trying not to smile. "I don't think I can fake that. We could join the mile high club."

"Really?" Her lips pressed into a thin line as she glared at him.

"I mean how do I know if you're a noisy lover or quiet? What about positions? Are there things you won't do? Are there things you will do that I haven't asked about? Was I the first for anything or has everything been done before—"

Her hand covered his mouth again. "One, we will not be

discussing our sex life with my mother. Two, definitely not that detailed. Three, if I hear one peep out of you about it to anyone, I will personally throttle you and give you the worse purple nurple of your life."

Logan lifted his hands to cover his nipples. "Geez, just kidding. No need to get violent. I never figured you for a kinky one."

"Just remember I grew up with brothers. I know how to hit you to hurt, but not hard enough to show Mom what I did." Her dark eyebrow lifted and the slightly evil glint in her eyes actually turned him on a little.

"Okay, okay. So you're a little kinky. Back off, She-Ra." Logan gave her an easy smile. "What about PDA?"

"What about it?" Claire took a deep breath and stared straight ahead.

Logan slipped his hand over hers. She snatched her hand away and held it close to her chest. He laughed.

"What are you doing?" Claire's eyes were wide.

"Yeah, a piece of paper is going to make us convincing." Logan rolled his eyes. "I've touched your hand before, Claire. Even held it at clubs."

"But I was always expecting it." She frowned and wouldn't meet his eyes.

"If we want to be convincing, we need to touch each other as though we always touch each other." Logan rubbed the back of his neck. They had perfectly good role models for the type of expected behavior. "You've seen the others around the office. Just those hints of intimacy. Morgan leans into Drew when they sit close. If Lacy is around, Jonah touches her hand or pulls her into him. Even Phoebe and Aiden have little things that show how much they just want to touch each other."

Claire lifted her worried gaze to his. "Fuck, you're right."

"So where do we stand on PDA?" Logan gave her a smile

and held his hand out on the armrest. His fingers spread wide and he flexed them. "Holding hands? Pancake or waffle?"

She narrowed her eyes at his hand before lifting her gaze back to his. She slid her hand into his.

Her hand was warm and smaller than his but as soon as their fingers interlocked it felt right. His chest thumped funny, but he ignored it.

"Waffle, it is." He smiled. "Relax. We'll hold hands and I'll probably hold you some. Nothing X-rated. Don't worry. I'll keep it strictly PG."

She smirked. "As long as we don't go for an R-rating, we'll be fine."

"PG-13. Brief nudity. Cool." Logan wiggled his eyebrows at her, trying to ease the worry creasing her brow. "We should be able to convince them without kissing. Unless you're okay with kissing?"

Claire didn't drop her gaze, but she gave a slight shake of her head. "No kissing. I don't think I ever saw my parents kiss, so we don't have to be *that* couple."

Logan dropped his gaze to her full lips. He wouldn't mind kissing Claire. He'd imagined more than kissing her in the past. Not that he would tell her that. Fuck, she'd probably castrate him if she knew some of the things he'd imagined and what he'd done while imagining those things. What could he do? He was a guy and she was fucking hot. She was the whole package.

Logan settled into his chair and closed his eyes. "Great. Now that's settled. Quiz me on your people."

"Honestly, everyone will be lenient about you knowing names." Claire's voice sounded light and breezy. "The only person we'll have to worry about is my brother, Sean. He isn't supposed to be there, but he could always tell exactly what I was thinking and he knows when I'm lying. If anyone questions us being together, it would be Sean. But only if it gets Mom off his back."

"But he's not going to be there?" He tipped his head her way and opened his eyes. His fingers tightened around hers, trying to reassure her.

She bit her lip and shook her head. "Nah, he's too busy."

He nodded and then smirked.

"I know about the flower tattoo on your left butt cheek, but any other tattoos or birthmarks I should know about?" Logan raised his eyebrow and let his gaze drift over her. He'd never seen her in a swimsuit and she'd told him to bring a couple. That might make this trip worthwhile.

Claire glared at him. "How'd you know about the tattoo?"

He held up his hands, afraid she'd hit him. "Drunk Claire doesn't really consider her skirt when she falls onto the bed. I already know you like thongs too."

He smirked and she narrowed her eyes. Then she laughed and the tightness in his chest loosened.

"I don't think my mom even knows about my tattoo."

"See, we'll be perfect."

CHAPTER 3

"SEAN!?" Claire gave Logan a panicked look as she hugged her brother. *Oh shit. Oh shit. Oh shit.*

"Isn't it exciting?" Her mother clapped her hands together. "All my kids in one place for a whole weekend."

Claire stepped away from Sean and ran into Logan. Before she could scoot away, he caught her shoulders and didn't drop his hands. Holding her upper arms, he pulled her back into his heat. She only resisted for a split second before relaxing into him. Sean and Logan shook hands with her in between them.

"This must be Logan." Her mother held out her arms and wiggled her fingers at him to come get a hug. "Get over here, you hunk."

Claire turned to gauge Logan's reaction. Logan raised an eyebrow at Claire, but she just shrugged. That was her mom. Logan went in for the hug. Claire rubbed her arm, suddenly a little cold.

"If I were twenty years younger. . . ." Her mother rested her head against Logan's chest and wrapped her arms around his waist. "What's it called when an older woman goes for a younger man? A puma?"

"A cougar, Mom. And back off. This one's mine. Find your own." Claire shook her head.

Sean leaned against the stair railing. His dark hair had grown longer and his dark eyes that matched her own didn't miss a thing as they swept over Logan and their mother. Fortunately, Claire could cover any awkwardness by claiming to be nervous about Logan meeting the family for the first time. She'd never brought guys home.

Mom pulled away and held Logan at arm's length. "My, you're a good looking one. You can call me Grace or Mom, whichever suits you. I'll answer to either."

But she didn't let him go. Her gaze went over all of him to the point even Claire was uncomfortable.

"Thank you, Grace." Logan looked like he wanted to run out the door back to the car they'd hired to drive them from the airport.

Claire stepped in and pried her mother's hands from feeling up Logan's arms. She slid her hand into Logan's. "Where should we put our bags?"

Mom's face lit up. "I had to do some last minute shuffling with Sean coming, but I was surprised I didn't think of it before."

She headed up the stairs, and they followed, each carrying their own bag. Stopping at a door, Mom pushed it open. "Here you go. I'm not naïve enough to think the two of you don't already sleep together, so I figured you wouldn't mind sharing a room."

Stepping into the room, Claire could feel the heat on her cheeks as she stared at the queen size bed that took up the majority of the floor space in the room. Logan wasn't a small man. The bed would fit them, but she couldn't guarantee they wouldn't touch during the night, which a king size would have prevented. And there wasn't room for anyone to sleep on the floor. A door led to an attached bathroom, so at least they would have a little privacy. The rooms down the hall shared a bathroom.

"I made sure to stock the rooms." Mom's voice went a little higher than normal and Claire turned to narrow her eyes at her. Her mom was full on blushing and gesturing. "The essentials are in the drawer in case you forgot anything. I might have had a little too much fun shopping, but I figured what the hell. You only live once, right?"

Claire was almost scared to see what her mother deemed "essentials." *Please just be extra toothbrushes.*

"I'll leave you two to settle in." Mom grinned and looked over Logan again. When she returned her gaze to Claire, she winked and said, "The walls aren't shared so you two will have complete privacy."

She tugged the door closed and her footsteps moved away.

"Could my mom be more embarrassing?" Claire sat on the edge of the bed.

Logan landed on the bed next to her. "Didn't know we'd be sharing a bed, Claire Bear."

She turned to glare at him. "Neither did I, Wolverine."

He hated that nickname, but he didn't seem fazed as he smiled at her. "Shall we see what treats your mom left in the drawer?"

She didn't bother to look as he opened the drawer.

"It's probably toothpaste and soap. Maybe cologne."

The soft purr of a vibrator made Claire's eyes pop out of her head as she swung her gaze to Logan's laughing figure. He tossed the penis-shaped vibrator at her. "Cologne, sure. Man, your mom did have fun."

He started emptying the drawer onto the bed. Condoms, an assortment of lubes and body lotions/oils, some silk ties, and a pair of fuzzy handcuffs. Claire couldn't seem to close her mouth. What the hell was her mother thinking?

"I think someone wants someone to get laid." Logan brought his laughing eyes up to hers.

"She'd be seriously disappointed to learn we won't be needing any of these." Claire shook her head and shoved the pile back toward Logan. "Put it all back."

He held up the vibrator. "You want to put this in the shower? Sleeping next to me all night will likely give you a lady boner. Wouldn't want all this to go to waste."

"I doubt you'll give me a lady boner." She pushed at his hand holding the vibrator.

He shrugged and smirked. "It's here in the essential drawer when you need it."

He held up a handful of condoms and stuffed them in his pocket. He winked at her. "So your mom will think we've been busy."

"I wouldn't use those. Mom wants grandkids."

"The box was sealed. I think we'll be safe." Logan took out one of the packages and inspected it. He held it up to the light. "Let's at least give the woman some hope."

Claire rolled her eyes. "My mom doesn't need any help thinking we're up to something."

"By the way, I don't wear pajamas." Logan stood and shut the drawer. "I generally sleep nude."

"Me too." She gave him a flirtatious wink as she stood and stretched.

His eyes darkened for a moment and she laughed.

"You're such a perv. I brought pajamas and you'll be good in a pair of boxers. Don't try to tell me you didn't bring any. I won't believe you." Claire shook her head at him.

"Fine." He raised an eyebrow and swept his hand down his front. "I don't know how you're going to resist all this though."

"Geez, I don't know. Maybe I'll just remember your personality." She stuck her tongue out at him. "I'm going to use the bathroom and then we can head down. We usually have a cookout the first night."

"Will have to check out the local candy." Logan smirked.

She hit his arm and he let out an *ow*. "No checking out anyone, but me. Especially around Sean."

"Fine, but don't be surprised if you can't handle all of my attention." He gave her a look she knew probably made women's panties burst into flames.

"Don't hold your breath."

LOGAN HELD Claire's hand as they made their way down the wood stairs. Since that first time, she'd been a lot more relaxed about him touching her. He didn't know why he'd slipped a condom into his pocket. The handful had been a joke for Claire. Who had given him the appropriate eye roll. He left the rest on the nightstand.

It wasn't like he'd be needing a condom this whole weekend. He'd keep his dick in his pants for her. Especially with her older brother around.

The "cabin" was a two-story house. The décor definitely screamed vacation home with little kitschy phrases on wooden boards and knick-knacks on every surface. But it was comfortable and had a lived-in feel to it.

As they started across the kitchen, the buzz of voices got louder. Logan tugged Claire to a halt and leaned down to her ear.

"Exactly how big is your family?"

Her hand pressed on his chest. He lifted his head to look into her dark eyes.

"They aren't all my family. Neighbors, friends." She

shrugged. "Practically the whole lake community shows up this weekend."

A tendril of her dark hair had escaped her ponytail. Logan brushed it off her face and tucked it behind her ear. His fingers trailed along her jaw and her lips parted slightly. From any other woman, he would take that as an invitation to lean in and capture her lips, but this was Claire.

He swallowed and dropped his hand from her face. "Ready?"

Her lips pressed together and she nodded. She led him out the patio doors and into a mass of people. The lake was at least half a football field away from the back of the house and every inch of yard space was occupied.

"Come on." Claire gave him a pretty smile and tugged him along. People stopped them as they went through. Claire would introduce him as her boyfriend and then they would chat about the great weather they expected for the weekend or how the lake should be the right temperature for swimming or how tomorrow night's bonfire should be much busier as people continued to arrive.

The last one perplexed Logan. This wasn't all of them? He shook his head. Finding a spot that wasn't already taken, Logan pulled Claire next to a tree. He backed her into it and leaned over her like they were making out. In sight of enough people, but meant to look like they were trying to hide a little.

"You do this every year?" He leaned down so his mouth was next to her ear. "I don't know how you breathe with so many people in one space."

Claire lifted her hand to the back of his neck. Her fingers brushed against his hair, sending sparks trailing down his spine. "It's no different than a busy club. I haven't been back for a few years. Work made it difficult to take the time off."

Her breasts brushed against his chest and for a moment,

he forgot what they were doing. That this was all pretend. In a club, he would be focused on the other women and Claire would be focused on the guys. Right now, they were both focused on each other.

No pretenses. Just him and Claire.

Her breath tickled his earlobe. His fingers tightened on her hips and he barely stopped himself from drawing her into him. He could trail kisses along her earlobe and down that proud jawline of hers until he finally captured those pouty lips.

He'd watched her apply cherry Chapstick to her lips, but not lipstick. Her makeup was light. It made her look fresh and young. Her hair smelled like peppermint and rosemary. He wanted to bury his nose in it.

This felt intimate and so fucking natural, like something he wanted was right here, and she was waiting for him to draw her into him and take it.

"Hey." Claire's voice was soft as she tapped on his chest.

He straightened to look down into her dark brown eyes. He could get lost in those eyes, following the starburst pattern created in black, brown, and even hints of light gold. Her breath touched his lips. Her lips were right there. His for the taking.

"You okay?" Claire's eyes were tight and worried. "You're looking a little flushed. Why don't we go get a couple of beers?"

Fuck. Logan nodded and stepped back as Claire wove her hand in his and pulled him toward the coolers. She was his best friend and coworker. She glanced over her shoulder a few times. The same concern lingered in her eyes. He tried to smile, but it must have come off weird because her eyebrows drew together. He should be used to wanting her but not actually having her by now.

She dropped his hand as she leaned over to grab two beers. Twisting off the top, she passed one to him.

Logan took a deep drink before inhaling. Usually he was able to push off his desire for his friend, but things weren't so black and white right now. He needed to focus on Game Day Claire with her oversized shirt and her stinky jeans. That time she bet she could belch the entire alphabet. It didn't always do the trick, but it helped him focus on her being his best friend and not a woman he wanted to fuck.

"Better?" She raised an eyebrow.

He smirked. "Much."

"Claire!" The masculine voice came from behind him and he turned to watch another male replica of Claire striding toward them.

"Travis." Claire practically beamed as she walked into the guy's arms. "I thought you weren't coming until tomorrow."

Travis grinned at her. "I couldn't let you deal with Sean all by yourself."

Claire squeezed his arms and pulled him in for another hug. Her happy eyes landed on Logan and for a moment, he forgot how to breathe. She was absolutely stunning. She pulled away and pushed her brother toward Logan.

"This is Logan, my be—boyfriend." She only winced a little at the almost slip.

Travis didn't appear to notice as he held out his hand. "I have to admit I was a little surprised when Claire told me she was dating you. Last I heard you guys were just friends."

Logan took his hand and shook it. "I must have been blind to be just friends with Claire."

No lies here. But he knew better than to pursue a woman. Even one who was his best friend.

Travis laughed and held up his hands. "No details, man. I don't want to lose my lunch."

Claire drank from her bottle and raised her eyebrows at Logan.

"Are you a player, Logan?" Travis asked. His attention somewhere to the side.

Logan choked on his beer. "Excuse me?"

Travis gestured to the cornhole game set up. "I could use a partner."

Logan glanced at Claire and she gave him a subtle nod. "Sure, as long as you tell me how to play."

"I like this one." Travis clapped him on the back and urged him toward the boards.

"I'll catch up to you later," Claire said after them.

Logan looked back at her and took a deep breath. This weekend would be a lot harder than he thought. Being close to Claire had unlocked a whole lot of want that he usually ignored. He took a drink and Claire winked at him. He didn't know how long Game Day Claire would be enough to hold him back from messing up their friendship.

CHAPTER 4

"I don't think the plumber could distract you from that piece of man candy. Logan's arms and chest are solid rock. Good job."

"Mom," Claire chastised. Some days she wondered if her mom partook of Travis's weed stash.

Sean chuckled, making her want to hit him, but she could ignore him.

Claire kind of understood why her mom cared. Her mom and dad had had the kind of love written in fairy tales. It had been years since her father passed away, but the only dating Mom was interested in was her children's.

"I'm pretty sure I saw little Parker Grant around here." Her mom went up on her toes to look around. "Of course, she's not so little anymore. When that girl hit puberty, puberty hit her hard in the parts that matter, Sean. With Claire taken, I can focus all my attention on you."

"I don't know," Sean said slowly, as his hand stroked his short beard thoughtfully. "Looks like Claire's man candy can be distracted. Maybe you will have to call that plumber, Mom."

Claire followed Sean's gaze. Logan stood at the cornhole game with Travis, but to the side of him stood a cute blonde in short shorts and a crop top that barely covered her breasts. She grinned and thrust her chest at Logan. Claire almost chuckled. Logan definitely had a type: blond and ditzy.

"Huh." Sean took a drink, pulling Claire's gaze.

"What?" Claire took a sip of beer. Sean just wanted their mother completely focused on Claire's love life and not his.

"It's like you don't even care." Sean smirked. "If I had a girlfriend—"

"But you don't," Claire interrupted. "I trust my boyfriend. Where is little Parker Grant anyway?"

"Maybe Sean is right, Claire." Her mother gave a worried look Logan's way and then she started to scan the crowd. "Betty said Alan made it into town. You know Alan Thomson, right, Sean? He would have been in your grade in high school."

Claire could feel the licks of flames on her ears. She didn't want her mom pushing anyone else on her. She didn't even really want a boyfriend right now. This could have been all avoided if Sean just kept his mouth shut. Fucking Sean.

"Oh, yeah." Sean nodded and grinned slyly at Claire. "Alan's a stand-up guy. He'd be perfect for Claire. Especially since she's not that interested in claiming her territory with that Logan fellow."

"Fine." Claire shoved her beer into Sean's chest. He automatically caught it. "You want me to claim my man."

She stalked across the yard. Fucking Sean trying to get Mom to set her up when she barely got Logan to agree to come with her in the first place. The last thing she wanted was for her mom to start *Parent Trapping* her and Alan fucking Thomson. God only knew what that woman would do to ensure her daughter ended up with a doctor.

All she asked Logan to do was keep his fucking eyes off any hotties while he was supposed to be dating her. And the first time she left him alone, he practically eye fucked a freaking blond bimbo.

"Oh hey, Claire," Travis said. "Do you remember Hannah?"

Claire ignored Travis as Logan turned to face her with that smug smirk he always got when he tried to get laid. Fuck him and fuck that.

She grabbed his shirt and tugged him down. She squeezed her eyes shut as their lips crashed together. Anger had carried her here. Sean's prodding and Logan's wandering eye had made her take them from PG to PG-13.

Logan's arms wrapped around her and his lips took control of the kiss. Her hands were trapped between them when somewhere in her anger-fueled mind, she realized she was kissing Logan O'Connell. Her best friend. Her coworker. The guy who was supposed to be off limits.

Fuck, he was a good kisser.

His hands squeezed her ass as he drew her into him. Her lips parted and he made good use of her lack of control to explore her with such thoroughness she completely forgot where the fuck they were and who he was meant to be. Heat flooded her body. His hardness pressed against her stomach made her eyes pop open. Logan. It was still him and, fuck, tingles racked through her whole body. Still kissing the shit out of her. Her eyes slid shut as she gave in to the lust flowing in her veins.

"Geez, get a room. I don't need to be scarred by watching my older sister eating her boyfriend's face off." Travis's voice penetrated whatever fog had surrounded them.

Logan lifted his mouth from hers. His honey-colored eyes were hooded as he searched her eyes. Her heart attempted to pound its way out of her ribs. His hands still cradled her ass, holding her against his erection. The heat of him had her body pulsing hot, needy, and empty. Shit.

He touched his forehead to hers for a moment and took a deep breath. His eyes were closed. His hands moved to her waist. As he lifted his head from her, his darkened eyes opened and caught hers. Fuck, her forehead fell to his chest. What the hell had that been?

Logan cleared his throat. "So, Claire, you've met Travis's girlfriend, Hannah, right?"

Oh, shit. That fuckhead Sean had set her up. He knew she'd do anything to get Mom off her back. The fucker. She'd get him at some point over this weekend. When he least expected it.

Claire lifted her head, forced a non-psychotic smile to her lips, and unclenched her fists out of Logan's shirt. "Sure. Hannah."

Logan's eyes danced when his gaze locked on hers. If it weren't for his erection pressed to her stomach, she would think the kiss never happened. He dropped a quick kiss on her forehead before spinning her to face her brother and Hannah.

Now his hard-on rested against her ass. If her cheeks weren't already red, they'd be burning right now. Had she caused that or had he already been hard talking to Hannah?

Travis laughed. "It doesn't take much to rile up Clarice."

"Clarice?" Logan's question was directly in her ear and shivers coursed through her.

"My brothers thought it would be fun to pretend to be Hannibal Lector. They usually include the creepy sounds with it." She made the comment over her shoulder before leaning forward and punching her brother in the arm. "Knock it off."

"Fuck, you still know how to hit." Travis rubbed his arm. Hannah came over to him with her face scrunched up in concern and took over the rubbing. Travis lifted his gaze to hers and smiled.

Why did happy fucking couples surround Claire all the fucking time? Logan rested his chin on her shoulder. She'd worn wedge sandals that brought her up closer in height to him. His hands rested on her hips as he pressed his cock against her ass again which made her suck in a breath. This one was totally her fault, but they needed to have a discussion about what was appropriate in public when they were finally alone.

"Claire packs a mean punch when she gets mad at you." Logan turned his head slightly and the scruff of his five o'clock shadow dragged against her neck. "She's a bit of a hot head."

Travis laughed and he might have even said something more, but Claire had lost focus.

Holy shit, Logan's scruff against her neck was intoxicating. Add his heat and she'd be the one looking for a guy to get laid to take the edge off. Which would be catastrophic because Mom would likely find out and start a new campaign to either keep Claire and Logan together or find ways for Claire to sneak around with the other guy. She could never tell which way her mom would go.

Probably whoever charmed her mom more.

Travis and Hannah returned to the cornhole game. Claire barely stopped herself from rubbing like a cat against Logan. He hadn't released her and the longer he held her the greater the craving became. She turned her head toward him.

"Want to get another beer to cool off?" She tried to give him a smirk, like this was all pretend and nothing had changed.

His voice was low when he said, "My dick is so fucking hard right now. If you move, your mom is going to get an eyeful."

Claire glanced toward her mother who had her eyes on them with a smile while talking to Betty.

"What do you usually do to call him off?" Claire asked, returning her gaze to Logan.

His eyes dropped to her lips for a moment and her insides grew warm. That kiss was a huge mistake. They were both sexual people. If they wanted someone, they didn't usually hold back.

"Promise not to hit me?" He winced to prepare himself for her attack.

She arched an eyebrow at him. "Not now that you asked."

He dropped his head to her shoulder. His scruff rubbed against her bare skin, and she almost moaned at the sensation. They'd done body shots with each other and she hadn't responded like this. But that kiss had unlocked something potent.

"I think of Game Day Claire, belching the alphabet." His tone sounded miserable like he knew she'd give him shit for it.

She laughed. The sexual tension uncoiled within her a little. She turned in his arms and leaned back a little. "What? You don't find that sexy?"

He grinned as he shook his head. "It usually reminds me that you're my best friend and mostly does the trick."

"Nice. Good to know we have a good balance." She still snickered a little remembering that day in the bar. One of the old timers, Billy, who hung out there, had made her a bet she couldn't do it. Even Logan took up the bet. Logan had a mixture of disgust and being impressed written on his face by the time she got to Q. "Need a repeat performance?"

He reached out and tucked a stray hair behind her ear. Her breath caught and her smile froze. She felt helpless as his eyes locked her in place. Her lips parted and her insides churned.

"Nope, I think that did the trick." Logan's hands released her waist and he wove his fingers through hers. "At least it's down enough to not be so obvious."

"Glad to help." She swallowed and tamped down her own desire that had stirred. At least hers wasn't as obvious. They started across the field toward the beer. The sun had begun to set to the west of the lake, making the sky and lake shine with soft reds, oranges, and purple. Sunrise and sunset were her favorite thing about lake trips.

He dipped down close to her ear and said quietly, "Didn't know you were that good of a kisser."

She flushed with heat but scoffed. "Please. Of course, I'm good. Loads of practice makes perfect."

He chuckled and moved away slightly, letting her breath return to normal. "Didn't take you for the jealous type."

He grinned at her and she stopped at the beer coolers. "Sean made me mad. He thought I didn't care about you flirting and tried to sic Mom on me with Alan Thomson."

"Alan Thomson, huh?" Logan glanced over to where her mom still stood with Betty. His hand curled around the back of her neck. He pulled her in close until their lips were a hair's breadth apart. "When are we going to meet the man who could take you away from me?"

Her breath caught, and she tried to keep her eyes open, tried to follow the conversation, but she got lost again in his smiling eyes.

"We'll have to work harder to put on a show." His eyes flicked down to her lips before capturing them.

She swayed into his body and almost whimpered when he pulled away much too quickly. Her heart ricocheted in her chest. This was Logan, her best friend, but damn, her body didn't give a shit who the hell he was as long as he kept kissing her.

"I've had practice too." His thumb traced her lower lip.

Her breath rushed out of her. She barely resisted the urge to dart her tongue out and lick his thumb. What the hell was she thinking?

"Have I ever told you I love the taste of cherry Chapstick?" His words whispered against her lips like a caress. He lifted his head and gave her a wink before grabbing them two beers like he hadn't just blown her mind. She drew in a deep breath and held it for a moment.

He handed her one and she slowly released the breath. Flashing him an easy smile she didn't feel, she drank a good portion to calm the parts of her that were now way too interested in parts of Logan. And in what the amount of "practice" they both had would be like together.

"Slow down, Lake," Logan said, under his breath. "Don't want to start belching in front of these nice people."

That and his goofy grin cooled her off. Normal, that was friend normal. Chuckling, she shook her head to rid herself of the burn of desire still thrumming deep inside. "You're just embarrassed that a girl can belch louder than you."

He held his hand against his chest in mock disbelief. "Are you calling me out?"

She shook her head. "Come on. We better mingle more."

He grinned and took her hand. "Gotta find that Alan Thomson. Check out the competition."

She laughed as he dragged her along.

LOGAN DEFINITELY HADN'T THOUGHT this through. He stood in their bedroom in just his boxer briefs. Claire had ducked into the bathroom as soon as they made it into their room. *Fuck. Their* room. Three nights of laying next to Claire, him practically naked. Her warm body within reach. All those soft curves close enough to strain against him.

His lips still buzzed from that kiss. He hadn't expected it and hadn't wanted it to end. And this thought train would lead to a similar situation below his waistband. He wasn't sure how long their friendship could really hold him back. He didn't even really mind the belching. It just helped shake loose the sexy image she always portrayed. Especially when he thought of the way she sucked her fingers after she ate wings. Yup, not helping.

He sat on the edge of the bed and put his head in his hands. Claire was his best friend. One he didn't want to take for granted and didn't want to use for sex. Sex was a fucking game to him. How many girls could he rack up like points? He enjoyed each and every one of them. Every woman was unique, from her smell to the softness of her hair to the taste of her lips. He appreciated their differences and worshipped them with his body.

But Claire wasn't one of them. Logan and Claire knew each other on a different level. They traded fucking sex stories like boys in a locker room. They spent more time together than anyone else he knew, and he didn't want to fuck that up because his dick hadn't gotten the memo that she was off-limits.

"Need an Advil?" Claire's voice drew his attention over his shoulder to her.

She had woven her hair in a braid. Her face was freshly scrubbed. She'd applied that damned cherry Chapstick to her lips as he watched. It took him back to his first kiss with Andrea Zimmer in sixth grade. She'd worn cherry Chapstick and they'd made out every day that summer.

His gaze dipped down and he almost groaned. Claire wore a sleep tank top with no bra on. It held her breasts up like an offering. Her nipples poked against the stretchy fabric, causing his dick to rise to the occasion. It wouldn't have been so bad if the top didn't stop right above her belly button and her shorts that barely qualified as sleep shorts didn't start until below her belly button. Her bare, slender waist made his fingers itch with the need to trail over the exposed soft skin. The shorts clung to her hips like they could fall off at any moment. He considered begging her not to turn around. Her ass in those shorts. . . fuck. He'd die.

And her legs. He almost bit his knuckle to keep from crying. Her smooth, long legs were deliciously bare from where they joined at her hip to the tips of her painted toenails. Yup, Bedtime Claire had just moved to the top of his Claire chart. The only thing that might be better was Naked Claire.

Fuck.

"Advil?" Claire asked again and crossed her arms beneath her breasts. It wasn't fair.

"What?" Logan finally forced his focus on her eyes. He was a shit friend.

"You looked like you might have a headache." She gestured toward him and sat on her edge of the bed.

"No, just thinking." The sooner he got under the covers the better. Unfortunately his boxer briefs would leave little to the imagination with his throbbing erection pressing against the fabric.

She smiled and laid back on the bed. He stifled a groan.

"Sorry about the heat. The air conditioning does work, but Mom has always kept the thermostat set higher than needed." She kicked the covers down to the bottom of the bed. "You don't mind, do you?"

"No." He cringed. Why would he protest her not covering up that glorious body of hers, or wanting the covers to hide exactly what his body thought of hers?

She propped herself up on her elbows and lifted an eyebrow at him. "Are you going to lay down?"

Her breasts thrust up with the motion and he stood. If he

laid down next to her, he'd be on her. She'd willingly participated in the kiss and might be willing to do more than that. Right now, he wouldn't be able to sleep next to her without sinking into her over and over again.

Which wouldn't be good for their friendship. And he wasn't sure how much longer that particular problem would hold him off.

"I'm going to take a shower." He moved quickly to hide the fact his erection was leading him.

"Okay?" She blew out a breath as he closed the door.

A cold shower and jerking off would make this night go much easier.

CHAPTER 5

CLAIRE TURNED on her side and stared at Logan's still form in the pale light cast by the moon between the curtains. His chest rose and fell steadily, but not slow enough to indicate he slept. She should leave well enough alone. When he'd come out from his shower, he seemed less tense. But she couldn't sleep.

"Logan?"

Opening his eyes, he turned his head on his pillow to face her. "Yeah?"

"Are we okay?" She bit her lower lip. Please let him understand and not ask her to explain. She didn't want to lose her friend over a kiss. But that kiss seemed to change things.

He rolled to his side so his body faced hers. Her gaze dipped to his lean muscular build. All his muscles were beautifully defined but not over developed. She'd seen Logan without a shirt on before, but that kiss made things different. It made her look at him differently.

She wanted to taste his skin, run her tongue through

those groves that made up his abs, especially where they slipped under his tight boxer briefs.

"Claire?" He waited for her gaze to return to his. "If you keep looking at me like that, we won't be."

She sighed. This was the issue. "Fuck."

They'd crossed a line and suddenly it was like she remembered he was attractive. Not that he hadn't always been hot, but it had stirred up an attraction she'd either dismissed or put to the side for their friendship. Now it was front and center again.

And that kiss had tossed enough wood on the fire to let it burn way too hot.

"Yup." When Logan fell on his back, his hands went beneath his head. "I knew you couldn't resist all this."

She scoffed.

He glanced at her and winked. "But could you try upping your gross friend game?"

She smiled at the easy tone in his voice. It settled something in her chest. "What do you think would help?"

"Honestly?" He shook his head and gestured toward her body. "I'm not sure what would do it. I mean, have you seen Bedtime Claire?"

She glanced down at her outfit. He made her sound like a Barbie doll. "Yeah, sorry. It's always hot here. I packed accordingly. I didn't even consider she'd put us in the same bed. Though I should have. I've never voluntarily brought someone home before."

"Do you have any disgusting secrets? Are you truly hideously disfigured under. . . what barely qualifies as pajamas?"

She raised her eyebrow. "Would it matter if I were?"

He released a negative noise. "Got any STIs?"

"Ew." She tugged his pillow out from under his head and wacked him with it.

He reached for the pillow. She held it away to protect herself from retaliation. He leaned over her and his eyes dipped to her lips and groaned. "Try belching the National Anthem."

"Is it the patriotism that will do it for you or the belching?" She grinned up at him. "I would need beer to do it anyway. Not feeling at all gassy."

"That's a shame because gassy might have done it." Logan glanced down. "I hate to say it, but you have complicated the situation."

She followed his eye line and gulped at the bulge in his shorts. "By any chance, did you stick a salami in your underwear?"

He fell back on the bed, chuckling warily. "No room with my massive hard-on in there."

Sitting up, she held his pillow against her chest. The subtle scent of fresh-cut grass mixed with something heavier and rich and all Logan made her ache. Fuck, that smelled nice. Logan always smelled good, but the darkness of the room mixed with his scent had her in a tailspin.

"What do you want to do about it?" The words slipped out of Claire's mouth. She should take them right back, but everything in her was keyed up and turned on. Maybe it had been the kiss or the fact the bathroom wasn't exactly soundproof. He'd gotten off in the shower not long ago.

Hearing him get off had turned her insides to liquid and she honestly couldn't sleep. For a few minutes, she'd considered grabbing the vibrator and taking it into the bathroom after he came back out, but she didn't want hard silicone. Not when the real deal was available. She bit her lip.

Logan put his arm over his eyes. "Fuck, Claire."

Before she could think better of it, she set his pillow aside and straddled his waist. Her hands went to his chest as she hovered above him. His hips spread her fairly low so only an inch separated her from the heat of him. Gah, it felt good.

This was so wrong on so many levels. They were friends. This could mess up everything for them. She knew better. Sex complicated things. Maybe it wouldn't for them, but it might.

But she couldn't bring up the ability to care about that right now.

His hands reached out for her hips, holding her there, stopping her descent into madness. A mere inch away. "What are you doing?"

His touch was exquisite. She wanted his hands everywhere on her, spreading his heat like wildfire across her skin.

"Haven't you heard the saying 'friends fuck'?" Some guy in high school had tried to convince her such a thing existed. Unfortunately for him, she didn't reach the same conclusion as he had. But right now, the saying had some merit.

"Doesn't that always go sideways?" Logan lifted an eyebrow. "How many movies have been about friends with benefits, but someone always starts feeling more than the other and they end up either hating each other or loving each other?"

"Do you love me, Logan? Do you secretly want to marry me?" Claire teased, trailing her finger along the side of his abs. The muscles tensed and flexed beneath her fingertip.

"No." His tone was breathless as he held her firm above him.

She raised her gaze to look him in the eyes.

"I don't love you, Logan. Not as anything more than a friend. I haven't secretly been plotting to get with you." Claire flattened her palm above the elastic band of his underwear. His muscles tensed beneath her touch. Her pulse increased. She lifted her gaze to meet his. "You're an attractive guy, but when we decided to be friends, I stopped looking at you as attractive."

"Way to stab at my ego." Logan grinned. His fingers tightened slightly on her hips. This could go either way. He could push her off or drag her down at any moment.

"Honestly, your ego could take a stabbing and still be fucking huge." She rolled her eyes.

He chuckled. "You know it."

She covered his mouth with her other hand. "What I'm saying is usually these things go sideways because someone has feelings they haven't expressed for the other. We don't have that. We just have huge libidos and a craving. An attraction that laid dormant for a while. I don't see the harm in exploring that."

He licked her hand and she pulled it away with a disgruntled face. She wiped it on his bare chest as he smirked up at her. "Are you saying you want me, Claire Bear?"

"Would you rather jerk off in the shower again?" She raised an eyebrow at him. She started to move to the side, but his hands held her in place.

He groaned. "You heard that?"

"Did you not want me to hear that?" She couldn't stop her cocky grin. "Look, we're both adults. We obviously have at least a passing interest in each other, which would be more than enough at a club. We can't exactly hookup with someone else this weekend. We can either take turns using the bathroom or. . . ."

"Or fuck each other's brains out." He blew out his breath and narrowed his eyes at her. "Just this weekend?"

"Why not?" She tapped him on his chest. "It's not like we could catch feelings from having sex. Have you ever thought about sex with me?"

His lips pressed into a line and he looked off to the side.

She slapped his chest.

"Ow, woman." His eyes snapped to hers. "What was that for?"

"Honesty is how this will work." She looked down at his hands still holding her hips. She raised an eyebrow. "Mind if I sit?"

He eyed the inch between them and groaned. His eyes lifted to hers. "Are we really going to do this?"

"Not if you keep cockblocking." She smirked at him. "Come on, Logan, my thighs are getting tired."

"Fine, in the interest of saving your thigh muscles, but no funny business." His hands lifted from her hips and he held them up like she was robbing him.

"Not until we finish our conversation," she agreed and moved a little forward so she sat on his abs. "Better?"

He put his hands behind his head. "If you took off your top, it would be a lot better."

"Yeah, sure." She shook her head. "All right. Since you've avoided the question, I'll admit I've thought about it."

His eyes widened. "You've thought about you and me. . . ." He made a crude gesture.

She narrowed her eyes at him and her fist clenched.

"Easy, tiger." He laughed and grabbed her hand and used his fingers to unclench hers. His fingers started massaging her hand, sending warm tingles flowing up her arm. His hard abs pressed against her intimately and the air around them changed slightly. A little less playful as the craving settled deep within her.

"I think about sex with you a lot, but I'm a guy." Logan met her eyes and held them. "You know you're hot."

Her brow furrowed at the *a lot*. But then his fingers dug into a tight spot on her hand, she released her breath. Her eyes slid closed slightly. She forced them open and met his darkened ones. "Have you caught feelings from fucking someone before?"

He shook his head. "You?"

"No." She hadn't. The guys she actually liked as more became more sometimes, but the guys who were just attraction stayed that way. Logan really wasn't either. He was something else entirely. They were buds, friends, coworkers. But the attraction lurked below the surface until she'd unlocked it with that fucking kiss. Now she couldn't get enough.

His fingers interlaced with hers and he pulled their arms above his head, pulling her down to him.

"Can we be done with discussion time?" The words brushed her lips and heat pooled between her thighs. Her breasts brushed his chest. This should be awkward as hell, but it felt so right.

"Quick recap?" She tipped her head to line up their lips better but didn't close the gap.

"Just sex. No love. Nothing changes, except I get to see you naked and finally feel those magnificent breasts of yours." His eyes dipped to look down her body.

"This weekend only. Once we fly back, everything goes back to normal. But for now, we'll work out the kinks in our relationship." She clenched her hands in his.

Logan twisted and suddenly Claire laid on her back with Logan hovering above her. His hands pressed her hands into the mattress beside her head. Her pulse raced. His hips surged between her legs and his firm cock slid against her sex with way too much fabric in the way. It still felt fucking fantastic. A moan ripped out of her from the sensation.

He leaned in until his mouth touched her ear. "Which kinks would you like to explore, tiger?"

"Why don't we see how sex goes before complicating it?" Claire arched against him.

He lifted his head and his dark eyes searched hers. "Vanilla sex, it is. Maybe."

She shook her head and wrapped her legs around his waist. "Just shut up and kiss me."

He lowered his head to hers and their lips finally met. Heat flooded her. The sparks all pooled, concentrating where his cock pressed between her legs. His lips opened over hers and he nipped lightly on her lower lip. Opening her mouth under his, she slid her tongue along his. His hands tightened on hers.

This should be more awkward. With anyone else she knew in the office, it would have been. Even if they were actually available. But this was Logan. She trusted him to have her back at work. She laughed with him at stupid ass movies. They never missed a chance to watch a game together. They danced with each other. Talked about fucking other people. Spent more time together than anyone else since they met.

It felt natural to add this to the list of things they'd done together. Maybe in the light of day she'd feel differently. Maybe she wouldn't. But she was willing to let all those worries slip away and just feel for tonight.

LOGAN TOOK his time exploring Claire's mouth. She tasted like cherry Chapstick, mint and something sweet that was all Claire. Since that kiss earlier he'd wanted nothing more than to get his lips back on hers. Envisioning that kiss had been enough to get him off earlier. He couldn't wait to get her firm ass back in the palms of his hands. That or finally those luscious breasts. He hadn't been joking about wanting to touch her breasts. They were natural, more than a handful, and completely perfect.

Mostly he wanted to sink his cock into her and see how many times he could get her off.

But he had time and he wanted to take advantage of every second. Claire wasn't shy when it came to sex and he thanked God for that. She explored his mouth with confidence and need. Their tongues tangled multiple times. Her fingers twitched around his and he knew she wanted to touch him, but he wanted this to last. The minute she touched him he'd lose all control.

Lifting his head, he waited for her to open her eyes. "You trust me?"

"Yes." Her tone was confident, but she lifted a questioning eyebrow at him.

He rolled off her and opened the drawer. The silk ties were somewhere in the dark drawer. He turned on the lamp and a soft light filled the room. Perfect, because he didn't want to miss a thing. She propped up on her elbow to see what he was doing. He moved most of the contents of the drawer to the top of the nightstand. He'd have to remember to thank Grace for her forethought.

Claire's fingers traced a line down his spine, leaving a trail of sparks in their wake. His cock twitched in response.

Fuck, her touch was intoxicating.

"What's the plan, Wolverine?" The teasing tone of her voice settled his throbbing heart. Right now, they were still the same Claire and Logan. He wanted to stay in this moment before they did anything to change who they were to each other. Sex would change things. Everyone knew that, and he knew it would change something between them. Even if they didn't fall in love with each other, something would change.

But he wanted what she offered. He wanted her but had always denied himself for the sake of their friendship. He wouldn't deny it anymore. Not with her looking at him like he was a five-course meal and she was starving.

"Wolverine?" he asked and glanced over his shoulder as he drew the silk ties through his fingers.

Her eyes widened slightly before her lips curled into a smile. She gave him a shrug. "You called me Claire Bear."

He shook his head with a slight chuckle. "I think I prefer calling you tiger. Much more fitting."

Before she could reply, he lifted her hips and shifted her into the center of the bed. Her hands grabbed his wrists, but she didn't stop him.

"What are you doing?" No concern in her tone.

"Making this last." He flipped his hands around to take hers. He straddled her and pulled her arms close to the wrought iron headboard. "Let me know if it's too tight."

"Afraid I might try and run away," she teased. Her hips wiggled beneath him.

He had to let go of one hand to tie the other. Claire took advantage and her hand trailed down his chest. He sucked in a breath and forced his concentration on the knot.

Her fingers dipped below the elastic of his waistband and traced the head of his cock. Finishing the knot, he glanced at her face. Her teeth held her swollen bottom lip as her darkened eyes lingered on his mostly covered cock. He froze at the longing in her eyes as she lifted her gaze back to his.

Fuck, this definitely wouldn't last long if she had access to touch him.

Her hand slid down the outside of his boxers and traced the outline of his erection. If she kept that up, he'd come before he even had a taste of her. He captured her wandering hand and moved it to the headboard with the other tie.

She pouted up at him. "Not fair."

He chuckled. "Next time can be all you. I'll even let you tie me up."

"I'm holding you to that." Her gaze trailed down his abs to

his cock as she licked her lips. He had to stifle back a moan. Fuck. He tightened the knot.

"Comfortable?" He sat back on his heels to admire her. Her arms stretched above her with her fingers wrapped around the headboard bars. Her dark hair fanned out on the pillow like a fallen angel. Her dark, hypnotic eyes followed his every move. Her pouty lips were swollen from their kiss. He could spend all night looking at her like this.

"Typical Friday night." She shrugged with a sassy smile.

The position caused her breasts to thrust up and tugged her short top farther up her torso, leaving the smooth skin of her stomach on display. Her nipples strained against the fabric, making his fingers ache to touch them. His gaze followed the dip of her waist to the swell of her hips down her long legs.

"Logan?"

He lifted his gaze to her eyes.

"Did you just want to tie me up and that's it? Because seriously, I was hoping for a little more. All that constant bragging about sex with this woman or that woman and how much you got them off. Not that I'm complaining. . . much. This is hot, but you know, I like to be touched."

She glanced over at the nightstand. She raised her eyebrow in challenge. "I guess you could untie one of my hands and hand me the vibrator. I can just get off and go to sleep."

"Worried I won't be able to get you there, tiger?"

She rolled her eyes. "I think I almost prefer Claire Bear. At least it makes sense in a nonsensical way."

He trailed his hand from her calf to her thigh. The muscles tensed beneath his touch. "You don't think you're a tiger."

"Never really considered the question of what animal I would be. Didn't think I'd be having this conversation with you after we both agreed to have sex either." She arched her eyebrow at him.

"Fine. I get it." He smirked at her. "You just can't wait to get all this."

She shook her head. He moved back to the nightstand and grabbed a bottle of lube that was also massage oil. He needed to slow things down before he burst.

"Your mom—"

"Really?" Claire asked with an eyeroll. "That's sexy talk right there."

He chuckled and poured some of the oil in his hands, rubbing them together to warm it. "Your mom had some really inspired ideas. Honestly."

"I don't want to talk about my mom. Or tell her we used anything in that drawer. It will only encourage her in the future." Claire gave him a mutinous look. "I'm about ten seconds from calling this whole thing off."

"Good thing you're all tied up then." He scooted to the footboard near her feet and leaned back against it. "You don't like anticipation? That's part of the thrill of fucking a stranger. Isn't it?"

"You mean less talk and more doing?" She stared up at the ceiling. Impatient beast.

Logan took her foot in his hands. She jerked a little on it, but relaxed and continued her staring contest with the ceiling. She was wound so fucking tight. They could get it over with like she wanted, but it wouldn't be half as pleasant as getting her to relax and enjoy herself.

Chuckling lightly, he worked his thumb in circles around her instep. "When you fuck someone you know, all these things start to get in the way."

"Like talking?"

"We had to establish boundaries to feel comfortable, but we still aren't falling on each other—"

"Because of you—"

"*Because* we are clueless about where to begin and how to get around the fact that we've been friends."

She made a dismissive sound. Her lips pressed into a thin line as she returned her gaze to the ceiling. He kept working her foot and hitting spots that were tighter before he changed to her other foot. This time she didn't jump at his touch. Progress.

"Our boundaries tell us that as friends we don't touch each other like this. So for a second it feels wrong even though it feels good."

She gave a little moan as her muscle relaxed beneath his touch.

"Strangers though. Think about it. You're in the club, dancing when you notice someone or they notice you and that first sizzle when you make eye contact." He slipped his hands up to her calf, massaging the muscle with the oil. Her leg muscles were tight and strong. He loved watching her walk in heels, but they had to wreak havoc on her calves. "When you finally make your approach, you have to decide: is this going to be a one-time thing or are you going to make him wait?"

"I've had one-night stands that lasted for days or weeks." Her voice was a little breathless, which made him smile. Her breasts lifted and fell in time with her breathing. Mesmerizing to watch, knowing he could do what he wanted with her and she'd let him.

He slid his hand over her other calf, releasing the knots in the muscles with slow, steady circles. "But you can never recreate that first time. Where you know nothing about this person and they know nothing about you. You can try anything because you don't know what they'll like. You don't know how far they'll let you go."

Not taking his hands from her leg, he knelt between her

knees. His fingers slid in slow languid circles beneath her knee. Her breathing hitched. He smiled at her sensitivity.

"Have you gone down on a stranger, Claire?" Logan applied more pressure behind her knee and her eyes fluttered closed and her lips parted. Her hips lifted off the bed slightly. His fingers slid to the backs of her thighs, his thumb teasing circles on her inner thigh. "Have you?"

Her eyes were so dark when she opened them he couldn't tell where her pupils began. She licked her lips and nodded. His fingers slipped farther up her leg as a reward.

"Did it excite you?" He kept his tone low. "Did you get wet while sucking on his cock?"

His fingertips edged along her shorts and she moaned. "Yes."

Fuck, she'd always been sexy to him, but seeing her helpless before him, trusting him with her body. He was lucky he didn't blow in his shorts.

"What turned you on? Was it because you didn't know what would happen? If he would sit back and let you do all the work? If he would grab your hair and fuck your mouth? If he would warn you before he came and give you the option or just blow in your mouth without warning?"

"Fuck," she hissed as his fingers worked near her shorts. She lifted her hips as if in offering.

The sweet scent of her arousal surrounded him. He wanted to strip her bare and bury his face between her legs, taste her with his tongue. But he needed her beyond caring about who he was and who they were to each other. He didn't want her to hesitate for a moment, but give in to the pleasure they would share.

"For me, every woman is different. Their smell. The way they move. The way they taste. Every kiss is different. Different pressure. Tongue or no tongue. Aggressive or timid." He removed his hands from her legs and she opened her eyes. Pouring more oil in his hands, he rubbed his palms together. "Even where women are sensitive isn't the same. Some women can orgasm just from having their nipples played with. Some don't orgasm at all, but they still enjoy the feel of my hands over their bodies. My cock sliding deep within them."

Logan skipped over her shorts, and his hands massaged her stomach and waist. She whimpered slightly. But without her touching him, he was in control. He could make this last and not take her like an untried schoolboy.

His hands moved in large circles from the bottom of her shirt to dipping under the waistband of her low-slung shorts. Her breath came in small pants and her legs stayed open with him kneeling between them. He wrapped his hands around her waist to reach her lower back with his fingertips.

"I've done things with strangers I'd never do with a woman I saw on the regular. When a woman goes down on me, I've fucked her face and given her no warning before coming. I've gone down on her even when she protested about not being groomed properly and pushed her over the edge with my tongue." He leaned over and kissed Claire's belly button. His fingers latched onto the waistband of her shorts. "A little dom/sub play. I've played both sides for women when they've asked."

She whimpered again and lifted her hips. He loved this game, but he wasn't sure how much longer he could play it. As her control whittled down, so did his own.

He dragged her shorts down an inch and pressed a kiss to the skin that was exposed. "The thing about strangers is you aren't as concerned about them getting off. I mean, you want them to, of course, but the main goal is to make sure you get off. And with a stranger, you aren't as concerned about what they'll think about you in the morning."

His fingers rubbed her exposed hipbone as he dragged his

tongue back up to her belly button. He raised his head to capture her eyes. "That lack of fear of judgment frees me to do what I really want to do."

"What about now?" Claire's voice had lowered and she practically panted the words. Her fingers tightened around the iron posts as she strained up toward him.

"With you?" He dragged his thumbs up her sides, catching her shirt and lifting it to just below her breasts. He held her gaze as he massaged the muscles he'd exposed. His thumbs came dangerously close to her breasts, skimming along the underside.

"Do you fear my judgment?" Claire asked. She bit her lip as her dark eyes held his.

"Judgment? No." He didn't fear her judgment. He knew her inside and out. He knew Game Day Claire and Pizza Appreciation Day Claire. PMS Claire which usually happened after Pizza Appreciation Day Claire. He'd seen Happy Claire, Relationship Status Claire, Clubbing Claire, Fuck Boy Claire, and even Dumped Claire. She turned to him when she needed someone to lift her back up.

In return, he'd told her things he'd never told anyone else. About his family. About the women he saw. About his future. Usually when drunk, but something about Claire made him trust her, because she trusted him with every piece of her. Somehow, she knew he'd remain her friend even when she showed him who she really was.

She hid Game Day Claire from the poser guys at first. The ones toting her around like she was a fucking trophy. When she invited a guy to game day, it was a big deal. They didn't always last long after game day though. On more than one occasion, Logan had met one of these guys out and about and fucked with them for fucking with her. He couldn't beat them up—he didn't want to go to jail, but he could royally screw their day with an "accidental" spill or a few well-placed words or just stealing the girl they were with. Those were the best times.

They didn't deserve any female if they couldn't keep Claire for whatever fucked up reason their fragile ego had come up with. They wanted a fucking trophy and not an amazing woman.

"Hey." The word was soft as her knee bumped his side.

He focused on her eyes. His hands stilled on her waist.

"I won't, you know?" Claire's eyes were fierce as they stared into his.

"Judge me?" He had to think about what he'd said before he fell into a rabbit hole filled with Claires. He had the real Claire in front of him, waiting for him to do something more than tease her.

She shook her head. "We don't judge each other. That's not who we are. Now. Are we done with erotic story time? Can we move on to actual action? Because I don't think my lady boner could get any harder." She grinned at him and his heart settled into a steady thump because she was still his best friend.

He couldn't help returning her grin. "I do aim to please."

CHAPTER 6

CLAIRE HAD NEVER BEEN SO TURNED on in her life. Her lady bits were about to combust. Logan's hands on her skin, his words in her ears, his mouth on her stomach. Fuck, he needed to get on with this and touch her somewhere that would actually get her off. Not that the massage wasn't nice. He had really great hands.

If her hands were free, they'd both already be naked.

His fingers hooked into her shorts and underwear again. She lifted her hips, hoping this time, they'd come off. She wanted every bit of clothing off her body right now.

Who knew Logan would want to take things slow and easy? Meanwhile she was ready to start gnawing at the ties around her wrists.

His eyes held hers as he started to lower her shorts slowly. Fuck this. He wasn't the only one who could talk about sex.

"I don't have any qualms about you sticking your face in my pussy." Claire figured mouthing off would be the only way to get Logan to speed things up. "Even if I spend an hour doing hot yoga and things are a bit ripe, you want to go down on me? I'm always down for it. I will say I did get a wax before this weekend because swimwear and pubes are a bit hard to manage, but normally I leave a little greenery."

He dropped his head to her stomach and took a deep breath. "For fuck's sake, Claire. I'm trying to make this last."

She couldn't erase her smile as she wiggled her hips to encourage him to take her shorts down. "How about we go for quantity over quality? I mean we're going to be here three nights total. Probably could get away with *sleeping* late and having a couple of *naps* during the day. If you're going to take this long though, I might have to make do with the toy a few times to get off quicker."

He shook his head against her stomach. His velvety hair brushing against her skin made her insides hotter. Which she didn't believe was possible. He chuckled. The sound rumbled against her stomach.

"You do realize I could just keep you tied to this bed the whole weekend." He lifted his head and inched her shorts down a little more until they reached her pubic bone. "I'm sure I could convince your mother we need time to work on our relationship."

"She'd have a wedding planned by the end of the weekend." She arched her eyebrow at him. "She'd also need your mother's number because she'd want to meet the in-laws before the nuptials. She'd be your new best friend on your phone, social media, and when she came to visit, she'd expect you there twenty-four seven to take care of her."

"Maybe we pass on the mother." He shrugged. "How about I get to take my time now and drive you out of your fucking mind with orgasms. And I'll make sure we get some quickies later."

"Stop bringing up my mom or I'm going to lose my lady boner." She glared at him. "And take off my fucking clothes. This isn't a strip tease."

He laughed. "Here I'm trying to be sexy and turn off your mind so you won't worry about what this means and you just want me to stick it in already. Which one of us is the girl again?"

"Obviously you are." She gave him a wink. "But if we get naked, maybe we can figure it out."

He got a wicked glint in his eyes that meant trouble. She almost tried to take back everything. Logan hovered over her until his mouth was a breath from hers. "This is why I tied your hands. You always try to rush things."

"I bet you wouldn't say that if I had your dick in my mouth."

His lips crashed against hers and his cock ground against her pussy. She pushed back against him, thankful for the pressure. It wouldn't take much to push her to the edge. His hands skimmed up her tank top on the side of her breasts. Oh, shit, that felt good. His head lifted and she caught that mischievous look in his eyes before her tank top covered her face from the nose up.

"Really?" she cried out.

His chuckle did nothing to make her feel better. Especially when he didn't move the material out of the way.

"Uncover my eyes, Logan."

"There wasn't a blindfold included in the drawer, so I'm making do." His hands went down her hips pulling her shorts and underwear off.

She had nothing she was ashamed of, but she would have liked to see the expression on his face when he saw her body for the first time.

The bed dipped between her legs again. His fingers wrapped around the back of her knees and lifted them.

"Logan, move my shirt," she pleaded this time.

"Shhh, I'm busy." He didn't move his hands from holding her knees so she knew he wasn't exactly taking naughty pictures for his spank bank. Mental images, yeah, but not actual digital memories. But just knowing he was probably looking over every inch of her exposed body made her insides melt.

She took a deep breath.

"Fuck, Claire. You have no idea how often I've thought of you naked." His hands travelled up the outside of her thighs. "I've seen your bare legs and even your waist and your cleavage so many fucking times. But I think Naked Claire is my new favorite Claire."

Another breath flowed through her and his words were like molten lava through her veins. His hands skimmed over her hips and up her waist. His thumbs paused beneath her breasts.

Her breath caught and held. Not sure what would happen next. His mouth closed over her nipple and she arched up into him. She gasped as his hand stroked over her other breast, circling her nipple. Liquid heat flooded her and knocked away any more thoughts she might have had.

He consumed her nipple and breast until she squirmed beneath him. Then he released it, just to take the other into his warm, wet mouth. She understood how he could make a woman come from just touching her breasts. His tongue and fingers were divine, sending sparks of heat to wrap around the center of her.

Her insides pulsed and throbbed with each tug on her nipple.

He released her. "Perfect."

His hands cupped and lifted her breasts. She could almost picture him watching. His eyes would be dark and filled with lust. His lips would be shiny and full. She moved her hips, trying to find friction to get her the rest of the way there.

"Patience. We can go hard and fast next time," he whispered next to her ear. His chest brushed against her nipples and she could feel the weight of his bare cock against her stomach.

Fuck, she wanted that between her legs. She wanted to see his cock. Touch it. Taste it. But mostly she wanted it to slide inside her and take her over the edge into oblivion. She had never been so turned on in her life. She wanted and needed release.

He lifted from her again. She held her breath waiting for his next move. His hands grabbed her hips and a moment later his breath scorched her inner thigh. It was all the warning she had before his tongue slipped down the center of her.

He held her hips while he took his time exploring her pussy. Her grip tightened on the bars above her head. All her focus went to his mouth and the divine things he did with it. His tongue thrust inside her. He pushed her higher and higher and all she could do was hang on for the ride.

When he sucked on her clit, she fell apart. His finger slid inside her, taking her higher and forcing her over the edge into oblivion again. But he didn't let her come down. He brought her right back up to ride the edge. His tongue and fingers worked together to destroy any sanity she had.

Most guys would move up after one orgasm or, you know, just be done with that portion of the evening's entertainment. Whether she got there or not. But Logan seemed content to just keep at it. Changing the way his tongue and fingers worked together to keep her on the edge.

She heard herself begging him for release. Words falling from her lips that normally she wouldn't say. She wasn't a beggar, but it was too much. He tormented her with pleasure and she wondered if she'd ever be the same. When she went over the edge again, finally he eased her down.

Her fingers released the bars of the headboard and she

took in shuddering breaths. Her whole body trembled in the aftermath.

His body moved over hers and his mouth found hers. Her shirt moved off her head to her arms as he continued to kiss her. Her breasts brushed against his hard chest and his cock rested against her pussy. He lifted his head and she opened her eyes to his.

"Still with me?" Logan brushed the hair from her face.

She nodded, not trusting her voice as she searched his eyes. "Good."

He reached up and untied her hands, dropping her shirt on the floor. Rubbing his hands over her arms to help ease the ache, he gave her a crooked smile. "Ready for more?"

Was she ready? She turned her head and grabbed a condom from the nightstand. After tearing it open, she reached between them and stroked her hand over his cock. The smooth skin warm against her palm.

"Next time I'm tying you up." She lifted her head and took his mouth, thrusting her tongue inside.

He groaned against her mouth as she worked her hand over him. She made short work of the condom before shoving him over onto his back. She straddled his lap and took him inside her in one move.

"Fuck," he whispered.

Giving him a smile, she grabbed his hands and held them against her breasts. "Enjoy the ride."

CLAIRE RIDING his cock was his new favorite thing. Logan knew the minute he released her hands, she wouldn't give him back control without a fight, but he was more than willing to hand over the reins to her. She wasn't sweet and gentle, or shy and discerning. That had never been Claire, and he hadn't expected her to change during sex.

She hadn't disappointed him. He'd nearly come earlier when she begged him for release. Now with his hands over her breasts as she rode him, he was grateful he'd managed to hold back.

"Can I at least get visitation rights?" Logan cupped her breasts together. They were perfect.

Claire stopped moving and stared down at him. "What?"

He groaned at the lack of movement. "Your breasts. I don't think I'll be able to give them up after this weekend. Maybe I could feel them up every now and then."

He winked at her and she laughed. He could feel her laugh through her whole body.

"Seriously, you have issues. Do you do this with all the women you fuck?" Claire tilted her head at him like he was a zoo exhibit.

"Hey, I'm just trying to last longer than any other guy you've been with." He looked around. "Did you start a timer, because I want to make this official."

She shook her head at him, but she also relaxed enough that he grabbed hold of her and rolled her under him.

"Hey."

"Again, it's not your turn yet." He captured her lips to keep down any other protests and grabbed her legs to help her wrap them around his waist. He slid out and then back in deeper than before.

She moaned against his lips as he continued his slow thrusts into her. Her hands curled around his neck while his cradled her ass cheeks. There wasn't a part of Claire Logan didn't long to touch. Getting his fill of her in three days may be impossible, but he was willing to try.

He lifted his mouth from hers and met her dark eyes. "One more time, tiger."

She arched against him as he kept a steady pace. One of her hands slipped between them and he could feel her stroking herself and his cock at the same time while he continued to thrust. If she didn't come soon, he would lose it.

"Fuck," he whispered, trying to hold it together a little longer. One more time from her, that was all he wanted.

He took her nipple into his mouth and bit it gently.

"Logan," she cried out as she came. Satisfaction filled him. Her arms wrapped behind his neck as she held on while he increased the pace of his thrusts to find his release. When she captured his lips, he fell apart, slamming into her one last time as he exploded. He collapsed on top of her, trying to catch his breath.

No one had ever felt that good before.

"Bloody hell," Logan muttered as he lifted off Claire and rolled beside her. He put his hand over his heart as he worked to catch his breath. His other hand found hers and wove his fingers through hers.

She turned her head and gave him a smile. "Tomorrow night, I get to tie you up."

His dick twitched at the thought and he groaned. "I should have been quicker."

"Payback is a bitch." She smirked at him before rolling to her side of the bed. When she stood and stretched, all he could do was admire all those perfect curves. She glanced back at him. "Are you going to join me in the shower?"

She laughed as he scrambled to his feet. He grabbed a handful of condoms. The bathroom wasn't huge and neither was the shower, but it was big enough for both of them. Mostly.

"You know it's a shame," Logan said as Claire was pressed against his front while he rubbed soap down her back. Water flowed over both of them.

"What is?" She kissed his shoulder and rested her head against it. Her wet curves fit against him.

"My shower at home is definitely big enough to have an orgy in, while this one barely qualifies for two people." He finished with the soap and wrapped his arms around her. "We'll never get to have real, good and dirty shower sex."

Her fingertips smoothed over his back. "Nope. That is a shame. I don't think I've ever done it in a shower before. I mean things would get heated, but I think we always ended up back in the bed."

Logan turned her under the water stream and then pulled away to take her in. Fuck, she was temptation itself with water caressing every curve. He might be able to work something out. "We'll have to be more creative."

Claire yawned and nodded up at him.

"Tomorrow." He shut off the shower and grabbed a couple of towels. He wrapped one around Claire before quickly drying himself off. Then he dried Claire off as her eyelids drooped. "Definitely tomorrow."

He led her back to the bed and made sure everything was put away in case someone came into their room. Claire snuggled into the bed without putting on any clothes. Chuckling, he joined her.

"I really do sleep in the nude," she mumbled as he gathered her in his arms.

"Me too." He kissed her lips briefly. "Go to sleep."

"We're still good, right?" Claire opened those beautiful brown eyes and met his.

He brushed a wet strand of hair off her face and something soft settled in his chest. "Yeah, we're good."

CHAPTER 7

Claire slipped out of bed before the sun had a chance to rise. She thought about waking Logan, but he curled up around her pillow and let out a loud snore. Trying to be quiet, she dressed in shorts and a T-shirt and put her hair up in a messy bun before heading down to the kitchen.

The whole house still slept which Claire loved. It used to be her and her dad's time. They both were early risers. They'd grab a cup of tea or coffee or when she was little, hot chocolate, and go out to the dock to watch the sunrise on the lake in silence. Some of her best moments with her dad were quietly watching the sunrise.

With her cup in her hand, she crossed the dew-coated lawn in her bare feet, down to the dock the houses next door shared with her mother. As she approached the chairs, she noticed someone was already in one. She started to turn around.

"Wait," a male voice called out quietly.

"I didn't want to interrupt." Claire turned back.

The man unfolded from the chair and gestured to the multiple chairs. "Plenty of room for both of us."

She squinted up at him. He was tall, probably around her age. His blond hair was in a classic male haircut. She could just make out the blue in his eyes from the lightening sky. He wasn't bad looking and his body was in shape, but she couldn't quite place who he was.

"I'll be quiet. I'm used to being up early. It's just so peaceful out here." He gestured to a chair and reclaimed his own, lifting a cup of coffee to his lips.

Why not? She relaxed into the chair and drank from her tea. Her eyes on the horizon, waiting for that moment when the sun would finally break over to the new day.

"I'm Alan Thomson." He held out his hand to her.

She laughed softly and took it. "Claire Lake."

"Ah, so you're the hot commodity Betty has been telling me about." He grinned at her. She remembered her mom saying he was staying with Matt, Betty's son.

"And you're the doctor my mother thought I should meet." Claire kept her eyes on the rising sun. He didn't score bad on the attraction scale, but guys usually fucked up if you talked to them long enough.

"I see my reputation proceeds me." He relaxed into his seat and his gaze went to the horizon. "I hope you know I didn't ask for a set up. Didn't even know about it until we got here and last night all Betty could talk about was how I was too late. That little Claire Lake was already taken."

He gasped and covered his shocked mouth before smiling. He had a nice smile, gentle.

Claire chuckled. "Yup, that's me. Taken."

Not really, but she had been last night. She glanced back at the window in the house Logan still slept behind. Would sex really not change their relationship? Even now thinking about it, she could feel that rush of butterflies in her stomach and a happy buzz between her thighs. He'd definitely aimed to please last night.

"It's a shame, really." Alan's voice drew her back to the sunrise.

"Don't tell me you were hoping for a set up? Because my mom and Betty can definitely find you someone. I'm surprised they didn't have a whole casting call waiting for you here."

He chuckled, a rich, dark sound. "No, not the set up. It's a shame you're already seeing someone. But I'll get bonus points if they know at least I've met you and realize my loss."

"If you want even more bonus points, you could come talk to me today in front of everyone." Had she met him last night she wouldn't have said anything like this, but somehow in the quiet light of dawn, Alan seemed like an okay kind of guy that she wouldn't mind getting to know better. Especially since no one was forcing her into a closet with him.

He smiled. "They'd love that, but what about your boyfriend?"

She shrugged. "He's not the possessive type."

Because she wasn't his girlfriend. No woman with half a brain would believe that Logan O'Connell would settle down with her. Well, not rationally at least. Sure, Lacy at work had had a crush on him, but it really wasn't on Logan, but the guy she thought Logan could be.

Claire didn't have any illusions when it came to Logan. He liked his life the way it was. He liked having sex with women, whether it was a one-night stand or someone he called often. No one woman could hold his interest for long.

She was lucky because she didn't classify as one of his women. She was his best friend who he'd tried to fuck the brains out of last night. How the hell would she get back at him for last night? Just thinking about him keyed her up. She actually wouldn't mind going back up and *sleeping* late this morning.

After the sunrise of course.

"Betty said you work at an advertising firm around the corner from St. Peter's Hospital where I work." Alan's voice tugged her back to the dock. He worked near her? That was surprising.

"I didn't know you lived near me. I figured it was another effort on my mother's part to get me to move back here, settle down, and give her grandkids." Claire took a sip of her tea and set the cup down. "She has many great qualities, but her quest for grandkids has brought out her dark side."

"I don't know how to deal with people like Betty and your mother." Alan set his coffee mug on the dock and put his hands over his trim stomach. "I heard them conspiring on the phone once last Christmas. Thankfully I still had Liz then, so they weren't focused on me. But they were planning on getting a whole lot of mistletoe—"

Claire laughed and it rang out in the quiet morning air. "That one wasn't exactly the best idea. They have lots of elaborate traps to try to get couples together. They were lucky everyone didn't come down with mono that year."

"Maybe that's why they invited me this year. Backup for an epidemic." Alan's smile lit up his whole face. He was quite handsome, to be honest. Of course, he wasn't trying to hard sell her on him as a candidate because he thought she was already taken.

"Don't sell yourself short. These mothers don't usually have an attractive doctor to pawn off. Usually it's just the local plumber." Claire shook her head. That poor man had just been there to unclog her mother's toilet. Of course, Claire wouldn't put it past Grace Lake to purposely clog the toilet to meet an eligible bachelor for her daughter.

"Attractive, huh? You sure you aren't single?" He raised an eyebrow. "Because I think I'd be willing to be put through the gauntlet for a chance at someone like you."

Warm fuzzies started in her chest but she tucked it away.

Yes, Alan may have turned out to be attractive and she may want to get to know him better, but her mother would have a fucking field day if her matchmaking efforts ever brought about an actual couple. So Claire let the conversation slide into quietness as the hint of light brightened slightly.

"Oh, this is my favorite part." Claire gestured to the sky as the glow began to rise, filling the sky with oranges and pinks. Her father called it the paintings of God. That if you had a moment, you should admire the painting before it faded away. Every day was a new canvas and something special to share.

"Beautiful," Alan said.

Smiling, she turned to Alan, but his eyes weren't on the sunrise, but on her face. Heat touched her cheeks. She usually wasn't one to blush, but it'd been a while since someone had commented on something other than how hot her body was. In the light of morning, she could see the blue in his eyes matched the early morning sky.

She turned her gaze back to the sunrise. Who knew? Maybe she'd get Alan's information for a doctor visit of her own when she got back to town. It definitely couldn't hurt.

AFTER THE SUN filled the sky with light and her tea was gone, Claire headed inside, still wondering if Alan might actually be single and would want to go out with her sometime. Sure, the mothers had been all hell-bent on matchmaking but that didn't actually mean the guy wasn't tied up in some sort of relationship or not looking for something real. Alan could have a hookup back in the city for all she knew. Or some woman that he wanted but couldn't have right now.

Men weren't always upfront with her.

Also Claire would, of course, have to break the news that

her "boyfriend" was really her best friend, who she coerced into pretending so she wouldn't have to spend all Saturday locked in a bathroom with the plumber.

She also wouldn't be able to tell any guy that she and Logan had hooked up. Even if it was just for a weekend. Guys got insecure about her having a platonic male best friend in the first place.

As she headed up the stairs, no one else appeared to be up yet. Which worked for her. She liked the quiet of morning. While she didn't get a chance to commune with her deceased father at the sunrise, she'd met a good guy. Maybe it was a sign from her father.

Pausing on the stairs, she couldn't help but wonder what her father would think about her and Logan. Not that they were a couple but would he prefer her to be with someone like Alan? Alan seemed like a decent guy. Down to earth and not a flirt or player like Logan.

She opened her bedroom door to Logan stretched naked on her bed. Still asleep, but part of him was definitely waking up. Now this was one work of art she wouldn't mind exploring more of. She smirked as she closed and locked the door before stripping out of the clothes she'd put on. Shyness and modesty weren't things she'd ever been good at. Even when she was younger, she'd always been the first one to strip for skinny dipping in the lake.

Leaning back against the door, she let her eyes flow over Logan's naked body. Of course, she knew he worked out and had a good body long before they had sex. They had hugged, and she'd seen him in shorts and a T-shirt. But nothing quite compared to Logan naked sprawled on her bed.

Hers for the weekend.

Her engine definitely purred for him.

Quietly, she crossed the room and sat on the bed beside him. He didn't stir, not even when she lightly brushed his leg with her hand. She kept her eyes on his face as she trailed her hand higher until she stopped before touching his cock.

Still nothing. Fuck it. He was hers and she was his to do with what they pleased this weekend. They needed to get their fill of each other because it was temporary. She'd been serious about not catching feelings, but temptation and longing could be just as dangerous to their future friendship.

Last night had been awesome. She didn't know if he could keep up with that level of orgasmic bliss, but she was definitely willing to let him try. And give him a taste of his own medicine.

Her hair was still pulled into a messy bun as she leaned over him and took his warm, hard cock into her mouth. A hiss released from his lips, but he didn't open his eyes. She ran her tongue along the vein on the underside before engulfing his head again in her mouth, sucking gently. Her hands caressed his balls as she moved on the bed for a better angle.

She took him down her throat and hummed slightly. He hardened even more. As she came off, she swirled her tongue around the tip. She bobbed back down on him and his hand caught her bun. Stilling, she glanced up at his face to see his eyes opened and latched onto hers. She cocked her eyebrow at him.

"It's still early, Claire," he chastised, but his darkened eyes sparkled with desire. His sleep-deepened voice sent shivers through her body.

Keeping her eyes locked on his, she sucked on him and he groaned. Like he gave a fuck what time it was when she had her lips around his cock. How many times did he envision this, she couldn't help wondering. Had he fantasized about her taking him deep into her throat and getting him off? Because she'd had some dreams about this. . . . She raised an eyebrow at him again, daring him to pull her off and tell her to go back to sleep.

His hand on her hair started moving her up and down slightly on him. As if he were testing her. She relaxed under his touch and let him control her movements. He held her eyes captive as he pushed himself deeper into her throat and she hummed again.

"Fuck, Claire." His eyelids lowered slightly, but he didn't close them, like he didn't want to miss a thing.

Logan wasn't the kind of guy that sex-shamed a woman after. Sure, they'd talked shit about past lovers. Occasionally they'd laugh over something that happened during sex. Like the time a woman's cat had curled up under Logan's chin while the owner went down on him. Or when Claire's bracelet had gotten stuck in a guy's pubic hair. But Logan wouldn't use having sex now against her in the future like some guys would. That wasn't how Logan rolled.

She trusted him fully. Even now, he watched her carefully for any signs that she might not be okay with what he was doing. She had to admit heat flowed through her knowing how much this turned him on. He continued to fuck her mouth slowly a few more times.

Suddenly, he lifted her head off his cock entirely and sat up to take her mouth with his. They both rose to kneel on the bed. Skin met skin and sparks ignited across her where they touched. Their tongues tangled as the kiss consumed both of them. His fingers trailed over her breast before slipping down between her thighs.

"So fucking wet," he said, breaking off the kiss and smiling at her. Three of his fingers slid inside her and she almost came, but he drew them out and tasted them. "So fucking sweet."

His mouth claimed hers again as his fingers slipped back inside her. Her hands skimmed over his abs down to his cock. He tipped to the side slightly as he reached for something. His fingers left her and she almost whimpered at their absence. He pushed her hand off his cock as he sheathed it with a condom.

With a smile and a nip at her lips, he gripped the back of her neck. She let him guide her to face the headboard. He placed her hands on the top of the headboard and whispered in her ear, "Don't move these."

She shivered at the desire in his voice.

Once behind her, he nudged her knees wider with his own. Her head hung between her elbows as she waited. Anticipation buzzed along her skin. She was practically dripping for him. Ready and willing to do whatever he wanted. He hooked his arm around her waist to angle her better.

The heat of his front rested against her back and his lips found the spot where her neck met her shoulder. Her lips parted on a gasp. The scruff of his unshaven face scraped along her delicate skin. He nibbled and sucked the skin there until she could barely think, knowing that she'd have either a hickey or beard burn or both where his lips were. Marking her as his for everyone to see.

She couldn't find it in herself to care. All she wanted was him inside her, filling her, making her explode all around him.

He positioned his cock at her entrance.

"I could fuck you all day long," he whispered. He surged into her and bit her neck at the same time. She gasped as he filled her completely.

"Oh, fuck." She bit her lip.

As he began to pump his hips, she matched his movements. Nothing was slow and easy about him this morning. She couldn't get enough as he thrust in and out, hard and methodical.

His hand reached around and squeezed her bundle of

nerves, pushing her over the edge suddenly and dragging him with her. He groaned his release next to her ear as he rested his forehead against her shoulder. Their breathing remained heavy in the air.

"What's on the agenda for the day?" His stubble scraped across her shoulder as he peppered it with kisses. Aftershocks shuddered through her at the barely-there touches.

As he pulled out, she groaned at the loss of him and collapsed on the bed. "Breakfast, probably some swimming or sunning, maybe a game of volleyball. I don't know what all Mom has planned besides the bonfire tonight."

Logan sat on the edge of the bed. His dark eyes wandered over her naked body, heating her in every spot those eyes lingered on. Her nipples tightened and her spent body throbbed back to life, just from his fucking eyes. Dangerous.

"What?" she finally asked.

He smirked at her. "Can Naked Claire stay around? I mean, I know we said just this weekend for sex but can Naked Claire come to Sports Center night. I'm more than willing to bring Naked Logan."

She laughed at his eager expression. "You basically want Naked Sports Center?"

"Why not?" He leaned closer to her and pressed a kiss to her lips. "It would make high fives more interesting and do wonders for our friendship. We should definitely consider chest bumps instead of high fives."

His gaze dropped to her breasts. She shook her head. He really was hopeless.

"Obviously neither of us has a problem being naked." He gestured between the two of them as he lifted his gaze to hers. The mischief dancing in his eyes almost made her laugh.

"Except for Logan Junior, who probably wouldn't get the

message about no sex." She gestured with her hand at his cock that had already started to recover.

Logan frowned down. "Logan Junior? Seriously that's what you want to call my dick?"

"What have other girls called your dick?" She crossed her arms under her breasts and cocked an eyebrow at him.

"Wolverine." He winked at her. "Because he never goes down."

She laughed and pushed him away as she got off the bed. "We're going to need a spare room for your ego."

"Come on." He came around the bed, holding a condom up. "I think it's time to experiment in the bathroom."

"Most injuries happen in the bathroom." She backed up to the bathroom door and held it open.

"Yeah, but what about orgasms? No one ever talks about how many orgasms are had in bathrooms. They only advertise the bad stuff." Logan pulled her in with him and lifted her to sit on the counter. She wasn't a dainty woman, but without her heels, he towered over her and made her feel almost feminine and tiny.

She put her hands on his shoulders, still not sure what they were about to do. Okay, that was mostly a lie. She knew they'd have sex again, but she wasn't quite sure how Logan thought they'd manage it in this dinky room.

"Wait here." He turned on the shower and came back to her. "While that warms up, let's get you warmed up."

"Logan this seems like a bad—"

His lips on her breast cut off her words as she moaned. Gah, his tongue was fucking heaven. His hands pulled her hips into his. His cock was almost as hard as when he'd been inside her not that long ago.

"At least give me shirts and skins night," he said between kisses as he worked his way up her neck. He pressed his lips against hers. "We'll do a coin flip. Heads I win, tails you lose."

She laughed and shoved at his shoulder. "You're incorrigible."

"Yeah, but I'm going to fuck you on this counter and then bring you to a boiling point in that shower and then fuck you on the bed after."

She scoffed. "I bet you can't get it up again after fucking me on the counter."

The glint in his eyes should have warned her. "What are we betting? Because I'm willing to place shirts and skins night on the table."

CHAPTER 8

LOGAN SMIRKED as they headed down to breakfast an hour later. Claire glared at his smirk because she'd lost. Sore loser. Whatever. He'd won the bet, meaning they both technically won. Two more times. Three for her. The shower may not be big enough for actual sex, but he still made her come on his fingers.

Claire put on a tight smile for her mother.

"Good morning, you two," Grace exclaimed as they entered the kitchen.

Logan grabbed a piece of bacon from the plate next to the stove and gave her his most charming smile. "Morning, Grace."

Claire's mom blushed. "I hope you two slept well."

"Never better." Logan winked at Claire and she narrowed her eyes at him. Unfortunately for him, she never took him up on the bet, so he still didn't have Naked Sports Center on the books. Yet. He'd wear her down eventually.

Sean wandered in half asleep rubbing his stomach. He filled a cup with coffee and then blinked a few times at Logan. "You still here?"

Strange question. "Yeah?"

"Shut up, Sean. I don't scare away every man." Claire lowered herself into a chair and pushed out the chair next to her, giving Logan a look.

Ah, boyfriend duty. Fun times. He snagged another piece of bacon before scooting the chair closer to Claire and sitting down. His arm draped over her shoulders. His fingers played with the strap of her tank top, stroking along the marks he'd left on her golden skin. Love bites and beard burn. Fuck, he wanted to leave them everywhere on her body and show them off to everyone.

"Fortunate for me. I don't scare easily," Logan said to Sean.

Claire gave him a slight glare, but he smirked at her and kissed the tip of her nose. Maybe she thought he was acting for her family. After last night, he didn't really feel the need to act. He wanted his hands on her as much as possible.

She should be practically glowing after the night and morning they'd had. Floating on an orgasmic high like he was. But he wasn't used to Claire around her family. Or really Morning Claire, when they weren't at work.

Though he could definitely get used to Claire's idea of a wake-up call. Her lips around his cock had been ten times better than he'd imagined when he watched her suck wing sauce off her fingers. Whenever she sucked on her fingers from now on, he guaranteed he'd have a raging boner remembering this morning.

"I don't think there is anything Claire could do to make me leave." Logan rubbed his thumb over the love bite again and she shivered beneath his hand. It wasn't a line. She was his best friend and no matter what he'd stick by her. Sex or no sex.

But he preferred with.

Sean scoffed and drank his coffee. "We'll see."

Logan glanced at Claire but she wouldn't meet his gaze. She had trouble keeping guys, that was fairly public knowledge. Plus the fact that she could hang out with him pretty much whenever, meant she didn't have anyone steady these past few months. They'd both gone home with other people though, so it wasn't like she didn't get action. But she hadn't dated anyone seriously that he knew of. Besides those douche nozzles she'd brought to game day those few times.

Logan was selfish and enjoyed his time with Claire. If she had a boyfriend, she'd have less time to spend with him. Besides, what guy would be okay with Claire hanging out with a player like Logan?

If a future guy made her choose, would she choose him or the boyfriend?

His chest tightened and he gripped her shoulder like he could keep her from having to make that decision.

"Sean, stop teasing your sister and sit down to eat." Grace set multiple platters filled with breakfast foods on the table. Was she expecting an army? She glanced over her shoulder. "Where are Travis and Hannah?"

"Hannah's staying here, too?" Sean snagged the platter of sausages before Logan could get a few. "You running a brothel I should know about, Ma?"

"Watch your mouth." Grace smacked the back of his head before turning a smile to Logan. "Excuse my ill-mannered eldest child. He believes couples should abstain when in the presence of their parents' homes."

Logan choked a little on his bacon and Claire thumped him on the back. Claire's mom had left them a veritable buffet of dirty times in their room. Maybe she was running a brothel.

"I'm hoping you get a chance to run into Parker Grant today, Sean. She's such a sweet girl." Grace sat at the table but looked over her shoulder again to search for Travis.

Sean rolled his eyes and ate a sausage link.

"Want me to run up and get Travis, Mom?" Claire stood before her mom had a chance to answer.

"Yes, sweetie. That would be nice." Grace watched Claire disappear out of the kitchen. Her accessing eyes landed on Logan. "Sooo, Logan. . . ."

"Here we go," Sean whispered as he leaned back to watch what would probably be, in his mind, fireworks.

Logan wasn't worried. He cut into his pancakes and took a bite before saying, "Yes, Grace?"

"Claire says you come from a family back East? Do you get to see your folks fairly regularly?" Grace lifted her coffee mug but didn't drink. She held it between her two hands.

"Every Sunday practically." Logan grinned. Fuck, he'd been certain she'd throw him a curveball, but that pitch was as easy to hit as a meatball. Straight across the plate. "Mom wouldn't have it any other way. She loves having us kids around her dinner table."

"Has she met Claire?" Grace's eyebrow raised slightly.

"Claire's been to my family dinner a few times. Her and my sister Kit are thick as thieves." He'd actually been a little terrified that Claire got along so well with Kit. Any girl he'd dated in high school had gotten the stink eye from Kit, but Claire genuinely impressed her. Probably because Claire *wasn't* dating him. "During football season, she hangs out with us on game day. Says it's better than being in a bar."

Sean stopped shoveling food in his mouth and raised an eyebrow at Logan. "You and Claire watch the game together?"

"Every one." He lifted an eyebrow. No need to lie at all. "Sometimes at one of our apartments. Sometimes at a bar. Sometimes at my parents.'"

Sean put his silverware down and wiped his face with a

napkin. Clearly something was on his mind. Sean smirked and leaned forward. "Have you seen the jeans?"

"Sean!" Grace chastised and glanced at Logan nervously.

Logan laughed. "Of course, I've seen the freezer jeans. It wouldn't be game day if Claire didn't wear them."

Sean narrowed his eyes at him. "What about the drinking and swearing?"

"You mean when she turns into a dude for a few hours." Logan took a bite of his pancakes as he watched Sean's face. Apparently, he was surprised that Logan knew Game Day Claire. Probably thought he was one of those guys who displayed Claire like a fucking trophy. "We've been together for a while now. We do pretty much everything together, so yeah, I've seen that side of Claire. Like I said, I don't scare easy. Besides, who doesn't like a gorgeous woman who's into sports."

Sean grunted and picked up his fork. That felt like a homerun for Logan.

Grace seemed to relax into her seat and drank some of her coffee. Her eyes took on that far off gaze look. "Game day was always big at our house. My husband, Kyle, loved sports and it ended up being a family day for the kids and him. A real big to-do."

Claire walked in with Travis dragging Hannah behind him. Hannah's face was bright red, but she had a huge smile on her face. Claire sat next to Logan and he draped his arm over her shoulders again. This time she gave him a slight smile before she added bacon to her plate.

"What's the plan for today, Mom?" Travis pulled Hannah into the chair next to him and started filling his plate from the platters.

"No plan."

Three similar faces popped up from their food to stare at their mother with open mouths. Logan chuckled and used his finger on Claire's chin to close her mouth. She grabbed his finger and put it down in her lap.

"What do you mean *no* plan?" Claire asked.

Grace shrugged, nonchalantly. "Just that. I'm just glad to have all my babies under one roof for a weekend. I don't need to choreograph the entire weekend."

Travis put his hand on his mother's forehead. "You sure you feel well, Ma?"

"Knock it off and eat your food." Grace gave each of them that look your mother makes when she wants you to do something. "The world is not ending. I'm just adjusting. You all are grown-ups and can do what you like. I'll probably go have a talk with Betty and hang outside, but you guys can do whatever."

"It's a trap, isn't it?" Sean looked around worriedly like ninjas were going to drop from the ceiling.

Claire released Logan's finger. She took a bite of food and then said, "I was thinking about hanging out in the lake for a while. Maybe some volleyball?"

"That sounds like fun," Hannah said. She was really cute. If Logan had met her in a bar, he would have tried to take her home. He didn't take other guy's girls though. Well, unless that other guy had been a douchebag to Claire, then they deserved what they got.

"See, you guys are capable of taking care of yourselves." Grace smiled and sipped her coffee. "Now eat so you have energy to keep busy today."

"Thank you for cooking, Grace." Logan gave her a smile and pinched Claire's shoulder slightly.

"Yeah, thank you, Mom." Claire also smiled, but then pinched Logan under his arm.

Claire turned to him and popped her eyebrow up at him, daring him to retaliate. Oh, he would. Just later, when she least expected it.

CLAIRE HAD MADE sure to put her bikini on before they left the room so she wouldn't have an excuse to drag Logan back to bed. Because she had a feeling if they went back there, they wouldn't be leaving anytime soon, given the look of determination in his eyes after breakfast.

Logan went back upstairs to change into his swim trunks, while she headed into the backyard. The air was still cool and thick with the morning dew evaporating. It would heat up as the day progressed. The sand volleyball court stood between their yard and Betty's yard.

"Hey, crazy girl."

"Matt." Claire turned. Her neighbor and childhood friend engulfed in a bear hug that lifted her from her feet. She just managed to see the twinkle in his green eyes before he grabbed her. She laughed and pounded on his back. His longish brown hair tickled her nose.

"What are they feeding you in that city? You must have gained fifty pounds." Matt set her on her feet but held her shoulders. He had seven inches and probably a hundred pounds on her.

She punched him lightly in the stomach and he pretended to double over. "Haven't you learned not to comment on a woman's weight, Matty?"

She threw out the nickname as a gauntlet, knowing he'd hated it since the beginning of high school.

"Now, you've done it." Matt slipped his flip flops off his feet and took up a starting running position. "It's dunking time."

Claire had already started running toward the lake. "No, Matty! Wait until I get my clothes off."

She made it all of ten feet before he swept her off her feet and threw her over his shoulder.

"You know this is a family lake during the day, kiddo. No skinny dipping." Matt swatted her ass and hauled her down toward the dock.

"Seriously, let me down." Claire laughed. "I still have my shoes on."

"Oh, I'll put you down." Matt's voice sounded anything but reassuring. His hand settled on her ass again and she had a second to take a breath when they were both airborne before they went under.

She kicked to the surface of the lake and sputtered. That bastard had jumped in the lake with her on his shoulder. He came up in front of her, laughing. She splashed him in the face.

"I still have on my shoes, you ass." She swam for the dock, but he grabbed her leg and tugged her back. She glared at him. "Oh, really, is that how it's going to be?"

He grinned at her as she got closer. She put both her hands on his head and pushed him under the water. While he scrambled for the surface, she got away and grabbed the ladder on the dock to pull herself up.

When her feet hit the dock, a towel appeared in front of her. She glanced up at Alan Thomson's smiling face.

"Figured you could use this." His smile was sweet. His lean figure looked good in board shorts and no shirt. He wasn't as clearly defined as Logan but he definitely wasn't a slouch.

"Thanks. Could have used a hand prior to the dunking." She raised her eyebrow at him as she took the towel.

"Sorry, Matt is more than most people can handle. Me included."

"That's right. I'm the king of the lake," Matt said, directly behind her.

She spun around and pushed him off the dock back into

the water. He almost grabbed her arm, but Alan pulled her back at the last minute, his hands on her hips.

She turned and grinned up at Alan. "Thanks for the assist."

His light eyes darkened slightly as they dipped down to her body. "Anytime."

She stood in front of him dripping wet in her shorts and tank top and her Keds.

"Come back in, crazy girl. I love it when you're feisty." Matt wolf whistled as he treaded water.

Claire rolled her eyes. "In your dreams, Matthew Miller."

"You know it, Claire." He blew her a kissy face before going into a back stroke.

"Old friends?" Alan asked, clearly uncertain about what type of relationship she'd had with Matt in the past.

"The oldest. Our mothers are besties. Matt and I are practically siblings." Claire sat on one of the deck chairs to tug off her shoes. "He could have waited until I got my shoes off at least."

Alan sat next to her. "It's like he's regressed to high school again."

"Hopefully not." Claire shuddered. "Otherwise we'll be out here skinny dipping tonight."

"Did someone mention skinny dipping?" Logan's voice came from directly behind her chair.

"Don't get any ideas." Claire glared up at him as she set her shoes to the side and stood.

Logan smirked. "Why would I get any ideas when someone mentions getting naked and wet?"

She shook her head.

"I thought you said you already had on your bikini?" Logan's gaze roamed over her wet clothes plastered to her body.

"Yeah, the evil neighbor boy threw me in the water."

Claire unbuttoned her shorts and let them fall in a splat to the ground.

"Are you the evil neighbor boy?" Logan's gaze turned to Alan.

"No, I'm just his friend. Alan Thomson." He held his hand out.

Logan walked around the chair to stand next to her as he took Alan's hand. "The competition?"

Alan laughed. "I take it you're the boyfriend."

"Logan O'Connell." They shook each other's hand while Claire lifted her shirt off and dropped it to the deck with a splat. She'd have to wring the damn things out and hang them on a chair.

This was the part she never had any trouble getting. Males stood up and took notice of her curves and her bikini highlighted the best of hers. Both the men paused to look at her as she rubbed the towel on her skin.

"Did you grab the sunscreen?" Claire met Logan's eyes and heat scorched through her. She could almost see in his eyes all the naughty things he wanted to do to her. She cleared her throat. "Sunscreen?"

Logan grinned and held up the bottle. "Ready and waiting to be rubbed on."

Alan cleared his throat. "I think I'll join Matt in the water."

Logan closed the distance between them as Alan went to the end of the dock and jumped in.

"Alan seems nice." Logan's voice against her ear went straight to her core. Sex, three times this morning, obviously wasn't enough to cool her jets when it came to Logan.

She turned and he was right there. So close she could feel his breath caress her lips.

"He also has a boner for you." Logan lifted his lips into a

teasing grin. "You sure you want to have a boyfriend this weekend?"

"Did you want me to stop having a boyfriend this weekend?" She lifted her hand to pluck imaginary lint from his shirt. "Because you seemed to really enjoy being a boyfriend."

"Fuck, Claire. You're making things very *hard*." He kissed her and she practically melted. He lifted his head and grinned knowingly at her.

That knowing look had been pissing her off all morning. She batted her eyes up at him and reached for the sunscreen, easily taking it out of his hand.

"Let me make sure you're thoroughly covered," she whispered against his lips.

His eyes widened and he pulled his T-shirt off over his head with one hand.

As soon as he had his back to her, she shoved him off the dock into the water. "Hope you cool off, sweetie."

He hit the water and went under. The other two guys laughed. But Logan didn't surface right away. Ha ha, very funny. She waited a moment longer before setting down the sunscreen and jumping in after him.

The lake water was a little murky from everyone jumping in. Hands wrapped around her waist and pulled her to the surface. Warmth engulfed her back. Logan's laugh was the first thing she heard.

She tried to get his arm off her, but he held her tight.

"What's wrong, Claire Bear?" he said softly so only she could hear him. "Worried you almost drowned me?"

"Wishful thinking on my part. Are you going to let me go?" Their legs tangled together as they treaded water.

"I like holding you when you're all wet." His lips touched the side of her neck and she automatically tilted her head for him to have better access. Below the water surface, one of his hands slid down between her legs. Very quietly so the other guys wouldn't hear, he said, "Always so fucking wet for me."

"Logan," she practically growled. She grabbed his wrist and pulled his hand away.

"Cannonball!" The word was the only warning they had before Travis flew over them and splashed everyone near the dock. Matt started a splashing fight with Travis.

"I need sunscreen or I'll fry." She tipped her head back to rest on Logan's shoulder. "I won't be much fun if I'm burnt to a crisp."

That got him moving. Logan headed for the dock still holding her. When they got to the ladder, he helped her onto it before following her out. She went to the towel and dried off again. Logan grabbed the sunscreen and sat on one of the lounge beach chairs. He spread his legs and held out his hand to her.

Apparently all business now that a burn might put her out of commission. She shook her head and sat with her back to him.

"This would have been easier when you were naked." He squirted lotion onto his hands.

"If we did this while we were naked, neither of us would leave the room and we would have no use for sunscreen." She arched her brow over her shoulder at him.

"Who needs sun?" His hands came down on her shoulders and he methodically rubbed the sunscreen into her skin. He dipped below her straps and below the back of her bikini bottoms. Then he started on her arms.

Either the sun had started to get to her or he was stirring up a fire within her.

"I'll get my front." Her voice sounded strained as she held out her hand. Instead of giving her the bottle, he squirted some sunscreen in her hand.

"You know I'd do a more thorough job." He dropped a kiss on her shoulder and a shiver coursed through her.

"You'd turn us from PG-13 to X-rated if I let you rub lotion on my breasts."

Logan groaned. "With the exception of your brothers, I don't think anyone else would mind."

Claire looked out at the lake. Alan and Matt both looked away quickly, while Travis just shook his head at the two of them. She chuckled. "At least they'd enjoy the show."

"That's my show for the weekend. They can find something else to watch." The words were practically growled in her ear. Fuck, that turned her on, too.

CHAPTER 9

After Logan finished slathering Claire with sunscreen, she helped get his back for him. The guys weren't as interested in watching him get lotioned up. Fucking pervs.

"Well, hello there," a sultry voice called out.

Logan looked over his shoulder. Claire gave him a pointed look.

"Remember to behave," she whispered harshly.

He had no doubt she'd leave him high and dry tonight if he didn't play along with the whole boyfriend illusion. Though that hadn't stopped her from getting cozy with Alan Thomson before he came down.

The woman walking toward them had to be in her early twenties. Blond hair. Green eyes. Bikini barely covering her tight little body. If this were a club, he'd have been on her in a heartbeat.

"I didn't know Claire would bring eye candy." The woman's eyes lit up and took Logan in from head to toe and obviously wasn't disappointed in what she found.

"Let me guess? Little Parker Grant?" Claire's tone was a bit standoffish, but not off-putting.

"Hardly little, Claire," the woman said with a smile that didn't quite hit her eyes. Then she turned those green eyes on Logan. Fuck she was sexy. "Hi, I'm Parker. I assume you're Claire's friend?"

"Boyfriend," Claire said as she moved to his front, continuing to rub sunscreen into his skin. Places he could clearly get on his own. Not that he'd ever complain about Claire's hands on him. He glanced down at the top of her head, but he couldn't get her to look up.

"Logan," he said to Parker.

"Climbing up the evolutionary scale on this one, aren't you, Claire?" Parker pursed her lips as her hot gaze followed Claire's movements.

Fuck, he hated catty women, but if it got Claire to keep rubbing on him, why not have some fun?

"Did you bring any friends, Logan?" His name rolled off Parker's tongue. Yeah, if they were at the club, he'd hit that in a darkened corner and leave with another hottie. That body would be worth it; that attitude would not.

"Nope, just myself. But I'm usually more than enough to go around." He winked at her.

Claire's hand slapped his side. She glared up at him. "Whoops, bug."

"Thanks, baby." He chuckled as she continued to work the lotion down around his waistband.

She rolled her eyes at the endearment.

"I guess I'll just have to settle for watching then." Parker brushed by, intentionally sweeping her hand against his. She turned back over her shoulder and gave him a wink.

"I think I'm beginning to recognize the crazy," he said softly.

Claire met his gaze. "What?"

He grabbed the back of her neck and kissed her. Not a small little peck, but an all-consuming, we-should-be-somewhere-fucking-right-now kiss. When he lifted his head, her eyes were dark pools of lust. Yeah, he did that. Not fucking Alan Thomson.

Parker sat at the end of the dock with her feet dangling over the water. She glanced at Logan again and her eyes were heated as she watched him. That chick was trouble with a capital T.

"All done." Claire slipped from his touch and set the sunscreen with the towels Logan had brought down.

"Now we get in the water?" Logan walked over to Claire and leaned over her. "Or do we find a private spot. Just the two of us."

"Definitely water." She shoved him back slightly.

He gave her a grin before he headed to where Parker sat.

"You know, I could use some lotion too." Parker held her hand over her eyes to look up at him. Yeah, not touching that with a ten-foot pole. Not this weekend. "I'd hate to burn."

He glanced up and saw Sean heading their way. "Hey, Sean. Parker needs sunscreen. You want to handle that?"

Logan gave a quick smile to her angry eyes, before he jumped into the lake, splashing water up on her legs. He swam out to the floating dock where the other guys were and climbed onto it.

"Yo, dude. I'm Matt," a big guy with a cheeky smile said.

"Logan." He held his hand up and sat down.

Travis handed him a can of beer from the cooler. "Met Parker?"

"Yeah."

"She's always been a firecracker." Travis wiped down his beer before opening it. "She got around in high school, especially after the twins showed up."

"The twins?" Alan asked.

Travis held his hands in front of his chest. "The twins."

Everyone nodded in acknowledgement.

Hannah came down and sat next to Parker on the edge of the dock. Claire stood for a few moments near them, chatting about something. Parker might have nice breasts, but Claire had nice everything. Claire's hair was tied up in a bun leaving her long neck bare.

"Dude." Matt hit Logan's arm with the back of his hand to get his attention.

"What?" Logan turned to see Alan's and Matt's eyes on the trio of women. Parker was more like the type Logan usually went after. Hannah too. But Claire outshined both those women in her red bikini.

"Claire." Matt nodded and smiled at Logan, expectantly.

"Jesus, Matt, that's my sister." Travis shook his head.

"What am I missing?" Logan turned and looked at the guys. Travis rolled his eyes. Alan just shrugged. Matt looked like a hopeful puppy.

Travis made a dismissive sound. "Claire is hot."

"Okay." That was a universal truth. Logan still didn't know where this was going.

"And intimidating as fuck," Matt added. "Like in high school, guys wanted her, but asking her out? Fuck, man. She'd probably tear off my balls if I even looked at her funny."

Logan leaned back on his hands and watched as Claire climbed down the ladder and swam toward the floating dock. Her arms and legs cut through the water effortlessly.

He got what the guys were saying. Claire was everything a guy could want and not every guy could go for that. She said what she wanted. Took what she needed. And fuck if she wasn't gorgeous while she did it. She also could hang with the guys and just be herself. She didn't put on a show like Parker. At least not with Logan.

Claire pushed up onto the deck as water flowed over her curves. Yeah, not every guy could watch his woman being ogled by every other male around without feeling insecure. Logan didn't miss the appreciation in either Matt's or Alan's eyes. Fuck, they could look all they wanted, but she was Logan's for the weekend.

"Travis, pass me a beer." Claire took the beer and sat next to Logan.

"You gonna belch the National Anthem?" He kept his voice low so she'd be the only one to hear.

She laughed, loud and uninhibited. "You need me to?"

Her grin alone made him want to drag her to somewhere private.

"Not sure it would help at this point." The words slipped from his lips, but then he gave her a smirk to take the edge off.

"So what are you guys talking about?" Claire glanced around as she took a drink of beer. "We were talking about anything but politics and landed on a discussion on why Party Pink is better than Bubblegum Pink for nails."

Logan chuckled. "Did you drop the stats for number twenty-four and blow their Cotton Candy Pink minds?"

"I don't think they follow football quite the way I do." She grinned and chugged a little beer. "Now Matt's little sister Emily can talk football all day long and we have on occasion."

"Did you see the preseason game last Monday?" Travis asked.

Claire went into a full rundown on why the referee had been fucking blind and that epic pass and kick. Then she went into her Fantasy football league and why her team was going to hand the other teams their own asses. Matt got into the discussion as they talked about this season and how the preseason went.

Alan drank his beer and hung back a little. He interjected some knowledge here and there but he wasn't a hardcore fan like Claire. Logan laid back on the dock and stared up into the clear sky. This was the shit he and Claire talked about every day, so he didn't feel the need to participate. Eventually the topic changed to Alan's rotations at his new hospital, giving Alan the stage.

Apparently the other girls had grown bored of just being eye candy and finally swam to the dock to join them. Even Sean came out. Probably to follow Parker who made eyes at all the guys. Her eyes settled on Logan last, but he tugged Claire down to lay on her stomach next to him.

He didn't catch the new topic. Some show that a few of them had watched or something.

"You having fun?" Logan rolled his head to look at Claire.

She pursed her lips and turned to meet his gaze, squinting against the sunlight. "I'm having an okay time. You?"

"Not club level fun, but pretty damn content." Not something he would usually feel, but the sun was warm, the company interesting, and Claire's skin brushed against his. He couldn't think of a better place to be at the moment.

She smiled and his pulse kicked up a notch. "You want to head in for lunch and maybe a nap?"

Except maybe that. He raised an eyebrow at her. "A nap or a nap?" The only difference between the two was his intonation.

She turned on her side, giving everyone else her back. Her gaze dipped down and then back up to his eyes. Fuck, her dark eyes were hypnotic. "The kind after a nice, long, hot shower."

Logan sat up and looked around at the others just hanging with their beers. Claire sat up too.

"We're going to head in for lunch," she said.

"Sand volleyball this afternoon. Right, my man?" Travis held up his fist to Logan.

"Sounds good."

LOGAN SAT NEXT to Claire at the table. She'd put back on her tank top and shorts over the bikini and he'd put back on his shirt, but heat still lingered between them that had nothing to do with the sun. Grace had premade sandwiches and put them in the refrigerator. Bags of chips sat in a bowl on the table.

"So, Alan, huh?" Logan started before he took a bite of his sandwich.

"What about him?" Claire sat back in her chair and popped a chip into her mouth.

"You sure you don't want to be stuck in a bathroom with him?" Logan watched her face carefully.

She shrugged. "He seems like a nice guy, not like the assholes I usually attract at the club."

"He doesn't like sports."

She smiled. "You caught that too?"

"The guy looked shook watching you spout out stats." Logan took a bite of his sandwich. The poor guy would never survive Game Day Claire.

"A guy doesn't have to like sports to date me."

Logan scoffed. Yeah, right. Half of Claire's life was sports. Didn't matter what season it was, she was into it. What the hell would she and Alan have to talk about? Work?

"He doesn't." She insisted and pushed his chair with her foot. "I've dated guys who weren't into sports."

"What happens during the season? They become a sports widower?" he teased.

"They don't usually last through a season." She shrugged and her face fell a little.

"Hey." He tipped up her chin with his finger and looked her in her eyes. "If they don't get you, they don't deserve you."

"Easy for you to say." She drank some water. "You could get any woman you wanted and they would probably feed you grapes while you watch the game. Guys don't want girls like me. They either don't like me spending so much time on sports or aren't confident enough to handle other guys looking at me. I'm too much for them."

He never felt that way about her, but they'd never dated. Both Matt and Alan seemed slightly in awe of her. Frankly, Logan adored the sports side of Claire. It was one of the reasons they became such good friends. Of course, Game Day Claire could potentially scare a lesser guy. Someone who only wanted Claire as arm candy. And if they were into her for sports, he could see a guy being intimidated by her sexuality.

"You don't need a guy who's into sports. You have me for that." Logan smiled at her and she returned his smile.

"You do realize if I do get a man, he won't like us hanging out." Claire picked at her sandwich a little and tossed it on the paper plate.

"Because I'm devilishly handsome." Logan leaned back in his chair.

"Guys tend to be possessive and figure any guy friend a gal has is trying to get into her pants." Claire shrugged.

Logan stood and pulled her to stand with him. "He wouldn't be wrong. I'm definitely looking forward to getting into your pants."

"Jesus, my eyes." Travis walked in and held his hand over his eyes. "Can't a man come into his own home and not find a guy fondling his sister?"

Logan just chuckled and threw away their plates. "Probably not when your sister is Claire."

"Like I didn't find you going down on Allison Perkins on the living room floor my senior year of high school." Claire shuddered. "Talk about scarred for life. My sixteen-year-old brother was getting some when I wasn't."

"Yeah." Travis got a dreamy look on his face. "Good times."

"I'm going to defile your sister upstairs." Logan took Claire's hand and tugged her after him.

"Unnecessary information, man," Travis yelled after them.

Claire giggled a little as they went upstairs. As soon as they were through the door, Logan backed Claire against the door.

"You giggled like a little girl." His hands went to her ass that he'd been wanting to grab since he saw it in that bikini. Fuck, he always wanted to grab her ass.

"Newsflash." She tugged on his ear. "I am a girl."

"I think I'm going to need more proof." Logan lifted her shirt over her head. "Have I told you how much I admire this bikini?"

"No, you have not." She lifted his T-shirt and he helped her pull it off over his head.

His fingers went to the snap on her shorts and opened them. They slipped over her hips and fell to the floor onto her bare feet.

He stepped back and sat on the edge of the bed. "Fuck, Claire. I mean, how you don't spend every day just touching that body of yours is beyond me. I've been given a limited license to visit and I want to touch you all fucking day long."

She leaned against the door. Her fingertips trailed up her sides. "If you were me, how would you touch me?"

"Your neck," he said and swallowed hard. Everything about Claire was sexy, but this side of her, holy shit. If he'd known, the only girl in a club he'd have left with would have been her. Every fucking time. "It's graceful and I love marking it up so other guys can see how desirable you are."

She trailed her fingers up and ran them down her throat,

tipping her head back and parting her lips. Those fucking fantastic pouty lips asked, "Where next?"

"Your breasts." His voice deepened and his cock had long ago stood at attention. It literally wept when her hands slid down to touch her breasts over the bikini that left little to the imagination. "I'd slip my fingers under those cups and tease your nipples."

Her dark eyes watched him while she did exactly what he said.

"I love to feel the weight of your breasts in my hands." His words were solemn as she followed through. "Slip your hands down your sides to the ties on your bikini bottoms."

Her hands slid along her sides. Her fingers tangled in the ties. "Like this?"

"Undo them." He swallowed against the lump in his throat. He was right on the edge, but he wanted to see how far she'd go, and he wanted to be the one to take her there. Every fucking time.

She released the knots and her bikini fell to the floor.

He wanted her completely naked. "Take off the top, too."

Claire's chest rose and fell as she did what he asked. She rested against the door completely naked, willing to do whatever he wanted.

"Trail your hands over your stomach down to your pussy." Logan couldn't take his eyes off her. "Touch yourself and tell me how it feels."

Her lips parted as she did what he said.

"So fucking wet." Her words were breathy.

Fuck. He wouldn't be able to play this game much longer.

"Dip a finger inside. Just one."

Her eyes fluttered shut as her moan filled the air. "Logan. Please."

He grabbed a condom and dropped his shorts before

crossing the floor. He slid the condom on but stopped before he touched her.

"Take my hand and show me what you want," he whispered in her ear. Heat radiated off her skin, scorching his own, though he didn't touch her anywhere.

He straightened. Her eyes opened and locked on his. With her free hand, her fingers wrapped between his from the back. Holding him captive with her eyes, she ran his fingertips over her nipple in a circle before dragging it down over her trembling stomach.

His fingers joined hers between her legs, slipping into her wet folds. Her eyes darkened as his finger joined hers inside of her. She controlled their fingers as she fucked herself with them. Her lips parted and he barely stayed where he stood.

"Please," she cried as her core squeezed around their fingers.

He took both of her hands and brought them against the door next to her head. He drew her hands up above her head on the door and held them with one of his.

"What do you want, Claire?"

"You."

When his mouth took hers, her legs wrapped around his waist. His free hand helped lift her into place. His cock pressed against her entrance. Lifting his mouth, he rested his forehead against hers.

"You're so fucking sexy." He slid inside her, slow and easy. Her lips parted on a gasp. "All those guys want your hot little body, but you're mine."

She whimpered as he thrust in and out of her. Her dark eyes opened and he almost lost it at the longing in them. He could lose himself in her so easily.

"They only get to look at that red bikini and imagine fucking you." He stroked harder in her as he spoke. "I would have fucked you right in front of them. Let them see what they're missing. I'm too selfish to do that. I want to keep this part of you all to myself."

"Logan." She tipped over the edge into ecstasy. He did that to her, not any of them. His cock. His words. His name on her lips.

"Hold on, tiger." He released her hands and used both his hands on her hips to guide her.

She wrapped her arms around him as he thrust harder and faster into her. "Oh, shit, Logan, I'm going to come again."

He captured her mouth and felt her shatter all around him, drawing him into his release. They stood there, panting against each other as they came back to themselves. Fuck, that had been intense.

Still holding her, he lifted her from the door and walked toward the bathroom. He paused and grabbed a few condoms.

"What are you doing?" she asked.

He kissed her nose and smirked. "I'm feeling cocky and have a plan for the shower."

CHAPTER 10

"Holy fuck!" Claire lay on the bed panting. "I might need an actual nap now."

Logan chuckled next to her and patted her hip. "We have sand volleyball."

Claire stared at the ceiling, trying to get her breathing under control. "I think all my muscles are fatigued to the point of not working anymore. Maybe I'll sit on the sidelines and cheer you on."

"Like a real girlfriend?" Logan gave her a cheeky grin.

She grabbed a pillow and smacked him with it. "You're ridiculous."

"All I know is neither of us is leaving here without putting on sunscreen." Logan took the pillow from her and dropped it on the floor. "Much as I love putting on a show for the guys and gals, I'd prefer to follow through after rubbing you down."

"You can't possibly get it up after that." She waved her hand in the general direction of the bathroom. He'd fucked her standing up with her wrapped around him again. Pretty much the only position that shower had space for.

Logan rolled to his side and ran his hand over her breast. "Wanna bet?"

The mischievous twinkle in his eyes made her simultaneously laugh and groan. "Look, you may be able to get it up again, but my lady bits need a break. And I definitely won't bet with Naked Sports Center on the line."

She narrowed her eyes at him while he laughed.

"I'm pretty sure I'm going to win Naked Sports Center before this weekend is through." Logan got off the bed and held out his hand to her.

She eyed it warily but sighed and took it.

"Please tell me you have another bikini that will blow those guys' minds enough that they can't focus on sand volleyball."

"I could just show up naked." She held her hands out to the side.

He groaned. "I'd never be able to focus if Naked Claire shows up."

His hands grabbed her hips and pulled her into him. His mouth claimed hers and with their naked bodies pressed together, she almost wanted to say fuck it and go at it again, but they'd already been up here over an hour.

She pulled back and tried to take in a deep breath. "Down, Wolverine."

He laughed and swatted her ass. "Grab the sunscreen, tiger."

It took them forty-five minutes before they were outside. Claire had on her black string bikini with only a pair of cutoff shorts over it. Logan wore another pair of board shorts that were swimming trunks.

They definitely had sunscreen almost everywhere. Which had led to oral sex for both parties involved. Claire gave Logan a side glance. He had this cocky grin on his face. Of course, she couldn't wipe the smile off her own lips. The guy had a very talented tongue.

He held her hand as they walked toward the volleyball court where Matt, Alan, and Travis were tossing the ball around. Parker and Hannah sat on the sidelines, chatting. All Parker seemed to want to talk about was makeup and hair. But Hannah had a sneaky sense of humor.

Claire's buzz was way too good right now. She could probably handle a little girl talk. Hannah waved her over with a huge friendly smile.

"It's about time. We thought about sending a rescue party after you." Travis flinched. "But no one really wanted to go to your door."

Logan laughed and released her hand. He snatched the ball out of the air. "Are we going to play volleyball or gossip like women?"

Claire smacked his side.

"My apologies." He grabbed her with one arm around her waist while the other held the volleyball. He kissed her quickly and released her again. "I'll try to be less sexist."

"More like too sexy," Parker whispered loudly to Hannah.

Claire dropped down beside her and pushed her sunglasses up her nose. "No such thing."

The boys were in their own world while they discussed rules and teams and such.

"As too sexy?" Hannah asked. Unlike Parker, who wanted to start something, Hannah was just curious.

"Nope. Logan is sexy, definitely. But too sexy? Would you want him to be less sexy?" Claire glanced over her glasses at Parker.

"Of course, he's sexy. I mean, even the guys would probably agree." Parker thrust her tits out more as the guys glanced over at them.

"Logan definitely would." Claire chuckled. Logan's ego

seriously couldn't get any bigger. He knew he was sexy. He flaunted it and used it to get in any woman's panties he wanted to. A little shiver raced down her spine as his dark eyes paused on her.

You're mine. Those words, fuck, those words. He didn't add *for the weekend* or *for now.* In that moment, she had been his. Happily.

"So he's conceited?" Parker asked with a little snarl in her tone.

"He's confident." Claire shrugged. "He is what he is and he doesn't care what anyone else thinks about him."

"I'm glad Travis isn't like that." Hannah glanced at Claire. "Not that he isn't confident, but he's not so. . . over the top."

"I'd be worried about Logan going off with another woman if he were my man." Parker's eyes tracked Logan as the guys started to play.

"I'm not worried." Claire met Parker's gaze and held it. Claire wasn't worried. Logan kept his promises and he'd promised to only have eyes for her. They weren't dating, but as long as they were fucking, he wouldn't fuck anyone else. Their friendship meant a lot to both of them. It would be hard to go back to just being friends, but right now, they were on vacation from their normal lives.

When they got back to their normal world, things would go back to being the way they'd always been. And that meant sleeping with other people. Parker could just cool it with the insinuations that she could take Logan. Not this weekend.

"Yeah," Hannah said, "you don't have to be worried when you look like you. And those looks Logan gives you." She fanned herself. "I can feel the heat from those looks."

"I just need someone to take the edge off." Parker's gaze went to the other guys. Matt and Alan were both eligible guys. Both good looking. Single and probably would be down.

Of course, Claire's brother Sean was somewhere around here. But he might have someone he was sneaking around with for all she knew. As long as Parker didn't try for Logan, Claire would be happy.

Claire's gaze fell back on Alan as Parker asked Hannah about her haircare routine. Alan was a good-looking guy. No one could outshine Logan, but Alan held his own. He'd been thoughtful and kind this morning. She might not have noticed him in a club, but she had noticed him here. Unlike Logan, he seemed to be searching for a girlfriend. Someone to spend his life with. If her mom could be trusted.

Logan only wanted sex. Right now, he wanted it with Claire. But once they got home, he'd find it with girls like Parker. Maybe Claire should get to know Alan better. See if there might be something there.

THE BALL WENT OVER THE GIRLS' heads.

"I'll get it," Logan offered. He ran past the women and Claire's eyes remained on Alan. Fucking Alan.

He picked up the ball and walked back to the court. He tossed Travis the ball before dropping to kneel in front of Claire.

"Yes?" Claire tipped her sunglasses down to look at him. Her eyes drifted down his sweaty body and he could see the heat stir within them. Good.

"Just wanted to say hi to my girlfriend." He lifted an eyebrow at her.

Parker cleared her throat, trying to get his attention. He didn't bother looking at her. Yeah, he'd noticed her checking him out. Fuck that noise.

"And you're still here because. . . ." Claire waved her hand for him to continue.

He leaned in and kissed her. He pulled back an inch and said, "For that."

Claire shook her head, but the little smile on her lips made his heart thump harder.

He smirked at her as he stood and joined the guys back on the court. "It's too bad there isn't another girl. Then you guys could play too."

"What about Emily?" Alan asked Matt.

"My teenage sister?" Matt glared at Alan like he'd offered to throw her to the wolves. Maybe he had. Who knew what Matt's sister looked like?

"Emily's in college, not thirteen. I'm sure she would play volleyball with us." Alan shook his head. He held up his hand to Logan and Travis. "Give me a minute and I'll see if I can get her."

Alan ran off into Matt's house.

"No one check out my sister." Matt held out his finger at Travis and Logan.

Travis laughed. "Why not? You check out my sister all the time."

Matt flushed red and rubbed the back of his neck. "That's different. She's your older sister. And besides, Claire doesn't mind."

"You drool over her like a sixteen-year-old boy." Travis stepped toward the net.

Logan laughed.

"You don't mind him looking at your woman?" Travis asked with a glare sent Matt's way.

Logan shrugged. "He can look. She's fucking sexy as hell. I'd be shocked if he didn't look. But when it comes down to it, she's with me."

Logan looked back at Claire. Her eyes had widened and her mouth was in a little o. Fuck, he wanted to kiss her again. Longer and without an audience. He wasn't sure why she was surprised though. He loved the way guys looked at her when Clubbing Claire was on his arm. They were envious she was with him. Sure, eventually someone had the balls to hit on her, especially when he wandered off to hit on some sweet piece of ass. But for a moment, in those guys' minds, she was all Logan's.

"Dude, I don't think I'd be as cool with you checking out my woman *or* my sister," Matt said as he looked back at the house. Probably worried that Logan would steal away what was Matt's. Right now, Claire wasn't stealable and neither was he. Not even for a hot piece of ass.

Alan stepped out the sliding glass door followed by a young woman. She had on jeans shorts and a pastel plaid button down shirt tied at her waist. She was cute with brown hair in a ponytail and light blue eyes. Too young for Logan's taste.

"I guess that means we're all in too." Claire stood and brushed her hands over her bottom. That ass was currently his.

"I would have done that for you, baby." Logan gave her a smirk.

She rolled her eyes and walked to stand next to him. "I'm sure you would have."

Unlike Matt, Logan didn't need to be insecure about Claire. She was his best friend. Always would be. At some point she might belong to another man, but some part of her would always belong to Logan. That was how friendship worked.

Though if Alan became that guy, he might not be cool with her hanging out with Logan. Especially as touchy-feely as Logan was this weekend.

"I guess I'm on this team too?" Hannah asked Travis and Logan.

Travis pulled her in and kissed her forehead. "Of course. I'd never pick anyone else over you."

She smiled at him sweetly and pursed her lips. He kissed her quickly before stepping back. They were so cute.

"Shall we play shirts and skins?" Logan caught Claire's eyes.

She shoved him back. "Fuck off, Logan."

Everyone laughed. As they all fell into positions for the game, Logan stayed next to Claire near the net, while Travis and Hannah took the line. Parker and Alan stood on the other side of the net from Logan and Claire, while Matt and Emily took the back of their side.

"Later then?" he said softly enough for only her to hear.

"Get in your spot." She gave him a gentle nudge away, but her smirk made him grin.

"So it's singles versus couples?" Matt called out.

"Speak for yourself, Matty." Emily grabbed the ball from Matt and headed back to the serving area. "I've got a man at college."

"I'm fine being single," Parker announced. Her eyes lingered on Logan again. "It just means I have more options."

Emily served and for a few minutes, following the ball kept everyone occupied. The women added an interesting dynamic and made it so the guys had to run less. Turned out Emily played volleyball in high school and could basically run that whole side of the court. While Hannah was scared to hit the ball.

"Just bump the ball." Travis had gone over to talk to her after another point had been scored when she failed to hit the ball. "Put your arms like this and—"

"I always wore sweatshirts on volleyball days in gym class." Hannah backed away from him and crossed her arms. She had on a crop top over her bikini. "Those balls bruise my arms."

Travis shook his head and looked around. "How about we take it down to three on a side? You guys can lose your ringer."

Emily flipped Travis the bird. "Whatever. Don't blame me because you suck."

"Grace has ice cream bars." Hannah walked toward Emily. "You want to grab one?"

"Sure." Emily handed the ball to Matt. "Good luck, sucker."

Matt looked at the ball for a second. "Fuck it. I want ice cream. Wait up."

He tossed the ball to Alan.

"Guess we're down to two." Alan glanced at Parker who just shrugged.

"Sure, why not." Parker dug her toes into the sand a little.

Logan and Claire looked at Travis.

Travis held up his hands. "Fine. Whatever. It's not like it was my idea to play or anything. I guess I'll go eat ice cream with my girlfriend."

Logan clapped him on the back as Travis passed. "We'll play one game and then we can go back to everyone."

Travis shook his head. "Not unless I find a sweatshirt for my girlfriend."

"Just you and me, Claire Bear." Logan gave her a wink and smacked her ass.

"What do you say, Alan?" Parker moved into the server position. "Wanna kick some ass?"

Claire moved off to her position, but her look said that she would get him back for the Claire Bear and the smack. He couldn't help but grin in anticipation of what she might do.

"We can certainly try," Alan said. His gaze strayed to Claire's breasts as she moved in front of him.

Claire gave Alan a smile that was sweet and soft and

fucking encouraging. What the fuck? Logan narrowed his gaze on Alan. He'd have to have a talk with Claire about the friendly doctor to see where her head was at when it came to Alan Thomson. Because if he can't look this weekend, neither can she.

Logan clapped his hands together. "Let's get on with this."

He had to admit he was pretty impressed with the women's bikini tops and that there hadn't been a nip slip yet. Both women seemed to be fairly decent players. Alan wasn't bad either. Anytime the opportunity arose, Logan spiked the ball down on Alan.

"Hey, Logan," Parker yelled as she moved to serve. "Wanna go for a swim after we kick your asses?"

He chuckled. "You know we're ahead by five points, right?"

She shrugged. "Not for long."

She served the ball and flashed him a nipple right afterward. Logan rolled his eyes as he hit the ball back. Was she seriously trying to distract him with her boobs? Had she not seen Claire's, which were ten times better than hers?

"Are you fucking kidding me?" Claire said under her breath.

Maybe he wasn't the aim of her frontal assault. Claire set up the ball and Logan spiked it down in front of Parker, who shrieked. Of course, Alan was too busy staring at Claire's breasts to help out his teammate.

All business, Claire held out her hand to the side and he slapped it. She gave him a nod as she moved into the service position.

Parker gave Logan a wink and a smile. He narrowed his eyes at her. She busied herself with brushing sand off her knees. Logan wanted to put her back in her place. He glanced back at Claire, but her eyes and smile were for Alan.

"You have something. . . ." Alan smiled at Claire and gestured to his cheek.

Claire walked to the net. Alan met her and brushed the hair off her cheek. She gave him that smile that Logan had seen her give guys in the club.

"Thanks." Claire touched Alan's arm briefly before she walked past Logan back to her spot.

Hot lava flowed through Logan's veins. Fuck that.

"Hey, Alan." Logan moved closer to the net and waited for Alan to join him.

"Yeah?"

"Who has the better tits?" Logan made sure both women could hear. "Claire or Parker?"

Alan glanced at both the women almost unintentionally and his face flushed. "Dude."

"What?" Logan smirked. "I'm sure the girls are dying to know what you think. I mean they're both on display in those luscious bikini tops. Obviously they both *want* you to notice."

Alan raised an eyebrow and narrowed his eyes. "What's your game?"

Logan held up his hands. "No game, man. Just wondering. No different than judging a wet T-shirt contest."

Claire came up with the ball under her arm. Her eyes on Logan. "You don't have to answer that, Alan. Not every man is only interested in the way a woman looks."

Parker strolled up behind Alan. "You're only worried that he'd pick me."

"Sure." Claire rolled her eyes. "Because he's been staring at your tits all game."

Alan swallowed and looked down at the ground. Yeah, this guy would never be Claire's equal. She had to see that.

"I'm afraid my decision would seem biased." Logan glanced between the two sets of breasts. Both very lovely, but there was no question Claire's were one hundred percent better.

"You're making Alan uncomfortable." Claire glared at him like he was the bad guy.

"Maybe Alan staring at your breasts makes me uncomfortable." His insides burned a little as his heart squeezed. "It's one thing for a guy to look and admire. It's another for him to stare long enough to memorize them."

"I think I'm going to go find some of that ice cream." Alan's voice got softer as he walked away.

"Like you haven't memorized women's 'assets.'" The ball dropped and both of Claire's hands went on her hips. Her breasts rose and fell with her breath.

"Much as I love drama, this one doesn't include me. So, yeah." Parker's voice was the next to leave.

"Like you don't with the guys at the club. What was that one guy's name? Owen. Didn't he send you a dick pic? Did you get off on it?" Logan couldn't seem to stop his mouth. Alan fucking Thomson had unleashed something Logan had kept tamped down for way too long.

"Shut up." Claire glanced around, suddenly aware of their surroundings. She grabbed his wrist and tugged him down to the dock. She dropped his hand, crossed her arms, and whispered, fury clinging to every word, "What the fuck is going on with you, Logan?"

"Alan eye fucking your breasts every chance he gets. You giving him encouraging smiles like maybe you don't mind the eye fucking." Logan closed the distance between them until they were almost but not quite touching.

"You mean like Parker eye fucks you?" Her eyes sparked like fire.

"I don't fucking want Parker." He brought his face down to her level. His heart pounded in his ears as he held her eyes. "I don't want to fuck Parker. I don't think about her like that.

The only woman I've memorized is you. Fuck, Claire. I've wanted you as long as I've known you, but I couldn't have you."

"What?" Claire took a step back.

He closed the distance. "I didn't care about those other guys because I knew they couldn't get you. Not fully. You show those guys this sexy version of you that is only part of who you are. And when you show them the parts of you that you only share with me, they fucking run away. I don't run away."

"You don't want me." She shook her head in denial.

"I'm hard for you twenty-four seven, Claire. I want you. Every fucking version of you turns me the fuck on. Even Game Day Claire with her foul mouth and her belching. I have wanted you since the first day you strolled into Taylor and King in that red dress and heels. You were a fucking knockout. Then you opened that mouth and told the dirtiest joke ever and I knew right then that I needed you in my life."

His heart pounded like he'd run a marathon.

Claire's eyes were wide and she barely blinked. Her fingers covered her mouth.

Fuck, what was he doing?

He inhaled and pushed out his breath, trying to calm the fuck down. "You're my best friend. I mean that. No matter what happens after this weekend. I will always want to be your best friend. I don't want a guy like Alan Thomson coming between us."

She took in a breath and stared at him hard. "So, what does all that mean?"

He grabbed her hand and smiled. "It means let me enjoy fucking your brains out while you'll let me. I know that part of our relationship is temporary and I'm good with that. Honest."

Some of the tension released out of her shoulders.

"But promise me you'll stay my friend and not let some guy make you drop me because he can't handle me being your friend." Logan straightened and ran a hand over his head. He couldn't bear to lose her. "I sound like a fucking girl."

Her lips quirked up into a smile. "I wasn't going to say it, but. . . ."

"Yeah, fuck you." Logan came down to her level again. Eye to eye. "I'm serious though. I know some guy is going to end up with you and you're going to be happy, but don't let them make you turn your back on me. You and me will be together too. I've never had a best friend like you."

She smirked. "One you could fuck, you mean?"

He smiled. "Well, I'm sure Marcus in college would have let me fuck him, but he didn't have quite the bangin' body you have."

She laughed and it made everything settle within him.

"Are we good?" Logan asked squeezing her hand.

"Yeah" —she poked him in the chest— "just stop telling people to look at my tits."

"I'm sorry about that. Fucking Parker and Alan, they're getting into my head. But, Claire Bear, your breasts are perfect. Why won't you share them with the rest of the world?"

She rolled her eyes, but a smile tugged at her lips.

"Come on." He tugged her hand. "Let's see if there's any ice cream left."

CHAPTER 11

THEY DECIDED to turn on a movie and sit in the air conditioning for the rest of the afternoon. Claire wasn't sure who suggested it, but everyone piled into the living room and took up their stations.

Travis and Hannah cuddled in a chair. Everyone else piled onto the sectional. Parker sat between Alan and Matt at one end, while she flirted with both the guys. Thankfully, Parker kept Alan occupied. On the other end, Claire sat on the couch while Logan sat on the floor between her knees. She couldn't keep her hands off his hair and ears. His hands trailed up and down her legs.

Every once in a while, he'd look up at her with banked heat in his eyes or he'd grab one of her hands and kiss it softly.

He'd always wanted her. His admission kept wrapping around her brain nonstop. It wasn't just her brain either. Somehow her heart had gotten in on the action. She couldn't even begin to analyze what he meant or what the underlying message might have been. It was just sexual, right?

They had this weekend. They'd play out their melodrama

and go home where things made sense. Where they were Claire and Logan, coworkers and best friends. Where they didn't kiss and definitely didn't fuck. At least each other.

Sure it might be hard to cram the genie back in the bottle, but this couldn't continue. If it did their friendship would suffer because he would eventually want to move on. She couldn't lose her best friend. She didn't want to evaluate her feelings for him, because it wouldn't matter. They had the weekend.

The group disbursed to change for the BBQ and bonfire. Logan took her hand as they headed up to their room.

Claire dragged him into the room.

"Is it time for the third shower of the day?" Logan reached for the snaps of her shorts.

She covered his hands with hers and looked up into his darkened eyes. "Not a communal shower."

"But we're conserving water and saving the planet." He smirked down at her. "Need some alone time? Can I watch?"

The heat of his body and his hands under hers made her want him to participate. Instead, she nodded her head. "I need some time to think. Alone."

His hands moved to her hips and pulled her in close. She wasn't surprised to feel his erection against her stomach. It seemed like a constant state for him. But the feel of it made her insides melt.

He lowered his head until his lips barely touched hers. "You sure?"

No. "Yes." Her voice barely a whisper. She was tight and needy and his heat seeped through her clothes to scorch her.

When his lips claimed hers, she whimpered. She was only so strong. Her arms wrapped around his neck as he lifted her slightly to change the angle of the kiss. His tongue swept through her mouth like a tornado: swift, thorough, and destroying everything in its wake.

He lifted his head and set her on her feet. She staggered a little, but he held her tight.

"Take your shower, tiger." His smirk at knowing what he made her feel should have made her angry. Instead it made her throb.

He pointed her in the direction of the bathroom and slapped her ass.

"Fucker," she hissed over her shoulder as she made her way into the bathroom.

"You like it." His laugh followed her in as she closed the door and leaned against it for a breath.

She turned on the shower and looked in the mirror. Her pupils were blown. Her lips were swollen and red. Her chest heaved with every breath. This was what Logan did to her.

She rested against the door. What would she do when they returned to their real life? How would she feel when they went out together and he left with another woman? Would she feel different? Would she be jealous?

She never had been before. Maybe a little put out if she didn't find someone else to hang out with, but jealous? Not really. It was just how they were with each other.

Checking the water temp with her hand, she sighed. She wouldn't know until they got there. To that moment when he chose someone else. It would happen. Logan wasn't going to change just because they had sex. She stripped off her clothes and checked the marks on her neck.

Worse than a horny teenager. She grinned at her reflection.

She didn't waste any time in the shower before stepping out in a towel. When she opened the door to the bedroom, Logan sat on the edge of the bed closest to her, leaning back on his elbows. His dark eyes took in every inch of her, covered by the towel or not.

"Give me a minute." He stood and dropped his shorts to

the ground in front of her. Seriously, the man had a gorgeous cock. He tipped up her chin with his finger and brought his face level with hers. "Hold that thought."

He stepped around her and without shutting the bathroom door, turned on the shower and stepped in. Unable to resist, she leaned against the doorframe and watched him rub soap all over his body and rinse himself. Fuck, he was a beautiful man.

Every inch of him was sculpted to perfection. It ought to be, since he spent a decent amount of time at the gym. She did her share of working out too. They'd even gone together a few times. Of course, he'd gone home with someone else and she'd received a few numbers herself.

"What's that smile for?" Logan ran the towel over his body efficiently, his short hair practically dry already.

Her fingers itched to feel the smooth prickly texture beneath them again.

He hung up his towel and stalked slowly toward her. Unabashedly naked. His heat coated her like a warm blanket. The fire burning in his eyes held her entranced. His fingers closed around the edge of her towel. "Want me to hang that up for you?"

She released her hold on the towel covering her. The terry cloth rubbed against her skin as it fell away, only held aloft by his hand. His gaze flowed over her slowly. He took the towel and turned to hang it up.

Her breathing started again as his eyes released her. Her gaze dropped to his backside. Seriously, it should be illegal to look that damned good. When he turned and their eyes met again, she knew he could see the fire burning in her own, matching his.

They moved as one, but not toward each other. He stepped closer, stalking her, and she retreated into the bedroom. His steps were larger and he closed in on her as the back of her knees hit the mattress. She stopped, still standing.

"How much time do we have?" His hand reached out to brush her hair behind her ear.

"How much time do you want?"

"All of it." His voice was soft and unhurried. When his lips claimed hers, her arms wrapped around his neck, pressing herself into his heat. He coaxed her down onto the bed, never relinquishing her lips, until he held himself above her.

The kiss went on and on, like they'd never kissed before and would never kiss again. The lust between them lingered, but it remained in the background. No rush. Just tasting and feeling. She could spend all day kissing Logan.

Her hands cradled the back of his head. His hair was soft velvet on her palms. His hands trailed down her sides. She parted her legs more and his cock nestled against her intimately, but he still wasn't in a hurry. His every movement was slow and the kiss endless.

He leaned to the side with his arm outstretched. The sound of the package opening filled the room. She shivered in anticipation. He knelt on the bed between her legs but didn't give up her lips. Following him up, she refused to give his up either. She wanted him so bad. Needed him to fill her. To ease the ache he created just by being himself.

He nipped at her lip, drawing her attention back to the kiss. She followed his lead and lost herself in the taste that was purely Logan. His body shifted above hers as they fell back to the bed. He slid inside her in one powerful move.

She gasped into his mouth, but he still didn't stop kissing her. The tension wound tighter and tighter with his every thrust. Slow and steady. Tearing her apart and putting her back together in slow motion. Without warning, the tension burst.

He caught her cry with his lips. But he remained unrelenting, driving her back to the edge with the slow, methodical thrusts of his hips. Dragging himself across every nerve ending until she couldn't think, just matched him thrust for thrust until she shattered, coming apart at the seams while he tried desperately to hold her together.

She pulled away from his lips. Needing air. Needing space. Still matching his hips in their slow dance.

His dark eyes opened to meet hers. Longing, lust, and something darker lingered in those depths. Something tantalizing and frightening.

"I can't. . . ." She gasped as he pushed her closer and closer to the brink again. She shook her head and closed her eyes. It was too much. Her being swirled with emotion and she couldn't grasp what she felt. Every time it got close, it slipped through her fingers. "I. . . ."

"Look at me, Claire." His words were hypnotic.

Unable to resist, she opened her eyes and lost herself once more to his dark depths.

"Let go." His voice was husky and strained as if he was holding himself back.

Her body no longer belonged to her. On his command, her body released. She strained up against him, letting the waves pull her under as they crashed on her one after the other until she couldn't breathe.

"Ride it out, love." The words barely registered in her as he gathered her closer to him and found a new pace. His forehead pressed against hers and those eyes held her captivated. "Stay with me."

She never came down from her orgasm, following his hips with her own. He kept thrusting until his own release gripped him. The tortured pleasure twisted his face and made him real. His eyes softened as he drew in a breath.

He claimed her mouth again as they slowly floated back to themselves. Tasting, exploring, taking everything they each had left to give. Releasing her lips, he shifted so his weight wasn't on her and she let out a breath, staring up at the ceiling. She wanted to ask him *what was that?* But she couldn't find her voice.

That had been intense and not playful like the other times they fucked. She closed her eyes. Something had changed. Something had shifted. And she didn't know what. She was afraid to examine it too closely.

But she wasn't catching feelings for him. They weren't falling for each other. What they were doing didn't mean anything. It was just sex. Slow, methodical, mind-fucking sex.

THE BONFIRE WAS ACTUALLY multiple bonfires around the side of the lake where the houses were. Every house had a bonfire with some sort of food to eat and people wandered from yard to yard. Coolers of drinks were everywhere. People milled about as children played tag through them.

Logan held Claire's hand as they strolled through the yards. It was peaceful even in this chaos. He felt content. Grace and Betty followed them to the next bonfire.

Claire hadn't talked much to him after sex. They'd gotten dressed and headed down to help Grace put out their offering for the night. A large chocolate sheet cake and the makings for S'mores. Then they'd followed Hannah and Travis around to the first few fires before the other two got stuck in a conversation with some old high school friends.

"So, Logan," Betty's voice was high pitched and a little nasally, "what is it you do again?"

"I work with Claire at Taylor and King, a boutique advertising firm."

Claire squeezed his hand and pulled away to go to say

hi to another woman. His hand chilled immediately. He sighed as she walked away. Nothing about this weekend was as easy as he'd thought it would be. He took a swig of his beer.

"You two look good together." Betty stopped next to Logan with Grace on her other side. "Almost too pretty together."

"What's wrong with two pretty people together?" Grace crossed her arms and glared at her friend.

"It makes it harder for the rest of us." Betty shrugged.

"Who?" Logan asked giving Betty a flirty smile. "The other pretty people?"

Betty blushed and touched Logan's arm. "Stop. I'm old enough to be your mother."

Her hand lingered on his arm and her eyes widened.

"Never too old." He flexed his muscle under her hand. Squealing, she took her hand away. He gave her a wink.

"Hey, Betty." Alan walked up to their group. "You look like you could use a refill."

Betty took the glass Alan offered and smiled. "Such a thoughtful young man. I sure wish we could find someone to pair you up with."

"What about Parker?" Logan's response drew everyone's eyes.

Grace shook her head. "No, no, Parker is ear-marked for Sean."

Logan almost laughed. *Did Parker know that?*

"But," Betty said thoughtfully, "if they aren't a match, they aren't a match."

"Stop, right there, Betty Miller," Grace said, turning so they were face to face. "We discussed this. Parker is for Sean, and Alan was for Claire."

"Well, Claire has this fine piece of man right here, so Alan and Parker would be perfect together." Betty looked around.

"I haven't even seen Sean today. He's probably creeping around with some other woman."

Alan bumped Logan's arm. When he had Logan's attention, he gestured for them to leave the bickering women behind. Logan nodded. Not that Alan would be his first choice, but better than the matchmaking mamas.

As soon as they were some distance away, Alan asked, "So what was that about at the volleyball court?"

It took Logan a minute but he remembered. "The breast thing?"

"Yeah." Alan rubbed the back of his neck. "I don't mean to look at Claire's breasts. They're just—"

"Why not?" Logan shrugged. "They're fucking awesome and it's not like she intentionally hides them or is embarrassed by them."

"Then what was that—"

"Parker flashed me her boob that last round. I thought maybe she was trying to distract me, but I know it was to fuck with Claire." Logan took a sip of beer. "I asked you that to get back at Parker."

Mostly.

Alan released a breath and smiled slightly. Though in actuality Logan had wanted to point out to Claire how Alan couldn't handle being with a woman like her. Not many men could. She was feisty and loud and gorgeous and sexy. She stood up for herself and put Logan in his place whenever she felt he got out of line. Most women just simpered at him and let him get away with being a shithead to them. Not Claire.

"We've got a few more days here and I didn't want to stir any trouble." Alan glanced back at the mamas still bickering. "I actually got excited to meet Claire before we came. Betty had nothing but good things to say about her. I was almost engaged a year ago and figured it was time to start dating again."

Logan nodded and his gaze sought out Claire, still talking with some woman. She'd pulled her dark hair into a loose bun, showing off her long and supple neck. Her top was loose and flowing over her denim shorts. She wore a pair of wedge sandals.

He always loved when she wore heels because then he could rest his chin on her shoulder. Though barefoot had its advantages too. She was by no means short, but shorter than he was.

"I didn't even know Claire would be so beautiful. When I met her this morning by the lake, I told her I worked at St. Peter's around the block from where you guys work. I've been there this past year. My sister even moved there to be close to me and find a job."

"This morning?" He'd slept in a little until she woke him up. Fuck, her lips around his cock, taking him deep. Shaking the thoughts from his brain, he couldn't lose himself right now in that memory.

"She came down to watch the sunrise. I was already there." Alan shrugged and held up his hands. "I swear I didn't do anything inappropriate."

Logan laughed. "Not sure why you seem scared of me. If you did anything inappropriate, Claire's the one you should be afraid of."

Alan's lips pressed together. "I hoped that when we get back to our real lives, you guys might want to hang out sometime. I have more downtime than I thought I'd have, and my sister is always after some guy or another. It would be nice to have friends outside of the hospital."

"We watch the game on Sunday evening at Legend's Bar. If you have it off, you're welcome to join us." He'd made the same offer to Lacy once. Of course at the time, he'd been a little more intrigued by Lacy and wanted to get to know her better. When Jonah arrived, suddenly Lacy got a lot more noticeable and that made Logan curious. Probably wouldn't have gotten to the point of actually being with Lacy though. They weren't really on the same level.

Alan seemed like a nice enough guy. But the first time he went out with Claire and suddenly all eyes were on her, Alan didn't seem like one of those guys that tried to make a confident woman like Claire feel less than, so she wouldn't try to stray. Of course Claire wouldn't put up with that shit. Nah, Alan wouldn't put her down, he'd just drop her entirely.

And if Sexy AF Claire didn't deter him, Game Day Claire would end whatever boner he had for her. It always did with the guys who preferred her as a piece of arm candy and not a rage machine yelling at tiny men on a football field.

"That'd be great." Alan smiled and he brightened considerably when he looked over Logan's shoulder.

Logan could almost feel her coming near him like a wave of heat. When Claire stopped at his side, she linked their hands together and smiled up at him before facing Alan.

"How's your night been going, Alan?" Claire leaned her head against Logan's shoulder. It was so effortless like they really were a couple. His chest ached slightly.

He fought the urge to swing her into his arms, kiss her senseless and drag her back to the cabin like a caveman. Who cared about Alan's night when they had a whole night to explore each other's bodies ahead of them?

"Barely dodging the matchmakers, but eating way too much. How about yourself?" Alan took a drink from his beer.

"Catching up with old friends. Thinking about heading to our house where there's cake and S'mores." She smiled at Logan. "How about it?"

"I'm game," he said, softly for her only.

Heat flared in her dark eyes. The two of them were combustible.

"I love S'mores," Alan added. He'd relaxed considerably

since he first approached Logan. As they started toward their cabin, Alan said, "Logan mentioned game days on Sunday at Legend's. My first Sunday off, I'll definitely try to meet you guys there."

Claire pinched the inside of Logan's arm and when he turned to her, she had a forced smile on her lips for Alan. "That would be great."

Yeah, that wasn't what her eyes told him. She'd give him hell for that later.

CHAPTER 12

"No, it was Toby Watts who started it." Claire pointed at Matt on the next log over. "You just went along with it because you thought you were being cool."

It was down to the younger adults around Claire's family's cabin bonfire. There were a few more people hanging out here besides the seven of them that had hung out during the day. A few other kids of families, grown now with some of their friends. Claire recognized a few of them. Like Parker, Claire didn't really know her, but Parker knew of Claire. A couple years younger made a bigger difference when they were kids and teenagers. A few bonfires over sat a group of older adults including Betty and Claire's mom.

Logan's hand trailed up and down her back as she leaned forward to talk with Matt about the first time they dared to skinny dip at the lake.

"What's not cool about skinny dipping?" Matt gestured to the lake. "We're just lucky we didn't get caught."

"Who was it that cried on the dock the entire time?" Claire pressed her finger to her temple to try to remember.

"Allison. Her parents moved away last year. I'm surprised

they didn't at least stop in to visit this weekend." Matt shrugged. "She really wanted to jump in but was too afraid of getting caught."

"Her crying almost got us caught."

"Only because I heard something," Travis chimed in, "and came to investigate. A bunch of naked teens in the lake wasn't exactly what I thought I'd find. Don't worry. I made Allison feel better."

"Ew, no, bad Travis." Claire threw a marshmallow at Travis's head.

He caught it, held it up like a trophy before he popped it in his mouth.

Logan's fingers trailed along the back of her waistband and a shiver raced through her. His touch was potent. The other bonfires had died down and some had even gone out. A bunch of goodnights filled the air as the other holdouts headed back for their homes.

Mom dropped off Betty before stopping beside Claire's and Logan's log.

"You all having fun?" Mom asked, looking around the circle.

A chorus of nods and yeses answered her.

"I already put away all the food," Claire said to her mom.

"Thank you. I can't wait to hear what you all have planned for tomorrow." Mom smiled and glanced at the house. "But that can wait for breakfast. I'm knackered."

Everyone said goodnight and the general noise of conversation increased again.

"Have you had a good day?" Logan's breath tickled her ear.

She smiled and looked down at her lap before turning to face him. "Better than I expected."

"Good."

"No making out around the fire," Travis yelled, while Hannah giggled on his lap.

"We could play spin the bottle," Parker suggested. She was once again between Alan and Matt on the log. Sean was no where to be found.

"I'm not playing spin the bottle with my sister." Travis sounded disgusted.

Parker rolled her eyes. "You would get to spin again if it landed on her."

"Aren't we all a little old to be playing that?" Logan asked. His tone was bored, but his fingers dipped into the back of Claire's shorts, tracing the edge of her panties.

Matt laughed. "Something about this place always makes me feel sixteen again."

"Maybe it's because your mom is doing all the house-work," Travis called out.

"I don't know." Claire looked around. "It's not just mom. It's this place. We grew up here. I don't know about anyone else, but I had my first kiss on this property."

Matt, Travis, Parker, and even Hannah all nodded and said yeah.

"Who was your first kiss?" Logan asked. His fingers skirting below her panty line now, heating her insides.

"Robbie Benson." Claire let her eyes unfocus on the fire as she remembered the sloppy kiss behind the trees.

"Ew, Robbie? My best friend?" Travis exclaimed. Hannah tapped him on his shoulder and gave him a disapproving look.

Claire stuck her tongue out at Travis.

"Who all has gone skinny dipping in the lake?" Matt asked. Most everyone put their hands up.

Hannah looked around. "By the time I was old enough, you all were too old."

"Well, we can fix that." Matt stood.

"How much have you had to drink, Matty?" Claire shook her head at him as he pulled off his shirt. No one around the fire was exactly sober at this point. But still. . . . "We're adults now. Not kids."

"Who's going to rat us out?" Matt lifted his eyebrow before dropping his pants to the ground.

The crowd groaned and simultaneously looked away as Matt streaked down to the water and jumped in.

He popped back up. "Come on, you chicken shits."

"Fuck it. Why not?" Travis stood and chucked his shirt on the log. He held his hand out to Hannah. "You never got to, so why not now?"

She put her hand in his and said, "How about we go out of the firelight to get undressed though? I'm not really into streaking."

"I'm all in." Parker took off her shirt. Her lace bra didn't do much to hide her assets. Her eyes landed on Logan as she took her bra off and slipped out of her shorts. She swayed slightly on her feet as she turned to Alan. "You coming, Alan?"

She sauntered off and by the look in Alan's eyes, he most definitely would be coming if he hadn't already. Alan's face was flushed from drinking already. Claire hid her face in Logan's shoulder to chuckle.

"What do you think?" Logan's voice was for her ears only. "Wanna break the law with me?"

"You want to get naked with a bunch of other people in a lake?" She lifted her eyebrow at him. She'd had just enough alcohol to make bad decisions.

He shrugged. "I'm not ashamed of my body. And I know you aren't ashamed of yours. I'll even keep the guys away from you if you want."

Logan's eyes twinkled with mischief in the firelight. Her breath quickened and her pulse pounded. She'd rather get naked somewhere with Logan alone. But hell, this was already a crazy weekend.

A bunch of splashes filled the air followed by giggles, both male and female as a bunch of the others joined in the fun.

Claire pressed a kiss to Logan's lips. "Okay, but I agree with Hannah. I don't need to be an exhibitionist."

"Why not? Your body is a work of art." Logan's grin was a little crooked. They were both happily buzzed.

"Have you been picking up Phoebe's lame pick up lines again?"

He tugged her to stand with him. "Maybe."

She rolled her eyes and he led her down closer to the water where they chucked their clothes before he grabbed her hand again. When they reached the end of the dock, Logan wrapped his arms around her and pulled her into the lake with him.

His lips crashed over hers before they went under and his hands slipped down to her ass. For a second she enjoyed the kiss, but then the water pulled them apart. They broke the surface and she glared at him a little for pulling her in. Not that she could stay mad at him. She sprayed him with water.

He chuckled and swam up next to her. "Want to do the back stroke together?"

"No." Claire glanced around. Most everyone was out by the floating dock, hanging onto the edge. Matt got out and jumped back in behind some girls who screeched at the water spraying them.

"Shall we join them?" Logan held out his hand and started in the direction of the floating dock. She shrugged and caught his hand. They slowly made their way through the water keeping their bodies underwater. Besides Matt, everyone else kept low in the murky water. Claire didn't want to inadvertently flash her brother.

"Travis, where are you?" Claire called out.

"The opposite side."

"Good, stay there."

Everyone else chuckled. Claire grabbed onto the dock and smiled at Logan before looking over her shoulder to see who was behind her.

"Oh, hello, Alan." She turned to face him, careful to stay mostly underwater. The water was dark and murky so it hid most of her.

Alan's face was still almost beet red. "Claire. Logan."

"First time?" Claire smiled softly. Poor guy. Call it peer pressure or too much alcohol because Alan didn't seem like the guy to go skinny dipping at all. Maybe she didn't need a guy who could handle all of her. Maybe she could make concessions for the right guy. Not that Alan was the right guy, but maybe he could be.

Alan nodded as Parker brushed up against him. Her white teeth gleamed in the pale moonlight. He didn't seem used to these shark-infested waters.

"Don't worry, we'll be gentle," Parker pulled up next to him on the dock. Her eyes searched out Logan. "How about you, big boy? Is it your first time too?"

Claire raised an eyebrow at the big boy comment, but then Logan's heat engulfed her back and she felt his big boy against her ass. The term was apt, at least. The water was warm from the day, but there were some cold undercurrents toward their legs which wouldn't be kind to those particular boy parts. But the coldness didn't seem to deter Logan's hard-on.

The thought that he could slide inside her right in front of everyone and they wouldn't know aroused her. Of course, skinny dipping meant no condoms so. . . that particular fantasy would not be happening.

"Skinny dipping? No, it's not my first time." Logan's breath blew against her ear and that shiver coursed through her again. His arm banded around her waist and drew her tight against him. All those hard muscles pressed against her were making her wish she'd called "out" and dragged him upstairs instead.

"Too bad. I've never had a virgin before." Parker smiled prettily at him before turning to Alan. "Have you ever had sex in the water, doctor?"

From Alan's wide-eyed expression, Claire suspected Parker wasn't exactly holding the dock with her other hand.

"What?" Alan let out.

Claire almost felt sorry for the man. But then Logan's hand slipped down between her legs, briefly. Just a hint of a touch to remind her who would be with her later tonight. She relaxed back into him as his mouth found her neck. So fucking potent.

Matt climbed back on the deck and squatted close to where they all were holding on. There were certain angles the human body should not be viewed from when that body was naked. Claire turned around into Logan, pressing her face into his neck. Her breasts flattened against his chest. His hand pressed into the center of her back, shaking from laughing.

"How are you guys hanging?" Matt bobbed his head.

"Dude, it's called skinny dipping, not get out and shove your junk into other people's faces." Claire lifted her head, deliberately keeping her gaze on his face.

Logan bit Claire's shoulder to keep from laughing out loud. His body shook next to hers.

"Hey, I'm not shy. It's not like I have a raging boner and the water isn't all that cold to make me shriveled." Matt shrugged and stood. "You don't want me on the dock? Fine, just remember you're in the splash zone."

"Things you don't want naked men to tell you," Logan whispered in Claire's ear.

She laughed right as Matt jumped off the dock, splashing their side.

"Why did we think this was so much fun when we were younger?" Claire pushed against Logan's chest. His hand cupped her ass, pulling her closer. The look in his eyes tantalized her.

"Because being naked with women is fun?" Logan smirked.

"We also swam around more and tried to cop a feel," Matt said as he swam closer. "I guess we all got a little more inhibited as we got older."

"Speaking of inhibited. Hannah and I are going in. Claire, avert your eyes." Travis yelled. Everyone chuckled as they very discreetly made their way to shore. A few more people headed back in laughing. But Claire refused to look until she knew her naked brother wasn't going to be in front of her.

The bang of the sliding door finally made Claire look up.

"Come on, Claire." Matt moved closer.

Logan's arm tightened around her waist and his chin rested on her shoulder.

"You never used to be a prude." Matt swam back a little. "Don't you remember playing Marco Polo."

"Usually in the shallow part of the lake." Claire's voice was a little breathless with Logan pressing his naked body against hers.

"We can play out here." Matt turned around. "I'll start."

Claire glanced at Alan and Parker. They both shrugged and moved away.

"Logan?" Claire whispered.

"I'm sticking with you," he said in her ear.

"Fine." She shoved off the dock and he followed her. They moved around the dock and held on in a spot blanketed by shadow.

Logan held on to the dock around her, shielding her. She opened her lips, but he shushed her.

"All right, here I come." Matt's voice got farther away from them, splashing around loudly.

Logan took her mouth, stirring up craziness within her. She held onto his shoulders as their legs tangled together. Kissing his way to her ear, he whispered, "Stay here."

He winked before he took off. Every inch of her was turned on and he left her.

"Marco," Matt yelled softly. They didn't really want to draw out the adults. Not that they weren't adults, but they were a little drunk and acting like kids.

"Polo." Logan's voice sounded from far off. Alan sounded like he was around the edge from Claire. Neither she nor Parker had made a sound.

"Come on. Play fair. I know Parker and Claire are out here still too." Matt splashed around in the water some more.

Parker giggled softly near where Alan was. At least, she hadn't gone after Logan.

"Marco." He was far enough away.

Claire rolled her eyes. She swam around the corner where Alan and Parker were. Giving them a grin, she called out, "Polo."

She swam off as Parker cursed. Hands grabbed Claire's waist and tugged her into a warm body.

"That wasn't very nice," Logan said against her ear and she relaxed into him.

"I have a feeling this could take all night." Claire glanced over at the dock where Matt was going around the outside.

"Come on, let's go in." Logan tugged her hand in the direction of the beach.

Fuck it. "Going in, Matty boy. They are like right behind you."

Matt turned and Parker squealed as Matt grabbed her.

"You good, Parker?" Claire called out in a moment of "never leave a gal behind."

"I'm good," Parker practically purred.

"Have fun." Logan held Claire's hand to help her up to the beach where they left their clothes.

"Um, Logan?" Claire started to look around the dock, but their clothes weren't there.

"Shit." Logan glanced around. "Travis?"

"Probably." That little fucker had run off with the clothes of everyone left in the lake. "I'm going to kill him."

"At least we got out first." Logan drew her against him. "That way I don't have to share your naked body with anyone else."

Heat pooled low and heavy in her as she met his eyes.

Parker still giggled on the other side of the dock. Shit, they should tell them.

"Hey, guys," Claire whisper shouted.

Parker stopped giggling.

"Just FYI. Someone took our clothes so you'll have to streak back to your places." Claire shivered as the breeze blew across her wet skin.

Logan pulled her against him.

"Fuck," Matt yelled. "Was it Travis?"

Claire shrugged even though he couldn't see her. "Probably."

"Can we talk about payback tomorrow?" Matt asked.

"Sure. Have fun, you three." Claire couldn't help the smile on her face as she and Logan snuck up the yard and past the dying bonfire.

Logan opened the glass door while she stood behind him.

"Towels on the chair," Sean's voice said in the darkened room.

"Thanks." Logan grabbed the towels and passed her one.

Once they were wrapped up, they entered the kitchen. Sean sat in a kitchen chair.

"Skinny dipping? Really?" Sean's dark eyes settled on Claire.

She just shrugged. "Why not? Where were you tonight?"

Sean shrugged and locked the sliding door. "Are you two the real deal?"

Claire's breath caught in her throat. "What do you mean?"

"I mean I know you, Claire. You don't bring guys home. You've told us about your *friend* Logan for months and now suddenly you two are dating?"

Logan put his arm around her waist but before he could say anything, Claire stepped forward.

"Why does it matter? What if we are serious? What if we're just fucking around? Why does it matter to you? I thought you came home to spend time with your family, but every time I turn around you're gone. So who gives a fuck what Logan and I are to each other? I want to know what you've been doing that's more important than family."

Sean's eyes locked down. She'd pushed too hard, too fast. He wouldn't talk now. After one more look at her, he stormed out of the kitchen. After a few minutes, she heard the click of his bedroom door.

"Fuck," she whispered. Sean could be such a dick sometimes.

Logan came around her and pulled her into a hug. He didn't say anything but just held her there for a minute. She took a deep breath. Sean trying to pick apart her relationship just made her angry. He showed up to the family cabin and then disappeared during the day. Off doing God knows what or who.

Logan rubbed his hand down her back over the towel and rested his cheek against her hair. Her heart skipped in her chest as her anger flowed away. How easy had it been to start to lean on Logan? To start relying on him? He'd never let her down in the past. But their friendship had been one with open doors to go out when it got to be too much.

He lifted his head and she tilted back to look up at him. What door would he use when it got to be too much?

"Let's go to bed." He took her hand and she watched herself automatically thread her fingers with his.

She looked at him and felt her heart thud against her chest. Something had changed between them and she wasn't sure it wouldn't destroy what they had before. But she let him take her to their room and when they fell into bed naked, she imagined this was more than just fucking. Each touch meant something. Each kiss held a promise of more.

Maybe she just needed to believe that someone who knew the real her could want her in his life as more than a friend. Maybe it was the way Logan's touches kept hinting at more. Maybe it was the dark something in his eyes when he slid into her and held her gaze captive while he pushed her over the edge time and time again.

Maybe it was the way he held her when they slept. Maybe it was nothing but a fantasy.

CHAPTER 13

LOGAN WOKE when Claire started to slip out of bed. "Where are you going?"

She crept away from the bed for a few moments. He heard the rustling of clothes, but then she leaned down over him.

"Just down to the dock." Claire kissed him. "I'll be back."

That kiss cleared the haze from Logan's mind. He grabbed her arm as he sat up and tugged her back to him. Instead of being naked as she'd been when they fell asleep, she had on a pair of shorts and a tank top. Seeing her dressed woke him up the rest of the way.

"I'll come with." He scrubbed his hand down his face and pushed the covers off.

"You don't have to. Really." She tried to push him back down, but he gave her a grin and kissed her. This kissing bit was nice—being able to kiss her whenever he wanted, but he wondered how long it would be once they got back before he would slip up. Grab her hand or kiss her in front of their coworkers. Or during a game.

"Two seconds, I promise." He pushed off the bed.

She sighed and waved her hand. He went into the bathroom and brushed his teeth. When he came out, he pulled on shorts and a shirt.

"Done."

She shook her head and held her hand out for him to go through the door. In the kitchen she stopped and grabbed two cups. "Coffee?"

He nodded while stifling a yawn. Morning wasn't the best time of day for him. Especially after a night of drinking beer followed by long, hot sex with Claire.

The programmed coffee maker had a pot hot and ready to go. She handed him a cup and grabbed her own as she headed out the sliding door and onto the dew dampened lawn. She didn't hold his hand, but that wasn't unusual for them normally, so he didn't think anything of it. Not that anything they currently did at this point was usual.

The dock was empty. He remembered Alan saying he'd been here yesterday morning. When he'd met Claire. Naturally, Logan was curious about this early morning ritual.

Claire stood at the edge of the dock, staring out into the water.

"Are we going to sit or swim or fish or what?" Logan took a sip of coffee and looked at her expectantly.

"Sit."

He nodded and set his coffee mug on the table before grabbing her hand. He sat down on the dock chair and pulled her to sit between his legs. For a moment, as tense as she held herself, he thought she might get up, but then she relaxed back into him. She sipped her coffee with her eyes on the horizon.

He took his own mug and followed her gaze. The sky had lightened in the distance, but the sun wasn't quite ready to make an appearance.

"What's the great mystery of coming down here every morning instead of staying in a warm bed with me?"

She sighed against him.

"When we came here growing up, my dad and I would always be the first ones up. Most days actually." Claire's voice was quiet and almost reverent. She rested her head back against his shoulder. Logan wasn't typically a cuddler, but with Claire, he liked when they touched. Right now, he loved how she relaxed into him and felt comfortable enough to share about her father.

Wrapping his arm around her waist, he said, "You don't talk about your dad much."

"I know." Claire sighed and sipped her coffee. Maybe that was all she wanted to say.

He respected that. The morning air was cool and had a freshness to it. A glass door creaked behind them and they both looked around the chair to see who was up so early. Still in yesterday's clothes and holding her shoes, Parker slipped out of the house Matt and Alan were in. She winced as she shut it and looked around before scurrying back to her family's house.

Logan chuckled. "Skinny dipping paid off for one of those guys."

"Maybe both of those guys." Claire shrugged as they fell back to watch the sunrise. "That type of thing happens all the time around here. Dad used to count the number of walks of shame and tell mom when she woke up. Not who, of course, just how many. Then mom would spend the rest of the day trying to figure out who and from what house."

Logan relaxed back into the chair with Claire's weight pressed against him. He didn't want to move a muscle or leave this moment. Even though he knew he was intruding on maybe a private moment of Claire's, he wanted to be a part of it. Part of him wanted it because Alan had been a part of it. A part of Claire Logan hadn't seen yet. The other half of him wanted to know more about her, know everything about her. Not just because of some jealous urge.

"What happened to your dad?"

"He died five years ago. Sudden heart attack. It wrecked my mom. Mom and him were everything to each other. My dad was loud and obnoxious at times, but in the mornings. . . . Out here. . . . It was like church. He'd make me a hot chocolate and himself coffee, and we'd walk out here quietly and sit to watch the sunrise over the lake."

"Sounds like a nice way to start the day." Logan kissed her head and tightened his arm around her. He knew about her family game day traditions with her father, but he didn't know the other parts of it.

She nodded and went silent again for a little bit. Drinking her coffee and watching the horizon, she never let her gaze fall away. She breathed in and out, and her hand stroked along his arm almost absent-mindedly.

"He loved all of us the same. I didn't get special treatment just because I was a girl." She paused and smiled softly. "Except here. At the lake. In the mornings. We were always the early risers even at home, but here meant everything."

Logan drank his coffee, wanting to hear more, but not wanting to press. His and Claire's relationship right now seemed like it was on quicksand, constantly shifting and constantly changing, and he wasn't sure what to hold onto anymore. Or if he hadn't already slipped under the surface to the point of no return.

"We talked about sports most other times, but on these mornings, he asked me about my life. Like the other parts of my life. How school was going. My friends. The guys I dated. What I thought I'd wear to prom. Instead of being one of his boys, I was just Claire."

She sniffled lightly. "I miss him so much. I know my

mom does and so do my brothers but when I have a complicated problem, I just want to be able to go to him and ask him to sit on the dock and drink with me while I work it out."

"Are you trying to work out a complicated problem now?" His tone was light, but he wanted to be here for her like that. Be her best friend. Logan inhaled the fresh morning air and Claire's light scent of mint and rosemary.

She picked at his shorts hem. "Not sure. I think I'm here more to just feel him again. Be in this moment and hear his voice tell me how cute Robbie Benson is. How my hair would look fabulous in an updo with my prom dress. How getting a C in AP English didn't mean I wouldn't go to college."

"I have to disagree with that last one. A C is a big deal, Claire. You need to focus on your studies and less on Robbie what's his name."

Giggling, she drew her feet up on the chair and curled into him with her face still aimed at the colors bleeding into the sky.

"I think my dad would like you," she said softly. Her head over his heart.

"Most dads like me. I'm a fucking dream. A catch, really."

"You're too cocky." She chuckled.

"You didn't mind that last night."

She hummed while she sipped her coffee. She waved her hand before she had a chance to swallow and finally said, "This is my favorite part."

Logan glanced at the sky but it didn't draw his attention like Claire's enraptured face. Freshly washed and bare of even a hint of makeup, her face looked younger in this moment than she usually did. One of those plastic claw hair clips caught her hair into a bun on top of her head. As the sun rose, the colors flowed over her dark eyes, reflecting a darkened image. Her lips parted slightly as awe settled over her.

Another chunk fell in his chest, locking into place. Tendrils escaped her bun and swayed in the breeze around her face. Suddenly he didn't want to share her with anyone else today. Not Alan or Matt or Parker. Not even her family.

"Want to do something today? Just me and you?" Logan swallowed as a tinge of worry filled him. What if she said no?

She glanced at him and wiggled her eyebrows. "Did you have something in mind?"

He couldn't resist kissing her full lips. He meant to make it a brief peck, but she turned on his lap and opened her mouth to him and he was lost. She tasted of mint toothpaste and bitter coffee and that unique taste that was all Claire. Fuck, he'd never get enough of her.

Even after basically a day of sex then rest then more sex and last night keeping her up until practically a couple hours ago, driving her out of her mind with orgasms and sliding into her over and over, he wanted more. Needed more.

But he didn't know what to call it. Or if he could give her more than sex in return. He just didn't want to stop this.

Claire broke off the kiss and traced her thumb over his lower lip. She met his eyes. "Can we discuss after. . . ?"

She leaned in like she was helpless to resist and pressed her lips against his. He stood, lifting her with him. Her arms tightened around his neck and her legs wrapped around his waist. She nibbled on his shoulder and neck as he walked them up to the house and up the stairs to their room.

He laid her down on the bed, pulling the clip out of her hair to let her dark hair fall all around her. She tugged him back down to her lips and he shifted them more fully onto the bed.

"I don't know if this weekend will be enough," he admitted as his finger rubbed her lower lip. What they had now, he wanted it all the time. Holding her, kissing her, fucking her. Talking to her in the early morning about her father. Learning about her from her family.

She made an impatient noise in the back of her throat and whispered, "It has to be."

CHAPTER 14

"Your big plan was mini golf?" Claire pursed her lips. "We could be having more sex, but instead we are going to play mini golf?"

"We can have sex again later." Logan brushed his lips against hers briefly before grinning. "And it's not just mini golf. They have bumper cars and go carts."

If it hadn't been for the amazing orgasm he'd given her twenty minutes ago, Claire would think Logan was a twelve-year-old boy. He was definitely way too enthusiastic about this play park thing he found.

"Come on, Claire Bear."

She rolled her eyes as he tugged her hand.

"I'm competitive. You're competitive. We light up our competitiveness and pettiness through the field of challenge and then go home and work out our aggression against each other." Logan leaned down so he was in her face. "Naked, of course."

"Of course." Claire didn't sound so sure and she wasn't. Yes, they were both highly competitive people, but they also usually ended up bickering when they competed against each other for something.

"There's even an arcade if we get too hot and a snack bar filled with all those calorie-filled carbs you love to hate," he tempted.

"Fine," Claire finally relented. He pulled her into him and kissed her.

She followed Logan through the arcade that smelled vaguely of popcorn and dirty socks, to the counter. The little blonde behind the counter at least looked in her twenties as she flirted with Logan. He gave the blonde that look. The one that smoldered and made women flock to him like crazy.

Claire leaned back on the wall next to Logan so he could see the condescension on her face. Yes, they weren't with anyone from the lake. But still, he was currently fucking her. He shouldn't need to flirt with everything in a skirt. He just winked at her as he got the putters and golf balls. He started out and she kicked off the wall to follow him.

Not many people were around this early in the morning so they pretty much had the mini golf course to themselves. It wound its way over a pretty sizeable area with lots of nooks and crannies to make it seem like you were playing alone even when it was crowded.

Logan held out a club and the balls to her. She picked the blue ball just so he'd have to play with the pink one.

As he started to line up his first shot, Claire crossed her arms and asked, "So what is it with you and blond-haired, blue-eyed chicks? I know you've gone home with some that don't fit that bill, but you definitely seem to have a type or at least a pattern. If a blond-haired, blue-eyed chick is around, you're going to make a play for her."

Logan flinched, put both hands on his putter and held it above his head like a barbell. "I'll tell you what. . . ." He smirked and a challenge lit in his eyes. "Every time we get below par on a hole, the other player has to give you one truthful answer to a question. But if you go above par, you have to give up something embarrassing."

"Like truth or dare mini golf?" Claire raised an eyebrow and gave Logan a doubtful look.

"Sure." He closed the distance between them and dropped his head so they were eye to eye. "If you don't want to tell something embarrassing, you can take a dare. To be completed within the game."

She glanced over the course and the score card. Nine holes. She didn't suck at mini golf. She'd be able to get a few truths out of Logan without giving away too much of herself probably.

"What the hell. Sure."

He kissed her, before heading back to his ball. "Agreed."

He lined up his shot and hit it. The ball skittered down the green and into the hole. He glanced at her over his shoulder with a wicked grin.

"Did I ever mention I worked at the mini golf course every summer through high school?" Logan gave her a mischievous smirk.

"Of course you did." She narrowed her eyes on him while she placed her ball on the circle to start. He wasn't the only one with a secret like that. She putted and the ball rimmed the hole and then fell in.

She blew him a kiss. "My dad had me on the golf course by the age of four. We mini-golfed a lot."

With his eyes sparkling, he closed the distance between them. His heat surrounded her. "So we're evenly matched."

"It would seem so." She straightened her spine and tilted her chin up at him. "I guess we're going to be spilling a whole lot of truth during this round of mini golf."

"Hmmm." He dipped his head like he was going to kiss her again, but then he backed up and went to get their balls.

"Tease." She followed him to the second tee.

He handed her the ball and grinned. "So we each have a question that the other will answer truthfully."

She nodded. "What's up with the blond-haired, blue-eyed type?"

Logan rested against a tree and his gaze flowed over her. According to his usual, she definitely wasn't his type. Dark hair and dark eyes. Sure, her body had curves in all the right places and the chemistry between them was intense, but Logan had a type. She'd seen it over and over again. Some hot little blonde would show up and he'd be all over her.

Claire walked over to look up at him. Her sneakers had her feet flat on the ground and gave him a definite height advantage on her. She put her hands on her hips. "Well?"

"Abby Crane." Logan closed his eyes and sighed. "You can't share this with anyone."

"Cross my heart." Claire dragged her finger over her chest in an X.

"It all started with a valentine." He blew out a breath and looked to the sky.

Claire arched her eyebrow. She didn't realize this would lead to story time, but okay. . . .

"Third grade. I spent all week working on a valentine for Abby Crane. She had blond curls and the biggest blue eyes. I wanted her to be my girlfriend." Logan rubbed the back of his neck and dropped his gaze down to the ground.

"Okay?" Claire didn't see what the big deal was. "So you had a girlfriend in third grade—"

"No. I *asked* her to be my girlfriend, but another boy gave her a stupid store-bought valentine and she went with him. After tearing up my valentine." Logan lifted his gaze to hers.

"I don't see how this became a thing. I mean, a valentine?" She tossed the ball in her hand and caught it. "That's like a guy saying he doesn't get you flowers because in second grade Betsy threw his flower on the ground. Yeah, it's sad, but doesn't explain—"

Logan's harsh chuckle stopped her. He glanced up at her with a smirk before looking down again. "The story doesn't end there. I didn't stop chasing her. In fourth, she asked me to the Sadie Hawkins dance and also asked Billy Palmer. When he said yes, she told me she only asked me because she knew Billy didn't like me. By high school, she'd use me to cheat on her boyfriends, and I ate it up, thinking *now she really likes me*. Because she made out with me. When they'd break up, she always found someone else to be with and then cheat on the new guy with me."

"That's fucked up." Her heart ached for Logan.

"By college, when girls started to pay attention and want me, I went after every blond-haired, blue-eyed woman I could. But I never kept them. It just became a thing, I guess."

"Fuck, Logan." If Claire had been there, she would have kicked that bitch's ass. She hadn't let anyone get away with humiliating her brothers back then. Logan was her best friend.

"I don't know." Logan pushed off the tree. "It's sort of messed up if you think about it. When I started getting feminine attention, I let it go to my head and I basically revenge-fucked every Abby Crane I could find."

"Did you ever fuck Abby Crane?" Claire walked over to the tee stand for this hole and put her ball down on it. When she lifted her gaze to him, Logan's eyes were filled with remorse.

"Summer between freshman and sophomore year in college. We were both at a party. She'd recently broken up with some guy. I used my newly found skills and got her to sleep with me. She told me she should have dated me as I got dressed after. That I was the only one who really wanted her.

That same night I fucked another chick at the party. Abby never looked at me again."

Logan closed the distance between them and Claire met his eyes. She could see the hurt deep inside them. That soulful part of his brown eyes. What kind of girl/woman would do that to a guy? String him along only to tear him down every time.

"I was a dick. If she came up to me now, I might apologize because it was hurtful. Even if she teased me throughout high school." Logan's hand went to the back of Claire's neck and held her in place. He smiled softly. "That was two questions so you better be as good as you think or you'll owe me one, Claire Bear."

"Don't worry. I've got this course locked." Claire wet her lips with the tip of her tongue, drawing his gaze down. He could kiss her. They'd been kissing all morning, but he didn't move. "How about you? What question do you want me to answer truthfully?"

His eyes almost flinched, but he didn't release her from his hold or his gaze. "Are you attracted to Alan Thomson?"

She pressed her lips together and then released out a breath. She shrugged. "He's a good-looking guy. I could see going on a date or two to see if we had anything worthwhile. As attraction goes. . . ."

She bit her bottom lip and really thought about it. Even the first time they met, he was good-looking and there might have been a hint of something that could have turned into attraction, but. . . .

She refocused on Logan. Her body practically melted at his touch. When he looked at her, she wanted to feel him against her in some way. Whether he held her in his arms or kissed her or fucked her. Gah, the way he fucked her.

She shook her head in his hand. "No, not now at least."

"But you could be?" He lowered his head and her breath caught.

"Ahem." A young male voice sounded beside them.

Both their heads swiveled toward the sound. A teenage boy with red cheeks stood there with a teenage girl giggling beside him.

The boy cleared his throat. "Do you mind if we play through?"

Claire laughed and stepped away from Logan, not missing the flare of heat in his eyes, promising they weren't done. She shook off the shivers that coursed through her.

"Yeah, go ahead." Claire picked up her ball. "We wouldn't want to hold you up."

Logan and Claire stepped back and watched the two play the hole. They definitely weren't playing to win as they giggled and flirted with each other. Logan's hand snuck around Claire's hip and pulled her back against him. She swallowed hard trying to maintain her composure in front of these teens when all she wanted to do was melt into Logan.

When the teens both got their balls in the hole, the young man held up his ball and said, "Thanks."

"No problem." Logan's voice was low and a little rough in her ear as they disappeared to the next hole.

"Whose idea was it to leave the cabin and go out in public?" Claire turned toward him with a gotcha smile.

"I didn't think it would be very busy." He shrugged. "Figured I could have my way with you where no one else would find us."

Claire put her ball down and lined up her shot. "Don't you know they always find us, Logan."

He grunted in response. This particular hole was pretty easy with a par three. Claire got it in two, while Logan got lucky and got it in one.

When she opened her mouth, he shook his head. "Nope, you already got your second question, so you'll have to wait."

She conceded and tried to imagine what else Logan would ask about. A little worried, but they'd talked about all sorts of things before they came here and started to have sex. There was very little they hadn't already addressed.

"Why aren't you dating anyone?"

"What?" She squinted her eyes at him to try to make sense of the question.

"Seriously." Logan gestured at her. "You're fucking gorgeous. You're amazing in bed. You'd rather talk about sports than nail polish and makeup. So what gives?"

"Ah." Claire straightened. "You're looking for the flaw. That big nasty secret that makes men run the other way."

Logan scooped up their balls and headed to the next tee. "Exactly. I mean what man wouldn't want to keep you. You're the whole package."

Her heart squeezed violently in her chest. "Gorgeous?"

"Yes. And sexual. Fuck, Claire, I don't think I'll ever be able to be near you and not have an erection." Logan lined up his shot. This particular hole was one of the more complicated with a tunnel and uneven green. The par was five.

"It's not hard to give men erections, Logan." She shook her head at him. He should know that.

"Pun intended?" He smirked at her as he took his first swing. She ignored that.

"And what did you say helped you lose that erection?" She swallowed, but held her head high. He already knew the answer to this particular question. It stared him in the face.

"It used to be Game Day Claire." He followed his ball and lined up his next shot. "You might as well be a huge, burly dude on game day. You belch. You cuss out the refs. You chug down beer with the best of the guys."

"You told me belching the alphabet—"

"Turned me off," he said slowly and lifted his eyes to hers. "Fuck. I'm sorry."

"Don't worry. You aren't the first man with that opinion." Claire pressed her club against the Astroturf. "If they're okay with guys checking me out, and my sexuality, then when I finally let them see me on game day, they prefer to just categorize me as one of the guys."

Logan had done it. Well, he'd put them in the friend zone early on. It made sense because they worked together and no matter how attractive she found him, he was a fuck boy. They might have had a hot minute together. There had been this pull and attraction, but after the lust faded, he would have gone for other women and she might have gotten hurt.

Their friendship made sense back in the office and out and about in the city. They cared about each other, but they didn't fuck each other. They went home with other people and didn't have a hint of jealousy between them. Now they'd tangled up fucking with liking each other and she wasn't sure whether they'd ever be able to completely untangle it.

"Fuck them." Logan's voice brought her head up and she met his angry eyes. "Seriously, fuck those posers. They let the idea of you intimidate them and so they used the excuse of Game Day Claire as a reason to sluff you off. Fuck that."

She narrowed her eyes. "You said—"

"What I needed to say to keep my hands off you." Logan lined up his shot and finished the hole. He came back to her. She still didn't know what to feel or say as he defended her. "I've fought against fucking you since we met because we're friends. You're amazing and I worried that if I got a taste, I'd never want to stop."

Claire swallowed as he closed the distance between them and got in her face.

"Those guys just wanted an excuse because they were insecure when other guys looked at you. They wanted an excuse because you were too much for them. Too beautiful. Too sexual. Too fucking awesome."

His hand cupped the back of her neck as his thumb trailed over her jawline. "I needed an excuse not to fuck you, because I like you. You're my fucking best friend and watching you suck on your fingers after eating wings got me hard. Watching you dance at clubs left me with an ache I used other women to ease. Hanging out with you made me want you. But I didn't want to fuck our friendship up."

She couldn't speak. Fuck, she could barely breathe. Her head spun with everything he said. Those other guys hadn't mattered. Not really. She may have been hurt, but it didn't last long. Logan searched her eyes and she knew she had to come clean.

"I started using game day to drive guys away when they seemed to get too close." Her voice was soft and her chest ached at the confession. She dropped her gaze to his lips. "I had guy friends through college and none of them were brave enough to ask me out. Only egotistical asshats who wanted arm candy seemed to be willing to try to date me. And after a while, they became too much. I knew they'd never accept the real me."

"Fuck them," he whispered and kissed her. His hands cradled her neck and face like she was the most precious thing to him. Her heart attempted to break free from her chest as she fell into the kiss. She wanted to give in to the crazy feelings inside her, but she knew the only thing down that path would be pain.

Logan wasn't long term. He never had been. No matter what he said about settling down because his parents did. That wasn't who he was and she couldn't sit back and wait for him to be ready. She enjoyed living fast and free, but at some point, she wanted more.

She wanted what her parents had.

She wanted something real and deep. She wanted teasing in the kitchen and hot sex in the bedroom. At some point she wanted children who would groan at how much their parents loved each other. Kissing Logan made her realize all these things.

Just fucking him wouldn't be enough. She wanted all or nothing and Logan wouldn't be the guy to give her that. She'd keep him as her best friend, but it would never be more. Deep in her heart she knew that's all they could be.

But Monday evening was early enough to return to reality and figure out how to find a guy who would suit her. Without her mother's help.

Right now, though? This weekend, this was enough. Kissing Logan, being with him was enough. For right now.

CHAPTER 15

Logan watched as Claire walked over to the tee on the eighth hole. He had decided to tone down his questions from then on. She had followed suit. First crush. First fuck. Most embarrassing place she'd fucked someone. Bathroom at a Wendy's for her. His had been in a car in an automatic car wash.

The game had been easygoing up to that point. But then the sabotage had begun.

Sure, Logan started it. He could at least admit that. A couple holes ago, Claire had been lining up her shot and he'd come up behind her and held her hips mid-swing.

She'd retaliated last hole by working him into a frenzy with the things she'd whispered into his ear. Fuck, the mouth on that woman. Any man who didn't hold onto her like she was fucking gold deserved to live a miserable existence without her in their lives.

She gave him the look to stay away from her when she settled in to shoot this particular hole. It was easy. She could make it in one shot, which would put her in the lead. Of course, this was the most hidden-away hole on the course. A cave-like structure around it cut it off from the rest of the course and gave the players a little shade from the sun. And gave Logan a whole lot of privacy to do what he really wanted to do.

The teens ahead of them had finished a little while ago, but there were more people starting the course now. No one had caught up to them and for the moment, they were secluded.

"Don't you fucking dare." Claire put her hands on her hips as she looked at him.

"What?" He held his hands up but couldn't stop his slow grin.

"I know that mischievous look in your eye. I'd rather not spend the whole day playing mini golf. It's getting hot."

"You can say that again." He grinned and closed in on her.

Her lips parted and the heat between them flared to an uproar. "You're bad."

"I tell you what." Logan reached out and grabbed the back of her neck to draw her into his embrace while he hid them more securely from anyone else's view.

"What?" She still eyed him warily.

He leaned in until his mouth was next to her ear. "If you let me fuck you right now in this cave, I'll tell everyone you won."

"Seriously, I'm about to kick your ass and you think I'd rather fuck you in the middle of a mini golf course than win fair and square." She leaned back to meet his eyes. Hers were dark and stormy. Yeah, she'd like to fuck him. That wasn't even a question.

"We're losing our window of opportunity, Claire Bear." Logan glanced over his shoulder.

"Oh, gee, that sounds swell." She gave him a fake cute look. "A quick fuck in the cave? Gee, thanks, mister."

She arched an eyebrow at him.

"Fine." He lifted his hands from her and strolled to the other side of the cave. "I don't have any more truths to tell you besides lame shit from my childhood, so why don't we make this interesting?"

She crossed her arms under her breasts and tapped her toe. "I'm listening."

"If you win, you pick time and place to fuck. When I win, I pick time and place to fuck. No matter where. The more public the better. No worrying about prying eyes or whether it'll be quick. Any time and any place. The more public the better." Logan laid out his terms. He wondered if she would be bold enough to take them. He would have put Naked Sports Center on the table, but she'd laugh that off.

"Fine. Do we need to stipulate time frame? We only have one more day here."

He closed the distance between them again but didn't touch her. "*Any* time. *Any* place. If you win and want to get it done quickly, that's up to you. If I win and in a week I want to call it, then it's still valid. If I wait a month, still valid."

Claire pursed her lips and looked at the score card. They were neck and neck with two holes left. He wanted that open loophole. He didn't want this to end, but he didn't know how to convince her to carry on once they returned to their real world. He didn't really date women. So he didn't know what he could offer her besides sex.

"Any time. Any place." She held out her hand to shake his.

He took it and pulled her in for a kiss, backing her up against the wall while he savored her lips. He lifted her legs up and she wrapped them around his waist as he claimed her lips as his. Tasting the sweetness of the soda she'd been drinking and that flavor that was unique to Claire. Fuck, he couldn't get enough and wanted inside of her right now.

When he released her lips to trail down her neck, Claire inhaled, dropped her legs, and then pushed at him.

"This is a family place, Logan." Claire pressed him back. Her eyes glittered up at him.

"Ah, but if I win and this is where I want to—"

"Who says you're going to win?" Claire scoffed and went back to her ball. "You're going to lose so hard, Logan O'Connell."

She turned and didn't see the smirk on his lips. Fuck it. Either way he won.

With the stakes apparently raised, Claire got super serious about the game. Her ball went in on the first putt. The setup for this hole was one of those types he'd always had issues with. It took him two strokes which evened them up on score.

"What happens if we tie?" Claire asked as they walked to the next hole.

"Then both of us get one any time any place." He glanced over at her to see what she thought of that.

"So one hole decides it all?" She tipped her head to look at him. Logan raised his eyebrow and smirked. She narrowed her eyes.

"Yup." Logan went to the tee. "And I'm up first."

She stood back and watched him with her arms crossed. He actually hoped they tied because he liked the idea of her having the option to pull him aside for a fuck. And he definitely wanted the option. He wanted it more than once though.

He had to admit her casual wear distracted him. She wore tanks that showcased her cleavage and short shorts that highlighted her long legs. She'd pulled her hair into a high ponytail to get it off her neck. But all he could think about was wrapping her ponytail around his hand while fucking her hard from behind.

"Are you going to play?" Claire gave him a knowing smile as she cocked her hip. Fuck, she knew him too well.

"Yeah." He focused on the ball. The par was higher on this one but he knew the right angle would get him a hole in one. He wasn't sure what Claire would hit on this hole. He almost wished he was going second. Then he could whiff it if she got two strokes.

Logan lined up his shot and hit the ball. It went over the hill and hit the back wall and rolled slowly back to the opening. Almost too slowly. Fuck.

The ball hung right on the edge of the hole but didn't slip in.

Logan glanced at Claire as he walked to his ball. Her forehead scrunched in concentration as if mapping exactly what he'd done and how to correct it. He tapped his ball in and it disappeared down a tube.

"Two."

Claire sauntered over to the tee. Of course she was cocky. Her attitude might intimidate a lot of guys but to him it was sexy as fuck. He walked to the edge and off the course to watch her work. Her ass stuck out as she lined up her shot. She glanced at him and winked.

She hit the ball and it rolled almost exactly as his did, but as soon as it came off the wall the angle was a little off. It rolled to the hole and rimmed it before going past the hole. Logan released the breath he'd been holding.

"Looks like a tie." Claire walked over to her ball.

"You haven't gotten it in yet, Claire Bear." Logan smirked.

She shook her head. It was all of three inches from the cup. If she missed this, he would rib her for ages about it and she knew it. Logan could see it on her face. How she concentrated on lining up just right. It would just take a tap. Anything more might push it past the hole.

"Stop looking at me like you're running commentary in your head." Claire didn't lift her eyes from the ball.

"But I'm so close to winning."

She scoffed and tapped the ball in. "Yeah, right, like you could beat me."

"What do you say?" Logan fell in step with Claire as she headed toward the club return. "Wanna bet on some other things? Bumper cars? Go karts? I wanna wrack up a bunch of these chits so I can throw them around like dollar bills."

"I think I'm out. Betting with you is always a losing proposition." Claire opened the door and they went through. They left their clubs on the counter and headed into the arcade area.

"You won, too. What about games?" Logan lifted his eyebrow.

She shook her head and chuckled. "How about a nap?"

He put his arm around her shoulders and tugged her into his side. "A nap sounds good."

She tipped her face to his. "The kind where we sleep, or at least I sleep."

"I don't mind if you sleep during."

She smacked the back of her hand against his abs.

"Ow." It didn't hurt at all, but he rubbed his stomach.

"I still think we should have put a time limit on the execution of the winnings." She glanced up at him. "I'm not one of your women you can add to your call list."

"Of course not." He squeezed her shoulders. He gave his stupid grin. "You're my girlfriend. I would never add you to a list. You'd be the list."

"I'm not your real girlfriend." Shuddering a little, Claire glared. "How about if either of us enters into a sexual relationship with someone else, the bet is null and void?"

They walked out the door to the parking lot and headed to the car they borrowed from Grace. Logan backed Claire into the side of the car and bent down to her level.

"So if I put my dick in another woman, I can't use my winnings?"

She flinched but nodded. Interesting.

"And if someone else puts their dick in you, I don't get to use my winnings?"

She nodded.

"Malarkey! We made a bet so I want my winnings." Logan narrowed his eyes.

"So use them now." Claire shrugged and her lips tugged into a slight smile.

He grinned. "I see what you're trying to do. Nope. I object to your caveat and provide a compromise."

Now she looked worried. "Okay?"

"I won't fuck anyone else until I use my any time, any place. You do the same and we'll be golden." Logan stared into her dark eyes as she weighed his words.

She pursed her lips and narrowed her eyes at him, before shoving against his chest. "Fine, but I still need my nap."

Logan's chest felt lighter as he walked around the end of the car to get in. Now he just had to figure out how to earn more chits to use.

CLAIRE LAID on the bed staring up at the ceiling while Logan had slipped into the bathroom to take a shower. Her fingers tapped on her stomach. What game was Logan playing? She got the idea of the win, but he was willing to go without until he used his?

Not that she kept count of how often he fucked someone, but he didn't spend a lot of nights alone. And they'd barely made it a few hours without fucking each other since they'd been here. Hell, they didn't even last one night before they were on each other. If she decided to hold out on using her any time any place, how long would he hold out before fucking some random?

It could be an interesting experiment. Like a free pass but with each other. Logan might not make it off the plane though before using his. She chuckled.

"What's so funny?" Logan stood in the bathroom doorway with a towel haphazardly hanging from his hips.

Dripping wet and practically naked, Logan was every woman's fantasy. Claire might not make it off the airplane without calling in her chit. The man had just the right combination of muscles and pretty boy looks. No wonder he was drowning in pussy back home.

He sauntered toward the bed. "Like what you see?"

"You know you look good." She put her hands behind her head and admired the view. He was hers for another night.

"I have confidence." He sat next to her on the bed. A drip made its way off his shoulder to flow down his chest to his abs. She could follow that drip with her tongue. Suddenly so very thirsty.

"And an ego for days." Somehow her mind merged "ego" with "abs for days," but it wasn't wrong.

"At least I'm not a weak fuck." His eyes flared hot.

"That you aren't." Her entire being sparked with the need to reach out and touch him and to have him touch her in return. This was bad. She closed her eyes. She needed to find some control before tomorrow when they headed home.

His fingertips traced the skin exposed between her tank and her shorts. She sucked in a breath. "Admit it. You like my ego."

She opened her eyes. His fingertips traced over her skin. He remained sitting on the edge of the bed. Looking sexy as fuck. "Yeah, I like you."

That had never been a question, but they'd crossed this line and she wasn't sure there was a way to go back to what they were before.

His fingers stopped on her shorts button. He flicked it

open and her breath caught. She watched his fingers work down the zipper. When she lifted her gaze back to his eyes, her chest rose and fell heavily. His dark eyes traveled down her body to her shorts.

"How tired are you?" His tongue darted out to lick his lips.

Her core clenched as his hand slipped inside the back of her shorts to cup her ass. His touch was electrifying. "Less so now."

He smiled. His hands slid her shorts down her legs, leaving her in her thong. He sank to his knees beside the bed and tugged her body to the edge. Her breathing hitched and she stared up at the ceiling with her hands beside her head. Anticipation filled her.

He dragged her panties off and lifted her thighs to his shoulders. He stayed like that for a moment. Her heart skipped around, waiting. Knowing his eyes were taking in the center of her made her insides melt. His mouth brushed her inner thigh, tickling her. She jerked a little.

"Shh, tiger." His breath was hot on the center of her, making her whimper. "Let me make you feel good."

She curled her hands into the blankets. His tongue stroked along the center of her. Her breath caught as he focused all his attention between her legs. His hands gripped her hips to hold her in place as he explored every inch of her with his tongue and lips. Licking, nibbling, sucking. His scruff teased the sensitive skin of her inner thighs as his wicked tongue made breathing normal an impossibility.

He kept it slow and steady, pushing her closer and closer to the edge, but not tipping her over. It wasn't a frantic need like before, but a soft, quiet need that bloomed like a rose. Unfolding under his direction. The need built until she couldn't stand it anymore. Out of her mind with longing, she writhed, but he held her hips tight, not letting her take control of her pleasure. His chuckles against her most intimate parts set her spiraling with desire. So close.

When he slid a finger inside her combined with his tongue over the heart of her, she flew over the edge on a harsh cry. He didn't relinquish his hold on her, but kept up his maddening rhythm to keep her needing more. Her breathing remained harsh and her mind melted, until the only thing that existed for her was Logan's tongue and fingers doing wonderful things between her legs.

Grabbing a condom, he rose over her. She opened her eyes to stare into his. The dark honey of his eyes had almost disappeared within the deep pools of desire. His lips crushed hers as he slid inside. His warmth covered her as they pressed together chest to chest, hip to hip. He reached up to take her hands and pressed them into the bed beside her head.

Her hips followed his until they moved together in sync. She couldn't hold back her moan as he claimed every part of her, so easily, so fully. Every time they came together like this, she couldn't imagine not doing it again and again and again. Until they both couldn't move anymore. She never wanted to leave this room. This space where they were just Logan and Claire.

He lifted his mouth from hers. "Look at me."

She opened her eyes to meet his. The lust and need in his dark eyes combined with the intimacy of this being Logan inside her drew her into her release. Tipping over the edge and free falling, pulling him with her. He moaned his release. She loved that sound. His satisfied grin was the last thing she saw before he collapsed over her.

She welcomed his weight on her, though she wished they'd taken off her shirt at some point. She loved how his naked skin felt against hers. But even with her half clothed, the weight of him pressed against her body felt good. Way better than any other guy she'd slept with before, but Logan didn't need to know that. She didn't need to feed his already huge ego.

"Fuck, you're like my favorite thing to do." Logan lifted and gazed down at her. He brushed some hair off her face and gave her his cheeky smile. "I seriously think this adds to our friendship. I feel closer. Don't you?"

"That may be because you're still inside me and that's about as close as two people can get." She patted his cheek.

He flexed his hips. His cock still hard inside her gave her aftershocks. She gasped at the sensation.

"You like it too. You could try to deny it, but we both know I'm right about this." He dropped a kiss to her lips and stayed there for a moment. Just a small kiss until his mouth opened against hers and his tongue traced the slit in her lips. She opened beneath him and he slid his tongue inside. His exploration made her lightheaded and started to feed the craving again. He lifted his mouth from hers.

"I need a little nap, Logan. At least twenty minutes." She started to move, but he didn't release her, still buried inside her.

"We could nap like this." He wiggled his eyebrows at her like a cartoon villain.

She shook her head. "Unless you're going to get off again, get off."

"Tempting." He brushed his lips over hers before he rolled to the side. He took care of the condom and returned to her. His fingers plucked at her tank top. "Why is this still on?"

Before she could shrug, he pulled it off her and tossed it over the edge of the bed. He drew her back into his arms. "Now we can nap."

Skin to skin. It almost felt too good. She shook her head again and snuggled into his arms. Tomorrow would be soon enough to worry about stopping this.

EVEN THOUGH LOGAN hadn't needed a nap, sleeping naked with Claire was amazing. When they woke, they got dressed for the BBQ tonight over at the Millers'. Claire wore this sundress that made him want to drag her into a dark corner and have his way with her. Being able to access so much of her without getting her naked had him searching for that dark corner. He wore a pair of cotton shorts and a light shirt. Seeing her in that dress, he'd stuffed a couple of condoms in his pocket. Just in case.

When they finally made it outside, the mass of people surprised Logan.

"There's like twice the number as the first night."

"Some people couldn't make it until tonight." Claire grabbed a plate and filled it.

He followed her example and she led him over to one of the set up picnic tables. They joined Matt and Travis. Parker and Alan came over shortly after they sat down. Hannah found them a little later and sat on Travis's lap. She nibbled off his plate.

"Where were you guys all day?" Matt asked. His eyes met

Logan's with a look of knowing they were off having sex somewhere.

"Mini golf." Logan took a bite of his BBQ pork sandwich. When he looked at Claire, he almost laughed at the BBQ sauce smeared beside her lip. Instead he reached over and swiped it with his finger before putting his finger in his mouth. She gave him a sly smile.

"I love mini golf. Babe?" Hannah turned to Travis. "Why didn't we go mini golfing?"

Travis glared at Logan before smiling at Hannah. "They didn't let me know. They were gone before we even woke up."

"Sneaky." Parker smiled at Logan. Not as much heat in her eyes toward him as yesterday but still a willingness he wouldn't even consider.

"Almost as sneaky as coming out of Matt's house at five forty-five. Don't you think, Parker?" Claire raised an eyebrow at her with a satisfied smile.

Both Alan and Matt flushed. Huh, Claire had been right about all of them together then. Good for them.

Laughter burst out of Hannah and she covered her mouth.

"You didn't tell Mom, did you?" Travis asked Claire. "It'd break her heart."

Claire shook her head. "Nah, that was Dad's thing. Not mine."

Logan rested his hand on Claire's thigh. She turned and gave him a soft smile. Something locked up in his chest. Shit, he might have actual feelings for Claire. Like beyond friendship and more than sex. Though the sex was definitely part of it.

Sean stopped at their table and everyone turned to him. His gaze bounced between Claire and Travis. "Haven't seen you guys all day."

"If you were actually around, you might have seen us." Travis glanced over to where their mother sat with Betty. "Maybe stop trying to hide from Mom."

"Alan!" A female voice that made the hairs rise on the back of Logan's neck burst through the crowd. Crazy-eyed Kelly strolled over to their table. Right into Alan's arms.

Fuck. Logan swore his balls tried to crawl their way into his body at the sight of her. She was still hot, but the crazy definitely outweighed the hotness.

Claire's hand dropped on his hand still holding her thigh and squeezed. At least, they had told her they were boyfriend and girlfriend, but who knew what the crazy chick would do or say. She'd practically gone off when she found out he'd cheated on Claire with her.

Not that it had really been cheating.

"Hey, guys, I want you to meet my sister. Kelly, this is everyone." Alan's grin stretched across his face.

Logan wondered if it was too late to run as Kelly's eyes swept over the group.

"Hey, sorry I'm late. My mom wanted me to spend time at home, but when Alan told us how much fun he was having, I had to come over for the barbeque." She still hadn't let her eyes settle on Claire or him. But he knew she'd seen them because she tensed and her lips puckered like she'd tasted something sour.

"You should grab a plate and join us." Matt made room next to him and patted the bench.

Alan arched an eyebrow at Matt and got that look older brothers had when you hit on their sister. "Maybe you could sit on the other side of Parker."

"I'll start with the plate." Kelly smiled forcefully and said out of the corner of her mouth, "Why don't you come with, Alan?"

Her gaze met Logan's and she narrowed her eyes at him. Fuck, this was a shit show waiting to happen.

Sean sat in the seat opened up by Matt.

"What the hell, dude?" Matt scooted farther away. "That wasn't for you."

"Do you know her, Logan?" Sean ignored Matt and turned to Logan. "Because that look she gave you, seems like she knows you."

Fuck. It wasn't like Logan was sweating bullets or anything. He kept his cool under pressure, but this was a fucked-up situation. "She's probably seen me around somewhere. Claire and I like to go out to clubs."

Claire's hand squeezed his and she leaned a little into him. Number one rule of lies: stick as close to the truth as possible. This wouldn't fall apart because of something he said. It all depended on how Kelly decided to act. But who knew what would come out of her mouth? Again, crazy girl.

Sean didn't look like he bought it, but he turned to talk to Matt, who still wasn't happy about Sean sitting next to him. Parker's eyes were on Logan and they were probing.

Logan leaned into Claire and whispered in her ear, "Should we get out of here?"

"Right." Kelly put her plate on the table next to Parker. She turned to Parker and asked, "So what's been going on? What have I missed? What juicy gossip is there about all these people?"

Kelly's eyes clashed with his again and he flinched. He couldn't be lucky enough for Sean to have missed that.

Parker caught it. She smirked as if she figured something out. "Let's see. First night was kind of lame. Yesterday we went swimming and laid out for a bit. Played sand volleyball. Bonfires at night and then we all went skinny dipping."

"Not all of us," Sean added. Like that mattered. Not when Logan was so fucked right now.

"Oh, so what did you do today since yesterday was so packed?" Kelly ate her sandwich while Alan sat on the other side of Parker and shot glances at Claire. Fuck, Kelly had probably told him about how she and he had a fling while Claire and Logan were supposedly dating.

Logan tuned out the conversation about today.

Alan seemed pissed, like he really wanted to say something. But if Claire already knew about Logan's cheating ways, what good would it do to bring it up in front of all these people? Right?

"And. . . Claire, is it?" Kelly's smile bordered on manic. "I see you're still with the cheating pile of shit Logan. So, what is it? Low self-esteem or daddy issues?"

"Are you fucking kidding me?" The words left Logan's mouth before he could think better of it. She could attack him all she wanted, but she needed to leave Claire out of it.

"You cheated on Claire with my sister. At least that's what Kelly said." Alan apparently grew a pair.

"Once a cheater always a cheater." Parker joined in the dog pile on Logan fun. Of course she also winked at him as if she didn't mind. She probably thought she had a chance now.

Logan had to think. Maybe they would buy that he and Claire were on a break.

Claire opened her mouth, but before she could say anything, Sean stood. He pressed his hands against the table and gave Logan a dark look. "You cheated on my sister?"

He said it loud enough that people surrounding their table heard and stopped talking. Logan started to stand, but Claire stopped him.

"No, he didn't." Claire squeezed his hand before standing.

"Well, he fucked me last weekend." Kelly twirled her fork in the air. "Or were you guys *on a break?*"

Claire glared at Kelly. "We are all aware that you fucked Logan. Thank you."

"If it was last weekend, then what the fuck, Claire?" Travis set Hannah aside and stood with Sean. "That sounds like cheating."

"Stay out of this." Claire straightened and turned to Alan. "Did you know your sister stalked Logan to our office? The place we work?"

Alan's forehead scrunched. "Kell, you didn't tell me about that."

"That's how I found out he was cheating on her with me. Like multiple times. I didn't even know he had a girlfriend and she—" Kelly pointed at Claire with a shaking hand. "She knew. She knew he cheated on her and she didn't even seem to care."

"Fuck." Logan put his head in his hands and shook it. They hadn't planned for anything like this. Sure Logan got around, but how many women that he slept with would hop on a plane to come here of all places. Apparently the craziest of them all.

"Explain, Claire." Sean had his arms crossed. He closed in and looked down on her. Travis was right on his shoulder. Ganging up on her. That was enough of that.

Logan stood and shifted in front of Claire. "This has nothing to do with you two."

Claire touched his back gently, but he wouldn't let them railroad her. This was his damn mistake. Of course, because they were lying about their relationship, it made both of them look bad, but he wouldn't out her like that. He'd take the brunt.

"Our sister has nothing to do with us?" Sean's face grew a little darker as he clenched his fists. He was a big guy and had a few inches on Logan.

Logan had fought a few times in high school, but he usually tried to charm his way out of it. "Look why don't we all just take a breath—"

"Logan." Claire's voice sounded defeated.

Fuck, this was a nightmare all around.

CLAIRE STEPPED around Logan and turned to look at her mother, who watched with her hand over her mouth. Yeah, this had gone way too far. This scheme had seemed so simple when really it would have been easier and less confusing if she'd just come home and told her mother she didn't want to be set up. But how could she break her mom's heart like that?

Their father's death had already shattered her. Claire could deal with a setup if it made her mother happy. Except Claire hadn't been able to deal with the setups and the traps. She'd stayed away instead, which also wasn't good for their family.

"How can you defend him?" Sean asked, shaking his head. He still looked like he wanted to punch Logan.

"You don't understa—"

"What don't I understand, Claire? That your boyfriend fucks other people and you're okay with it?" Sean leaned in a little. "You deserve respect from your boyf—"

"He's not my boyfriend!" Claire covered her mouth. A few people gasped. Logan's hand landed on her shoulder and gave her a reassuring squeeze. She almost leaned back into him.

"What?" Travis asked.

Claire looked at her brothers and then over at her mother.

"You three follow me." She turned around to Logan and took a deep breath.

He watched her face. He stood close and was prepared to defend her. It made her heart pound so hard. But this was her situation to resolve.

"Not you," she said softly. She put her hand over his heart. "Just wait here."

His lips pressed together and his hand went to her hip. She closed her eyes at his touch.

"Claire—"

"Just wait here please." Claire dropped her hand and stepped away from him with a look that said *please just do this one thing for me.*

He nodded curtly and sat at the table. Claire led the way with her family following her back to their cabin. She left the patio door open and turned on the kitchen light. When the patio door closed, she turned and met each of their eyes. Sean, Travis, and Mom.

"Have a seat."

"What's going on, Claire?" Mom asked, still a little confused. She probably didn't hear the whole thing. Maybe not even her outburst.

"That new chick, Alan's sister, fucked Logan last weekend and Claire knew about it." Sean took the seat and crossed his arms. His eyes shot daggers at her. "And then she tried to lie that he's not her boyfriend."

Claire rolled her eyes. Now he believed Logan *was* her boyfriend. She needed to think. She needed to figure out how to salvage this situation.

"My god, he cheated on you?" Mom dropped into the chair like she'd lost a family member. "I knew he was too good-looking."

"Would you all just be quiet?" Claire yelled and added in a normal tone, "Please."

"What great excuse do you have for lying about your cheating boyfriend?" Travis even looked belligerent.

Claire took a deep breath. Fuck it. "He's not really my boyfriend. So he didn't cheat on me."

"What?" Travis stood.

Sean laughed knowingly.

Mom's eyes narrowed and her mouth pinched.

"He's my best friend. I spend a lot of time with him and Mom would always call when we were together."

"You sleep with him?" Travis asked, still actively upset.

"No," she rushed out and then blushed. "Not usually."

Claire could feel a little heat in her cheeks. They had really screwed this up. Not only had they lied to her family, but they'd slept together. Something they had never done since they became friends and wouldn't have done if she hadn't asked him here.

Sean scoffed.

"Explain, Claire Elizabeth." Mom brought out the no-nonsense voice.

"I let Mom believe we were together as girlfriend and boyfriend so that she would stop siccing guys on me every time I was around," Claire burst out.

At her mother's hurt look, Claire's heart ached. She didn't want to hurt her mom.

Sean nodded. "I knew it. That first night, you didn't give two shits that he checked out Hannah."

"When?" Travis asked and started for the door.

Claire grabbed his arm, but he tried to shrug her off. "What? Are you going to beat him up for looking at your girl? How old are you again?"

"Shut up."

"Travis, sit down." Mom stood and went to get a glass of water. She took a drink as everyone settled back at the table.

"Logan *is* my best friend. We go out together all the time. We just don't go home together. At all. I spend more time with him than I do anyone else. So when I saw the opportunity, I grabbed it. He needed someone to make Kelly back off —who is crazy bananas by the way—and I needed to get through this weekend without being locked in the bathroom with a plumber or tricked into spending time with Alan Thomson."

"You locked her in the bathroom with the plumber?" Travis turned his incredulous eyes to his mother.

"Not the plumber." Mom came back over and sat down, but she didn't deny locking Claire in the bathroom with a man. "Is it so wrong to want to see my grown children settled down already? Your dad and I were married by the time I was Claire's age. Why wouldn't I want that for my kids?"

Her eyes welled with tears that she didn't shed.

"Don't you think we want that?" Sean said. "But on our own terms, Mom. I don't need you shoving Parker in my face every time I come around. Trust me when I say, she and I would not mix."

"But you don't know her that well," Mom protested.

"Trust me, everyone knows Parker that well," Claire said with emphasis on the *everyone*. "She practically propositioned Logan every chance she got, and this morning she came out of Matt's house, and I'm pretty sure she wasn't just with Matt last night."

Mom's face flushed.

"The fact is," Claire started and took a deep breath to steady herself, "I don't want to get married right now. I love my life the way it is. I'm discovering myself before I attach myself to some man. My life is fun and exciting. I'm not lonely."

"But sharing your life with someone—"

"Is a possibility. Down the road, but I don't need a man to define my life. Maybe you should stop letting Dad define yours." Claire reached her hands toward her mother and waited until her mom slipped her hand into hers. "I know it's been hard with Dad gone and us all out of the house. Maybe you should put all that matchmaking energy into figuring out how you want your life to be now."

"Definitely do that." Sean tilted on the back legs of his chair.

"Fuck off, Sean," both Travis and Claire said at the same time. Claire punched Travis in the arm.

"So what's the deal with you and Logan then?" Sean asked.

Mom straightened. "I don't want to be matchmakey but you two do seem pretty close."

"Really close," Travis added and flinched away before Claire could hit him again.

"We're friends." Claire tried to make herself believe it, but friends don't go at it like teenagers or make sex bets with each other. There would be fallout from this weekend, but she'd deal with that Tuesday at work.

Sean made a disbelieving noise.

"What now?" Claire put her hands on the table and glared at him.

"I don't have any friends that I treat the way you treat him." Sean shrugged and gave her a knowing look.

Travis moved his chair away from her before he added, "I definitely don't look at my friends the way he looks at you either."

"Seriously?" She stood and looked at both her brothers. "You two want to dissect my relationship with my best friend? Fuck that and fuck you."

"Did you want me to set up the couch for Logan, sweetie?" Mom had a glint in her eyes as she said that.

She couldn't bring herself to tell her mother off. She was raised better than that. "No. It's just one more night."

Sean chuckled, but she kicked the back leg of his chair out. The resounding crash as he and the chair hit the floor was music to her ears.

"Fuck, Claire."

"Language," Mom said. Sean's mouth dropped open and everyone started to laugh.

"I miss when Dad would say that after dropping the f-bomb multiple times." Travis sat forward and put his hands on the table. "I miss Dad, period."

"Me, too," Sean said as he stood and righted his chair. "He was the only one that could keep Claire in line."

Claire laughed. "That's because he'd tell me what a great job I'd done after I supposedly got yelled at. God, I miss him."

"I do, too." This time the tears slipped down her mom's face. "So fucking much."

They all came together to hug their mom. Claire wasn't one hundred percent sure her mother would back off the matchmaking, but even a brief stall would be nice. Claire had enough on her plate. She had to figure out how to untangle the sex back out of her relationship with Logan.

And she needed to figure out how to mean it.

CHAPTER 17

"So, you are available." Parker slid in next to Logan at the table.

"No." He stood, moved away from where Parker sat, and looked toward the door Claire had disappeared into with her family. He wanted to be in there with her to support her, but he knew this was a family thing. And he respected that.

"No?" Parker followed him. Her hips swayed like they could hypnotize him into submission. Not today, Satan. A sound almost like a female growl emitted near the table. Logan glanced back. Kelly's eyes dug holes into Parker's back.

Save him from crazy women. Fuck. How long would Claire take?

"I'm not interested in you, Parker." He tried the direct approach.

Kelly brightened and looked like she would come over.

"Or you, Kelly."

She flipped him off. That was about right.

"But Claire isn't your girlfriend?" Alan asked with way

too much hope in his voice. "This whole weekend was just a ploy?"

Fuck. He wanted Alan to back the hell off so he could figure out what this thing was with Claire. She said she wasn't attracted to Alan, but she'd hesitated. Logan could tell there was a hint of something that could grow. He wanted to stomp it into the ground before it became something real and threatened whatever might happen between him and Claire. Alan could never handle all of her.

Logan just glared at Alan. He didn't owe Alan Thomson an explanation. Logan turned on his heel and went over to get a beer instead.

A bunch of coolers had been set out with a variety of drinks in each of them. Logan found the one with beer and grabbed himself a bottle.

"Yo," Matt said as he held out a hand for a beer.

Logan passed him one before opening his own and taking a long drink. Fuck this night. He only had one more night with Claire. They could have acted all couply and even made out, but now. . . . Fuck, he didn't even know what Claire would want to do now.

Go back to being friends? Was that even possible? Maybe he could offer friends with benefits and sleepovers and cuddles.

Fuck, he liked the cuddling.

"Man, that was crazy." Matt settled in to stand beside Logan as he took a drink.

Logan could only nod. Yeah, Claire had blown their cover. Now it would be weird if he held her hand or kissed her or dragged her off to a corner to have his way with her. Just when he'd finally located a dark enough corner to take advantage of that dress. Fuck.

He might still try the corner thing, but he doubted her brothers would let him near her now. Especially Sean.

Maybe Logan should just get wasted.

"Why'd she do it?" Matt asked, nonchalantly as if he asked about the weather.

"Her mom kept trying to set her up." Logan shrugged.

"Brilliant." Matt took a drink. "I should do that next time. My mom is almost as bad as Grace when it comes to getting her kids settled."

"What mom isn't?" Logan nodded. His own mother had been on him the past few years about when would he bring a girlfriend around. But what could he do?

After graduation high school, the whole idea of having a girlfriend gave him hives It took time to develop a relationship that could lead to marriage. And he never committed much time to the women he saw because none of them held his interest. The only woman he spent that much time with was Claire.

His mom had even dropped some hints about grandkids and that he didn't have to be married to have one. That woman. He loved her to death, but when she got a hair up her ass about something, it would definitely become his problem.

"Is there something between you and Claire?" Matt didn't meet his eyes after asking that. Sneaky bastard.

"Why?" Logan narrowed his eyes.

"Hey, no hard feelings, but Claire's hot. I've been trying to tap that since I was in high school." Matt gave him a smirk. "I figured this weekend might be my chance until you showed up with her."

"I'm still here." Logan marked his claim as loosely as he could. They were practically a couple anyway, at least until the bet played out because they'd promised not to fuck anyone else until they both used their chits. What if she made him use his chit tonight? This was supposed to be a freebie, but he wouldn't know the new rules until Claire came back out.

Matt held up his hands. "I know I can't compete with the likes of you, so I'll just go see if Parker wants another go or if Kelly is willing."

"I should warn you Kelly is a bit crazy."

"I like the crazy ones, my man," Matt said loudly as he walked backwards toward the picnic area.

Logan shook his head at Matt's back. This whole thing was crazy. Claire was off. . . what? Having a conversation with her family about why Logan wasn't a cheating bastard, but a guy who took advantage of the situation? That probably wouldn't put him much higher on the scumbag scale.

"Hey." Hannah stopped next to him. "So this is weird, right?"

Logan nodded and took a drink.

"I mean, shouldn't we be in there, too? I'm Travis's girlfriend and you're—" She stopped and looked at him. "I mean, what are you now?"

"I'm Claire's best friend." And. . . *lover* sounded too weird. Fuck buddy, maybe. Logan shrugged.

"You two seemed so hot and heavy. I was a little jealous because Travis doesn't look at me the way you look at her." Hannah gave a little shiver.

"How do I look at her?" Logan couldn't contain his curiosity.

"All possessive, like you want to consume her. In a good way of course." Hannah smiled. "Like fuck her brains out."

"Nope." Travis strode across the lawn and fit in between Logan and Hannah. His arm went around Hannah and he turned to Logan and said, "Mine."

Hannah giggled and wrapped her arms around Travis's waist.

Logan rolled his eyes. "How'd the talk go?"

He turned to see if Claire was headed back yet, but just Travis had appeared.

Travis shrugged. "All right. Sean seemed fucking cocky, saying he knew it all along. Mom cried because now she won't have stunningly gorgeous grandchildren. Her words, not mine. I just need you to keep your eyes off my woman."

Hannah giggled again. She'd wanted possessive.

"Trust me. I don't want your woman. Not that you aren't lovely, Hannah, but I've got my hands full right now." Logan glanced toward the house again.

"She keeps saying you guys are best friends. I don't know if you'll get out of the friend zone, man." Travis smirked. "I guess you made a little progress this weekend, but if you hurt her, Sean will kill you."

Logan lifted an eyebrow. He'd probably say the same to any guy his sister brought around. "What about you?"

"I'm a lover not a fighter." Travis squeezed Hannah who giggled a little more. "I'll let Sean do the dirty work, but I'll help him hide the body because that's what family does."

Logan shook his head. "You think they'll be in there much longer?"

Travis shrugged. "Can't say, but we might as well find a good spot to drink because I think we all need to get drunk after that drama."

Travis bent down to the cooler and passed out new beers to Logan and Hannah before taking one for himself. He nodded his head in the direction of the dock and tugged Hannah in that direction. Logan glanced once more at the house before following Travis.

CLAIRE WALKED DOWN to the dock a while later. She had a good heart-to-heart with her mother after Sean had vanished again. They even got out an old photo album to reminisce about Dad. They'd laughed and cried a little, but overall, Claire's heart felt good.

She still missed her dad and always would, but reconnecting and being honest with her mom had done both of them good.

"Claire Bear!" Logan's boisterous voice boomed as she neared the group on the dock. Parker and Kelly had their feet dangling in the water, while they arched their backs in what looked like a competition of whose boobs were bigger.

Matt, Travis, and Logan all sat in the chairs with quite a few bottles of beer scattered around them. Each looked a little more drunk than the last. Someone had brought down one of the coolers to the dock. Hannah sat on Travis's lap, playing with his hair. Alan stood leaning against one of the poles on the entrance to the dock.

Alan was closest to her and he gave her a smile. "Everything okay?"

Claire smiled and nodded. "Everything's good."

Nodding, Alan ducked his head. Yeah, she didn't want to stick around to find out what he thought of her being single, because right now, she wasn't actually available. She had this weird thing going on with her best friend, but eventually Logan would do what he always did and go off with some other woman.

Logan held his hand out to her and gestured for her to come join him. He swayed in his seat. When she didn't move fast enough for him, he said, slurring his words, "Claire, come here. You need to catch up. This woman can handle her liquor. I think she's drank me under the table at least once. Was it once, Claire Bear?"

Matt and Travis looked up at her with hazy eyes and sloppy smiles.

"How much did you guys drink?" Claire made her way between the bottles and stood in front of Logan.

"A lot." Matt belched.

"Oh, Claire, you should belch the National Anthem." Logan's dark eyes were glassy and he kept waving her over to him even though she stood in front of him.

"It's the alphabet that I can do, and I'm nowhere near the level of drunkenness that would require." Claire shook her head at Logan. He didn't usually get wasted when they went out. If she got wasted, he always made sure she got home.

Logan stood and swayed on his feet for a second. He held up a finger and belched quietly. "You need to catch up."

Travis held out a beer to her. "Here ya go."

As she took the beer, Logan grabbed her hips and turned her around.

"Logan," she chastised as he tugged her down to sit on the chair with him. She sat between his legs. For a second, she thought about getting up and finding her own chair.

"Shh. Just go with it," he murmured in her ear and nodded his head toward the other women.

Both Parker and Kelly looked at her disdainfully. Oh, so they thought he was back on the market. She held up her middle finger to them and smiled as she rested back into Logan's hard chest. His heat engulfed her and she fought against snuggling down into him. This she would miss. The cuddling and the kissing. The sex, too, but she'd still have her best friend.

He wrapped his arm around her middle. She drank some of her beer and took a deep breath, inhaling his sinful scent. It filled her with longing and desire. This would be hard to give up. God, she hoped she'd still have her best friend.

"You can't tell me you two are just friends." Travis held his hand out and moved it up and down toward them. Hannah grabbed his hand and brought it back to her hip.

"Best friends," Claire said and took another drink.

Logan chuckled, darkly. His fingers drew circles on the outside of her sundress at her waist. Suddenly she wished she wore shorts and a tank top because then his fingers would be on her skin. His skin against her bare skin. His mouth pressed to hers. His cock filling her. Shit.

Yeah, going back tomorrow would be a problem. The warm tingles never stopped when he touched her and just made her want more. Maybe they just should end the fucking portion of their relationship now.

His lips caressed her bare shoulder and dragged up the nape of her neck. She sucked in a breath as heat raced through her veins and pooled between her thighs. Or not. Fuck.

The conversation carried on around them and the beer kept coming. Every now and then, Logan or Claire would add something, but otherwise Claire just enjoyed being close to Logan. This part would definitely end. Tuesday she'd go into the office and see all those couples being all cute with each other and feel. . . completely and utterly jealous.

Because this thing between her and Logan would disappear. It had to. They weren't faking it for anyone anymore, but he still held her close and kissed and touched her like she was his. But she wasn't.

"I don't want to go home tomorrow," Matt groaned. Everyone added an affirmation of that statement. It was like he had read Claire's mind. The ache in her chest meant nothing. It couldn't.

"Work in less than two days. Ugh." Parker sat against Matt's leg on the dock. She'd kept up the tug of war between Alan and Matt most of the night.

"But it will be nice to be back in the city," Kelly piped in. Of course, she would say that. She just got here. Everyone booed her. "What?"

"It's beautiful out here," Alan said to his sister. "So quiet and peaceful. Has anyone watched the sunrise besides me and Claire?"

Logan's hand had been drawing teasing circles on her side, but it stopped. His hand gripped her hip, almost possessively. Her heart ratcheted up a beat from the lazy throb. "Claire and I watched it at six this morning. It was spectacular."

"I'm not waking up at six o'clock for anything." Travis pulled Hannah closer in a hug.

"We could just stay up," Matt suggested and then he belched.

"It's been a while since I pulled an all-nighter," Travis added. "Why not?"

The others were all agreeing. Claire tipped her face so she could see what Logan thought. She'd already planned for an all-nighter of a difference sort. After all, this was their last night together. Their last night of sanctioned sex.

His eyes found hers. He had slowed down drinking when she arrived an hour or so ago. Nursing a single beer. So his eyes weren't glassy anymore. In fact now, they darkened and pulled at that part of her that only Logan had touched.

Yes, she'd had sex before. Good sex, bad sex, amazing sex, over the top sex. Nothing she'd done with Logan was particularly unique. Except, something about sex with Logan was different. In a good way. In a crazy, addictive way. Deeper.

Fuck it.

"If we're going to stay out here, I need to change and use the bathroom." Claire didn't look back at Logan again. Saying bathroom around drunk people usually had a herd effect. Suddenly everyone would have to go.

"Oh, me too!" Hannah raised her hand.

Claire stood. Logan's hand trailed down her body to tease the hem of her dress. She glanced at him for a second. His dark eyes locked on hers. Her lips tilted up into a smile and she subtly moved her head into a "come on" motion before heading up to the house. The group followed her up and she lagged until she fell behind them. A large familiar hand slipped into hers and tugged her off to the side into the wooded area next to their lawn. Logan's heat surrounded her in the darkness. Shapes and shadows were the only thing she saw. He backed her into a tree and she could feel his body crowding hers.

Patio doors slipped open and closed in the distance as everyone tried to be quiet. His head dipped down next to hers.

"I've been thinking about this dress all fucking night." His words were hot against her ear and she fought against the shiver that racked through her. "You wouldn't deny me my fantasy, would you, tiger?"

Fuck, when he called her tiger, her core tightened in memory of all the orgasms he'd given her over the past few days. She could try to blow him off. Make him use his chit from today, but fuck that. She wanted this. She wanted him.

His lips trailed down her jawline as her hands found their way to his shoulders to hold on for what was guaranteed to be one hell of a ride. She'd worn wedge sandals which brought her up a few inches, so he didn't even need to bend as he kept kissing down her neck to her shoulders.

His fingers gathered her skirt, slowly inching it up her legs. The fabric caressed her thighs as his lips worked their way back to her ear.

"Do you want to stay out all night with everyone or spend our last night here upstairs fucking each other's brains out?" He bunched her skirt at her waist while his hand slipped over her thong.

She sucked in a breath. "That's not really a fair question right now."

He smiled against her cheek as his hand slipped under her panties and his fingers stroked along her slit.

"Who said anything about fair." He stopped so his lips hovered over hers. "You're already dripping wet from me, Claire. I could slide in and ease both our aches."

She whimpered and tried to close in on his lips, but he evaded her. His fingers parted her and slid inside. She hissed, unable to move the way he held her.

"What's the answer, Claire Bear?" He leaned in and licked her lips, while his fingers rocked within her. "Stay or go fuck?"

Her brain seriously short-circuited, but she could play dirty too. She skimmed her hands down his chest and opened his pants. Her hands slipped inside and took his hard cock into a firm grasp. He groaned and his forehead tipped to rest on hers.

She licked her lips and stared at his shadowed face in the darkness as she stroked him. "We could do both."

His lips took possession of hers. Hard and demanding. She opened under his assault and followed his lead. He removed his hands from her and she could feel him dig in his shorts pocket. He dropped his shorts and underwear. She kept up her exploration of his cock, following the ridge of his head with her fingertip, until his hands removed hers.

A package ripped. His lips never gave up hers. Feeling him putting the condom on, she wrapped her arms around his neck. He grasped her underwear and ripped them off. She gasped into his mouth.

Grabbing her thighs, he lifted her, and her legs wrapped around his waist. He nudged his cock against her entrance. He pulled away from her lips. Both of them breathed heavily. His forehead rested against hers and she could almost see his eyes in the darkness.

"So greedy," he chastised. "You want sex and friendship."

"Stop teasing, Wolverine," she bit out, hanging by a thread.

"What a novel concept." In one stroke he was deep inside her. "Both."

When he didn't move, she let out a whimper. She pressed back against the smooth bark of the tree and tugged him deeper with her legs. "Shut up and make me scream, Logan."

His chuckle rippled through her, taking her higher.

She tugged his mouth back to hers and showed him what she wanted. She rolled her hips against him. Rough and quick. She was already so close. She just needed him to take her.

He pulled out slower than she'd like, but when he thrust, it was hard and fast. And he didn't stop doing it, like he wanted to consume her. His tongue and his lips took advantage of her open mouth as she rode his pistoning hips. Every nerve ending quivered with anticipation.

Climbing higher and higher. His hands gripped her hips so he could go faster and deeper. Her orgasm came at her like a speeding train and he covered her mouth with his as it hit her. He captured her scream and kept going. She clung to him as he worked toward his own release.

She caught his groan with her lips over his, still riding her own waves.

His hips stopped with his cock deep inside her as he came. His lips took on a softer, almost tender touch against hers. Her heart couldn't slow down. Her fingers stroked the back of his neck and played with the velvet of his hair.

This wasn't the end. They both still had a chit to cash in. Any time. Any place. Something tickled at the back of her mind. Something Logan had said about both. Friendship and sex. Would he bring it up again? Could she be friends with benefits with Logan?

How would that even work? Because she wouldn't play sloppy seconds to any other women.

He lifted his mouth from hers.

"You should go change," he said softly against her lips, but he didn't let her down. She opened her eyes. In the darkness she could barely see his eyes.

"You have to let me go," she whispered. She stroked her hand against the stubble on his cheek.

His hands tightened on her hips and he pressed a soft kiss against her lips.

"Never." The word was so soft she wasn't sure she heard it, but it made her heart skip a beat.

When he pulled out, she wanted to draw him back inside her. But she bit her lip as he set her back on her feet. Her skirt fell around her knees. She looked down at the dark ground.

"Looking for these?" Logan finished fastening his pants and held out her thong. She went to grab it, but he shook his head and slid it into his pocket. "Nah, this is mine."

She couldn't help envisioning a drawer full of his conquests' underwear. Fuck, that was like a bucket of cold water. She stepped away from him, heading toward the house. His hand caught hers and tugged her back into his arms. His mouth claimed hers in a possessive kiss.

"Stop overthinking, Claire Bear," he whispered in her ear.

He released her and walked back down toward the dock. She stared at his back. This guy she didn't know. Sports Logan. Drinking Logan. Partying Logan. Work Logan. She knew all those guys, but the guy who fucked her senseless. . . . He was a mystery to her.

She wanted to know him better, but at what cost?

CHAPTER 18

STAYING up all night sounded good on paper. Logan rested back in the chair with Claire between his legs, her torn panties in his pocket. His hands teased the skin between her tank top and shorts. He never wanted to leave the dock if it meant he could continue to touch her like this.

Matt snored in the chair next to him while Kelly had taken up the station on his lap, curled into him with her maniacal smile on her lips as she slept. A shiver of horror traveled down Logan's back. Hopefully, she stayed away when they returned to the city. Alan and Parker were in a chair, quietly talking to each other. Maybe there was something happening between those two.

God, Logan hoped so, because he didn't want to have to deal with Alan thinking Claire was available. Logan stroked his hand over her back as she played with his fingers on his other hand.

Travis was still awake on the other side of Logan, but Hannah had curled up on him and her kitten snores were almost as loud as Matt's.

"You guys ready to go back to real life?" Travis asked.

Claire turned her face to Travis and nodded. "Work is waiting for us. It was good to come though."

Logan smiled against her hair as he pressed a kiss to her head. It was "good to come," and he figured they'd have an hour or two before they had to pack for the airport. If everyone else in the house stayed asleep, he could make her come a few more times.

He'd put the hint of sex and friendship in her mind. It would be up to Claire if they kept this going. He wasn't sure he was ready to claim her as a girlfriend. He wasn't even sure he could ask that of anyone. That wasn't the way he rolled usually. He'd be willing to exclusively fuck her though.

But that may not be enough for Claire.

"Should we wake up Matt?" Parker asked quietly. She glanced toward the lightening horizon. "This was his idea."

"Yo, Matt," Travis said loudly. Hannah squirmed on him, but settled back to sleep.

"Yeah, man?" Matt opened his eyes and looked around like he'd just dosed off.

Travis pointed toward the sunrise.

Matt gave a sleepy smile and nodded. "Thanks, man."

He nudged Kelly awake and soon everyone was awake and facing the sunset. Claire inhaled deeply and blew it out softly. Fuck, this time was for her to commune with her father, and so far she'd had it interrupted every morning they'd been there. Her head rested on Logan's shoulder. He dipped down to her ear.

"Do you want me to get them to leave?"

She shook her head and threaded her fingers through his as she wrapped his arms around her.

"No, Dad would have loved this," she whispered back.

He kissed her cheek and gazed out at the sunrise. Logan looked around at the people he'd spent the past three days with. Some of them he may never see again. If he did see the rest, it would be in a different context. He'd miss this easy vibe, but he was ready to go back to his real life and work.

Only one thing stopped him. Once they returned, he and Claire would return to being friends. Sure she'd agreed to hold off on sleeping with other guys until they cashed in their chits. But how long would that actually last?

Their appetites for sex meshed well. Which was why he never worried about her finding someone at the club if he found someone. But what would happen when the only one he wanted to go home with was Claire and she was done waiting?

Especially if they weren't actively having sex with each other. But then again, maybe once that door opened, would it be so hard to reopen it? She breathed again and relaxed into him further. He couldn't imagine returning back to girls like Kelly after having been with Claire. Fuck no.

Maybe he could convince Claire to keep fucking him until they had it out of their systems. Sure, this weekend had sparked something in him, but he was sure it would fade. The idea of putting himself out there emotionally made his chest tighten and his palms damp, but keeping it strictly sexual didn't bother him at all. In fact, it was rather brilliant.

"We should have done this every morning." Matt's voice was reverent as the sun peeked over the edge.

Travis yawned. "What time is everyone taking off today?"

"A few hours." Alan stretched and Parker cuddled into him. "I'm used to no sleep though."

"We head back after lunch." Matt shifted Kelly on his lap. She fell back asleep for the whole sunrise.

"I'll let you know about the game." Alan spoke to Claire and then glanced at Logan.

"You can get my number from Kelly. FYI, I have her number blocked." Logan shrugged.

"It's all right. I've got Claire's number." Alan smiled. It was a friendly smile and not at all smug. But that cut Logan. When had Claire given Alan her number? Was this thing going to happen? Would Alan date Claire? Probably in a heartbeat, but would Claire date Alan?

Travis set Hannah on her feet and got out of his chair. He fist bumped everyone as he passed them. He stopped in front of Logan and Claire. "Dude."

"Yeah?" Logan didn't release Claire's hands and his arms were still wrapped around her.

"You need to come to more family stuff. It definitely makes it more interesting," Travis said.

Logan nodded. "If I get the invite."

Travis bobbed his head and wrapped his arm around Hannah as they made their way back to the house.

"Time for bed." Matt stood still holding Kelly. She squealed a little and then wrapped herself around him like a monkey. Matt gave Alan a what-do-you-expect-me-to-do look. Alan just shrugged and shook his head.

"See you in the city," Alan said, holding Parker's hand. Parker gave Logan a pouty frown.

Logan just nodded to both of them.

"Great to meet you, man," Matt said.

"You too." Logan watched them take off for the Millers' house.

Claire sighed. She tipped her face toward him. "Should we try to sleep?"

"Plenty of time to sleep when we get back." Logan shifted her slightly so that she would feel how hard he already was, just being close to her. "Can't waste a second of vacation time."

"Mom might want to have breakfast in a few hours before we leave." Claire still didn't move to leave this chair. Maybe she felt the same. Maybe she would miss who they'd become while faking a relationship.

Maybe it wouldn't take much to have her want to continue to have sex.

"Do you want to stay out here a little longer?" He wished she'd left on her skirt now. They could have stayed out here and still played.

"Just another minute to soak it in." Claire's body blanketed his.

He nodded. He didn't want to think about later today or tomorrow. He didn't want to think about Alan fucking Thomson. He wanted to sink into her warmth until he couldn't think anymore.

He kissed the nape of her neck at her hairline and kissed all the way down to her shoulder. She sighed softly, but her hands tightened on his. He traced her neck muscle with his tongue and then nibbled at it before gently sucking it into his mouth.

She gasped and tipped her head for him.

"Logan?" His name was breathy on her lips.

"Mmhmm." He didn't release his hold but rocked his hips under hers.

"I think it's time to go to bed," she gasped out.

He lifted his mouth from her skin and saw the red mark he'd left behind. Heat flowed through him. "Let's go."

As soon as the bedroom door was closed and locked, Claire stripped out of her clothes and so did Logan. His hands were back on her and she fell into the bed with him on top of her. The whole night-slash-early morning had been enough foreplay for her. She wanted him inside her now.

She reached for a condom as his mouth closed over her breast. His tongue did this thing that made her toes curl as she tore open the package. Her hand closed over his cock and he gasped against her breast before drawing even harder on it.

"Fuck," she whispered, losing herself in his touch for a moment. Her core pulsed, hot and empty. She stroked his cock and he thrust it in her hand. She could do this all day long, but she needed this craving taken care of. Sheathing his cock with the condom, she pressed him over onto his back and straddled him.

His dark eyes stared up at her as she sank over his cock, taking him inside her. She moaned at the fullness of him. All day every day she could be down for this. Logan inside her, driving her crazy with need.

"Fuck, Claire." Logan's hand went between her thighs to torture her clit while his other hand cupped her breast.

She tipped her head back and lifted off him before coming down hard. This had to be enough. She needed to get this out of her system so they could return to their normal lives, where they didn't have amazing sex with each other. Reality was closing in on them. Reality was closing in on her.

Logan didn't do relationships. He went after anything with two legs and breasts. She had been convenient this weekend, but it couldn't last. But that didn't mean she wouldn't take advantage of it while she still had him.

His fingers worked her clit while she rode him hard. She could feel the wave of her orgasm coming at her. Logan tweaked her nipple and she bit her lip. She flew over the edge, riding the waves out over his cock until he grabbed her hips and thrust into her, pounding her from below.

Her breath caught in her chest. She came harder and dragged him into his release. His mouth opened as he squeezed his eyes shut. Ecstasy. His fingers jerked against her hips as she collapsed on top of him. She might have actually died a little there. Fuck. Their chests rose and fell together. Moving wasn't an option.

"Shower," Logan said, softly. She barely nodded, figuring he'd leave her here to die happy. He rolled them to the side and slid out of her.

She rolled onto her back while he went in and turned the shower on. She breathed in and out. How would they go back to being just friends? When he looked at her, she wanted him to touch her, and here, he usually did. They spent a lot of time together between work and hanging out. How long until she wanted more?

She glanced toward the bathroom at a noise. He came back out and scooped her up to stand against him.

"Together, tiger."

"There's not enough room," she protested as he dragged her into the bathroom.

"There's plenty of room." He tugged her against him, dropped his lips to hers, and stepped into the shower. He moved to the side slightly and pulled her under the shower head.

"This is ridiculous. It would go quicker if we each took a shower, separately."

Logan rubbed soap on his hands and ignored her words. His hands ran over her body. Occasionally stopping to get more soap. Every inch of her tingled beneath his touch. She was breathless when he started rinsing her.

But then he pressed her back against the wall of the shower and knelt before her. He drew her leg over his shoulder and his mouth closed over her sex. No warning. No soft kisses and light teasing touches. Just his tongue pressed against her clit. Her fingers wrapped around his head to hold on to something.

His tongue and lips brought her quickly to the edge. The soap had been all the foreplay she needed. When he thrust two fingers into her core, she cried out and shattered into a million pieces.

He rose to his feet and kissed her with a smile on his lips. So fucking cocky. But she couldn't get angry at him. He had good reason to be cocky. His hands stroked down her back while she came down and his erection pressed into her belly.

When she could breathe normally, she stepped back and filled her hands with soap, motioning for him to turn around.

Logan's body was beautifully sculpted including his back. She ran her hands over his muscles, washing every inch of him. The shower had them so squished together that her breasts dragged across his back with every motion. She especially enjoyed when he tightened his glutes as she soaped them up.

"Turn around," she commanded.

He did and she expected a smirk on his lips. Instead he looked completely captivated and it was so fucking hot. She soaped the front of him, paying extra attention to his cock and balls. He kept his hands to his sides, but every now and then, they'd twitch toward her. When she rinsed him off, he reached for her.

Before he could grab her and pull her in, she dropped to her knees and took his cock into her mouth.

His hands cradled her head as she met his eyes. Gauging his reaction by his face, she took her time, bobbing over him, using her hand, swallowing him whole. Giving him everything she had to give. All the while his dark eyes held hers. His hands rested on her head but didn't control her.

When he got close, he drew her away and lifted her to her feet. She panted with need as his lips captured hers in a kiss both passionate and tender. It called to her heart. Within seconds, he had on a condom. He pressed her against the wall of the shower and grabbed her knee, lifting it up, spreading her open for him.

One thrust and his cock was fully seated inside her,

pressing her into the tile. Gasping, she grabbed onto the top of the shower wall behind her for leverage, thrusting her slick breasts against his wet chest. They moved together. His eyes locked on hers.

"I don't want to stop." Logan's voice was low and rough as he continued to thrust into her.

"Then don't stop." She didn't want him to stop. She was hanging by a thread. Just a little more and she'd come.

"No way I'm stopping fucking you right now, tiger." That cocky smirk lit up his face as he changed his angle a little.

"Thank fuck." She gasped and stumbled to find the new rhythm.

"I don't want to stop this. Whatever we call it. I want to keep fucking you all the fucking time."

She couldn't answer him because she was coming. Almost animalistic sounds broke free from her lips as she hurtled over the edge. He groaned and gathered her in his arms.

He shut off the water and wrapped a towel around them both. "I mean it. I want to keep doing this. You want exclusive. I can give you that."

"What are you talking about?" Claire's core still throbbed around Logan's hard cock buried deep in her body. He was lucky she could string syllables together to make words right now.

He set her on the counter and she expected him to pull out. He started to but then he thrust back in, still hard. Aftershocks rippled through her.

"Didn't you come?" She sagged against him, not sure she could go more rounds.

"I held back." He grinned at her and slipped his fingers down to tease her clit.

Her body pulsed to life as if she hadn't just had multiple amazing orgasms already. "Are you trying to kill me?"

"I'm trying to convince you." He withdrew and thrust again.

She gasped as the tingles spread through her body. Convince her about what? That he could give her orgasm after orgasm? She already knew that about him.

"Answer me, Claire." He started a slow pace.

She couldn't help following his movements, drowning in the feel of his cock inside her. "What?"

Thoughts drifted away as the fire inside her burst into an inferno. He kept stoking it higher and higher. He lifted her, walking with her until the bed met her back, and he kept thrusting, coming down over her. Their pace quickened until she couldn't hold back anymore. She cried out as she climaxed harder than before.

He thrust inside her one last time and his eyes met hers as he found his release. Her arms dropped to the bed like a limp noodle as she gazed up at him. The eye contact seemed more intimate than what they had just done, but she couldn't care about that right now. He hovered above her, still deep inside her. His cock pulsed. She could stay like this forever.

"Tell me you aren't ready to stop doing this." Logan's voice was soft and dark. Even though the morning light peeked around the edges of the curtain, with him, it felt like eternal night. Like they had forever to fuck and climax and fuck some more.

His chest teased against her nipples. His breath caressed her lips. If she hadn't just been completely satiated, she would want to go for another round.

"I want to keep fucking you," he said. His lips coaxed hers to open to him, and she gave him everything she had. How could she not? He had laid her out bare before him, not just physically. His kiss was soft and tender. But she knew it was an illusion that would easily shatter.

When he lifted his mouth away from hers, his dark eyes

held hers. Fuck, he was serious. She figured he was, but Logan was rarely serious.

"You can't be serious, Logan." It was meant to come out as a statement, almost a joke, but it came out as a question instead.

He slipped out of her and fell on the bed next to her. He turned his face toward hers, but she was afraid to look at him. Afraid to lose herself in those eyes. For him to see into her in this moment.

"We fit together better than anyone I've ever been with." Logan's words might have been meant as a compliment, but it served as a reminder. A reminder of the many women who have had a shot at keeping Logan and none of them had succeeded. She wasn't special.

"You're just confusing things because we're friends." She shook her head and finally looked at him. "I don't need a fuck buddy, Logan. I'm over having fuck boys in my life. I want something more. Plenty of guys have offered to still fuck me even if they didn't want to date me anymore."

Logan's lips tightened. Maybe at the reminder that she too had her share of lovers. Maybe at her dismissal of being his fuck buddy. They'd shared details of exploits before. Both of them had their fair share of sexual partners.

She leaned up on her elbow. "Tell me honestly what you think will happen between you and me."

"I don't know." He put his arm over his eyes and sighed. "Right now, you're the only woman I can think about. I want you. I want to hang out with you, but I also want to hold you, kiss you, and fuck you. Why is that a bad thing?"

He uncovered his eyes and looked at her. She smiled softly at him and cupped his jaw.

"We're friends, Logan, and that's it. We took a weekend and fucked each other's brains out and it was amazing. But when we get home and you see all those women, you'll figure out you don't want just filet mignon every day, when you can have a veritable buffet of different meals." Claire fell back onto the bed and looked up at the ceiling. She wasn't wrong about this. "You're a fuck boy. That's what you do."

"What if I don't?" The words were soft and almost menacing. Shivers of delight coursed down her spine, but she shut that shit down hard.

She turned on her side and met Logan's eyes. She could see the stubbornness in them. Maybe a dash of hope. "This was supposed to be temporary. Just a way for us to keep from proving we were faking a relationship. Burn off the chemistry between us. We can't keep doing this."

He started to open his mouth, but she needed to shut him down. It took this weekend to show her what she wanted. She wanted it all.

"You don't want a relationship. But I do." Claire sat up on the bed and twisted to look down at him. "I want a boyfriend, Logan, not another fuck buddy."

CHAPTER 19

Fuck. Claire's words echoed in Logan's head while they packed and then headed down to breakfast with her family. He shouldn't have been surprised that Claire wanted a boyfriend. But the fist that had wrapped around his heart had surprised him.

"Did you have a nice visit?" Grace asked him as she passed the breakfast potatoes to Travis.

"Yes. Thank you for having me." Logan didn't know how to interact with anyone now that they knew about him and Claire faking a relationship. He couldn't move his chair closer or call her Claire Bear. No, that shit would be for her real boyfriend. The next guy she'd bring home. The real deal. Fuck.

"You know, you two do look good together and seem to have a good time—"

"Mom," Claire interrupted with a look.

Grace held up her hands and smiled. "You can't blame a mother for trying. At least Travis has Hannah."

Hannah smiled at Travis and they held hands on the table. If this hadn't blown apart, Logan could be holding Claire's hand. Teasing her wrist with his thumb until her lips parted and her pupils blew wide.

"Sean, I think you're off the hook with Parker Grant." Grace sighed. "It looks like she and Alan Thomson have hit it off. Though they don't live in the same area, so I don't see that going the distance. Maybe you can be there to pick up her broken heart."

Before Claire or Sean could say anything, her mother held up her hand. "If you want to. I'll learn eventually, just give me time. I'll find a hobby. Then you'll get sick about hearing about quilting fabric or knot tying."

"You're fine, Mom." Sean grabbed the sausage tray and set it in front of his plate. "We know you mean well."

"Besides, it's not like I stopped looking for a boyfriend," Claire said as she added pancakes to her plate. "I'm just busy with work. And I'll find one in my own way."

That fist on Logan's heart squeezed a little tighter. He rubbed at his chest. "Startups take a lot of time. We've spent more time in the office than out at the beginning, but we have more free time now."

Claire glanced at him with an uncertain smile. He smirked at her to try to ease the tension between them. They'd dressed and packed in silence before coming down for breakfast. They both had their chits and they'd shaken on it. No fucking anyone else until they both used their chits. He just had to make her crave it so she would use hers and then still want more. As long as he didn't give in and use his, she might eventually cave.

"Whatever you do," Grace caught Logan's attention, "stay away from that Kelly. She's got the crazy eyes."

"I'm well aware." Logan laughed. "Now."

Claire grinned. "Maybe steer clear of the stalking types period."

"Will do." Logan winked at her. Fortunately for him,

Claire wasn't the stalking type, but he may need to up his game to hook her back in. He couldn't stand being rejected for his feelings after high school, but he could weather a few rejections for fucking. Especially because he knew Claire would be fighting against this attraction.

They ate and talked with her family for almost an hour before it was time to leave for the airport. Their bags were already in the car when Grace came out. She hugged Claire and whispered something in her ear before pulling away.

Grace came over to Logan. "You get a hug too."

She jerked him into her tight hug, rocking him back and forth.

"Watch my Claire, please," she said in his ear. "She's so strong and solid that sometimes she forgets she's soft, too."

She squeezed his upper arms and released him from her hug. "You take care of yourself and remember you're always welcome here."

"Thank you, Grace." Logan kissed her cheek.

Grace blushed and hit his arm lightly. "Go on."

Logan shook Sean's hand and gave Travis a fist bump. He was actually going to miss these people.

"Come on, Logan," Claire said impatiently as she got into the car.

She's soft. Logan glanced at Grace and she nodded toward the car. He joined Claire in the back seat and the driver took off.

"Thank you for coming with me." Claire tilted her head back on the seat and turned her face toward him. "I know it kind of all blew up in our faces, but I think overall it was a good weekend."

"It was fun." He reached over and settled his hand over hers. At her indrawn breath, he said, "I'd do it again in a heartbeat."

"SHARE A CAB?"

Claire almost flinched when Logan's hand went to the small of her back. Her nerves were about shot. In the airport and on the entire plane ride here, Logan had found little ways to touch her.

She blamed it on the lack of sleep last night and the crash course of sex this morning. But every touch had her blood singing and all she wanted to do was pull Logan's head down to hers and devour his lips. But she had to be firm and draw the line somewhere.

They were still friends and all his touches were "innocent-adjacent" by friendship standards. "Sure."

He leaned in for a moment like he wanted to kiss her. She even lifted her face slightly before he bent down to pick up her suitcase. His permanent smirk was in place as he nodded to her.

"Let's go."

Fuck him, the fucking tease. She'd gone almost a year without having sex before. She should be able to go twenty-four hours without longing for Logan's dick in her. It would serve him right if she held out on using her chit. He probably wouldn't make it a month without sex. He might not even make it a week.

She trailed behind him to the taxi stand. He gave the guy her address since it was closest.

He turned to face her. "What's that smile for?"

"Waiting." She shrugged. After all, the waiting would be what finally broke Logan and made him go back to his fuck boy ways. And as soon as he did that, the chits were off the table.

The guy at the stand got their attention for their ride.

They both sat in the back seat for the forty-minute drive downtown.

"The bet we have. . ." she started and looked over at him.

"Yes?" Logan still had that smirk on his lips.

"You sure you don't want to put a time frame on using it?" She looked up at him through her lashes and gave him a half smile. "It could be a while before I cash it in and you'd have to hold off on all those women at the club."

"I'll hold off fine, and chit or no chit" —Logan leaned in until his cheek brushed hers and his lips were against her ear — "I'm always available to fuck you, Claire. All you have to do is say the word."

She breathed in his scent, that dark rich earthy scent. It did nothing to calm her throbbing lady bits. "I also have a very handy vibrator to take the edge off."

"What if you find your elusive boyfriend type before I cash in mine?" His cheek brushed hers as he pulled away a little. His face was still close enough she felt his breath against her lips. "Will you fuck me just to get it over with, so you can be with him?"

"Maybe." She shrugged and, unable to resist, ran her finger over his bottom lip. The soft skin made her warm inside. She lifted her gaze to meet his. "Maybe I'll make you both wait."

His eyes darkened. She'd been able to ignore their attraction before this weekend. She should be able to do that again, even if she knew what his lips felt like against hers or the way his skin tasted. It would just take a whole lot of time. Maybe a little distance.

"Did we say the weekend only? Because the weekend isn't over." Logan leaned in a little more and she put her hand on his chest to stop him.

"The flight home was our end date," she whispered almost

touching his lips with hers. "But if you want to use your chit. . . ."

His eyebrow lifted and he smirked as he sat back. "Tricky, tricky, Claire Bear."

"Whatever works, Wolverine."

He captured her hand and massaged it like that first night. His dark eyes caught hers. "I'll be nice. You don't wanna use a chit; you don't have to. You can hold onto it for a year. Even two. I can wait. But if you need something to ease the ache better than any vibrator, you have my number and I'll let you keep your chit."

Her breath stopped for a moment. Damn, she wasn't ready to play this game yet. She needed time away from him and his cock. Distance and time would help settle her lady parts into their new rhythm of not being pounded on multiple times a day.

She slipped her hand from his as the taxi hopped on the interstate. "We need to stop touching each other before we slip up at work."

"Ah, there's Serious Claire. I was wondering when she'd show up." Logan rolled his eyes and rested his arm along the back of the seat.

She narrowed her eyes at him. "One of us has to consider the consequences."

"Everyone else is boning each other at work. Why not us?" Logan raised his eyebrow and gave her a half smile that made her engine purr. "Everyone probably thinks we are anyway."

"Because we're best friends. We're not living together like Morgan and Drew or Jonah and Lacy or Phoebe and Aiden. They're in love. Are you in love with me, Logan?" She kept her eyes locked on his.

His lips tightened for a moment, but he shook his head. "We don't have to be in love to fuck, Claire."

He didn't exactly say that quietly and she glanced at the cab driver who seemed happily in his own little world. Thankfully. Not that Claire gave a fuck who overheard them.

"I know, but what I want and what you want are two different things." Claire shook her head. "Yes, I could fuck you all the time and it would be great and fantastic sex, but it would also keep me from finding someone who might actually want a future with me."

"Then why were we faking a relationship to begin with? Why didn't you let your mother set you up? You could have spent the whole weekend fucking Alan Thomson."

Oh, hell no. "Are you fucking kidding me right now?"

"Don't pretend like he wouldn't be perfect as a boyfriend. He's a doctor and settled. He already has your mother's stamp of approval. His sister is a little crazy, but whose isn't?" Logan crossed his arms and looked out the window on his side. "Besides you already have his number."

Claire pressed her lips together and stared at the tension in Logan's neck. Some of her anger drained. "Why do you care? You were the one to invite him to Sunday game day. Yes, I have Alan's number. So what?"

He stayed looking out the window. Oh, no, he didn't get to pout when the reality was he'd be the one to end them.

"At some point, we'll be at a club and you'll see some blond-haired, blue-eyed hottie and you'll forget all about me." *Like you always do.* She didn't add that, but it was there. It had never made her feel anything in the past, but she was afraid too many things had shifted between them. And next time it happened—and it would, it would cut her deep.

She let that sit in the air for a while since he wasn't talking to her. A new tactic from him, granted. She pulled out her phone and texted her mom she was on the way home from the airport. She glanced over her social media and then set her phone on her lap.

The cab had gotten off the interstate and was only a few blocks from her apartment.

"Maybe we should call the bet off. Maybe we should just finish this right now." She sighed and her stomach ached a little at the thought. It made sense, even if she hated the idea. "We need sleep and tomorrow morning we'll be back at work and everything will go back to normal."

At least as normal as she could get when Logan had touched every part of her body and made it sing just for him.

"No."

"What?" She turned to look at him as the cab stopped outside her apartment building.

His gaze swept over her before landing on her lips for a hot second before lifting to her eyes. "The bet chits stand. Maybe sleep is all we need right now, but fuck if I'll give up two more times with you."

Hours later, Claire woke up and looked at the time. Two am. She'd taken a shower in her reasonably large shower and ate a couple of slices of leftover pizza before falling into bed. Now at two am, she was wide fucking awake.

And her body was keyed up because of withdrawal. She'd had Logan between her thighs for three days and now her lady bits were unhappy with the current state of no nude male available to fondle for a little more action.

She grabbed her phone to text Logan like she usually did when she couldn't sleep. He was a perpetual night owl. But should she?

She'd never questioned it before. Why should she start now if she truly wanted to get back to normal with him? Sitting up, she opened their text conversation. Fuck it.

Any chance you're awake? she texted.

I'm always up for you. ;) was his reply.

She rolled her eyes, knowing he was making an innuendo. But that was normal. They always had a light flirtation going on. It was playful and didn't mean anything.

I went to sleep too early and now I'm up. Is it worth it to get out of bed to see what's on ESPN? That should take them back to normal.

They're playing some college football. Nothing too exciting. A repeat.

She let out a breath and smiled. This was normal. This was Logan.

Anyone worth watching? Falling back on her bed, she stared up at her phone.

There's a new tight end at Duke that they've tagged as the one to watch this season.

I do like a tight end. Is he hot? She bit her lip and hit send. But this was how they always interacted. Nothing new to see here. Just two friends discussing football.

I haven't checked him out yet. I could come over and we could start a new tradition of Naked Sports Center.

She smiled and shook her head. *Is Sports Center even on?*

If not, you have on-demand.

She could practically see the grin on his face. He probably wasn't even out of bed, lying naked on his sheets and talking to her in the dark with the only light being his cell phone screen. If she told him sure, he'd be over here and they would end up fucking while watching a repeat of Sports Center.

Fuck, that shouldn't make her warm inside. She glanced at her nightstand. She could take care of this herself and go back to sleep. It wouldn't be the same as him easing her ache, but it would do in a pinch.

How about it, tiger?

For fuck's sake. She wanted him, but she needed to draw the line they wouldn't cross. Oh, he'd cross the line as often as she'd let him get away with, but she couldn't start out by inviting him over just so he could make her orgasm.

It's late and we have work in the morning. I'll just drink some warm milk and go back to sleep. She sent it and then worried he'd say something about warm white stuff that could help her sleep.

Sleep tight, Claire Bear. Night.

Night.

She opened her drawer and took out her vibrator. Not quite as penis shaped as the one her mother had bought. Thinking about her mother buying vibrators was not helpful right now. So she just remembered this morning in the shower. Logan's hands running over her body. His tongue between her thighs.

CHAPTER 20

"How'd you sleep last night?" Logan stepped into the break room where Claire stood putting away the dishes.

Her cheeks pinkened slightly before she said, "Good. How about you?"

He'd had a raging hard-on after texting her, but after that was taken care of. . . . "I slept fine."

Not as good as he'd slept with her though. He headed to the coffee maker and began brewing a pot. When it was set, he sat at the table and watched Claire put away dishes. Work Claire had always been one of his favorites. Tight skirts, flowy blouses, and high fucking heels that put her on his level. Fuck, he needed a chance to fuck her in those heels. And only those heels.

If he called in his chit at work, would she allow it? Maybe he'd try later, but right now, he just wanted to talk.

"We on for the season opener on Thursday at Legend's?"

She glanced at him over her shoulder as she put away the rest of the cups on the high shelf. She always left a few on the counter for Lacy. "Hell, yeah. I've got my fantasy league all ready. I plan to win the pot this year."

Claire bent over the dishwasher to grab some dishes and her skirt tightened across her spectacular ass. Was she wearing a thong with that skirt?

"Mmhmm." Logan knew he should comment with something, but his fantasy had run rampant in his mind. Easing her skirt up around her waist. Pulling her thong out of the way. Driving into her while holding her hips steady. Why hadn't he taken advantage of that angle this past weekend?

He stood and went to grab a cup, adjusting himself to hide his hard-on. This was going to be a long day.

Claire closed the dishwasher, grabbed a cup, and leaned against the sink, waiting for the coffee to finish dripping. Her dark eyes were sharp this morning and they took in his business attire, pausing over his cock, before lifting to his eyes.

What kind of naughty thoughts was she having? And how could he convince her to let him fulfill them?

The door burst open and Lacy stepped in. A huge smile graced her face as she went for the coffee cups on the counter.

"Good morning," she sang.

"Someone got lucky last night," Claire said under her breath as she filled her coffee cup and turned to Logan with the pot.

He held out his cup for her to fill and gave her a knowing smile. Shaking her head slightly, she filled up Lacy's cup.

"How was your weekend?" Claire asked Lacy.

Lacy's cheeks flushed bright red. "Good."

Logan chuckled and Claire sat across from him.

"What did you guys do?" Lacy took a sip of coffee.

"Went to my family's cabin." Claire leaned back and crossed her legs. Fuck, her legs were magnificent.

"Both of you?" Lacy's eyebrows shot up.

"Yeah, Claire had me be her fake boyfriend so her mom

wouldn't set her up with a doctor." Logan ignored the glare Claire sent his way. "Nice people, really."

Lacy's eyes widened as she looked between them.

Jonah broke the silence when he strolled in. He paused behind Lacy and dropped a kiss on the top of her head before grabbing a cup and filling it with coffee. "Silence this morning? Nothing happening in the sports world?"

Lacy glanced at him and her cheeks turned red again. "Logan and Claire faked being a couple this weekend for her mom."

"Hmmm." Jonah took a drink and casually glanced at both of them. "Fun."

Logan laughed. Claire hit him in the arm and he turned to meet her narrowed eyes. "What? It's kind of funny. It's like one of those rom-coms you keep turning on, but then say you hate it, even though we watch the whole thing."

"Shut up," Claire said out of the side of her mouth to him before she stood and straightened her skirt. "Work waits for no woman."

She swept out of the break room before anyone could say anything else.

"So you and her a thing now?" Jonah raised an eyebrow at him. His eyes twinkled slightly.

"Not that I know of." Logan sipped his coffee. He smirked. "So what did you do to make Lacy all blushy this morning?"

Lacy practically squeaked and headed out of the break room.

Jonah laughed. "Just a little early morning wake-up call."

Logan shook his head. He wished he could have given Claire a wake-up call this morning, but no, they only had two times left. If Claire wouldn't be so stubborn, they could be as happy as these two were. Maybe not as practically hitched, but definitely fucking.

"Good on you, man." Logan rose and walked toward the door. "Someday you're going to have to tell me the whole story of how that happened."

Jonah smiled and shook his head. "Not in this lifetime."

EVEN THOUGH IT was technically Tuesday, they were having their Monday morning meeting. Claire sat next to Logan like she always did which made him happy. But he knew she didn't want to let on at work that something more had happened between them.

Logan perked up when Phoebe strolled in. Her red hair was caught up in a bun. Huge sunglasses covered half her face, and she held a venti Starbucks cup. Sighing heavily, she sank into the chair next to Morgan.

"It's not even Monday," she complained as she tossed her sunglasses on the table.

Aiden strolled to the table after her and sat on her other side. He propped up his tablet on the table. "You complain when it's Monday, too."

Morgan smirked at that and waited for Drew to sit before saying, "Okay, it's a short week but it's going to be a busy week."

She started listing off the client proposals that needed to be finished this week as well as a few new proposals they'd just been notified of. Nothing too new and everyone offered their status report.

"Logan and Claire, I need you guys to start work on the Noble Brewers campaign." Morgan fixed her icy blue eyes on him. "They want to do something special for their seasonal ale and with their new expanded distribution, they want to increase their ad spend. They want something new and sexy. That's your expertise. Today, you two need to finish up the ad campaign for the Fervor perfume from Violett Industries."

"No problem." Logan took down some notes. Noble Brewers was owned by brothers Sean and Ethan Brewer. Aiden had brought in the company for Logan, and Logan loved working with the up-and-coming brewery.

Claire paid attention to the meeting, tapping her pen against her notepad. The meeting went on with schedules and new clients that both Aiden and Phoebe were trying to bring in. The status on several clients that were past the proposal phase. Overall, business was booming and Logan was proud to be an integral part of Taylor and King from the beginning.

The meeting ended and they all spread out to their desks. Logan pulled up the files they would need to finish up the Fervor campaign and also downloaded the Noble Brewers files onto his computer. He and Claire definitely needed to put the final touches on the Violett Industries campaign quickly. It looked like it would be a long week.

Jonah and Lacy were discussing a puppy food campaign while Phoebe and Morgan remained at the conference table going over something. With the exception of Aiden and the owners, they all had desks in this common area, aka the pool, so collaboration would be easy. But sometimes the noise level rose a little too much.

Logan lifted his eyes to Claire across from him and waited for her to lift her gaze to his. When she noticed him looking at her, she raised her eyebrow in question.

"Do you want to get a room?" Logan wiggled his eyebrows.

Claire narrowed her eyes at him.

He pointed to the small conference room. "To talk about the perfume ad."

Glancing around the chaos of their office, she gave him a curt nod and picked up her stuff. By the time he came into the room, she had the interactive whiteboard set up with what they'd pulled together prior to the weekend.

Logan closed the door and sat beside her at the table to look at the board. "Intense desire and hot sex."

"Yup, that's what we're going for." Claire pursed her lips as she gazed up at the board. They had very little color on the board, wanting soft lighting and black and white stills for the final product.

"Can you pull up the images we were considering as examples?" Logan leaned back in his chair and peeked over Claire's shoulder at her screen. Black and white photos of artfully nude people filled her screen.

"We could just look at them on our own computers," Claire argued.

Sighing, Logan turned in his chair to face her. She reluctantly met his gaze.

"You want things to go back to normal, right?" He lifted an eyebrow.

She narrowed her eyes but nodded.

"Fine, then what we would normally do is put the images up on the big screen so we can sort out the ones that are definite noes." Logan could play at being Work Logan all fucking day long. He'd spent many days wanting her and not having her. Blocking out the desire had been easier for him before. Now, maybe not that easy, but still he could focus on work and not the subtle strains of mint and rosemary that teased his nose.

She hadn't wanted anything to change so he wouldn't. Hopefully that would make her realize that sex wouldn't change things between them. And fuck finding a boyfriend. He had all the dick she'd ever need.

"Fine." She cast the information onto the interactive whiteboard.

Logan studied the images. Couples in various positions and angles covered the screen. Just what they needed. Sexy photos to look through after spending a weekend fucking each other. He cleared his throat before asking, "What did we have as a tag line?"

"Make him want you with a Fervor." Claire leaned back next to him and stared at the images. He didn't dare look over at her or his cock would harden, which wouldn't be very Work Logan of him. He needed to be professional.

"Do we want to find more color?" she asked.

"Nah, the black and white adds depth without going over the top." They had over thirty images to go through. Logan pointed at the screen. "Get rid of three, five, and ten."

"Fourteen, fifteen, seventeen, and twenty are too much in my opinion." Claire blacked out those spaces.

"Twenty-five and twenty-nine."

They went through and whittled the list down until only five remained. Claire cleared the field and put the five remaining images on the board. These were the images that didn't show actual nudity that would get their ad pulled or not placed in some magazines or internet spots.

"Number five has too much side boob," Claire pointed out.

"Can you really have too much side boob?" Logan tossed his pen on the table and took in a deep breath. The first ones had gone fast, but the next few eliminations had taken them almost an hour to get it down to five.

"Picture one is fairly tame. Nude woman and man embracing. Woman's back to the camera. His head rests on her shoulder. Been there-seen it a few dozen times," Claire pointed out.

"Is the overuse a bad thing or a good thing?" Logan put his feet up on the table and tipped his chair back.

"It may be too tame for what we're trying to convey." Claire shrugged and marked it with an x to indicate it might get cut. "Okay, pic two. Man's and woman's hands clenched over their heads on the bed. Picture indicates they are in the throes of passion without showing anything risqué."

"It's safe. Won't trip any censors." Logan rubbed his hand over his jaw. "I like the lighting in number three. The darkness and shadows highlight what you can't see, while his hands pretty much cover her breasts. You get to see her expression of ecstasy."

"If we were selling to men, yes, number three would be good, but maybe not so much for a woman customer." Claire slipped off her heels and put her feet up on the table like him.

If he looked for it, he could see the edge of the hickey he'd given her yesterday morning down by the lake. He wanted to reach out and brush her shirt out of the way so he could trace the edges of it. If he wanted a picture of intense desire, it would be of Claire's neck and shoulder bared to him. Her dark hair swept to the side.

"Four is probably the most intense." Claire swallowed and Logan turned back to the image. She continued, "The only shown nudity is his ass. We could probably crop it mostly out. But with him pressed up against her on the wall, you see the work in his back as he holds one of her hands above them and the other hand holds her leg around his waist."

"Not a bad position," Logan said quietly. He'd done that to Claire. He wanted to do that to Claire again. Then added, "For the ad of course."

Claire chuckled. "Definitely not a bad position."

He caught her smirk out of the corner of his eye. He needed to keep it level during business hours. "But five is the side view with too much side boob, per you. The lighting manages to highlight the skin while hiding the censor triggers, but you can obviously tell they are fucking in this photo."

"Pretty much all the photos are either fucking or about to be fucking." Claire blew out a breath. "Great way to start the week."

"Definitely back to normal, right?" Logan put his feet on the ground and rested his elbows on the table to really look at the photos. "One is definitely out."

"Agreed." Claire lowered her feet and worked on her computer. "Three is tasteful but a little too edgy."

Logan nodded as she took it off the sheet. "I think we should keep number two in the mix in case the client wants something tamer, but we should definitely pick between the guy's ass and the side boob."

Claire shook her head and met his eyes with a grin. "Seriously? Ass or boobs is the choice?"

He tapped her on the nose. "Well, not everyone can have it all like you, Claire. So yes, sometimes you have to choose between ass or boobs."

"I say ass then." She drew away from him and put the two remaining pics up on the board.

"As a self-proclaimed ass man, I agree with your conclusion." Logan moved to grab his laptop and clicked down the lid. "You want to grab some lunch before we work on the Brewers?"

Her lips tightened for a moment like she would say no. His heart damn near stopped in his chest. But this wasn't out of the ordinary. This was their normal.

Her face cleared and she smiled at him. "Sure."

His chest loosened and he smiled. "We could go to Hooters."

"Fuck no." Claire stood and straightened her skirt while

she stepped into her heels. "I need somewhere I won't be tempted to get wings. This weekend was hell on my diet, and we have a game day this week, so I'm eating light."

He loved that her only objection to Hooters was it would be hell on her diet. "Fine, you pick the place."

CHAPTER 21

BY LATE AFTERNOON, Claire felt like everything had returned to normal between her and Logan. They'd successfully handled a very sexually charged campaign without any unnecessary innuendos and besides a playful tap on her nose, Logan had barely touched her all day.

That should be a win. But now as she sat at her desk across from him, she wondered if it was. What was he up to?

"Dinner tonight?" Logan asked. When he looked up and saw her watching him, he cocked his eyebrow. "Do I have something on my face?"

She shook her head. Fuck, what if she was the one who couldn't go back to normal after having sex? "Yeah, dinner sounds great. My place?"

The words slipped out before she could even think. They usually got takeout or delivery and ate at one of their apartments so they could watch ESPN and actually choose what they wanted to watch instead of a sports bar where the TVs were set to someone else's taste.

"Sure." He returned to working on his computer.

Okay. Yup, just normal Logan and Claire time after work.

As long as she didn't think about this weekend, she should be fine. Gah, maybe she was a girl.

She went back to working on the last thing on her to-do list for the day. Within ten minutes, she finished and took her cup to the break room. She didn't start the dishwasher since she wouldn't be the last to leave tonight.

Logan walked in. "I'm going home first to change. I'll be there in about twenty minutes. Do you want to order something for delivery?"

He stopped next to her and added his coffee mug to the dishwasher. She breathed in his scent and everything in her softened.

"Delivery. Yeah." She cleared her throat and headed to the door. "Anything in particular you want?"

She glanced back over her shoulder at him. His eyes had darkened and a string of tension drew tight between them. That undercurrent of desire they were both ignoring nearly snapped in the air. After a few seconds, he broke out of it first.

"Whatever you want will be fine."

She nodded and walked into the office. Jonah, Lacy, and Phoebe were in a heated discussion over some sort of. . . ice cream? Maybe?

Shrugging off the tension, Claire stopped at her desk to grab her purse. Everyone said a quick goodbye before going back to their conversation. Claire needed to get out of there before Logan came out of the break room. She couldn't ride down in the elevator with him. Not when her insides were still churning with need.

She liked to think that she'd be the strong one out of the two of them. But she knew she could fold just as easily as he could. One touch and that'd be it.

"Hey, Claire," Emily's voice stopped her at the door.

"Yeah?" Claire turned to meet Emily's pretty blue eyes.

Some of the panic eased from her chest and she took a deep breath. Claire was being ridiculous. She smiled at Emily. "Did you need something?"

Emily glanced toward the break room and took a deep breath. She leaned forward and whispered, "You mentioned you have a friend who is a lawyer?"

Claire stepped closer to Emily's desk. "Yeah, she does family law."

Emily glanced toward the office and took a deep breath. "Would she know how to declare incompet—"

"Ready to go?" Logan closed in on Claire and stopped with only an inch of space between them. She'd been distracted, but now her hair stood on her neck and goose-bumps covered her arms.

With her cheeks pink, Emily resumed her seat and smiled at the two of them. "Good night, guys."

What had Emily been about to ask her? When Claire started to open her mouth to ask, Emily subtly shook her head.

"Come on, Claire. Let's get this show on the road." Logan smiled at Emily then took Claire's elbow and steered her out the doors into the lobby. Dropping her arm, he pressed the button for the elevator. "Share a ride?"

Claire glanced back through the window, but Emily wasn't at her desk anymore. Too weird. She'd have to remember to text Emily her friend's number. Logan stepped in front of her, breaking her line of sight.

"Earth to Claire?" He brought his head down to her level so they were eye to eye and searched her eyes. "Do you want to share a ride?"

She blinked and nodded, then she put her hand on his arm. "Wait. Aren't you going home first?"

"It depends." Logan shrugged. The elevator stopped and the doors opened.

He gestured for her to enter and followed her in. She pressed the ground floor button.

"Depends on what?" Claire finally asked.

"What I feel like," Logan shrugged. He gave her a weary smile. "It's been a long day already. If I go home, I might be tempted to just stay there and climb into bed."

Claire nodded and leaned against the back wall of the elevator. "Didn't sleep well last night?"

"Slept very little," he admitted. His gaze swept over her before he closed in on her.

She lifted her eyes to his, giving him a look that asked, *what do you think you're doing.* Heat and lust swirled in his eyes as he stopped right before her. She couldn't catch her breath as his dark eyes held her hostage.

"I missed you last night." His voice was low as he caged her in with his arms, not touching her at all. But he might as well be surrounding her, as her every nerve ending stood on end, reaching out for his touch.

Finding her voice, she said quietly, "It was only a weekend, Logan. You slept fine before it."

He dipped his head toward her shoulder, still not touching. She tipped her head automatically, giving him access to her neck. He turned his lips toward her neck and she held her breath, waiting. Waiting for his lips to find her pulse and send it skyrocketing more than it already was.

"Seeing you all day and not being able to touch you. . . pure torture." His breath bathed her neck in warmth that settled low in her belly.

Closing her eyes, she held herself steady. Her fists clenched at her sides. She wanted to arch into his heat, pull his head down so his lips would be on her skin. But she'd made a line in the sand for a reason. So they wouldn't keep sliding into each other. As pleasant as that sounded at the moment.

"Are you using your chit?" She turned her head to look him in his eyes. Fuck, they were practically feral with need. Were her own eyes that bad?

His gaze dipped down to her lips, now so close to his. If he leaned in a little, they would be kissing. Her lips parted and her insides clenched. Just a taste. What could it hurt?

Logan lifted his gaze back to hers. "Not yet."

He pulled away as the elevator dinged their arrival. She swallowed the whimper in the back of her throat and resisted the urge to pull him back to her. So fucking potent.

She took a deep breath and tried to calm the rolling in her stomach. "I've got a car waiting. Let's go."

BEING hard around Claire was nothing new to Logan. He'd spent the past year stifling his urges when it came to her. Constantly reminding himself she was his best friend. She was like a priceless toy still in the original box. Pretty to look at, but he didn't want to destroy it by opening it.

But this weekend, they'd opened the box and she'd let him play with the toy. But now. . . . Fuck. Now, she wanted to put the toy back in the box and pretend they'd never had it out. Fuck that.

"Do you want another beer?" Claire got up from the chair and headed to her kitchen.

"No thanks."

She'd ditched her heels as soon as they'd entered her apartment. Now, she walked barefoot into the kitchen. She still wore her work clothes, probably afraid to get naked with Logan in her apartment. Normally, she'd change into some pajama pants and a T-shirt with a sports logo and sit with him on the couch, but instead she sat in the chair.

"You know what would make Sports Center more entertaining?" Logan said as she came back to the living room.

She eyed his smirk before letting out a resigned sigh as she lowered into the chair. She had to know what he was about to say, but she still said, "What?"

"Being naked. I mean, we spent all day in these clothes. Wouldn't you like to strip them off and just breathe." He tried to keep a straight face, but the grin just kept creeping up.

"I don't need your ass *breathing* on my couch." Claire took a drink from her bottle.

"Hmmm." He looked around considering. "We could put towels down."

Claire gave a little burst of laughter before narrowing her eyes at him. "I'm perfectly comfortable wearing clothes. I think we'd *both* be uncomfortable if we got naked."

"Aw, Claire Bear, do you still want me?" He kept his tone light and flirty when all he really wanted to do was bend her over her coffee table and fuck her until she admitted sex with him was the best she'd ever had. After all, he was willing to admit it to her.

She scoffed and took a drink. Her attention returned to the TV. "Thursday. Cowboys or Buccaneers?"

Back to football. She'd been pressing him to stay on that topic the whole night. Even while they ate dinner. Not that he minded. It was what their friendship was built around.

"Anybody but the Cowboys." He reclined on the couch and put his socked feet on her coffee table. Reaching up, he undid another button on his shirt. "You should know that by now. Trying to keep your mind off other things?"

He arched an eyebrow at her, but she pursed her lips and took another swig of beer.

"Can you really root for the Buccaneers?" Claire asked. Her toes curled into the area rug under her coffee table. She definitely wanted the toy put back in the package. Too bad.

"I don't have to root for anyone to enjoy the game." Logan shrugged and put his feet on the rug before sliding across the couch to be closer to Claire's chair. Her eyes were wide and wary. He leaned forward and trailed his finger behind her knee.

"Hey." She jerked her bare leg from him and glared.

He just smiled. "We also don't have to have sex to get off."

"What are you talking about?" She crossed her legs.

"We both have a sex chit for any time any place."

"I'm well aware—"

"I've already offered to let you take advantage of me whenever the mood strikes. Chit or no chit." He stretched up and cracked his neck to the side. "But if you don't want to have intercourse, I'd happily do other things to get you there."

Her eyes had darkened as he spoke. Her breath came in little hitches that lifted her breasts. Three days hadn't been long enough to properly worship those breasts.

"After all," he continued, "if neither of us can have sex with other people. . . ."

She leaned forward and set her beer on the coffee table. "That's why we have the chits. If you want to use yours, you're more than welcome. The sooner we use them, the sooner we can resume our normal lives. And get back to fucking other people."

Logan quirked up the side of his mouth.

"Ah, but that bet was for mutual satisfaction and getting to do the deed in a less than private space, like the cave at the mini golf course. I wouldn't want to use up my chit for an orgasm in your living room." He shook his head. "I wouldn't let you do that either. It would be quite the waste of the intended usage."

"Logan." She sighed and leaned back in her chair. "It's been a long day—"

He knelt on his knees in front of her chair.

"What are you doing?" She lifted her eyebrow at him, but she didn't pull away.

"Helping you relax after a long day at work." He winked at her and lifted her foot into his lap. Drawing her leg over his shoulder, he turned to sit between her legs with his back on her chair. He slowly kneaded the knots from her muscles.

"I don't think—"

"Exactly. Don't think. Just watch Sports Center." Logan kept kneading her foot in his hands, drawing her leg over his shoulder. "Just a friendly massage."

She released a little moan as he worked on a tight spot. "You should—"

"Shh. This is my favorite part." Logan focused on the screen while he slowly worked his knuckles into her arch.

With a huff, she finally sat back on her chair. When he finished with her left foot, he pulled her right foot into his lap and started the process over.

"What do you think of the new coach for the Bills?" Logan asked, easing his hands up to her calf.

"I'm hoping he ends up taking them all the way this year. It's the first time in a long time they've had a decent team to work with and with the new coach, it might be the push they need to have an undefeated season." Her voice was soft and a little breathy.

"That would definitely help your fantasy football league." He turned to lean his shoulder on her chair under the pretense of massaging her calf. His back pressed against her other leg. He glanced up at her.

Her eyes were latched onto the TV, almost desperately. Her breathing had quickened. Her lips were parted.

His fingers closed in on the back of her knee and she inhaled sharply. Her eyes fluttered, trying to close. Her hands gripped the arms of the chair. He smiled and pressed his lips on her inner thigh above her knee.

"Logan." His name came out as a question and a plea at the same time.

He shifted to face her, still stroking the back of her knee. He loved how responsive she was to his touch. Her dark eyes settled on him as she whimpered.

"What do you need, tiger?" He kissed her inner thigh a little higher this time, right at the edge of her skirt. He sucked lightly and licked the spot.

"Fuck," she hissed out. Her legs fell open as much as her skirt would allow.

He ran his hands up the outside of her legs, pausing as he hooked his thumbs into the hem of her skirt. He raised his eyes to hers and waited. If she wanted him to stop, he would. But damn he wanted to taste her again, to hear her cry out in ecstasy.

Helplessness and acceptance lingered in her eyes. She wanted this. She wanted him.

She bit her lip and nodded. He pushed her skirt up to her waist as she slid down a little on the armchair. She wore a black thong that teased him by covering what he craved most.

He pressed his lips to her panties. She clutched the arms of the chair and moaned. His fingers slipped under the straps of her thong and eased it down her legs before he tossed it to the side.

He pulled her hips to him, loving the feel of her ass cradled in his palms. Trailing his hands down to her knees, he lifted them to the arms of the chair. Opening her up to him. Her dark eyes tracked his every movement.

When his mouth closed over her clit, he couldn't help humming with pleasure. He could spend hours between her thighs. He slid his tongue over her, exploring every inch anew. Tasting. Teasing. Tempting.

The room filled with the sounds of her pleasure and the prattle of the TV. Nothing was better than giving her pleasure. She didn't act like some women who thought they didn't deserve it or were too shy to admit they wanted it. She took her pleasure in everything she did.

If this was all she allowed him, he'd take it. And often.

He slid his fingers into her core and stroked them back and forth within her. Her hips followed his touch. He flicked his tongue against her.

"Fuck, Logan. I'm going to come," she whimpered.

He sucked on her clit and she exploded all around him. He kept up the tempo of his fingers and his tongue to keep her suspended there for as long as possible. Her thigh trembled beneath his other hand.

Her fingers gripped his ears and pulled him away from her. He kept his fingers moving within her. She gave him a heated look that had his heart leaping in his chest. She wanted to give in. Good.

He withdrew his fingers from her and licked them clean. She brought her legs together and slipped down to straddle his lap on the floor.

"We can't keep doing this." She captured his lips with hers and he forgot to breathe. She pushed him over onto the floor with her on top of him. His erection pressed against the zipper of his pants. Her tongue explored his mouth and tangled with his own.

She lifted her mouth from his an inch and he opened his eyes, falling into her dark liquid eyes. She slid her hand between her legs to grab his cock through his pants.

He smiled. "Why stop something we're so good at together?"

"Shut up." She silenced him with a kiss as she stroked him over his pants. "Tonight only."

"I'm available anytime for you, tiger."

She shook her head and her dark hair fell like curtains around his head. Everything about Claire was sexy as fuck. He tangled his hand in it to capture her neck and pull her back down for another kiss. He never wanted to stop.

He released her lips and gave her a grin. "I'm not finished with you."

She raised her eyebrow and sat up straight.

"Tonight, tiger," he added to reassure her. Just to reassure her, because he wasn't finished. He wasn't sure he'd ever be finished with her. It was a problem, but not one he needed to look at deeply right now. If ever. "I'm not finished sucking on your pretty pussy. Bring that ass up here."

He guided her forward on him and helped her reverse herself over his face. She leaned over and undid his pants. When she drew his cock out of his pants, he lowered her onto his mouth, diving in again.

When her mouth closed over the head of his cock, he thrust his tongue inside her. He latched onto her clit and sucked as he thrust his fingers inside her. At the same time, she took his cock down her throat and swallowed. Her moan made his balls tighten. He almost wished he could watch her red lips around his cock, but this worked, too.

He dropped his head down and smiled. "Maybe this is a bad idea with how competitive we are."

She released his cock from her warm mouth and looked over her shoulder at him. "What, afraid I'll beat you to the finish line?"

"How do we even judge that? I mean if I come first, do I win or do you win?"

Claire chuckled. "I think we both win either way."

"How about another chit for the person who gets the

other one off first?" Logan wiggled his eyebrows at her and then he flicked his tongue out to trace her pussy. Her walls tightened on his fingers.

"What is with you and betting?" She shook her head at him.

"Makes things interesting." He chuckled. "Better get to work. I'm pretty sure I have a head start."

He stroked her gently, moving his fingers in and out. She closed her eyes and released a breath.

"Fine. I've already gotten there, so I'm pretty certain you're going to blow before I do." Claire smirked at him before turning and taking his cock into her talented mouth. She might not be wrong on this one, but he'd definitely try to make her come first. He wanted another chit.

CHAPTER 22

CLAIRE STRETCHED IN HER BED. Her fingers bumped into Logan's back. He rolled over and gathered her naked body against his own.

"Morning." His sleep-deepened voice tickled her ear before he nuzzled into her neck with his scruffy face. Tingles raced down her spine. Fucking potent.

Well, that happened. She kind of knew it would. Though she really thought she'd be able to hold out longer than a day. Being alone with Logan would always be a bad idea from now on. They'd spent most of last night tangled in each other's arms. Used God knew how many condoms. And her body was definitely blissed out on orgasms.

"We need to get ready for work." She tried to make herself get out of bed, but he'd started to draw lines down her back with his fingertips. All she wanted to do was sink into his arms and stay there as long as he'd let her. Fuck, that was dangerous.

"How about we hit the snooze button?" Logan rolled her to her back and before she could protest, his lips claimed hers. Everything in her went soft and supple under his touch.

Devastatingly slow, his fingers glided over her breasts, teasing her nipples into hard peaks, before carrying on downward. Over her trembling stomach to torment her aching pussy.

She arched into him. Never wanting him to leave, knowing it was inevitable. If she kept doing this with him, she'd be hurt even more when he left her for some random.

"Stop thinking so hard, tiger." His fingers stroked between her legs easy and firm, drawing her gently into release. Her body gave it up so easily, like it was more his than hers now. She gasped against his mouth. She wanted him to fill her again.

"Logan, please."

His fingers never stopped, drawing her closer to another edge. He rested his forehead against hers as he lifted his hand from her to grab a condom from the nightstand. She reached down and stroked him while he got the condom ready.

When he finished putting it on, he thrust in her with one smooth motion. Holding her hands next to her head, his forehead pressed against hers as their eyes met and held. Almost too intimate, but she couldn't look away. She couldn't close her eyes. She needed this from him. She wrapped her legs around his hips and held him there for a moment, relishing in the feel of him inside her.

"Fuck, Claire. Why do you want to stop doing this?" He pulled back and thrust inside again. "It feels so fucking good."

She bit her lip as he stroked in and out of her again. Every nerve ending twittered happily. "You want to have this conversation now?"

"Of course." He grinning and dropped a kiss to her lips as he thrust again. "I have a captive audience."

"Fine."

He rewarded her with another thrust. She gasped at the

impact. She wouldn't last long with the way he worked her body.

"Both of us have played the field," she said, inhaling. "Both of us have had fuck buddies."

"Right. But I'd be more than happy to be exclusive." Logan's dark eyes held hers as he gave her a few thrusts. Her shaking hips met him, thrust for thrust.

"What does that mean to you?" Her voice was a little breathless.

"That if I'm fucking you, I'm only fucking you. No one else." He dipped his head to her shoulder and sucked where her neck met her shoulder. She arched into him and pulled him tight into her body.

"I'm done fucking around, Logan," she whispered. He kept up a slow and steady rhythm of thrusting in and out of her body. Her hips met his with each stroke. Driving her out of her mind.

He lifted his head. His dark eyes twinkled. "Then fuck me."

She squeezed his hands. "I mean, I'm ready to look for something real. Something more than just sex. I want someone to come home to at the end of a long day. I want someone to share early morning sunrises with. I'm ready to love someone and have him love me."

Logan kissed her and it felt like her heart was breaking open. Because she was terrified of what would happen if she gave in to him. She would fall in love with him and he wouldn't return those feelings. No matter what Logan claimed about someday, she knew what he was like now. A kid in a fucking candy store who couldn't decide whether he wanted the chocolate caramel or the hazelnut truffles or maybe the licorice whips. So he had them all.

When he pulled back, his eyes dark and moody, she smiled.

"You're the reason I want that." Claire shook her head at his confused look. "Not because I'm in love with you, but because of how it felt to be in your arms and be on a team with you at the lake house. Where it was you and me against the world. I want that all the time."

He pressed his forehead to hers as he picked up the pace. "I don't know what to say. Fuck, Claire."

What could he say that would make a difference for her? He wanted to fuck her, but he didn't want a commitment. That wasn't what she wanted.

She lifted her lips to capture his. She was so close to the edge now. No one had ever made her want more than sex before. Anytime someone got close she'd driven them away. She thrived on driving weak or arrogant men away by being herself. But now, Logan had given her a glimpse of something that made her heart ache.

Maybe it had started with all the couples in the office, but he'd made it something tangible. Something real as they sat cuddled on the dock watching the sunrise over the lake.

He broke off the kiss and held her gaze while they both fell over the edge. He collapsed half on her, half on the bed. She dragged in a breath to slow her racing heart. He turned his face to hers. His eyebrows were all wrinkled like he was trying to figure something out.

"I'm not going to fuck anyone else until we use all our chits." He cupped her cheek with his palm and she leaned into it.

"My one and your two." She smiled but her heart wasn't quite in it. Three more times and then that would be it for them.

"If you want me, Claire Bear, no matter how often, you have me. I only want you."

Her heart squeezed. Those words did funny things to her

brain. She closed her eyes. "We should put a time limit on it, so that we can both move on."

She opened her eyes. It made sense. He could go back to his random hookups and she could find something that felt as real as this did. His eyes closed as if he were fighting something. Finally he opened them. "I would hold out forever if it meant you would fuck me when you wanted—"

"Logan—" She didn't need his temptation.

"The end of this month." He lifted off her and moved to sit on the side of the bed.

She sat up and stared at his back. His muscles tensed. She didn't want to let him go at all. This month wouldn't be enough time to let him go, but she had to. At least, the physical part of their relationship.

Not that they would be able to hold out until the end of this month. They barely made it a day without sex. She already felt more for him than she should. But after this, she'd still have her best friend. That should be enough.

He looked at her over his shoulder. "Less than a month to use the chits and then we go back to just being friends."

He reached out his hand to her, not to shake, but to hold, and she took it. She squeezed it and looked into his eyes. "Agreed."

Claire had been distant since yesterday morning. They had worked together, but last night, Logan had gone home alone to deal with whatever the fuck it was he was feeling. He didn't want to stop having sex with Claire. He didn't even want anyone else. But who knew, maybe that would change when sex with Claire was off the table again.

Tonight was the season opener and they would be heading to Legend's to watch the game like always. Like nothing had changed. Like they hadn't had sex at all. Like she didn't want more than he had to give. Like he couldn't give her what she needed. Because what if he wasn't what she needed at all? What if she wanted something he couldn't give her because he was broken? Fuck.

"Got a call from Alan last night." Claire glanced up at him from her laptop.

Logan's heart pounded a little harder. "Oh, yeah?"

Fucking perfect, Dr. Alan Thomson. He could give Claire what she wanted, what she needed. He had a house and two point five kids practically written on his stupid face. He didn't really know Claire the way Logan did, but maybe he could handle it. Doctors had insane egos, right?

Maybe he could deal with all of Claire without diminishing her or running.

"He still banging Parker?" The words tasted nasty in his mouth like he was snitching on someone. But he'd never make it easy on Alan. Not when it came to Claire.

Lacy gasped from her desk next to his. He grinned at her. "I could have said fucking. You're welcome."

Lacy shook her head. Her brown eyes still wide.

"It just startled me." She leaned in and whispered, "You sounded almost jealous."

"Not of Parker, trust me." Logan told her softly. The jealousy was definitely new and he wasn't sure it would go away when the sex stopped. The thought of Claire in someone else's arms ripped his insides to shreds.

"Anyway," Claire drew his attention back to her, "Alan says he can come to the game tonight."

Logan grunted. He had less than a month to convince Claire that having a boyfriend wouldn't be better than having him at her beck and call. And the one night he was supposed to have her all to himself, Alan fucking Thomson would be coming, too.

"So is Alan the *one*?" Raising an eyebrow, Logan met Claire's eyes. Perhaps his tone was a little more mocking than he should have been, but he didn't want her to go to Alan when they were done. Alan might be a nice guy but he couldn't handle her.

Her lips pressed together and she leaned back in her chair with a mutinous look. "Could be. After all, he's not looking to play the field or just looking for a good time. He wants to settle down."

"As long as you don't fuck him." Logan shrugged, but he held her dark eyes. They had a deal and that deal included not fucking anyone but Logan until their chits were used up.

Lacy's mouth dropped open. Logan turned to her and gave her a wink. Her mouth shut and she blushed.

"Are you done trying to shock poor Lacy?" Claire pushed her hair back from her face.

Logan grinned. "I'm just telling it like it is."

"Just ignore him, Lacy. He's an ass." Claire lifted her brow at him daring him to keep talking.

Logan stretched and turned to Lacy. "I'm sorry if I offended you with my abrupt language."

Lacy laughed. A sweet sound. "Language doesn't bother me. Usually I can follow your banter, but you seem to be on a different level today. Not that that's a bad thing, but just different."

Claire made a dismissive sound. But Logan grinned at Lacy. She gave him a small smile back.

"I like that," Logan told Lacy before he turned to meet Claire's fierce look and tipped his head to her. "I hope Alan likes football, for your sake."

THIS WAS A HORRIBLE IDEA. Claire sat at the high bar table at Legend's across from Logan, knowing that at any minute Alan would walk through those doors. They'd come straight from work. So no game day jeans and jersey. Just normal Work Claire.

Gah, even she thought in Logan's doll-like phrases now.

Even though this was the season opener, it wasn't an important game that Claire felt she needed to commit to watching. She could relax and just enjoy the company, so Alan joining them shouldn't affect anything. Except for Logan.

Well, and Alan would provide a much-needed buffer.

"Hey, guys." Alan approached the table and shook Logan's hand before turning to Claire.

She forgot about the awkward should-we-shake, should-we-hug, or should-we-go-for-a-cheek-kiss greeting dance.

Alan stuck his hand out and relief poured through her as she shook it.

"This is the secret clubhouse, right?" Alan took the stool next to Claire. "You two do this all season?"

"Sometimes we go to the game. Together or separate. But yeah, this is pretty standard friend stuff." Claire pushed a menu toward Alan.

"We usually get a few appetizers to share." Logan sent Claire a questioning look. Was it about the friend line, because they were still friends.

"That sounds great." Alan looked over the menu.

When their server stopped at the table, Logan ordered their usual apps plus beers for him and her. Then he looked at Alan expectantly.

"I'll have a beer and a side salad with dressing on the side." Alan handed the menu back to the server. "I hope you don't mind me snagging a few of your appetizers."

Logan leaned back in his chair and smirked. "What's mine is yours."

A slight twinge coursed through Claire. It was about the appetizers. Obviously not about her.

"How did pretending to be in a fake relationship pan out for you two? Still best friends, I see." Alan tapped his finger on the table as he glanced between the two of them.

"It wasn't my finest moment," Claire acknowledged, not daring to look at Logan. "But Mom is done with the setups for a while and will be finding a hobby to occupy her free time."

"I still can't believe you two weren't the real deal." Alan shook his head and smiled at Claire. "You were very convincing. Though I've done the 'friends that fuck' thing before during med school. No time for a relationship."

Claire could feel the heat settle in her chest as Logan's eyes practically singed the side of her face. "We've been friends for a while now, so it wasn't too hard to pretend to be more."

"How's Parker?" Logan asked out of the blue.

Claire cut her gaze to him, but he just leaned forward, all his attention on Alan. The waitress set down the beers and left.

Alan cleared his throat. "We really haven't talked since I got back. She didn't want to keep in touch."

Logan smiled like the Cheshire cat. "Huh. Must not have left a good impression."

"With work, I don't have time for a distance thing right now." Alan shrugged and his hopeful gaze caught Claire's. "Besides Parker and I didn't really talk about long term. Time and place, right?"

Claire gave him a smile. Sure he'd had sex with Parker, but she'd been fucking Logan the whole weekend too. And a few nights ago. And at least three more times before the end of this month.

"What do you guys do for the game? Eat, drink beer, and watch the game?" Alan lifted his gaze to the TV screens.

"Pretty much." Claire drank a little beer. "Thursday nights are a little busier than weekends."

Logan narrowed his eyes at her and pointedly glanced at her full beer. She rolled her eyes at him. Usually she was through with the first beer before the appetizers came. So what if she didn't want to guzzle down her beer.

"Do you follow football, Alan?" Logan turned his attention back to Alan.

"Not particularly." Alan glanced at Claire with a flinching look. "But it should be pretty simple to follow. I played on my high school team."

That perked Claire up. "Then we don't have to explain play by play. That's good. Not that I wouldn't have, but it can get complicated."

"Who's playing today?" Alan perked up as the TV volume went up and the pregame stuff started to wind down.

"Buccaneers and Cowboys," Logan said as the food arrived. The server left some plates on the table along with some napkins.

"Who are we rooting for?" Alan's gaze bounced between her and Logan.

Claire shrugged. "Neither, really."

"Then why are we watching the game?" Alan took a bite of his salad while she grabbed a hot wing and put it on her plate.

She used her napkin to wipe her fingers off and Logan shook his head at her like he was disappointed. Her insides bubbled when she remembered his comment about her licking the wing sauce off her fingers. Not everything had to be sexual. She narrowed her eyes at him.

"We like to watch as many of the games as possible during the season." How could she even begin to explain to a guy who didn't really watch football? Part of it was the excitement of the game. But a lot of it was because it was what her family did together. It gave her a sense of connectedness that living away from her family in a city full of strangers didn't give her.

Alan pressed his lips together and nodded. "I'm glad you have a best friend for that then."

Logan cleared his throat before putting a few wings on his plate. While holding her gaze captive, he brought his fingers to his lips and sucked the sauce off them. Her core clenched.

"Always willing to pick up your slack, Alan." Logan's smirk annoyed her. "Gotta make sure Claire's needs are met."

"With residency, I don't have a lot of free time." Oblivious to Logan's undertone, Alan glanced over the carb fest on the table and picked up some of the celery that came with the wings.

The man needed to pick up something unhealthy and quick or she'd be flagging down the server for a salad of her own. She hadn't noticed what Alan ate when they were at the lake house. Didn't really care much there. But surely he wasn't a health nut just because he was a doctor.

Meanwhile, Logan decimated his wings and pulled more of the fried goodness from the center of the table onto his plate. Claire's stomach growled. Logan held out the plate of mozzarella sticks to her. Smiling tightly, she took one and set it next to her one poor wing.

She took a sip of beer and glanced up at the screens. They were lining up for the starting kick.

"I was glad you texted." Alan pulled Claire's attention from the TV. "I was hoping to spend my free time getting to know you better."

Logan snickered but kept his eyes locked on the TV. He knew she hated talking during the game. But fuck Logan, she needed someone long-term and Alan was a good candidate.

"That would be nice, Alan." She smiled and picked up a carrot stick. She didn't even dunk it in the ranch before eating it. While she liked carrots, it tasted like sadness compared to the carbs within reach.

The bar went nuts and Claire swiveled back to the TV. Fuck, what did she miss?

"Buccaneers just ran the ball fifty yards." Logan nodded to the TV.

"Who caught it?" She squinted up at the screen.

"Rogers." Logan's attention was firmly on the game now.

Claire sighed. She would likely have to watch the replay tonight.

Alan just smiled at her. "What else do you do for fun?"

"Sometimes we go dancing at the clubs." Claire glared over at Logan as he ate a few more carb-based items while she glanced at her plate. What would Alan think if she shoveled the rest of everything on the table, except the veggies, into her mouth before Logan could?

"I don't go out much myself. Sometimes I'll go to the bar with the other doctors. I leave the clubbing up to my sister." Alan glanced over the food on the table again before turning his nose up at it. Maybe game day wouldn't be the best time for her to get together with Alan.

"How is Kelly doing?" Claire asked with a glance at Logan.

Logan stiffened at her name and looked around. When he was assured she wasn't in the vicinity, waiting to pounce, he returned to watching the game. Claire glanced up at the screen.

"She's doing great. She seems to be back on track now."

Alan glanced over at Logan. "Fortunately, she's off her obsession with Logan."

Something settled in Claire's chest. At least one thing had gone right. Crazy Kelly had officially backed off.

"Though she may have a thing for Matt now." Alan flinched and shook his head. "It may not go as far since they don't live close together."

"Bunny boiler," Logan mumbled as he stole another wing from the basket.

Claire chuckled but covered it with a cough.

"Don't you want the last wing, Claire Bear?" Logan held the basket under her nose. The wing sauce practically singed her nose hairs, but God, did it smell good.

"No, thanks. I'm good." She gave Alan a smile.

The crowd in the bar went nuts again.

"What now?" Claire looked up at the TV, hoping for a replay.

"Cowboys scored a touchdown." Logan snatched the last wing from the basket and licked the sauce trailing down his hand.

What a fucker. She glared at him, but he winked.

Alan kept up a steady stream of conversation which practically made watching the game impossible. At least for her. Meanwhile Logan happily ate most of the appetizers and got to focus on the game. She hoped his six pack abs turned into a keg.

Every time the bar went wild, Claire would try to see what had happened and Logan would thoughtfully tell her. Meanwhile, Alan rambled on about stuff from movies to work to music like this was a first date. Maybe he thought it was.

Fuck, maybe she wasn't cut out to date because this was killing her.

"I need to use the restroom," she finally cut into Alan's

monologue about the perfection of the original trilogy of *Star Wars.*

Alan nodded and took out his phone. "I should check for messages."

The restrooms were down a hallway and she had to wait for the women's to be free. As she washed her hands, she took a deep breath to ease some of the tension running through her. Normally, games relaxed her. Even yelling at the TV was almost cathartic.

This particular game wasn't an important matchup to her. None of her fantasy league were on the teams. Watching the recaps should be enough. So why was it bothering her this much?

Alan could be her future. He was a nice enough guy. Who cared if he didn't particularly like to watch football? It wasn't everyone's cup of tea, after all. She could behave herself for this one game and then make sure to ask him out to lunch or dinner instead of watching the game next time.

With her plan laid out in front of her, she left the bathroom and caught her breath.

Logan stood leaning against the wall, waiting for her, with a smirk. His sleeves were rolled up, showing his tight forearms. His shirt unbuttoned at the neck revealing his chest a little. Dark scruff lined his jaw. He was hot.

"Enjoying the game with your future husband?"

Claire's mouth opened but nothing came out.

"Excuse me?" A young woman gestured behind Claire toward the bathroom door.

Claire shifted out of the way and dragged Logan farther down the hall.

"Not everyone is into football," Claire reasoned. Sure, a lot of guys were into sports, but not every sport and not every guy.

"You can't watch the game." Logan closed in on her with

every word. "You've barely touched your beer." Her back hit the wall. "And don't get me started on the food."

She put her hand on his chest to hold him back a little. His heart raced under her touch, matching the frantic beat of her own.

His hand came over hers, holding it in place. She lifted her gaze to his.

"What do you want from me?" she ground out. His heat seeped into her, setting her blood on fire. "It's the only time he had free."

"We're twenty-six. We have plenty of time to dick around and find someone to spend the rest of our lives with. Later. You and I enjoy each other in multiple ways without you having to fake being something you're not." He tipped his head like he would kiss her.

She wanted him to and she didn't. She knew it would be bad to give in to him. To throw caution to the wind and say fuck it. How long would this last before it crashed and burned? A month, maybe two? At least she'd be thoroughly fucked while they were together.

But how long before she fell a little harder? A little deeper? Because she was close to the point of no longer caring. She was close to wanting to be with him no matter the cost.

He'd leave her for another woman. Someone new. Someone softer. Someone who didn't drink beers and belch with reckless abandon. Someone who didn't have a temper and throw things at the TV.

And it would destroy her. Because she could feel herself slipping down that slope. Maybe she'd already hit the bottom. Maybe she'd done the unthinkable and fallen in love with Logan O'Connell.

The boy who gave his heart away long ago and had it thrown back in his face repeatedly. The fuck boy with the gorgeous face and body that everyone wanted for at least one night, but no one dared to keep him.

Not even her.

"Are you cashing in a chit?" She threw it in his face. "Because if not, back the fuck off."

His eyes narrowed and his lips pressed thin, but he stepped back. Not enough to let her go, but enough that maybe she could breathe and think a little more rationally.

"How is Alan fucking Thomson going to be *it* for you?" Logan still held her hand on his heart. "Why give up this maddening beat between us? You and I are perfect together."

"We're friends, Logan." She took in a deep breath and met his eyes. "Just friends with a little pent-up frustration to work out. You only want me because you can't have me."

"That's the thing, tiger." He closed in on her again before she could react. His mouth hovered over hers as his eyes searched hers. Her breath caught. His deep voice was almost a siren song as he said, "I can have you and you can have me. Just say the word and I'll be balls deep inside you. Whenever, wherever you like."

His lips brushed over hers as he said those final words. The wall held her up or she'd be a puddle at his feet. His cheek brushed hers as he moved his lips to her ear.

"I'm yours, tiger."

CHAPTER 23

Logan left Claire practically panting in the hallway. He couldn't help the cocky smile on his lips as he joined Alan at the table.

"How's it going?" Logan asked and took a drink of his beer.

"Not bad." Alan slid his phone in his pocket. "Didn't quite know what to expect after last weekend."

"Yeah." Logan nodded and watched Claire walk toward them. He never knew what to expect from her now. Would she fight him or succumb to him?

"She's something else, isn't she?" Alan had turned to watch her too.

"Yeah." Logan swallowed the harsh pill that she didn't want to "waste" her time with him. She didn't say it expressly, but she'd already written him off as a lost cause. But maybe he just needed time. Maybe he could be what she needed if given time.

"I'm going to ask her out." Alan's tone was level and a little wary. "You guys seemed *close* at the lake. But you aren't actually dating, right?"

"She's a free agent." Logan tried a shrug but the tension held his shoulders too tight for the motion. Technically, she wouldn't be a free agent until Logan's month was up or they'd used up their three chits.

Fuck. He'd wanted to use one of his already, but he needed to wait. Needed to hold off as long as possible until she gave in to the lust between them.

Claire reached the table and slid into her seat. She glanced at the TV screens. "What'd I miss?"

"Mostly commercials." Alan shrugged, but he smiled at her like he'd done good. What a dork.

"It's half time. They should come back any moment." Logan chugged his beer and then looked around for their server.

That blond-haired, blue-eyed little flirt from last week sat a few tables over. She winked at him and he felt. . . nothing. He wasn't disappointed he couldn't go over to get her number since it was game day. He didn't want to ask her back to his place or go to hers. He didn't want to have anything to do with her.

Claire was the only one on his mind. He caught the server's attention and raised his empty glass. The server nodded.

Logan turned back to the table which had become the Alan Thomson Show. Again. Work Claire tried very hard not to slip into Game Day Claire. Her gaze darted between Alan, the sad wing on her plate, her neglected beer, and the TV screen.

Alan kept up the conversation like he hadn't talked to anyone in weeks. Logan didn't think the guy had talked this much up at the lake, but besides noticing Alan noticing Claire, he hadn't really paid much attention to him. Most of the time, Logan had focused on Claire.

Worst game day ever. Especially when he knew neither

Alan nor he would get lucky tonight. If Logan had wanted to, the chick at that table would let him blow off some steam, but he'd made a promise to Claire.

Besides, he didn't want that other chick. He wanted Claire.

Alan's phone buzzed on the table. He glanced at it and scowled. He met Claire's eyes apologetically and said, "I have to take this."

She just smiled at him like Little Miss Perfect and nodded. Alan went down the hallway away from the noise of the bar.

"Would you eat that poor sad wing now?" Logan lifted his eyebrow at her. "And drink your warm beer, so I can get you another one."

Claire glared at him, but she devoured the wing and mozzarella stick on her plate before glancing toward the hallway to see if Alan was on his way back and had seen her scarfing down her food.

Logan rolled his eyes and pushed her beer toward her.

She chugged like a champion and when she finished, she burped slightly. Not her normal belch but definitely more herself. Logan shook his head as he waved over the server to get Claire a refill. When he turned back, Claire's eyes were on the game.

He didn't dare say anything. This was Game Day Claire. When the server dropped off her new beer, Claire drank a third of it and then belched. Her eyes never left the game.

There was his girl. He smiled and drank some of his beer. Alan hadn't returned yet, so he watched the game with Claire like they usually did.

"Their new QB has a great arm," Claire said as she shoveled a few fries into her mouth.

"Who knows, maybe the Buccaneers will have a fantastic

season and I'll have a new team to root for," Logan managed to say with a straight face.

Claire laughed at him. Her dark eyes sparkled. "Yeah, right. Like you would be a fucking fair weather fan."

"You caught me. I'm a football team monogamist." Logan smirked.

Claire scoffed and laughed a little before watching the next play.

Alan came back out to the table with a frown. "I hate to run early but I have to deal with something."

Could the guy be more vague?

"That's okay." Claire smiled softly at him. "Thanks for coming out. It was fun."

"Good seeing you again, Logan." Alan held out his hand.

Logan took it. "Yeah. Have a good night."

Alan turned to Claire. "Walk me out?"

"Sure." Claire glanced at the TV and sighed softly while Alan looked through his wallet and threw a couple of twenties on the table.

When they walked away, Logan drank his beer and ordered another basket of wings. Thank fuck Alan was leaving. If Alan and Claire became an actual couple. . . Logan shuddered at the thought. Claire was open and vivacious and so fucking sexy. Alan was a good guy, but he didn't hold a candle to Claire.

The game had just gone to commercial when Claire came back to the table and chugged the rest of her beer.

"Alan ask you out?" Logan leaned back in his bar chair.

Claire nodded. The server brought the basket of wings and set it in the middle. Logan pushed the basket toward Claire. Her eyes lit up and her fingers danced in the air.

"Did you say yes?" A lump formed in Logan's throat.

Claire grabbed a wing and met Logan's eyes. "He's nice

and attractive. He's looking for something more serious than a hookup."

Her eyes rolled back in pleasure as she ate a wing.

"Is that really what you want?" Logan rested his elbows on the table and held her gaze. His heart froze like a rock in his chest.

"Yes. Of course." Claire picked up another wing and started eating it.

"Why didn't you eat when Alan was here?" Logan took a drink of his beer. "This is game day. Not talk about movies day. Not even date day. Is this who guys get when they go on dates with you?"

"What do you mean?" Claire sucked her finger into her mouth and Logan's thoughts popped like a fucking bubble.

He needed to be her best friend right now and not remember how good that mouth felt sucking his cock. He shook his head and refocused.

"Why didn't you drink and eat and tell him to shut the fuck up while the game is on? Who the fuck are you trying to be?"

Claire grabbed her napkin and glared at Logan. "Guys don't like women who scream at the ref or devour their food or belch the alphabet. So, yeah, I have to tone it down if I want to at least make it to an actual date."

She downed some beer.

"You hide part of yourself to make a guy like you? That's pretty fucked up."

"You're right." She narrowed her eyes on him. "It is fucked up, but I've had too many guys want to be just friends after meeting Game Day Claire or Clubbing Claire or Work Claire. So excuse me if I'm cautious. I'm pretty sure Alan wouldn't appreciate Game Day Claire."

"Seriously, men are morons." Logan was angry on her behalf. "You shouldn't have to hide a significant part of who you are to please a man. What kind of relationship would you build by leaving part of you out of it?"

"It's not a big deal." Claire took another wing. "Besides he doesn't even like football, so he doesn't need to get to know that side of me."

"You mean the side that connects you to your father?"

"Drop it." She gave him a warning look. Fuck that.

Logan took a breath and decided to go at this another way.

"You want to find someone for forever, right?" Logan gave her a cocky grin. "Because you've got me if you want someone for right now."

She rolled her eyes. "Yes. I want a relationship. Not a fuck boy."

"Then don't waste your time on Alan Thomson."

"It wouldn't be—"

"Yes, it would be wasting time." Logan glanced at the TV knowing the game would be coming back on. He returned his gaze to her. "You can't have forever with only half of you. You have to put your whole self out there if you want someone who can actually handle everything you are. That means letting them see Game Day Claire *and* Date Claire."

"You know Barbies are blond, right? I'm not some doll." She gave him that look to knock that shit off.

He grinned wider at her. "Claire Bear, you're so much better than any doll they make. Don't sell yourself short."

Claire shook her head. Her forehead creased as her attention got drawn into the game again. He didn't want her to find someone who would take her away from him, but he definitely didn't want her to have to hide a part of her away because she felt ashamed of it.

He stood and went to stand in front of her chair.

She pursed her lips before she lowered her gaze to meet his. "May I help you?"

"I like Game Day Claire. I'd fuck her."

She lifted her eyebrow and a small smirk came to her lips. "You'd fuck anything."

"I know I'm not a great catch. I barely had standards." Logan rubbed his hand over his short hair and held her gaze. He trusted Claire, but what if she didn't want anything more than his cock? How could he handle being around his friend if she rejected his heart? Not that he was in love with her. "If I could offer you a future, I would. But when I think about even asking you to be my girlfriend, I get all fucked up inside."

"Logan." She reached out her hand to him with pity in her eyes. He didn't want that.

"I know I'm not offering you much, but I'm offering what I have to give. At least right now." Logan took her hand in his and squeezed it. "Maybe it could be more. I know I want to spend time with you. However I can get it. I'd fuck Game Day Claire every fucking day if I could. Any Claire really."

She smiled at him which encouraged him because this shit was scary as fuck.

"At least think about it before you waste a year or more of your life on Alan fucking Thomson. Take a chance that I might be able to offer more."

His breath caught in his chest, worried that she'd reject him if he offered more. Afraid to offer more, but Claire would be worth it.

CLAIRE BARELY REGISTERED GOING HOME that night or the next day at work. Since it was Friday night, that meant office happy hour now. All night and all day, her brain kept swirling around Logan's words and what that meant to her.

What would it hurt to see where this thing between them went? Every time she asked herself that, her chest ached.

She snapped out of her daze at the bar. Not the whole crew this weekend. Drew and Morgan were off doing their own thing. Emily had to go to her grandma's. Claire still didn't know what was up with Emily the other day with needing a lawyer. And Ben, the quiet, sneaky-hot accountant, rarely joined them.

"It feels like a shot night," Logan spoke up from his seat next to her. Some of the ache in Claire's chest eased. That line was typical for her best friend.

Lacy groaned and shook her head. "No shots."

Claire grinned, remembering when Lacy got so drunk on shots that Jonah basically had to help her home. Even though she'd tried her best to keep up with the rest of them, Lacy hadn't stood a chance.

Jonah wrapped his arm around Lacy's shoulders and tugged her into his side. "No one would make you drink shots."

Lacy glanced up at him with an open expression. "But I want to be part of the team."

"It's okay, Lacy." Phoebe placed a hand on Lacy's arm before glancing at Logan. "I think we could all use a week without shots."

Logan just smirked. "Fine. Beers and margaritas, it is. Help me at the bar, Claire?"

He stood and held out his hand to her. Something he'd done a thousand times in crowded bars and nightclubs. She glanced up at his dark eyes, watching her, waiting for her to decide. She cursed her stupid heart for skipping before she forced a smile on her lips and slid her hand into his.

Heat travelled from his hand up her arm as she trailed behind him through the crowd. He pulled her to stand between him and the bar while they waited for the bartender's attention. Logan's heat surrounded her, making her feel all warm and gooey inside. She missed the sex, don't get her wrong, but she also missed the snuggling and touching.

"We going out this weekend?" Logan didn't even look at her when he asked, like it was no big deal. Maybe it wasn't to him. Maybe he was just trying to be her best friend instead of her maybe lover.

"I need to catch up on stuff this weekend. Tons of laundry and I haven't grocery shopped in weeks." She shrugged as nonchalantly as she could. "I also need to catch up on my sleep."

His gaze flicked down to hers on that, but before he could comment, the bartender drew his attention. She hadn't been lying. She needed a down weekend to catch up. Sleep had been evading her all week.

Mostly she needed space to think without Logan always being there. Without his scent drawing her in and his warmth making her want everything he had to offer even if it wasn't everything she needed.

He turned with a pitcher of margarita and three mugs for her to carry. "We still on for Sunday's game?"

She nodded and he grabbed the pitcher of beer and three more mugs. He gestured for her to lead the way back to the table. When they arrived, mugs and pitchers were passed around the table. Words flowed about the past week at work.

Claire tried to stay focused on the conversation, but Logan's leg pressed up against hers under the table. The heat between them brought forth the questions that had kept her up most of the night and distracted her all day.

Would she ever be enough for Logan? Could she do what no other woman could do and hold onto him? They were good as friends, but this made it so much more complicated.

He said he would be exclusive but couldn't offer her the

title of girlfriend. But that was just a label. A label she didn't need, right? What it meant though was he would be hers and hers alone until. . . . This was where the fantasy began to fall apart.

The "until."

Until he realized that she would always be loud and crass on game days. Until someone else caught his wandering eye and he realized she wasn't worth the sacrifice. No one ever wanted all of her.

"Is everything okay?" Phoebe's soft voice pulled her back to the present.

Logan had vanished along with the guys. Claire searched the bar and saw them at one of the dart boards. Lacy's large brown eyes were slightly glazed over, but she also gave Claire a concerned look.

"I'm sorry." Claire forced a smile. "What'd I miss?"

Phoebe sighed and gave Lacy a look. "You just seem off this week."

"Did something happen between you and Logan last weekend?" Lacy grinned and leaned forward. "I mean the friends pretending to date is one of my all-time favorite tropes."

"What?" Phoebe looked a little lost.

Claire sighed.

"My mom is notorious for setups. So to stop her machinations, I had Logan pretend to be my boyfriend for the weekend," Claire explained to Phoebe. "Well, my mom decided to be progressive and let us sleep together. That first night, I thought Logan was already messing up in front of everyone when he appeared to be flirting with another girl, who ended up being my brother's girlfriend, so in my anger, I kissed him."

Lacy sucked in a breath like this was the most fascinating thing she'd ever heard.

Claire glanced toward the guys at the same time Logan looked back. He smirked at her and gave her a wink. She shook her head but couldn't help the smile lifting her lips. That kiss had been epic. The whole weekend had been epic. She had him for at least another three times. Why was she holding herself back?

That achy throb in her chest returned.

"Let me guess." Phoebe took a sip of her margarita before continuing. "You and Logan played *pretend* a little too convincingly and now your mother believes you're getting married."

"Actually" —Claire returned her focus to the two women in front of her— "we ended up getting busted on Sunday by that chick that showed up in the office on Friday. So my family knows we're just friends."

Phoebe smiled and twirled her straw in her drink. "Friends who fucked."

"No, they wouldn't do that." Lacy shook her head. "The kiss is always the big shocker, but then there's all this repressed sexual tension."

Phoebe snorted. "Seriously, Lacy? This isn't a high school romance. This is Claire and Logan. Two very hot, very sexual beings, who had to share a bed for a weekend. Before Aiden, I probably would have hit that if I had to spend a weekend pretending to be a couple with Logan. Of course, I wouldn't have all the issues because we aren't also best friends besides coworkers."

Phoebe gave a brief nod to Claire. Claire took a deep breath and released it. Lacy's eyes widened.

"What Phoebe said." Claire gestured in Phoebe's direction. "We've never been attracted to each other before—"

Phoebe laughed and even Lacy grinned.

"No really." Claire scrunched up her face at their denial. "I mean Logan's always been good-looking, but I wasn't attracted to him. Not in that way."

"Sure, let's say we believe you." Phoebe's grin said she absolutely thought Claire was full of shit. "I could see you putting it on a shelf to maintain your friendship, but don't lie to yourself. I've seen you two out. When the other isn't looking. . . ."

Phoebe shook her head and smiled.

Claire had asked Logan if he'd ever been attracted to her. Warmth flooded her system as she remembered what he'd said after sand volleyball. *I've wanted you as long as I've known you, but I couldn't have you.*

She shook her head but her pulse ramped up at the thought. "Fine. There may have been an underlying attraction, but" —she held a finger up— "neither of us would have acted on it had it not been for that kiss."

Lacy beamed a know-it-all grin at Phoebe.

"Probably," Claire mumbled and put her head in her hands.

"Please tell me it wasn't bad?" Phoebe made a sour face and took a sip of her margarita. She glanced over at the guys. "Because that would just be a tragedy."

Claire lifted her face and raised an eyebrow at Phoebe. "Trust me when I say he exceeds his reputation."

Phoebe's face transformed into a slow grin. "The world is right again."

"So what's the problem?" Lacy looked completely confused. "You guys are friends. You're attracted to each other and you have awesome sex. I'm not seeing the problem."

Claire straightened and stopped herself from holding her hand out toward Logan. "He's Logan."

Phoebe sighed.

Lacy shook her head. "Yeah, so?"

"How many eyes right now are on the man? He could have his pick of the litter here. I've seen him take women from guys I've dated before without even doing much but give those women the time of day. He's a walking hormone and women know it."

Lacy leaned forward and started, "But you knew all this before last weekend."

"Last weekend." Claire finished the rest of her margarita as she tried to put words to what she'd felt. She leaned in and the other women moved in with her. "It wasn't just the sex. He was attentive and touchy. He held me and we. . . cuddled."

She said the word like it was the worst thing they could have done. Before Lacy could say anything or ask why, Claire held up her hand.

"It was all pretend. It was a show for my family and childhood friends. None of that was real, but it felt so fucking real." Claire inhaled. "I want that. I want a guy so smitten with me that he can't stand the thought of not touching me. That instead of sitting next to me, he wants me to sit in his lap or he sits between my legs while I play with his hair. Someone I can lean on and not worry that he might decide to take someone else home with him."

The other women leaned back and glanced over at their guys. Yeah, each of them had what Claire wanted. What Logan had shown her was missing from her life.

Sex was awesome with Logan. And that cuddling guy existed in him in some form. He'd brought him out at the lake house, but that guy couldn't be real. She knew Logan. They rarely went home at the same time and almost never with each other, unless they both struck out.

Unlike Logan though, Claire sometimes did date a guy longer than a hot second. She didn't tell every guy she slept with that she couldn't ever be more than sex. She didn't turn her nose up at the thought of monogamy right now.

Blinking back tears that had welled in her eyes, Claire grabbed her purse and forced a smile at the ladies. "I'm clearly overtired. I'm going to head out."

Phoebe caught her hand before Claire stood.

Her warm brown eyes caught and held Claire's. "Maybe he always chose someone else because he couldn't choose you."

CHAPTER 24

Logan spent Saturday running errands and catching up on chores around his house. He'd texted Claire after she left on Friday night to check on her. But she'd just said she was tired.

Saturday night crept up on Logan. He sat in his chair watching a highlight reel of the past week's games and smoothed his thumb over his phone screen. He wanted to call Claire. He didn't have a best bud to process his feelings with. He had Claire for that.

"Fuck it."

He pulled up his text conversation with her.

Please tell me your Saturday night is as boring as mine?

Three little dots showed up on his screen and he straightened on his chair as they disappeared. Maybe she'd decided to go out. Maybe Alan had the night off. He released his breath when he felt his phone vibrate with response.

It could be worse. We could be at a club where Kelly might stalk you.

Would Alan be there? Because that would make it perfect. He could stare at your tits and I could try to get a restraining order on Kelly.

She's only crazy because guys like you made her that way.

Guys like him? What the fuck did that mean? He typed, *WTF.*

The eclipses showed up again and faded. And then showed up and faded. He paused his show and hit the call button on the phone. It rang a couple of times even though he knew her phone was in her hand.

"Yeah?"

"The fuck does that mean?" he asked.

She sighed. "Look, you've been a player since high school. You don't promise women anything and they still sleep with you hoping that maybe they'll be the one to change you. So they let you into their lives and when you do exactly what you said you'd do and go off with someone else, they're devastated."

"Fuck." He ran a hand down his face. Somewhere inside he knew women did that. Thought they could make a guy change. Honesty didn't always work. But he hoped Claire didn't put herself in that category. He wanted things to progress with her, but he wasn't sure what that meant or what that even looked like.

Claire's voice brought him out of his thoughts. "It's not like you were the first to do that shit to her, but there are women who don't get a clue. They think it's a game they can win, not just something you play."

He blew out a breath. "Aren't you tired of this shit?"

Suddenly he was bone weary of playing this game. He just wanted Claire here in this chair with him while they fought over why one football player was better than the other. He wanted her warmth against his side. Her breath against his neck. Her leg crossed over his.

He just wanted her. But he had no idea how to tell her any

of that without giving her the power to hurt him. He'd put so many of his cards on the table while she still held her hand hidden from him. Yeah, she said she wanted more, but that didn't tell him what she wanted from him.

"I've been tired of it for a while." Her voice was soft. "I feel like I'm missing out on this big thing that most of the women in the office have found."

Logan thought about last night after the guys rejoined the ladies and Claire was gone. His chest had ached, but he'd stayed a while to drink and joke around with the rest of them, because the only thing waiting for him when he got home was an empty bed.

A few women had approached them while they played darts at the bar, but no one sparked any interest in Logan. They were just a body. He missed Claire.

"I miss you," he said softly. The words caught at his throat, but he couldn't hold them in. "You're my best friend."

"And you don't have girls as friends." The soft smile in her voice nearly did him in.

"Come over." He couldn't help himself. "Just come over and watch this crappy rehash of the college games with me? I have beer. We can order a pizza. Just come over."

He held his breath, wondering if he'd pushed too hard.

"I'm not putting on makeup," she said in response.

His heart started to beat again. "Then I'm not putting on a shirt."

"My hair will be in a messy bun and I'm wearing my laundry day sweatpants and T-shirt."

He cracked a grin. "Sponge Bob?"

"Sponge Bob," she said solemnly.

"Well, get over here then, Sponge Bob and all. I'll order a pizza."

Ten minutes later, Logan grinned as he opened his door for Claire. The oversized yellow T-shirt hung down over her hips. Her sweats weren't leggings, but actual baggie sweats that did nothing to reveal the shape of her legs. Her Converse shoes were worn and had a hole in the toe. Her face didn't have a lick of makeup on it and her dark hair was clamped on the top of her head with a clip.

She'd never looked more beautiful to him.

"Hey," she said and brushed past him into his apartment. She hooked her purse on the hat stand and toed off her shoes to reveal socks with eggplants all over them.

He shut the door and let out a breath.

He loved her.

Those words didn't scare him at all as his heart swelled in his chest. No, but saying them to her would be terrifying. Hearing her say he wasn't enough for her would break whatever was left of his heart.

Claire glanced over her shoulder at him as she walked to the couch. "Did you remember the bread sticks?"

"I thought you were trying to manage your carb intake during football season." He rested against the wall, just watching her move. She picked up the throw pillows and moved them to one side. He was so fucked.

"We're watching football, right?" She gestured to the TV.

She sank onto his couch and snagged the remote from his chair. All things she'd done before last weekend. She opened the guide and started scanning through the channels. Practically ignoring him.

He still hadn't moved. Just so fucking happy that his best friend was here. He loved all the Claires, but there was something special about Best Friend Claire.

She turned on the couch to give him an odd look. "Are you just going to stand there?"

Shaking his head, he forced himself to move and sat next to her on the couch. She lifted an eyebrow at him for a moment but then went back to studying the guide on the TV.

Casually he reached around behind her and snatched the remote from her hand.

"Hey!" She turned and watched him put the show he'd been watching back on. Her soft rosemary and mint scent drifted over him. He tensed but managed to ignore the heat from her body so easily in reach.

"My apartment. My choice." Dropping the remote on the coffee table, he leaned back on the couch with his arms spread along the back and finally looked at her.

Her eyebrow was raised and a small smirk played on her lips. "Fine."

She put her socked feet up on the coffee table and leaned back. The softness of her hair brushed his arm. But neither of them shied away from touching each other. What he really wanted to do was draw her into his side and rest his head against the top of hers, but he kept himself immobile as they relaxed in each other's presence.

For a whole ten minutes, they watched the commentators talking shit about this or that player and team before the door buzzed. He reluctantly got up to get the pizza.

He tipped the guy and closed the door.

"Aha!" Claire stood behind him on her tiptoes looking down at the pizza box or more specifically the bag of bread-sticks on top of the pizza box.

"What? You really think I'd forget the breadsticks?" He met her eyes and for a moment, just a moment, he wanted to kiss her. Just a brief peck on the lips would be enough for him, but instead, he cleared his throat. "Can we go back to the coffee table or do you want me to feed you over my shoulder?"

She chuckled and stepped away into his kitchen. He set the boxes on the coffee table. She came out with two beers and a handful of napkins. She handed him a beer before resuming her seat next to him.

His chest eased again that she didn't change seats. Things were awkward between them and he didn't like that. He took a drink of beer and opened the pizza box to pull out a slice while she started on the breadsticks.

"You think Anderson will go for the draft or finish school first?" she asked around a bite of breadstick.

The knot in his chest released and they eased into an easy rhythm of talking about the players while they ate.

When they finished eating, Logan took the leftover pizza to the kitchen and grabbed a couple more beers before returning to the couch. They hadn't talked about what was happening between the two of them the whole time, which was nice.

She hadn't answered whether she was willing to take a chance on him and he didn't want to press her. He handed her a beer before resuming his seat next to her.

"Thanks." She took the bottle cap off and put it on the coffee table.

He returned his arm across the back of the couch on her side and drank his beer. "You want to watch the recap of Thursday's game or change the channel?"

"This is good." She leaned back on the couch and tucked her feet up beside her.

When her hair touched his arm again, he wrapped his arm around her shoulders and drew her into his side. Stiffly, she glanced up at him, a little on edge, but he just smiled without taking his eyes off the screen.

She sighed and took another drink before snuggling into him to get comfortable.

This right here, this he could get used to.

～

CLAIRE SNUGGLED DEEPER into the warmth behind her. Until the warmth squeezed her around her waist. She opened her eyes warily and took in Logan's living room. She glanced down at her still clothed body and the arm wrapped around her waist.

She remembered snuggling up against him sitting up. It had been comfortable. Apparently too comfortable. She'd decided to come over because she missed her best friend. She figured she'd keep it completely platonic. And definitely not spend the night.

She took a deep breath and blew it out. At least they didn't have sex again. Though from the hardness against her ass, that part of Logan hadn't gotten the memo. The warmth that flooded her system also hadn't received the memo.

When she went to move off the couch, Logan's arm tightened around her, drawing her against him and his nose nuzzled the nape of her neck.

"Five more minutes." His sleep husky voice sent shivers down her spine.

She sighed and relaxed into him. "Don't you have to go to lunch at your mom's?"

"Mmmm." His nose traced along the back of her neck until his lips brushed the base of her skull.

Fuck. Her insides went liquid and her own leash on her control was slipping.

"Logan?"

His teeth scraped along her neck next. Holy shit, he did not play fair.

"I love it when you say my name."

Her heart pounded against her ribs and she wanted to give in so fucking bad. He knew how to make her feel good and it had been days since the last time she let him.

"I should go home," she said, trying her best to stiffen a little in his arms.

"You should shower with me." His voice held so much promise as his lips found that spot where her neck met her shoulder. It was like his own personal button to make her lust overcome all her sense. If only it didn't work so well.

"I should have gone home last night." She bit her lip to stop the moan that wanted to escape as he continued to kiss and tease that spot. She barely kept herself from grinding her ass into his hardness.

"Let me show you how shower sex is supposed to be done," he murmured against her skin. His fingers edged beneath her shirt and found the soft skin of her stomach.

"I—"

He stopped her denial with four words. "I'll use a chit."

"What?" Her brain nearly orgasmed at the mention. It was like a free pass. No decision had to be made on her part.

"Any time, any place." He traced her spine at the back of her neck with his tongue. "That was the deal. I choose now and in my shower."

Her body ramped up against her protests. She still should fight against this. "What happened to it needing to be public?"

In public, they would be one and done to not get discovered. If she gave in to him here, alone in his apartment, who knew how long they would go at it. Probably until right before he had to leave for his family lunch. Somehow the thought of going all morning didn't exactly cool her jets.

"If I thought you'd give in to me without using one, I would happily keep my chit." He nuzzled the back of her neck again. His warm breath bathed her in tingles. "But I only have a limited time to use two and I'd hate to have to jack off again this morning imagining you, when you're right here."

"We did have shower sex at the lake house." She twisted her shoulders slightly in his arms to try to face him.

"That wasn't shower sex." He kissed the tip of her nose.

"It was sex in a shower," she pointed out. This was all an excuse to have sex. Sure, it could be fun to have shower sex in a larger shower, but he was the one who added the stipulation that it needed to be public sex for the chits.

He slipped his hand down the front of her sweats and under her panties, cupping the heart of her, but he just hovered there. She sucked in a breath and waited for him to really touch her. Her heart lodged in her throat.

His teeth tugged on her earlobe and he whispered into her ear, "Chit. Now."

His fingers pressed against her and slid over her clit. Her lips parted on a gasp while her eyes slid shut. She pushed back into him as he teased her opening, circling his fingertip on the edge.

She could barely breathe as he continued to torment her. All her previous excuses flew out of her mind. When he touched her like this, she was his to do with whatever he pleased. And she knew he'd do whatever possible to please her.

His lips left butterfly kisses from her ear down her neck until he stopped on that spot again. Her breath caught and held. Waiting. Anticipating. His lips closed over the muscle there. At the same time he slipped his finger inside her, he applied suction to her neck.

"Logan," she breathed out in a rush of breath. She wanted to touch him and feel his naked skin against her own, but he held her back to his front as he continued to torment her. His body curled around her own as he stroked her higher and higher. His mouth continued to tease the skin of her neck with his tongue and teeth and lips, until she was practically panting.

A small part of her pleaded for sanity, to stop this madness, but her heart was all in. He could smash her heart to bits or tenderly take care of it. It didn't matter. Somewhere along the way she'd given it to him.

He bit her neck and twisted his fingers slightly and she couldn't stop the oncoming storm as she tipped over the edge. Her lips parted as her breath escaped. His heat surrounded her, amplifying the orgasm. Her core pulsed around his fingers as she tried to catch her breath.

"Easy, tiger," he whispered against her ear. "We're only starting."

Sparks lit across her skin as he eased his fingers out of her and kissed where he most definitely left another mark on her neck. She couldn't care about the marks.

Tomorrow when she got ready for work would be soon enough to worry about any marks he left behind. Because she was positive that wouldn't be the only one.

By using a chit, he gave them carte blanche. He took away the decision-making from her. After all, they'd made a bet and he wanted her to pay up. She couldn't wonder how bad it would be to give in to him again when he still hadn't offered what she needed for this to continue. He wanted now and she wanted forever.

Or at least the promise of a potential future. Because she could see losing herself in him for as long as he would have her.

She pushed those thoughts aside as his hands helped her sit up, and he followed her. When they sat beside each other on the couch, his dark eyes captured hers. His finger brushed a strand of hair behind her ear.

"You're beautiful." He brushed his lips across her lips, fleetingly and way too quick. "Smart as hell." Another kiss but to her jaw. "Sexy even in rumpled Sponge Bob."

She smiled at that and he kissed the corner of her mouth. Her mind gave up, knowing she would have sex with him, regardless of whether it was a good idea or not.

His hand wrapped around the back of her neck and held her still. His hot gaze roamed over her. "Fuck, Claire. I know you aren't perfect, but damned if I can find anything wrong with you."

"What about the belching?" She raised a challenging eyebrow.

He touched his forehead to hers and whispered, "It was the reminder that you were my friend before I knew how you felt beneath me. I don't think even that would be enough to hold me off."

She smiled softly. "Not even the National Anthem?"

"Not even." His lips closed over hers in a soft kiss. Tender and sweet. Not at all like Logan.

She pulled back, resisting the urge to reach up to touch her own lips, and searched his eyes. She wasn't sure what she expected to see, but this wasn't her best friend Logan. The guy who flirted and teased with no thought to the consequences. Right now, more lingered in his eyes as he looked at her.

He kissed her again before standing and drawing her up with him. Her heart pounded in her chest as he slipped his hand into hers and led her to the bathroom. Something had shifted even more between them.

The part of her that had been fighting this, whatever it was between them, suddenly stopped. Maybe Logan wasn't exactly perfect either. Maybe all he could give her was not dicking around on her. And maybe that would be enough for now.

CHAPTER 25

Logan turned on the shower and went back to Claire. She stood in the doorway to the bathroom looking so fucking uncertain. It made his chest ache. He stripped off his athletic pants, leaving him completely naked before her.

Her dark gaze dipped down over him appreciatively, but she made no move to touch him or to take off her own clothes.

"If you don't want to. . . ." He let the words hang there. He didn't want to stop this, but he didn't want to force her into anything either. Yeah, he'd called on the bet to have her, but he still wanted her to want him too.

She blinked and shook her head. Her eyes lifted to his. "I want to."

Relief swamped him. All he wanted to do was take care of her. Hold her in his arms, fuck her until she saw fucking stars, enjoy every minute of every day with her.

Moving behind her, he released the clip holding her hair up. He ran his fingers gently through the rich strands to ease it down her back.

Threading his fingers through her hair, he gently

massaged her scalp. Her head fell forward on a moan and he smiled. Being with her was as easy as breathing.

"You can keep doing that as long as you want," she mumbled.

He chuckled. "I would, but I have other priorities."

She pouted as his fingers left her scalp. He drew off her shirt and pushed her sweats to the floor. He knelt behind her as he lifted her feet one at a time to take off her socks.

When he stood, she was still in her underwear and a sports bra. He drew her back against him and wrapped his arms around her. Lowering his head to her shoulder, he took in a deep breath and released it slowly. This. This was what he wanted.

Her hands grasped his arms, but she didn't do more than touch him.

"Are you sure *you* want to do this?" Her tone was playful.

"This is part of it." He kissed her shoulder and squeezed her against him.

She glanced toward the slowly fogging mirror and he turned to follow her gaze. They looked good together. Sex with her was always amazing, but to be able to just hold her like last night. He'd never experienced anything quite like it. She'd fallen asleep on his shoulder and for a moment, he considered lifting her and carrying her to his bed.

But he worried she'd wake up and insist on going home. So instead he shifted them to a lying position on the couch. And he did something he'd never done in his life. Fell asleep with a beautiful woman in his arms that he hadn't just fucked. It was amazing.

"Logan?" Her voice was soft as their image slowly fogged over, becoming more and more obscure.

"Mmm?" He pressed his lips to her shoulder.

"Do you really think we can do this?"

He glanced at the shower but he wasn't sure that was what she meant. "This?"

"You and me?" She stepped forward so she could turn around to face him. Her dark hair surrounded her face in a tangle. "Exclusive?"

He took her hand and brought her knuckles to his lips. His heart swelled in his chest. Half in hope, half in fear. He had to be completely honest with her if they wanted this to work. "I want to try."

Her lips pressed together as she searched his eyes again. He hoped she found whatever she was looking for in them. Because right now, nothing was more important than having Claire in his arms. Not just for today.

"I don't want any other woman. I just want you, Claire." He stepped forward and brushed her hair over her shoulders. "I know you're looking for forever and I'm not saying that isn't a real possibility, but I don't know what that looks like."

He cupped the back of her head and tipped her face to look up at him. Her dark eyes were filled with desire and something he didn't recognize. Maybe fear, maybe hope, maybe something else entirely.

"I've never wanted to belong to anyone before. I never wanted anyone to be all mine. But with you. . . ." He dropped a kiss onto her lips before leaning his forehead against hers. "I want it all."

She inhaled and closed her eyes for a moment. He would give her as much time as she needed, but every second killed him a little inside. What would he do if she said no? What would he do if she started dating someone else? Taking someone else to her bed?

Her hand settled over his rapidly beating heart.

"I can be yours."

The words rippled through him like a shockwave. He drew her back in and his mouth claimed hers. All the slowness flowed out of him. Cuddling would happen later, but right now, he needed her. To be inside of her and to take them to new heights of passion.

He made quick work of removing her bra and panties. Grabbing a condom from the counter, he backed her into the shower and shut the door.

The water poured over them as he reclaimed her lips. Their lips, teeth and tongues met in a complex dance until he knew they'd need to breathe soon, but he didn't want to relinquish her mouth ever again.

She was his.

All his.

His hands slid over her wet curves, greedy for the feel of her hot skin.

Her hands slipped over his shoulders and to the back of his neck, holding him right where he was, keeping him kissing her. He made quick work of the condom before shuffling her back against the shower wall. Grabbing her waist, he lifted her against him and her legs circled his hips.

His cock sank home inside of her and they both let out a groan.

He pressed his forehead against hers. "I can't get enough of you."

"Me neither." She leaned in to kiss him and he lost what little control he had.

They moved as one, her rolling her hips and him pistoning into her. Their lips clung together as all the words he wished he could say played silently against her mouth. From the moment he met Claire, he'd known she was different.

He tried to keep them strictly platonic, even as they spent more and more time together. There had been moments. When he took her home when she was drunk. When they did body shots with each other. Every fucking time they went out to the club and she dressed to impress. It really didn't take much for her to impress him. When she acted like she was one of the guys when she really wasn't.

She was perfect.

"Logan." She broke away from the kiss.

He opened his eyes to find hers, drowning in need and want and desire. A fist closed around his heart. This was all uncharted territory for him. He didn't know how to just be with one woman. But she wasn't just one woman to him. She was a hundred different versions wrapped into one complete package. And he wanted all of her.

"Hey." Her hand touched his cheek and he refocused. The look on her face was enough to make him almost come, but he wanted her to fall over the edge first. He wanted to drown in ecstasy with her.

He smirked at her and readjusted his hold on her. He slowed down his thrusts and tipped his forehead against hers. "I'm all in."

"I know." She grinned at him. "I can feel you."

"Shall we discuss the terms of this new exclusivity?" He kept up his slow and steady pace. Her breath quickened with each stroke.

"Now?" She raised an eyebrow at him.

"When else?" He shifted slightly and her eyelids fluttered to try to shut.

"Logan." She moaned and grabbed the back of his neck tightly. Her eyes opened wide and her lips cocked a little. "Make me come and then we can have a discussion."

He lifted her from him and she made a disappointed sound as her feet hit the ground again. Pulling her with him under the shower spray, he turned her around in his arms.

"How about we discuss the points *while* I make you come?" His hands cupped her breasts and he ran his thumb over her nipples as water poured over them. He would never get enough of her.

CLAIRE KNEW Logan was just trying to torment her. But hell, they had all morning to mess around, so why not lean into it. Besides, she'd already come once and he hadn't. Two could play at his little game. She reached behind her and wrapped her hand firmly around his cock, stroking over the condom.

His breath caught and she smiled, leaning her head back against his shoulder.

"What's there to discuss?" She wanted him back inside her doing what he did best. "You don't stick your dick in anyone else and I'll gladly let you stick your dick in me."

"Naked Sports Center?" His voice was low and dark as his lips trailed over her shoulder.

"Negotiable." After all, it would happen. She wasn't stupid enough to believe it wouldn't.

His hands slid down her arms and took her hands. He held them both in front of her. "Awesome."

"I didn't say it was a given." She shook her head at his eagerness.

"But you didn't say no either," he said against her ear. Shivers raced down her. He took her hands and bent her over with his body to press her hands to the tiled wall of the shower. "Don't move your hands."

Tingles raced through her blood as his fingers trailed back up her arms and over her back down to her hips. Her core clenched in anticipation as he pulled her hips back a little. His foot nudged between hers and spread her legs wider. Fuck, she just wanted his cock in her now.

"We need to discuss time." His hands went to her hips and curved over her ass down between her thighs.

She inhaled and hung her head in her bent-over position. More fucking talking. "Time?"

"Obviously, I'm going to need full access to you at all times." His fingers teased her clit with a light touch.

Her brain short-circuited as her focus went to where his fingers continued to torment her, but not actually enough to make her come. Bastard.

"Full access?" she managed to ask.

"I'm willing to be at your beck and call." His fingers paused at her entrance, touching her lightly there. "To ease whatever aches you have."

He thrust his fingers inside of her and she groaned.

"But I don't want to just be your fuck boy." He pulled his fingers out of her and she whimpered. So not fair.

"So you want what? Boyfriend access without being an official boyfriend?" She glanced over her shoulder at him and almost fell apart. He stood behind her, stroking his cock while staring at her pussy. Water coursed over his shoulders and down those tight abs. She practically ached for him to be inside her.

His darkened eyes met hers and he grinned. "What can I say? I like fucking you, but I also like cuddling and kissing and spending time with you. I can't do labels. Maybe I'm just too fucked in the head for labels, but I know I want you and I don't want to share you with anyone else."

His hands grabbed her hips and his cock filled her with one powerful thrust of his hips. Her fingers curled into a fist at the sensation ripping through her. He stayed there, fully sheathed in her and she pulsed all around him. So close to the edge, a slight breeze could make her fall over.

"Logan, if you don't fucking make me come, I will take back everyth—"

He reached around and found her clit as his hips started

grinding into her. "Don't be like that, tiger. You know I always get you there."

He began to move in and out of her, dragging himself along every raw nerve. Rocking his fingers against her clit until she couldn't even think anymore. Her whole being focused down to where they were connected.

She cried out as she came. Her body tightened all around him. Her hands slipped slightly down the wall, but his arm came around her, holding her against his chest so that she wouldn't come apart completely. He ground into her and pushed her back up into the stratosphere.

"A little more, tiger," he whispered against her ear. His fingers stroked her clit as he thrust into her over and over.

His name passed over her lips as a scream as she finally couldn't take anymore and exploded one more time all over him. This time her orgasm drew his own out of him. He pulled them both to standing as his cock pulsed inside her.

"What the fuck was that?" Claire breathed out as she rested all her weight back against Logan. Her breathing was heavy and she was in some serious need for a nap.

Logan chuckled and an aftershock raced through her. "Just the beginning."

CHAPTER 26

Claire glared at Logan as they sat in the back of a car on the way to his mother's house. Honestly, she should be ecstatic or at least completely satiated. After fucking in the shower, they'd washed up and ended up having sex on his bed. Twice.

In between those two times, when she was blissed out of her mind on an orgasmic high, he asked if she'd come with him to his parents' house for lunch. She'd said yes, but in her defense, he had been stroking her to another orgasm at the time. That yes was more for the orgasm than a visit to his mother's.

"Stop pouting. It's not like you haven't been to my parents' house before." Logan squeezed her hand, which he hadn't let go of since they left his apartment and stopped at hers so she could change. "Besides, Kit will be there."

He also hadn't stopped smiling. Which made her insides melt and made it hard to stay mad at him for using sex against her. She did like his parents and his sister, so it wasn't a hardship to go with him.

"What are we going to say about this?" She held up their joined hands.

"Nothing." He smiled like an idiot. "If we don't bring it up, they won't."

Claire scoffed. "You don't know mothers very well then."

Logan opened his mouth to say something but the car stopped in front of his parents' house. No labels might become an issue real quick here. When they both were out of the car, he put his arm around her waist and drew her forward.

"It'll be fine," he said and the front door opened.

"Finally." His twenty-three year old sister, Kit, flicked her purple dyed hair over her shoulder. "Mom was about to start calling hospitals."

"I have a cell phone." Logan held it up.

Kit stuck out her tongue and said, "Then try using it."

"Very mature." Logan pulled Claire into the house and Kit pounced. This was the most normal thing about today.

Grabbing Claire's hand, Kit pulled her away from Logan. "At least you brought my favorite sister-in-law."

"I'm not your—" Claire started, glancing warily at Logan. He was the one with the issue involving labels. He smiled at her and his sister. Obviously not caring.

Kit tugged her into a hug and said, "Not yet, but someday."

Logan stepped forward. "Kit—"

"Don't mess this up for me, brother." Kit glared at Logan over Claire's shoulder. Kit touched strands of Claire's dark hair on either side of her face and winked at Claire. "If you don't marry her someday, I'll marry her just so she can be part of the family forever."

Logan shook his head. "I'm going to go see what Dad is doing."

"Good." Kit hugged Claire again. "I'll take care of our future wife."

Logan stopped and met Claire's eyes for a second. She rolled her eyes and shrugged. Kit was being Kit. He smiled at her before heading into the living room.

Stepping back, Kit pulled Claire into the kitchen where Logan's mom, Mary, worked on lunch. "I've got Claire."

Mary turned and smiled. "Great to see you again, Claire. Kit, add a place setting to the table please."

"Can I do anything to help?" Claire glanced around the smallish kitchen. Pots were on the burners, and Mary stood at the counter rolling out dough for biscuits. The air smelled of pot roast. That sense of coming home hit Claire in her chest.

This was the part she liked about coming to Logan's house. Claire couldn't see her own family often with work and being a flight away from them, but Logan's family had welcomed her with open arms.

Of course, if things went south between Claire and Logan over this thing, then she wouldn't just potentially lose his friendship, but she'd lose this surrogate family as well.

"You can keep me company." Mary smiled and gestured toward the kitchen table where a basket of towels sat. "And fold some towels."

Nodding, Claire sat next to the basket. Before she finished folding one towel, Kit came back in and sat next to her, grabbing a towel of her own to fold.

"How was your weekend at home?" Mary asked, cutting out her biscuits.

"It was good. We got to see a lot of my old friends and hang out." Claire didn't add that she and Logan had sex every minute they could. Or that they were still having sex and had a weird agreement to keep having sex, but not actually call it anything more than sex. But they weren't just fuck buddies.

Maybe friends with benefits? Had she made a mistake agreeing to his terms?

"Logan's always been able to fit in with a crowd." Mary moved the biscuits onto a cookie sheet. "I hope he didn't get into any trouble up there."

"None at all." Claire added a towel to the growing stack. "My mom and brothers enjoyed having him with us."

"That's good." Mary slid the biscuits into the oven and washed her hands. "You two seem to still be in a good place. Logan's never brought a girl home before you."

"I'm not really a girl in that sense. We're best friends." Claire felt almost like a fraud for saying that. But they were still best friends. Who fucked only each other. And held hands and cuddled. But they weren't boyfriend and girlfriend.

"For now." Kit snickered. "I think they are secretly madly in love, and Logan just doesn't want us to ruin it for him."

Claire tensed.

"Kit, stop teasing the poor girl." Mary shook her head and took the folded towels to put away. "A man and woman can be just friends. It is such a thing."

Kit raised her eyebrow at Claire, but Claire shook her head.

"Friends," Claire said, definitively, "that's it."

Logan came in and went to the fridge.

"So when are you going to make it official, big brother?" Kit grinned.

"Kit!" her mother and Claire said at the same time.

Logan turned with two beers in his hand. "Make what official?"

Kit jerked her head suggestively at Claire.

"Ohh," Logan said knowingly. He stepped forward and handed Claire a beer. He gave Kit a devious look. "You mean when am I going to ask Claire to be my best friend forever?"

Kit rolled her eyes. "You are the blindest man in the world. But I guess most man whores are blind."

"Kit, language." Mary flicked a towel at Kit's bottom.

"Hey." Kit scooted away in her chair with a fake pout. "He's the one running around sticking it to all the ladies."

Mary gave her the side-eye while hanging up the towel. Logan just ignored his sister.

"I'm pretty sure being best friends forever means we have to get matching tattoos." Logan leaned on the table next to Claire's chair. "We could get them right here."

His fingers brushed the collar of her black T-shirt. Right where he had left a hickey that she'd covered up as best she could. Her breath caught in her throat as tingles raced along her skin, and she tried to appear nonchalant.

"Or we could get those heart necklaces." Logan grinned, taking his hand away and drinking some beer. "What do you think, Kit?"

"I think you're ridiculous and Claire deserves better." Kit grabbed her own beer and came over to Claire again. She grabbed Claire's hand.

Claire stood and let Kit drag her into the living room where Logan's father, Joe, had the TV on.

Kit tugged Claire down onto the couch. Joe glanced at the two of them and nodded in acknowledgement at Claire. He also turned up the volume on the TV.

"Now," Kit began, "it's been what, a month since you last came to lunch?"

Claire nodded. That seemed right.

"Any hot guys in your life?" Kit settled back on the couch and took a drink of beer. "I gotta say the pickings around here have gotten a little slim. You still hanging out with that one guy? Willy or Dick or some phallic-like name?"

"You mean Peter?" Claire took a drink and looked at the pregame interviews on the TV. Peter seemed like so long ago.

Of course, she told Logan about him before her mother called about Labor Day weekend.

"Yeah, Peter." Kit snapped her fingers and looked at Claire expectantly.

"Let's just say he didn't live up to his name." Claire held up her pinkie and frowned at it.

Kit laughed. "That sucks. Come on, I have to live vicariously through you. The guys around here in the suburbs? Snoresville."

"Not much to tell. I hit a bit of a dry spell. Been too busy." Until last weekend and Logan. Claire drank her beer.

"I'm sure you went to a club last night and got all sorts of numbers. Poof. Dry spell over."

"Nope." Claire fixed her gaze on the TV. "No club last night. Too far behind with laundry."

"Laundry? That's so disappointing." Kit crossed her arms and pouted. "Honestly, I'm going to have to come spend the weekend with Logan in the city so you and I can go out and find you a new boy toy."

Claire pressed her lips together. She didn't need a new boy toy. But she couldn't even say she had a boyfriend to throw Kit off the trail. She'd want details. This was so damned hard. It would be easier if they could just tell their families her and Logan were boyfriend and girlfriend, but Logan didn't want labels.

That was the thing though. Why? Why no labels? Was this all about something that happened with that girl? As fucked up as that chick had been, Logan knew who Claire was and she wasn't like that. One, she would never cheat and two, she only wanted one guy right now, but it scared her to want him.

"Claire doesn't need a new boy toy." Logan crossed the room and sat on the other side of Claire, definitely closer than friends sat and a small zing of awareness zipped through her.

"What? I suppose you're willing to be her boy toy instead of her best friend?" Kit raised an eyebrow at him. "I know I joke around about you two loving up on each other, but honestly, I'm glad you're just friends. There needs to be some karmic balance in this world and two hot people dating each other is definitely not it. Besides, Claire's not stupid enough to be one of your girls."

Ouch.

"Dinner's ready," Mary called.

Kit got up, heading toward the dining room, before she turned back to Claire. "I saved you a seat next to me."

Joe left for the dining room and Kit grabbed his arm to go with him.

"Hey," Logan said softly. "She's just being Kit."

Claire blinked and turned toward Logan. Was she being stupid? She generally tried to avoid thinking with her lady parts. But when it came to Logan, her lady parts were pretty damn demanding.

"Claire Bear." He raised his eyebrow, knowing she hated that name.

"Wolverine." The name came out as her knee jerk reaction to him calling her that.

"Come on. Let's get lunch over with so we can go back to your place for the game."

MONDAY MORNING, Logan woke up in a tangle of sheets with naked Claire sprawled over him in her bed. They'd decided to watch the game at her place. They'd ordered in pizza—Claire got a salad, drank beer, and spent most of the commercial breaks making out. Best Sunday game day ever.

He needed to remember to bring a change of clothes to her place in the future. He stretched slightly, enjoying the feel of her warm skin against his. The sun had barely come up, giving the room a light, hazy look. His phone belted out his alarm tone.

"Turn it off," Claire muttered into his shoulder.

"I have to get up." He brushed her hair from her face and lightly traced his fingers over her eyebrows down to her cheeks. He hadn't gotten to experience waking up with her like this at the lake house. She always woke first. He could get used to it.

She sighed against him and propped her chin on his chest. Her dark eyes narrowed at him. "My alarm goes off in fifteen minutes. You suck."

"Only when you ask nicely." He tousled her hair as she groaned.

Her head went back down on his chest. She rubbed her face against his pec as her arms tightened around him. She was divine.

He traced his hand down her spine. "Wanna call in sick?"

"Pfft, that wouldn't be suspicious." She rubbed her cheek against his chest like a kitten.

He'd already been hard when he woke up, but now he definitely wanted to do something about it. He rolled her onto her back and hovered over her.

"Everyone knows we watched the game together. We could say we got food poisoning." He pressed his lips to the pulse point on her neck and scraped his scruff against her collarbone. Her fingers curled into him.

"We've got work that needs to get done," she protested, but then she parted her legs to wrap around his waist. "So if you want to do this—"

"You mean this?" He thrust his hips into hers so she could feel his hardness.

"Mmhmm." She bit her lip. She opened her eyes and the wicked glint in them made him almost groan. "You have ten minutes."

LOGAN ROLLED into work later than normal on a Monday morning, but he couldn't wipe the smile from his face. He would need to pack a few things in a bag before heading to Claire's for the game tonight.

He waved to Emily who was on the phone and strolled through the pool to get to the break room. Morning sex was a great incentive to start the day, but if he expected to keep his energy high, he needed some coffee.

Lacy stood like a zombie in front of the coffee maker waiting for it to finish brewing.

"Morning, Lace."

She grunted and held her cup to her chest.

Logan grabbed a cup from the shelf and sat at the table to wait.

Lacy didn't move much or even greet him. He tried to remember if he saw Jonah in the pool.

"Where's Jonah?"

"California." The coffee maker finished and she grabbed the pot.

Now Lacy's state made sense. Normally, Jonah made sure she had at least a cup of coffee in her before releasing her into the office. Before Jonah, this was almost a norm for Lacy. Jonah's family lived out in California.

"Everything okay?" Logan asked as he poured himself a cup.

Lacy nodded. "His father is having knee surgery. Jonah's sister will arrive later today and he'll come home."

Claire walked into the break room and paused. Her eyes

stopped on zombie Lacy. She glanced over her shoulder back into the pool and noted no Jonah. Releasing the door, she grabbed a cup and poured her coffee. She added creamer and a sugar packet to it and stirred.

"Talk like I don't exist, because right now I'm not sure that I do." Lacy waved her hand in the air generally and sipped more coffee. She sagged against the counter.

"Jonah's in California," Logan filled in.

Claire nodded and lifted an eyebrow at him. "Good thing we didn't get food poisoning then."

Logan smirked and shrugged his shoulders. The office would have been fine without them and he would have had Claire all to himself for a day. Suddenly, the weekend couldn't come fast enough. Two whole days of nothing to do but Claire and watch football.

Claire shook her head, but her lips tugged into a small smile. He couldn't get enough of her. Maybe he could convince her to spend the whole weekend naked in one of their apartments and fuck until it didn't feel like a raging need anymore.

"I'm going to go sit out there." Lacy pointed at the door as she walked toward it.

Claire grabbed the door's handle and held the door open for Lacy to walk through.

When the door shut, Logan closed the distance between them. "At least promise me this weekend will be a naked weekend."

Claire almost sputtered on her coffee. "Dude, uncool."

"What?" He grabbed a napkin and pressed it on the small drop of coffee on her chin. "We get to have sex now and I'm thinking the more we have it, maybe I'll get a little focus back."

"You are ridiculous."

He trailed his fingers over the love bite and mark he'd left on her shoulder with his scruff this morning. At her sharp inhale, he lifted his gaze from her skin to her lips.

"Can we kiss at work?" He started to dip his head.

She put her hand on his chest and pressed her lips together. "Behave. This is still a workplace."

"Lunch?" He raised an eyebrow.

Aiden walked into the break room. Neither Claire nor Logan stepped back from each other. His eyes trailed over them, taking in everything and then he nodded.

"Pardon me. I need coffee for when Phoebe comes flouncing in."

Claire dropped her hand and stepped away from Logan, taking a drink of her coffee before winking at him and heading out the door.

Logan cleared his throat and tried to think of something to get himself back under control. Even belching Game Day Claire would no longer do that particular trick.

Aiden jerked his head toward the door. "So that's happening?"

Logan smiled. "Something like that."

"Phoebe will be stoked," Aiden grumbled.

Logan's eyebrows drew together. "Why?"

"She bet me a hundred dollars that you two would start banging on the regular. Her words, not mine." Aiden took a small sip of his coffee and straightened his French cuffs.

Logan chuckled. "Phoebe's awesome."

"Yes, she is." Aiden's eyes grew a little glazed before he shook it off. "Shall we join the others?"

Claire and Lacy were seated at the conference table. Drew and Morgan came out of their office as Logan and Aiden made their way to the table. Once everyone was settled, Logan took Claire's hand under the table and linked their fingers together.

She didn't make any outward expression that anything had happened, but her fingers tightened on his.

Phoebe strolled in with her sunglasses still on and her Starbucks coffee in her hand. "Can't we have Monday *afternoon* meetings? This is practically barbaric."

Morgan rolled her eyes and everyone waited for Phoebe to join them at the conference table.

"Wait." Phoebe stopped before sitting. Her gaze scanned the table. Her eyes stopped on him and Claire for a moment and he swore she could see their connected hands. But without X-ray vision that was impossible. "Where's Jonah?"

Lacy put her coffee cup down. "He'll be back tomorrow. Family emergency."

"Everyone okay?" Phoebe took her sunglasses off as she took her seat.

Lacy nodded. "Just knee surgery."

"Good." Phoebe propped her elbows on the table and rested her head on her hands. A wicked grin on her lips as she looked at Logan and Claire. Her finger lifted to point at them. "Now, let's talk about this development."

Lacy looked at Claire confused. Claire just shrugged nonchalantly. However, Logan startled. So much for playing it cool. He practically gave it away. How the hell did Phoebe do that?

"Phoebe, can we keep focused on the Monday meeting?" Morgan put her hand on Drew's knee when he started chuckling. She gently shook her head at him. He just gave her a smile.

Phoebe pointed her finger again at Logan and Claire without lifting her head. "I knew you guys had sex over the holiday weekend."

"Fuck." Morgan threw her hands up and leaned back in her chair. "This isn't anyone's business but their own."

Phoebe grinned at Morgan. "Come on. This office is like

hookup central. Those two haven't so much as made a pass at each other in almost a year and suddenly they smashed. But then all week nothing, and today, hello!"

"Maybe your sex radar is off," Drew said and shrugged. "Can we get back to the meeting?"

Aiden took a hundred dollar bill out of his wallet and handed it to Phoebe. "Now can we get on with the meeting?"

Phoebe smirked, folded the hundred dollar bill and stuck it in her bra. "Please proceed."

Claire gave Logan a look that said they'd talk about this later. He shrugged and squeezed her hand. Most likely she'd yell at him later, but whatever, this thing between them would be common knowledge at some point. He wouldn't have minded if Aiden spilled the beans.

Of course, Aiden kind of did if the gloating look on Phoebe's face was any indication.

EXCEPT FOR THAT one hiccup at the Monday meeting, the week went by without a glitch. Claire had to explain to Phoebe what was happening between her and Logan, but besides that, everything had been quite normal to almost boring at work.

Of course, the evenings were very different. Logan had always been fun to hang out with, but adding sex to the mix seemed to make things even crazier. Some evenings they sometimes just snuggled in a chair while watching TV.

They did make a pact to not have sex at work. Figuring, they could control themselves for the day. Though they did have a few lunches in bed.

Happy Hour was cancelled this week. Too many people couldn't make it. So everyone decided to meet at a club on Saturday night instead to unwind after a busy week.

Claire made Logan get ready at his own apartment so they wouldn't be late. Any time they undressed or dressed near each other, sex happened. Instead, Phoebe and Emily had come over to dress and gossip before the club.

Claire smoothed her hand over her red A-line cocktail dress. The almost tame neckline contrasted nicely with the barely there back. The straps tied behind her neck in a halter style, but the beads on the ends of the straps trailed down her bare back to dangle almost at the top of her butt. Her red Jimmy Choos gave her the height where Logan could rest his chin on her shoulder.

Phoebe gave a wolf whistle as she came out of the bedroom wearing a black wrap dress. "If I didn't have a man. . . ."

Claire shook her head. "You'd find another one. We both know you like dick."

"True." Phoebe came up beside Claire in the mirror and fluffed her red hair. "But if I ever did decide to go the other way, you'd be on my list."

Claire laughed. "You'd have to get in line. Kit has claimed dibs."

Emily stepped out of the bathroom. Her blond hair was half pulled up into a messy bun. The rest fell over her shoulders. Her makeup was light, almost natural, but still highlighted her blue eyes. Claire needed to ask who made that wine-colored lipstick though. It was fantastic.

Emily's dark red Boho style lace dress had wispy sleeves and a plunging neckline down to the top of Emily's navel. The lace skirt was long with a high slit showing off her legs, but the underlayer was almost a mini skirt. Showing a lot more skin than Emily's typical long skirts and peasant blouses she wore to work. She had on gladiator sandals that stopped just below her knee.

"Sorry, Claire, I think Emily just blew my mind." Phoebe slow clapped. "Girl, you've been holding out on us."

"Was I supposed to wear something else?" Emily glanced down at her outfit like it wasn't a big thing. Maybe for her it wasn't. She looked comfortable in her own skin.

"You look wonderful, Emily," Claire reassured her as they walked over to Claire's living room.

Emily sat on the couch as Phoebe started pouring a few preparty drinks.

"Oh, did you still need that lawyer's name?" Claire took the seat next to Emily. Phoebe handed them both a Sex on the Beach.

"No. Not right now. I think." Emily pushed her hair over her shoulder and shrugged. She took a drink and sighed. "My grandma isn't doing well. And it may be time to look into a power of attorney and medical directive."

"I'm sorry about your grandma," Claire said. "If you need any help, let me know."

"Thanks." Emily took a drink. "Okay, enough sadness. You and Logan? It's official?"

It was Claire's turn to sigh. "I don't know."

"What?" Phoebe asked and sat forward. "You guys have been boning all week and you don't know if it's official?"

"It's complicated." Claire took a drink. "We're exclusive, but with no labels. Labels freak Logan out apparently."

"Huh." Phoebe sank into the chair and took a healthy drink. "He's never been in a relationship before?"

"Nope." Claire shook her head. "Honestly, it doesn't bother me. He's open to it becoming more and that's enough for me."

But is it? That stupid little voice in her head kept nagging her. All week it had been persistent. The only time it shut up was when Logan touched her, which happened often.

She still wanted forever, but she had what she wanted. Well, most of what she wanted. She had a guy who she liked, who knew everything about her, and the sex, the sex was to die for. She even had the cuddling.

Just not a promise of something more. But relationships were about compromise.

"That labels thing can get pretty sticky." Emily held out her cup to Phoebe for a refill. Her smile was a little crooked. "My friend had a guy who wouldn't label them and they went out for seven years before she finally asked if he was ever going to marry her. They broke up."

"Labels can be terrifying to someone who is used to no attachments, but Logan seems like the kind who will get over it." Phoebe took Emily's cup and set it aside. "Eventually."

And that was why that voice wouldn't shut the fuck up. How long would she have to wait for Logan to feel comfortable moving to the next level? A few months? A year? Five? If he even decided he wanted to. She had time, but how much of that time would she be willing to give to him?

Her chest ached. How much would he break her if he never wanted to go further in their relationship? Would time start to make her resent him for something he'd been upfront about from the beginning? Would she lose her best friend?

"Ugh, okay, I've got a car coming. Everyone out of your heads." Phoebe stood, filled Emily's cup and handed it to her. "Tonight we've got some pretty hot guys waiting for us at the club, so let's not overthink this. Forget about tomorrow and just have fun tonight."

Emily smiled and let out a *woohoo* as she stood.

Claire stood and took in a breath. Fuck it. It had only been a week, two if she counted the lake house. This didn't need to get solved now or even in the coming weeks. Tonight she'd just have fun and enjoy having Logan all to herself.

It would sort itself out. Unless it didn't.

This would be the first time they would go to the club with the intention of going home together. This could make or break them. It would be fine. He wanted her.

Smiling, she raised her cup and they all clinked them together.

∾

WHEN PHOEBE, Claire, and Emily entered the club, heads turned their way. Logan couldn't blame a single guy. Claire was gorgeous in red. From her heels to her dark hair pulled to one side, everything about her turned him on. Every guy in this club would wish they were with her. They'd fantasize about the body beneath that dress.

They could fantasize all they liked. Tonight the only one going home with Claire would be him.

Ben stood from the booth. He was a little older than most of them. Maybe even already thirty. He wore a black shirt and jeans with a pair of sweet looking dark brown leather cap toe dress shoes. His dark hair was cut with almost military precision on the sides with a little length on top. His close-trimmed beard never had a hair out of place.

The guy always dressed impressively at work, but Logan had never been out to the clubs with him. Ben could score big if he wanted to here.

"Hey." Claire stopped in front of Logan.

"You look stunning." He took her hands and held them out to the side to take in her red dress. He turned her around to see her entire back revealed.

Fuck. He couldn't resist sliding his fingers down the cord and beads hanging down her back, lightly brushing the skin of her spine with his knuckles. She shivered beneath his touch.

He wanted to cover every inch of exposed skin with his lips. Later couldn't come soon enough. He might be tempted to use a chit.

Sliding his hands around her waist, he closed the distance between his front and her back and whispered in her ear, "It's a good thing we didn't get ready together. We would have never made it out of the bedroom."

She smiled and tucked her chin before looking over her shoulder at him. "You don't think it's too showy? That I'm looking for attention?"

Logan spun her around in his arms. Pressing his hand against her bare back, he held her close against his chest. His gaze rested on her red lips. He didn't want to fuck up her makeup, but he really wanted to fuck up her makeup.

"Every guy in here wishes he was me right now. But I'm the only one who will fuck you tonight. I don't see a problem with that."

Her dark eyes looked at him through her lashes with a sexy smile.

"All right, you two. We aren't filming a porno." Phoebe smirked at Aiden while tracing his tie with her fingers. "Yet."

"Never." Morgan shook her head. "You mean never. I'm going to need a lot to drink to put up with my best friend's innuendos all night."

Phoebe laughed. "You miss my innuendos."

"Probably." Morgan tilted her head to the side.

Drew stepped forward and pressed a kiss to Morgan's shoulder. "I'll get us some drinks."

Jonah volunteered to help and the rest found seats around the table. Claire and Logan sat at the end near Emily and Ben.

"This place is so crazy," Emily spoke loudly to be heard over the music. "A lot different from the bar."

"Yeah, not so great for conversation, but awesome for dancing." Claire slipped her hand into Logan's under the table. Their thighs pressed together.

His heart warmed and settled. This amazing woman was all his. That thought should terrify him. He'd spent years avoiding being exactly where he was today. In a relationship. Of sorts. Yes, they didn't have the conventional labels, but he wasn't looking for anyone else.

Ben sat stiffly next to Emily with his hands clasped on the table and at least six inches between the two of them.

"A lot of singles come here to unwind on the weekend." Logan figured it couldn't hurt to put that out there for the last single people in the office.

Emily's eyes widened and a muscle ticked in Ben's jaw.

Drew brought over some drinks and set them down on the table before heading back to the other booth. Well, fuck if Logan knew what to talk about. He didn't know Emily or Ben really, and they wouldn't probably want to talk about the latest campaigns.

"How's school going?" Claire asked Emily with a smile.

"Oh." Emily's cheeks flushed with color as she tucked a strand of hair behind her ear. "It's different. I mean, it's just one class so far. It's been a while since I've been in school, but I'm excited about it."

"What are you going to school for?" Logan asked. He hadn't even known Emily had aspirations beyond receptionist.

"Marketing." Emily's cheeks flushed again. "Just trying to learn more about advertising. I've already talked with Drew and Morgan about getting some hands-on experience."

Ben took a drink of his beer. "Education is important."

Logan nodded his head as he took a drink. He studied Ben once more because that was odd. Ben didn't even glance at Emily, but she glanced at him every few seconds. Almost the same way Lacy used to look at Logan.

A familiar song came on and Logan turned to Claire. "Isn't this your favorite song?"

"It is." She gave him an impressed look.

"My duties as best friend as stated by yourself means we have to dance." Standing, Logan held his hand out to Claire. She took his hand. He pulled her into him and looked at Ben and Emily.

"You two coming?"

"I don't dance," Ben said, but he glanced over at Emily.

"I'm good." She held up her glass to her lips. Lacy leaned in to say something to Emily.

Logan shrugged and led Claire out onto the dance floor. Logan forgot about their coworkers.

Envious looks from both men and women surrounded them as he pulled Claire into his arms. Soon those people faded too as Claire and Logan moved together to the beat of the music.

Hips swaying as their eyes met and held, they danced close. Logan couldn't keep his hands from touching her every chance he got. Their bodies brushed together, making him wish they were alone.

Her eyes darkened to the color of the midnight sky as she looked up at him. Her lips slightly parted and her cheeks flushed with heat. Bolts of desire rocked through him.

She winked at him before she spun away to dance with Phoebe and Morgan.

Logan slipped his arm around Claire's waist to tug her back against his front. Her heels brought her to the perfect height. He brushed his lips against her ear.

"You're the sexiest thing on this dance floor." His other hand dropped to play with the hem of her skirt. "When we get back to your place, don't take this off. I want to fuck you with this stunning dress wrapped around your waist."

Claire tipped her head to the side so he could see her dark eyes. "Why wait?"

"You kill me, tiger." Logan groaned and pressed a kiss to her shoulder.

She turned in his arms. His hand rested against the center of her bare back as they continued to sway to the music. She lifted an eyebrow at him and gave him a sly smile. "I want to use my any time, any place. Here and now."

Those words went directly to his cock, which had already hardened with her grinding against him. At those words he was ready and able to attend to her darkest desires.

She touched his jaw and he dipped his head to hers. Before his lips found hers, she chuckled as she dodged his kiss. "Not literally here on the dance floor."

He lifted his head and saw Phoebe and Morgan over Claire's shoulder. He wasn't sure what kind of smile he gave them. It was probably quite feral, but he tried. Right now, he wanted to figure out a good place to fuck Claire. Fortunately, he was familiar with the nooks and crannies of this club.

Claire pressed her hand to his chest and then slid it down to take his hand.She looked up at him through her eye lashes. "Come on."

THIS WAS CRAZY. Claire knew it, but Logan had her so keyed up, she really didn't give a fuck. Finding a dark corner in this club that wasn't already taken would take a miracle, but she needed his hands on her and his cock inside her. Now.

Not tonight when they got to her place. Though it was inevitable that later they'd still fall on each other. Yesterday at work she almost broke their no work rule. They'd been in the copy room together. He kept his eyes on her ass and hadn't bothered to hide how hard she made him. She'd wanted to lock the door and have him take her. But she'd managed to hold off.

Tonight, a hundred greedy eyes watched Logan with lust and hunger, but they'd have to find some other guy to hit on. He wouldn't be going off with any of them. He was hers.

His fingers slid along the strings hanging down her back again, sending shivers racing through her. Heat pooled in the center of her, as he closed in on her from behind.

"Claire Bear, do you know where we're going?" His smooth tone should make her angry, but instead it poured over her like warm honey. She wanted to sink into him and let it cover her.

She shook her head.

With his hand in hers, Logan tugged her to a stop. His warmth engulfed her back as he closed the distance between them. He leaned close to her ear. "I know a place."

She glanced at him over her shoulder. How many women had he fucked already in this "place?" Technically, she'd made out with guys in the darkened corners of this and other clubs, but nothing full on. Not like what she planned to do with Logan as soon as they found somewhere isolated.

"The same place you fuck all your eager women?" She turned to face him.

He grinned and tipped her chin up with his finger. His thumb traced over her lower lip. He leaned in close to her ear. "The only woman I've ever wanted to fuck in this club is you."

Fuck, he was smooth and her body liked it.

He kissed her ear before moving away. She followed as he pulled her along by her hand. The club was a mix of light and shadows. Darkened corners and bright spotlights.

She glanced behind them to see if anyone had followed, but the majority of people were crowded on or around the dance floor. She noticed a few couples in tucked away booths as they passed.

Logan paused at a door and then opened it. After a second he pulled her inside and shut the door behind her. Darkness engulfed her. Only the muffled sound of bass penetrated the space.

"Where—"

Logan's lips took hers as he pressed her back up against the door. His lips were soft and firm against hers. She couldn't make out anything in the inky darkness. His hand slipped up the outside of her thigh under her skirt and her thoughts shattered as heat coursed through her from his touch.

She tugged at his dress shirt to untuck it from his jeans until she could put her hands under it and splayed her fingers over his bare abs. His warm skin tightened beneath her touch.

This was what she wanted. What she needed. Logan all to herself. Away from the prying eyes. Away from the other women who wanted him. Who thought they could own him.

His hand slid between her legs and he groaned against her mouth.

"Fuck, Claire."

She grinned and tipped her head back against the door. His fingers caressed her warm bare flesh. No barrier in the way.

His breath was warm against her earlobe as he whispered, "If you'd told me you weren't wearing any panties, we wouldn't have lasted five seconds out there. I would have found a dark corner and fucked you where anyone could see."

Even though they weren't the most romantic words, she melted. His fingers slid inside her and her knees went weak.

"You make me lose all control. You know that, right?" He pressed his forehead against hers.

"I like making you lose control." Her voice was almost breathless when she spoke.

His fingers went deep within her as his thumb circled her clit. The door against her back and his body pressed against hers were the only things holding her up. She bit her lip to stop herself from crying out as he stroked the fire within her higher and higher.

"Good." He captured her mouth. He groaned against her

lips as his fingers kept moving in her. "I can't guarantee this will last long. Definitely don't time me. But I'm going to make you come at least once first."

Her insides turned to liquid. His tongue slid into her mouth to tease her own. While he continued to thrust his fingers, his other hand cupped her breast, dragging his thumb across her already hard nipple, sending pulses of desire through her.

The bass of the music filtered through the door, but absolutely no light penetrated. Logan's lips left hers to trail down her neck. The scruff of his five o'clock shadow dragged across her skin. Her body clenched in anticipation and she felt him smile against her neck.

Her hips rode his hand, striving for the peak just out of reach. When he finally bit down and sucked on her neck, her whole being tensed at the precipice.

"That's it, tiger. Give me a little more," he whispered against her skin and drove her higher still. His mouth returned to hers and she exploded. His lips caught her cries of surrender as his fingers held still inside of her while she came down.

His hands moved away from her and she heard his zipper and the crinkling of a condom wrapper. His forehead pressed against hers.

"You okay?" he asked. His hand came up to cradle her cheek.

She leaned into his hand and turned and kissed his palm. "I'm good."

He captured her lips, and his hand dropped to lift her knee. Her core pulsed in need. His cock nudged at her entrance and she gasped against his mouth as he slid all the way in her.

"We'll go slow and easy when we get home," he promised against her lips.

Home made her heart race. Being with him felt like home.

Her arms wrapped around his neck as she nodded. He slid out and back in a few times slowly before he picked up the pace. Her legs were like liquid or she would have wrapped them around him too. His arm hooked one of her legs high, but all she could do was hold on to him with her arms as he strove for his own release.

Each stroke sent her higher and higher.

"If you want me, you can have me any time, any place. You don't need to win a bet to have me fuck you, tiger." He kissed her hard before leaning his forehead against hers. His cock slammed into her over and over again.

She leaned her head against the door as the tension wound tighter within her again. It was useless to hold back. Her body was addicted to his at this point. His free hand went to her hip to help hold her in place as he continued to thrust.

"Logan," she let out as she fell over the edge again.

He slammed into her one more time and captured her lips. He shook against her as he came. She didn't think she'd ever be able to let him go. Her heart hammered inside her chest as she tried to slow her breathing.

He withdrew from her. After a few seconds she heard his zipper and then his arms pulled her into him, hugging her. Warmth flooded her that had nothing to do with their slackened lust. Suddenly she realized how much of herself she'd already given Logan.

It was too late. He'd crawled inside her heart and he could destroy her now. Whether intentionally or not.

She couldn't exactly tell the guy afraid to commit that she was head over heels in love with him. That she couldn't imagine spending a minute of her life without him in it. He was her best friend and she loved him.

"You are perfect, Claire." Logan kissed her, but she pulled

away at least as much as she could against the door. Yeah, not so much.

"No, I'm not. I'm not perfect. I'm a fucking mess." She couldn't let him think she was this perfect thing. Even if he knew the parts of her that were imperfect, she knew how easy it was for guys to convince themselves that she had no flaws. And when those flaws came out, they ran.

"Trust me, I know you aren't this ideal woman, but for me. . . ." He paused and his fingers trailed over her lower lip slowly. He cleared his throat.

She wished she could see him. See his eyes to tell what was going through his head. Instead, she could only feel his warm body against hers.

"For me, every aspect of you is perfect. Even Game Day Claire, because she's fun and doesn't give a shit who's watching her or what they think of her. Work Claire gets the job done but she also has fun doing it. I've never wanted to go to work more until I met Work Claire."

Her heart skipped a beat as his words flooded over her.

"I thought Pajama Claire was going to be the death of me. Until I met Naked Claire. I would give my left nut to be with Naked Claire all the time. So sex confident, and I love waking up with her on me. All soft skin and tangled limbs."

Her breath caught in her throat. Her insides went soft again. She never wanted to leave this place. This time with Logan. She wanted to ask him to say it again and again.

"You're so fucking confident and so insecure at the same time." Logan's forehead rested against hers and he blew out a breath against her lips. "You have this huge heart and I can't help wanting to be part of it. You're my best friend in all ways. So yes, to me, you, Claire Lake, are perfectly imperfect."

CHAPTER 28

CLAIRE REAPPLIED her lipstick in the mirror of the ladies' bathroom. When Logan spilled all that on her, she'd been speechless. He saw her. Not as some prize to be won. Not as some fine piece of ass to make everyone else jealous. But her.

Maybe she'd been overthinking the labels too much. Maybe what they had right now was enough for both of them. Maybe it would grow and they would become more. Maybe they would have a future together.

She put her lipstick back in her clutch and fluffed her hair a little. This was the woman Logan O'Connell wanted to take home tonight.

And she couldn't wait to get him home to show him how much she appreciated his speech. She grinned at her reflection and headed out into the club.

The music still pounded out on the dance floor, but here it wasn't so bad. She could see their group at the table and she took a deep breath. Everyone knew that Claire and Logan were an item even if they hadn't said they were boyfriend and girlfriend.

Maybe the labels didn't matter as long as they had each other and everyone else knew it.

"Claire?" Alan's voice made her stop mid-step and turn. He walked toward her with a drink in his hand.

"Hey, Alan." She gave him a tight smile and looked to see if Logan was around. "What are you doing here? I thought clubs weren't your scene."

"Kelly convinced me to come out since I had the night off." Alan shrugged and glanced over his shoulder.

Claire almost bristled as Kelly came bouncing over. When Kelly saw who Alan was talking to, she slowed her step and glanced at her brother.

"Hi, Claire." Kelly stopped beside her brother and crossed her arms. "Where's your boy toy?"

Claire forced a smile. "Around here somewhere."

Kelly grinned. "You and him still hot and heavy?"

"Something like that." Claire glanced at Alan as he winced. Better he find out now than pin his hopes on Claire being single forever. He hadn't even called to schedule that follow-up date anyway.

"Really?" Alan asked a little tersely. "You and Logan? Because that guy has snake written all over him. Look what he did with Kelly and how did he handle it? Not like a mature adult, but using you to bail him out."

She'd used Logan for the same thing, so she just lifted her eyebrow at him as if to say, so what?

"Logan's not a one-woman type of guy." Kelly turned and looked out at the dance floor. "He told me that so many times. Just a few weeks ago he needed his freedom and the ability to chase whatever skirt he fancied. So are you putting up with that shit?"

Rage bubbled hot inside Claire and also a little wave of doubt. He really hadn't had time this week to see anyone but her, but what happened when they weren't able to see each other? She shook that thought out of her head.

"What Logan and I have isn't like what you and he had."

Kelly just smiled snarkily. "How do you know? Did you look at our texts? Did you hear him talk about how perfect I was?"

Fuck, that was a dagger directly in Claire's heart, but Kelly didn't need to know that.

"If you'll excuse me." Claire started to walk around them, but Alan grabbed her arm. She stared at it like he had scabies. He took his hand away and held it up.

"Look, Claire." Alan nodded a little toward Kelly in a gesture to ask her to leave.

Kelly rolled her eyes and walked back to the dance floor.

Claire crossed her arms. "We've known each other for about a week, Alan. What makes you think you know me or Logan?"

"You're right." Alan stepped back slightly. "But from what I saw he was really good at pretending to be your boyfriend. How do you know he isn't still pretending?"

"I—" Claire cut herself off and pressed her lips together. "At least he doesn't lie about who he is or what he likes. You came to that bar not because you wanted to watch the game, but because you thought that would be your in to get me."

Alan swallowed and looked away.

"I get that things are rough being single. I do. But I also know you and I would have never meshed well." Claire straightened and dropped her arms. "I need someone who wants to be my best friend, too."

"So someone like Logan?" Alan scoffed.

"Maybe." Everything in Claire wanted to say yes, but she didn't want to tell Alan fucking Thomson that. The only person she wanted to tell was Logan. "Now, if you'll excuse me."

LOGAN DECIDED to stop at the bar after escorting Claire to the bathroom to freshen up. If he waited for her, he'd end up finding another place to fuck her. They were here with their coworkers. Yes, the hookup was her idea, but still he needed to behave himself. They had all night after they got to her place. So he needed to chill.

Arms wrapped around his waist from behind and an unfamiliar feminine voice said, "Hey, you. I've been looking all over for you."

Tensing, he pulled the arms from around his waist and turned. "I think you've got the wrong guy."

The short blond-haired, blue-eyed woman looked up at him and gave him a cheesy grin. She stuck her barely-covered breasts out and trailed a hand over her exposed stomach. Her mini skirt barely covered her ass. Her pupils were dilated and her too tight clothes were a little rumpled.

She reeked of alcohol.

Her eyebrows came together. "You're Logan O'Connell, right?"

He tipped his head to the side and really looked at the woman in front of him. Nope. No clue who this woman was and he didn't forget women he slept with.

"I am. Who's asking?"

"Me. I'm Chloe. My friends have been telling me all about you." Her eyes raked over him, pausing on the front of his jeans.

"Not interested." He started to turn away but she threw her arms around him.

"But I'm your type." She hiccupped and grinned up at him like that would make it all better. "My friends say you always go home with someone like me, so here I am."

"I'm with someone." He started to back away from her, but she clung to his arm.

"Who?" She looked around, swaying as she did. "I don't see anyone."

Logan sighed and looked toward the table of his coworkers to see if anyone could help him. They were still far away. They probably didn't even see him.

"My boyfriend just dumped me, and my friend, Kelly—you know Kelly—said you would be able to help me get over him by getting under me." She paused and looked confused. "Get you over me? Get under you?"

Fuck. Logan blinked at the drunk girl now clinging to his waist. He leaned down to yell near her ear. "I'm sorry about your boyfriend, but I'm not interested. Maybe go find someone on the dance floor or, you know, go home so you don't do something you'll regret."

She pouted up at him and grabbed his face. Before she could plant her lips on his, Phoebe showed up and pulled the woman off him.

"Hey, that's my man candy," Chloe yelled.

Logan ran a hand over his hair and met Phoebe's eyes. "Thank you. Some women just won't take no for an answer."

"Claire saw you." Phoebe's words shot ice into his heart.

His heart sank into his stomach. Ice flooded all his limbs. Urgency trembled through him.

"Fuck. Which way did she go?" She had to know he wasn't doing anything wrong. The only woman he wanted was Claire. Even when they were just friends. How could she not know?

Phoebe pointed toward the exit, still wrangling the grabby woman.

Logan took off after Claire. He'd wanted to tell her he loved her in the closet, but it didn't seem like the right time. He didn't want to come off as needy. But fuck that, he needed

Claire. He couldn't lose her over a drunk girl he didn't want anything to do with.

As he burst through the doors, he saw Claire vanish into the back of a car. Before he could get to her, the car took off. He put both his hands on his head and blew air out into the night.

"Fuck!" he yelled as he doubled over.

Some women shrieked in the line to get into the club.

Ignoring them, Logan pulled out his phone. He tried calling Claire but it went straight to her voicemail. He opened up their text conversation.

That wasn't what you thought it was.

He looked around and didn't see any cabs. His heart pounded in his chest as the three little dots came onto his screen and then vanished.

Staring at the screen, he held his breath for her response.

No. This wasn't happening. He opened the Lyft app and put in for a ride to Claire's.

Claire still hadn't texted him. Fuck, that looked bad. That looked real bad when he thought about it. But he didn't do anything. He didn't want that woman on him at all.

She was drunk and Kelly told her to hit on me. I told her I was with someone. I don't want her. I only want you. I've only ever wanted you.

He sent the text and cussed again. A little quieter this time.

He fought against texting her that he loved her. He didn't want to tell her over text. He wasn't even sure he could tell her. The thought of it made his heart beat in triple time and his stomach clench like he ate week-old pizza.

Glancing over his shoulder, he remembered Phoebe and the others. Shit. He opened the car share app. The car was a minute away. He pulled up Phoebe's number.

Going after Claire. Sorry.

Good luck.

~

CLAIRE CLOSED her apartment door behind her and leaned back on it, as if the hounds of Hell had chased her down the hall. She drew in a deep breath and held her hand over her aching chest. Her phone buzzed again, but she didn't want to read anymore texts from Logan. Or even Phoebe.

She kicked off her shoes and put her phone and clutch on the table in the entryway.

She'd managed to hold off the tears that threatened. But she still felt like someone ripped her guts out in front of her and dragged them all over the club floor. Her heart stuttered in her chest and the weight of it crashed into her stomach.

All those other times she'd watched Logan hit on some girl played through her mind like a demented warning system. All of them stuck on repeat. No matter what she tried, she couldn't seem to shut it off.

Always the same. She and Logan would be dancing and someone else would catch his eye. He'd make his way over to usually a petite blonde with blue eyes. He'd lean in and whisper something in the woman's ear. Just like that woman tonight.

His chosen woman would giggle and put her hand on his chest. And then he'd leave Claire behind while he made his way to one of their apartments or maybe even that closet he'd pulled Claire into tonight.

Shaking the images out of her head, she went into the kitchen and pulled down a bottle of scotch to chase them away. Logan had followed her out of the club and was probably on his way here. She'd seen his early texts, but it didn't fill that gaping hole inside her.

She'd known this would happen. How could it not?

The alcohol should numb her insides enough that she didn't feel like crawling into bed and just laying there. If she did that, Logan would slide in next to her and she wouldn't find the strength to push him away.

She had to, though, for her own sanity. She grabbed a glass and put some ice in it before pouring a generous amount.

Not knowing how much time she had before he showed up, she drank the entire amount and refilled it. Bringing the bottle and glass with her, she went into her living room and sat in the armchair that faced the door. Her feet rested on the coffee table. Her ankles crossed. She needed all the liquid courage scotch could give her to say the things she needed to say to Logan O'Connell.

What was she thinking being with him? They'd stayed just friends for a reason. Did she honestly believe that he would miraculously change? For her? That she was the one? How stupid was she?

This was her own fault. She should have never let it get this far.

Keys rattled in the door and the door burst open. She drew in a breath and let it out slowly. Show time.

"Claire?" Logan's voice preceded him in the room. He gulped in air like he'd run up the stairs or something.

Watching him, she drank more scotch and wiggled the glass out in front of her. "Want some?"

His eyes narrowed on the glass and he shook his head.

She shrugged and filled her glass again. Her head and fingers had started to buzz slightly, so she let the scotch settle in the glass instead of downing it again.

"You didn't respond to my texts." He finally caught his breath and walked toward her. He sat on the edge of the couch, right next to her, but he hadn't touched her. Yet.

She didn't think she could handle him touching her right now. Not with what she needed to get off her chest.

"My phone's over there." She gestured with her glass.

"Did you at least read my texts?" Logan drew in a breath and rubbed his hand over his hair.

Claire shrugged like none of this mattered while her heart crumbled slowly to bits in her chest. She should have guarded her heart better. She knew better. Not let it get so vulnerable.

"She was this drunk woman," Logan said, "who just got dumped, and Kelly told her to hit on me as a sure thing."

Claire nodded. "She wasn't wrong."

"Fuck, Claire. Stop this. She was wrong. I don't want anyone but you."

"Okay, let's say I believe you." She leaned back in her chair, careful to keep her skirt from creeping up too high, and took a sip of scotch. She crossed her legs at her ankles on the coffee table. "You don't want a girlfriend."

He pressed his lips together. "I said I don't want to label us."

"Mmm, sure." Waving off his explanation, she set her glass down on the table. "You don't want a girlfriend because then you'd have to tell those women who think you're fair game that you have a girlfriend. By not labeling it, you're open to fuck whoever you want."

"I wouldn't do that to you." He shook his head. "Yes, I have issues with having a girlfriend, but that doesn't mean I want to be able to fuck anyone else. I can give you that. I can give you exclusivity. Why would I need anyone else when I have you?"

Claire took a deep breath and let it sit in the air between them. "Okay, fine. You only want to fuck me, because why? I'm convenient? After all, we work together and spend a hell of a lot of time together. We get along great and I'm really good at sex. So it would make sense. Definitely makes game day a lot more interesting."

She gave him a fake smile and a wink.

Hanging his head down, he ran his hand over his head a few times. When he looked up, he had determination glinting in his eyes. "What do you want me to say, Claire? I want to be with you. Only you. I know I have issues with commitment, but none of those other women matter to me. I want you."

Dropping her feet to the floor, Claire leaned forward and set her elbows on her knees, her hands clasped between her legs. She turned her head to face him. She had him on the rails. It was time to bring out the big guns.

"How about the future? Do you ever want to get married?"

"Whoa, where is that coming from?" He recoiled into the couch. "We've only been together for a week. Two if you count Labor Day."

"That doesn't answer my question. I'm not asking you for a proposal. I'm asking a basic question. Do you *ever* want to get married?"

"Why does it matter right now?" Logan's eyes met hers. She kept her expression blank. Logan breathed out. "Fine. Someday. Maybe. I don't think I'm opposed to marriage. In the future."

Claire sighed and reclined in her chair. She picked up her scotch and drank the rest of the pour to give herself a moment. It really didn't matter what his answers or excuses were. What happened tonight had been inevitable and she wouldn't survive when it happened again.

He could destroy her.

"Claire, talk to me."

"Our friendship isn't going to survive this." She set the glass down with a hard thump.

"What?" Logan grabbed her hand. "What are you saying?"

She cupped his cheek, feeling the roughness of his stubble against her palm. God, she loved that stubble. She smiled softly as she rubbed his jaw with her thumb. This man. If he were someone else, she'd risk it.

She'd let him peel pieces off her heart until there wasn't anything left. She'd just be with him with no hope for anything more than the present.

But he was her best friend. She couldn't have it both ways.

As his best friend, she needed to put her cards on the table.

"I love you, but I can't be this girl. The one who has to stand up to every girl out there who thinks my man can be had. All because some other girl told her he was a good time. Or he looked at her and she thought she could have him. Whatever the reason, I don't want to be that bitch."

She tracked her thumb over the edge of his lip and pressed against them when he started to part them to speak. She shook her head sadly. "Eventually, it would get old and you'd get tired of me, so let's just end this while things are on a good note. We remain friends and you don't have to worry about labels anymore. We're just friends."

He captured her lips with his. She didn't pull away. She couldn't resist one last kiss. The taste of his mint mixed with her scotch. Her heart thrashed wildly like a caged animal that only wanted to get out. But she couldn't let it.

Pulling away from him, she shook her head. She pressed her fingers against her lips to hold the feel of him against them one last time.

"We're good together." Logan clasped the back of her neck to keep her there. He pressed his forehead against hers and closed his eyes. "Damn good together."

She allowed him to hold her there because it wouldn't change her mind. Her heart jerked and tears pressed on the back of her throat. "I don't see how this is going to work. What I want, you aren't ready to give, and I don't think you'll ever be ready. We're better off as friends."

He searched her eyes and whatever he saw in them made that little hope inside him die. She saw the moment it hit him. His hand slipped from her neck and he stood.

Her heart reached out, longing for him to stay. She wanted more of him, but she wanted too much. She took a breath and leaned back in the chair, crossing her legs, clutching onto the arm rests to keep from following him as he walked to the door.

"What is it you want, Claire?" He turned at the door. His hand held the knob. "What is it that I can't give you?"

A tear slipped down her cheek, even as she smiled dejectedly. "Everything."

CHAPTER 29

LOGAN SHOWED UP AT HIS PARENTS' house on Sunday. He hadn't slept at all after he left Claire's. He'd found his own bottle of scotch and sat in his cold, dark apartment, drinking it straight from the bottle.

"You don't look so good." Kit wrinkled her nose as he came into the house. "Or smell too good. Did you bathe in alcohol last night? Didn't you shower today?"

Logan snorted. Like it mattered. Like anything mattered. He was doomed to play the whore forever. Tossed from one woman to the next. The only woman he wanted to hold on to wouldn't hold on to him back. Just like always.

"Mom!" Kit narrowed her eyes at Logan as he sank into one of the dining room chairs. "Logan's broken."

"What is it, Kit?" His mom came out of the kitchen wiping her hands on a kitchen towel. "Logan, sweetie, are you sick?"

Coming over, she pressed her hand against his forehead. He grabbed her hand and held it briefly against his cheek before releasing it.

He propped his elbows on the table and put his head in

his hands. For the first time in a long time, he wanted to cry. He wouldn't here, but maybe later when the alcohol wore off and the pain of losing Claire finally hit him.

Fuck, he was screwed.

"Kit, go finish stirring the gravy and pull the biscuits when the timer goes off." His mom waved Kit out of the room before she sat in the chair beside him. She took a deep breath and studied him. "What's going on?"

"I fucked up." Logan sighed.

"With Claire?"

Logan turned to her with a little surprise.

"Don't look at me like that. I'd have to be as blind as a bat to not notice things had become more serious between the two of you lately." His mom tipped back in the chair. "Give me a little credit."

"She told me she loved me, but that we were better off as friends."

"Did you tell her you loved her back?" His mother's eyebrow raised.

"What would be the point? I can't be what she needs me to be." He shook his head. He didn't think his love would help. He wasn't even sure why he couldn't define their relationship. It hadn't been a problem when they were pretending. So why did the idea make his chest feel heavy and the air too thick to breathe? "I want to give her everything, but I can't."

His mom rubbed his back and made a tutting noise. "I should have sat you down years ago and knocked some sense into you, but I assumed you'd figure it out on your own, given time."

Confused, he squinted at his mother. "What?"

"You do everything in your power to avoid being hurt. Even little things would make you withdraw when you were younger."

Logan sat back in his chair. "What are you talking about?"

"That valentine. Followed by the roller coaster ride with that girl. That was the last girl you claimed to love and she broke your heart."

"This is about Claire not Abby Crane." Logan shook his head. "She has nothing to do with this."

"Except she does." His mother wasn't making any sense. "When was the last time you asked someone to be your girlfriend, Logan O'Connell? And don't lie to your mother."

"Abby Crane," he grumbled.

"Exactly. You didn't like that feeling. Being rejected. Not once, but over and over again."

It had sucked. Cut him open and filleted his heart.

"I'm not sure anyone would be normal having their love thrown back in their face like that." She folded the napkin on the table in front of her. "That resentment grew within you. And then college girls started to fancy you. You let them fall all over you. Proving to that girl that someone else wanted you, but you never let them close."

"When did you become a therapist, mom?" Logan gave his mom a little smile.

"Shush and listen. You just never tried to keep one again. You could have fallen in love all over again. But you didn't want to risk a broken heart. After all, if you didn't want them, they couldn't hurt you."

That made a little sense.

"But then came Claire," she said.

The ache in his chest grew. He rubbed at it knowing it wouldn't ever go away.

"Logan, you loved that girl from the start. Going around saying she's your best friend, like you practically invented the words. You looked at her like she hung the moon just for you. But stubborn as you were, you kept playing around and pretending it didn't piss you off when she went off with other men. So you fucked around still."

"Jesus, Mom." He didn't want to talk to his mother about fucking.

"Watch it." His mother crossed herself before continuing. "You finally had her and what the hell happened?"

Logan flinched, knowing he was to blame. "I didn't want to label our relationship."

His mother shook her head at him in disappointment. "Every relationship needs a label. It doesn't have to be girlfriend, but it needs something to hold onto. Something to say I'm yours and you're mine. Something to bind your hearts together."

Maybe? But that feeling of suffocating. . . .

"She doesn't want me that way anymore. She just wants to go back to being friends." Logan picked at the napkin in front of him.

"Don't be daft." She snatched away his napkin. "You already had a label. Best friend was your label."

Logan stared at his mother.

"Have you ever called anyone else your best friend in your life?" She narrowed her eyes at him.

Logan thought back to his friends growing up. Never once had he called anyone his best friend. Just Claire.

"I see those wheels turning. Go get your best friend back." His mom stood and looked down at him. "But first, go home and shower. You stink. You're excused from family dinner. I'll make you a plate to take with you."

Logan shook his head as his mother made her way back into the kitchen. She made it sound so simple, but what Claire wanted was a future. Something more than being just friends. He stared at the wedding picture of his parents on the wall, surrounded by pictures of him and Kit throughout the years.

Claire wanted everything.

His mom came out with a plate. "Now go get her. You don't meet a girl like Claire every day."

His mother was right. Claire was his best friend and that meant something to Logan. He just hadn't realized how much until now.

"I love you, honey." She hugged him. "Don't fuck this up."

Logan smiled and looked at his mother. "I won't fuck this up."

CLAIRE DIDN'T SHOW up at Legend's on Sunday, but Logan expected that. He'd still gone. Had a few beers at the bar and talked with Brick during the game. She also hadn't responded to his texts, but he knew he'd see her at work on Monday.

Logan sat at the conference table with his coffee and iPad ready for the meeting to start, but Claire's chair sat empty next to him. His leg bounced under the table. He had no idea how he would play this. No idea how to explain to Claire that they already had a label.

She was mad at him, so he'd dial it back. Make sure she knew they were still friends and he would ease back into the relationship thing.

"Is everything okay?" Lacy asked as she sat across from him next to Jonah. She nodded toward Claire's empty chair.

His leg stopped bouncing. Logan took a deep breath and shrugged. He didn't know. Claire said she wanted to stop to preserve their friendship, so he took her at her word. They should still be friends.

He screwed up on Saturday, but he didn't. Yes, a woman had come onto him, but he hadn't reciprocated.

This was part of being who they were and she should

know that. It didn't matter if he was with the woman he loved, someone would always think he was fair game. Maybe he could just convince Claire to never go to bars or clubs and then they wouldn't have any problems like that.

"I'm not the last one here?" Phoebe walked in and stood somewhat shocked at the two empty seats as opposed to one. "You didn't leave Claire tied up somewhere, did you, Logan?"

"I haven't seen her since Saturday night." Logan rubbed the back of his neck and his leg started bouncing again.

"I'm here. I'm here." Claire swept in, hurrying across the office floor. She dumped her purse on her desk and grabbed her tablet. "I'm sorry."

Morgan straightened. "It's not a problem."

Logan drank Claire in as she claimed the chair beside him. Not a hair was out of place. Her brown eyes collided with his briefly before she turned her attention to Morgan and Drew. She wore a tight, black skirt and loose pink blouse.

He didn't know how to make this right. But he had to.

He could barely focus on the meeting as he tried to think of what he could do to prove to her that he was all in. He wasn't even sure offering to call her his girlfriend would do it at this point. But he had to do something. So friends. Start with friends.

CLAIRE WANTED to scream "stop staring at me with those sad fucking eyes," but she held off. Her chest felt hollowed out and sitting next to Logan without feeling an ache in her chest proved to be harder than she thought it would be.

The meeting seemed to last forever. As soon as Drew said they were done, she was the first one up and back at her desk. She couldn't risk going to the break room and being alone with Logan.

Yes, she wanted to stay friends, but she also needed a little time. Space to get over him and get her feelings in check so they could remain friends. It wouldn't happen overnight, but with time, they should be back to where they were before.

Maybe the same as before but without them going out to pick up other people.

The whole day felt like everyone else walked on eggshells around the two of them. She made sure to never find herself alone with Logan in any space. If Lacy went to the break room, Claire went too. When Lacy left, Claire did.

She didn't care if everyone noticed. Everyone had noticed Logan and that chick. They knew her reasons. She wasn't doing him wrong and he hadn't technically done her wrong. Not really. They just didn't work as a couple. It was that simple.

It happened that way sometimes. It didn't hurt any less, but they'd make it through. She'd been through plenty of breakups. Of course, this time she didn't have her best friend to lean on.

Claire sighed as she walked into the copy room a little after five. She needed to grab her report off the printer. She planned to stop and grab some ice cream on the way home, because she wanted to change into her pajamas and embrace the cliché tonight.

Logan hadn't approached her all day. Some of the tension had eased out of her as the day wore on. Occasionally she'd glance up and catch him watching her thoughtfully, but he looked away immediately.

Today had been hard, but hopefully tomorrow would be a little easier. She had a few more things to finish up before heading home and then she could drink herself to sleep. And do it all over again tomorrow.

Glancing through her papers, she barely registered the door opening. The snick of the lock caught her attention though. She spun around.

Logan stood resting against the door. His dark eyes met hers.

"What are you doing?" She didn't move from beside the copier.

"Using my last chit."

Heat flushed through her body as she registered what he said, but she shook her head. "No."

He cocked his eyebrow up at her and took a step in her direction. Her back was against the copier, she had nowhere to run to. His smile took on that lazy, seductive edge that made her panties melt.

"I didn't say no on Saturday night," he reminded her, taking another step.

Her heart clattered as her pulse leapt. Yes, she'd used her chit. It'd been more of a joke. She could have just asked him to fuck her and both of them knew he would have been down for it.

"I have until the end of the month, but I want to use it now." Logan closed more of the distance between them until his dark summery scent caught in her nose, filling her with memories of him pressed against her.

"Anxious to get back out there?" She braced herself against the copier, refusing to cower. His attitude toward relationships was why they weren't still having sex without the necessity of chits. Not wanting to label what they had felt like he had one foot out the door the entire time.

"Not particularly. But I am anxious to touch your breasts again." He lifted an eyebrow as his gaze dropped to her cleavage revealed by the V in her shirt. Her nipples tightened under his gaze.

"We can't. We're not together." She shook her head and

held her papers in front of her like a shield. "That's not playing fair."

He stepped closer and looked down at her papers with a cocky smile. "What's not fair is you trying to deny my right to my winnings. The chit had nothing to do with us being together. Besides the fact that I couldn't stick my dick in anyone else until all of them were used."

She cringed.

"Which I haven't done." His hand came up to her jaw. "I assume you haven't had anyone else's dick in you?"

"What?" She tried to back away, but her ass bumped the copier again.

He lowered his head so they were eye level. His words slow. "Did you fuck someone else, Claire Bear?"

"Of course not, but that doesn't mean I'm going to fuck you." Claire glanced around, trying to grasp at straws. She'd barely walked away after the last time they'd had sex. She wasn't a fucking saint. "We said no hooking up at work."

His smile didn't quite reach his eyes. "That was part of our exclusivity deal which is null and void as of Saturday night when you told me you loved me but didn't want to fuck me anymore."

She pressed her lips together. Those words bit at her heart, but she refused to let him see her pain. "So you want to fuck me in the copy room at work as what? Payback for taking away your toy?"

Logan smiled and his fingers traced her jaw up to her ear. His hand curled around the back of her neck and tilted her head back slightly.

"It's not payback for anything, Claire Bear—"

"Stop calling me that—"

"It's something I won fair and square. You owe me one any time, any place fuck before the end of this month." He inched in until his heat surrounded her. "And I want it to be here and now."

Her resolve was slipping. Her traitorous body reacted to his nearness like an addict to their favorite drug. Her lips parted. Desire throbbed low and heavy in her belly. Her skin tingled with the need to be touched.

"This isn't a good idea," she whispered. His fingers gently massaged the back of her neck. Her eyes fluttered closed.

"You agreed to the terms and conditions of the bet. But if you want to back out, I won't hold it against you." His hands dropped to his sides.

She opened her eyes as her body protested the loss of his touch. "I—"

"But here's the thing." Logan tilted his head. His heat still close to her. His eyes darkened. "As long as I have this chit, you'll believe I'm holding out to use it. Instead of the fact that I don't want anyone but you. So let me fuck you now so I can prove to you that you're the only woman I want to be with."

Claire sucked in a breath. "It won't change anything."

He wrapped his hand around the back of her neck and brought his lips a breath away from hers. Her papers fell to the floor as her hands went to his chest, but she didn't push him away. She wanted to grab his heat and drag it into her, but she waited. Her breath stuck in her throat.

His lips brushed softly over hers and she almost groaned. Her fingers curled into his shirt. He smiled against her lips and said softly, "But it will feel so fucking fantastic."

He claimed her lips with his and everything in her softened. From chest to knee, they pressed together. It seemed a tragedy that a quicky in the office would be her last time with Logan, but it made some sense too. They had met here, became friends here.

How many times had she imagined this?

Fuck it. She wanted him. She wanted this. Would it prove

anything? No, but he was right, it would feel fucking fantastic.

The sound of her skirt zipper almost startled her. The fabric fluttered around her legs as it slid to the floor. Thankfully she'd worn a thong today, so when he grabbed her ass to pull her against his hard cock, he grabbed her bare flesh.

He groaned into her mouth and she forgot to think anymore. Her fingers went to work on his buttons, spreading his shirt open to feel the tight muscles beneath. She undid her buttons and then pressed her skin against his.

Heat flooded between her legs. The copier pressed against her back uncomfortably.

He lifted his mouth from hers. "Okay?"

She opened her eyes and melted from the concern in his. "The copier is jabbing into my lower back."

His fingers tightened into her ass cheeks as he glanced around the room. His slow easy smile made her throb. "Come on."

He backed up, drawing her with him, until he stopped in front of an armless chair. "Undo my pants."

Her fingers went to work on his belt, button and zipper.

"Pull them down." His fingers massaged into her glutes, making her thong move intimately against her. He took her mouth and deepened the kiss. She was on fire for him.

She shoved his pants over his hips and then hooked her fingers in his boxer briefs and drew them down, freeing his cock. Her hand wrapped around him and stroked his length.

He lifted his mouth from hers. She opened her eyes and he searched hers. She could see the desire and longing in his, but also a hint of hurt. He lowered to the chair and then walked her forward to straddle his legs while standing. Her hands slipped under his shirt onto his shoulders.

He kissed her belly and it trembled. He lifted his gaze to hers. His hands lowered on her ass until his finger slipped under her thong and pressed inside her sex. Her hands tightened on his shoulders and her eyes fluttered shut.

"So fucking wet." His whisper was harsh.

Her core tightened around his finger. Heaven help her, she wanted Logan. Just as much as she did Saturday. This lust might never go away. That could be a problem. How could they stay friends when she knew he held this much power over her body?

He drew her bra out of the way and his mouth closed over her nipple. He toyed with her nipple with his lips and tongue. Her brain shut off, becoming all about the need, the desire, the want.

Even as he rocked his finger in and out of her, she could feel him reaching into his pocket with his other hand. When he switched to lavish attention on her other breast, his finger slipped out of her.

Gah, she needed it back. She needed him back. Inside her, driving her crazy.

Every pull on her nipple made her need more. His fingers tangled in the strings of her thong and when he tore them off, she gasped and looked down at him.

He lifted his face from her breast and met her eyes. "Ride me."

Her heart ricocheted in her chest. A condom covered his cock and she lowered herself down over him.

He hissed as she engulfed him. When they were fully seated together, he lifted her legs to wrap around to the back of the chair. "Find the rung."

Her heels hooked into the rung, giving her leverage. He grabbed her neck and pulled her into a kiss. He devoured her like he couldn't get enough of her. Like this was the last time they would be here, tangled together, drawing pleasure from each other's body. Like he loved her.

Her heart stopped and she lifted her mouth from his.

His eyes opened. All the teasing was gone. Logan's amber eyes looked lit from within. Holding her hips, he lifted her slightly up his cock and then lowered her back down. He did it over and over again, while staring deep into her eyes.

"Believe me when I say I only want you." He closed his eyes and shook his head. "I suck at this—"

She chuckled and using the back of the chair as leverage, she lifted herself more and then came down on him. "You do not suck at this."

He gave her a half smile. "I suck at the emotional stuff. I'm afraid to get hurt."

She started a slow pace of lifting and lowering, teasing both of them. "Everyone's afraid."

He took a deep breath and pulled her mouth back to his. Against her lips, he murmured, "I love you, Claire. I will do whatever it takes to prove that to you."

Her heart swelled in her chest as his mouth crashed over hers. No more room for anything existed as he helped her quicken the pace. She soared toward the edge, uncertain what the future held for either of them. Knowing once this was over, they would be over.

But for now, the need overwhelmed her ability to think. All she could do was wrap herself around the man she loved and succumb to the pleasure he always provided. Every inch of her skin touched his. His thrusts matched her lifts until they both fell over the edge into oblivion.

She collapsed against his shoulder as she tried to regain control over her erratic breathing. His arms tightened around her.

"I'm yours, Claire," he whispered. "For as long as you want me."

She allowed herself to bathe in this moment. To feel his love and her own, like this was meant to be. She wanted to believe. She wanted to have faith in him. To trust him with her heart.

It would be so easy to get carried away.

It already hurt. How much more would it hurt in a month or a year? Better to take this pain now.

She straightened and lifted off of him. He released her as he helped her up. She turned away, not willing to let him see the tears pooling in her eyes. He said he loved her. But it wasn't enough. She focused on getting dressed, and from the rustling behind her, so was he.

Finishing straightening her skirt, she finally turned around. Logan held out her papers to her.

"Thank you." She took them and held them to her chest.

"Anytime." His crooked smile held only a little flirtation in it.

"I still can't trust you." She turned her back on him and shut her eyes. She didn't know how he could prove to her that she could be enough for him, that he wouldn't leave her for someone easier. Too many nights of watching him walk off with someone else had scarred her heart worse than she had known.

"I know." The words were soft and resigned. "I love you."

It was a kick to her already bruised heart. She went to the door and unlocked it. Her hand on the doorknob, she turned back to look at him.

He stood with his hands in his pockets, next to the chair. When she lifted her gaze to meet his, she saw determination in them. Her heart skipped a beat and she left the room.

CHAPTER 30

Logan kept away from Claire for the most part during the week. He sent Claire texts at night saying that he missed her. Even though he worked with her every day at work. She didn't text back. Proving to Claire that he meant what he said was an impossible task.

He couldn't stop women from hitting on him, but he could control who he went home with. He could put a hold on his sex life to prove to her he was serious, but how long would that take to win her back? A week? A month? A year? Five?

He'd be willing to make it happen if he thought it would change her mind.

It was Thursday morning. When he walked into the break room, Claire was putting away dishes like every other day.

"Good morning, best friend." Logan prepared the coffee machine.

"Good morning." She didn't even glance his way as she put away the coffee mugs.

"Legend's tonight?" Logan rested against the wall across from the coffee as it brewed. "Giants vs. Washington. Wings, mozzarella sticks, French fries. As much beer as you can drink. How bout it?"

Claire closed the dishwasher. Even though she hadn't responded to any of his texts, he still sent them. Sometimes he talked about the college games he'd watched during the evenings.

"Wear your game day gear. I was planning on going home to change." Logan shrugged and tried to appear nonchalant, but this was what they did as friends. If they were really still friends, they could do this together. "I'll be on my best behavior and we can trash Washington Football Team and figure out what their new nickname will be."

She arched an eyebrow at him. "Anything is better than what they had. I personally like the idea of Warthogs. The mascot uniform would be hilarious."

A smile tugged at his lips. This was what he missed. Him and Claire just hanging out.

"So what do you say?" Logan asked.

"Sure. I could use a beer or five." Claire winked at him before she grabbed her coffee mug and filled it from the finished coffee pot. "It's been a long week."

She could say that again. Last week, he'd had Claire in his bed and the time had flown. This week his bed had been cold and lonely. No texts in the middle of the night asking what was on ESPN. No late-night discussions about who would most likely be drafted out of college ball next year. No Claire.

"Meet you there at eight?" Logan kicked off the wall and grabbed himself a cup of coffee.

Claire nodded and she took a sip of coffee. "Sounds good."

All day he fought the urge to hold her, press her up against a wall and kiss her until she remembered how good they were together. But he knew she remembered. It just wasn't enough to hold her to him.

He went back to his desk to finish up his day.

Logan showed up at eight and grabbed them a table at Legend's. He even placed their order before Claire walked in. She had on a Giants jersey over her game day jeans and sneakers. Her hair was slicked back into a ponytail, but she hadn't bothered to take off her makeup from the day.

As always, she was gorgeous.

She claimed her stool as the server set their beers down. "Nice."

He lifted his pint glass in a silent salute to her and downed half of it. When he set his glass down, she was still chugging. Her throat worked as she poured the entire contents down her throat.

Fuck, he needed something non-sexual to focus on or this whole evening would give him blue balls from hell. He listed Superbowl winners starting with last year's and stared up unseeing at the screen.

Claire seemed content to let him stare. She ordered another beer and it arrived with the appetizers. They didn't always talk before, so when the game came on, they both focused on that.

"That's my fucking quarterback, you deranged hippo." Claire threw her wing back down on her plate and glanced around the table.

"I don't think Brick wants you to throw *anything* at the TV." Logan gestured with his chin toward the bar. Brick stood behind it with his arms crossed, looking directly at Claire.

With a belligerent look, Claire wadded up a napkin and held it up to Brick. He narrowed his eyes on it, but then gave her a slight nod. She grinned and watched the screen until the "deranged hippo" defensive tackle showed. She nailed his image in the nose with her napkin.

"Feel better?" Logan ate a fry as Claire collapsed back into her chair.

"You want to trade?" Claire leaned forward on the table. If she were wearing anything else in her closet, he'd have a spectacular view of her cleavage, but not so much in a jersey. Small favors.

"Trade?" He met her gaze.

"My quarterback for your quarterback in fantasy football." She raised an eyebrow.

"Yeah, right. My guy is set to go to the fucking Superbowl, while your guy can't even cross the line of scrimmage. Let alone get off a good throw before that hippo takes him down."

"He's usually much better."

"But you don't want to keep him?"

Claire shrugged. "You can't keep everyone. Sometimes a trade makes sense."

Logan pressed his lips together. Shit. The parallels to their situation made him want to defend keeping her quarterback. The trade didn't even make sense to either of their fantasy leagues.

"Maybe give the guy a chance." Logan leaned back in his chair and gestured to the TV. "You can't judge a quarterback on one game and definitely not on a few plays. If teams did that, they wouldn't keep anyone around long."

Claire picked up a wing and devoured it, while glaring at the screen. "Sometimes when a guy shows you he sucks, maybe you should cut your losses."

Which was exactly what she did to him. Based on their history of hooking up together. He grabbed the mozzarella stick basket and devoured them as they returned to watching the game. But his mind wouldn't settle on the game.

His whole sex life had been about the next conquest. Sure he screwed around multiple times with some women, but he never gave them anything more than a good time. No promises.

Falling in love with Claire hadn't been sudden like a lightning bolt strike, but he'd always known more was there.

His best friend. His confidant. His other half.

If she hadn't made the first move that night, would he ever have been bold enough to reach out to her? Ever?

Fuck.

He honestly didn't know. Fear had wrapped itself around his heart and held it away from anything that could potentially hurt it. Anyone who could possibly reject him.

Sure he'd been rejected by chicks at the club or bars for sex, but none of them meant half as much as Claire did to him. Claire didn't just make him want to fuck her, he wanted her in his arms. He wanted permission to just reach out and hold her. To snuggle with her and watch a movie. To be the one she turned to when she needed someone to listen to her.

He didn't want just right now with her.

He straightened in his chair. He knew what he needed to do.

"I've got to go."

Her gaze pulled from the screen. "What?"

He smiled and put a few twenties on the table. "I have to go."

"But it's the third quarter?" Her eyebrows twisted and she gave him a look that said he was being weird.

His heart swelled in his chest. "Yeah, something important came up and it can't wait another minute."

By ten the next morning, Claire was worried about where Logan had taken off to, because he hadn't shown up to work.

Last night it had just started to feel like old times. Watching the game and hanging out. Talking about the game.

Then without warning, he had to leave. No phone call. No text alert. They'd been talking about the quarterback and fallen into a comfortable silence. And bam, gotta go. Logan out.

Claire glanced over at Logan's empty chair and then the closed door of Morgan and Drew's office. Phoebe was in a meeting with Aiden in his office. Lacy and Jonah were in deep discussions about the use of a clown in a dog food commercial.

As he was against the use of clowns, Jonah kept showing clips of *It* to Lacy.

Where the fuck was Logan?

Claire stood and grabbed her coffee mug, intent on a refill. But instead of the break room, she went up front to Emily.

"Emily?" Claire felt stupid being up here, but that didn't stop her.

Emily lifted her head and smiled. "Hey."

"Has Logan called in?"

Emily shook her head and gave Claire an encouraging smile. "I'm sure he's just running late or on a project or something."

"You're right." Claire waved her hand like it wasn't anything. She headed into the break room and filled her mug. She needed a minute. A minute to gather her thoughts and not worry about Logan's whereabouts.

She sank into the chair and stared at the door. The radio silence from Logan drove her nuts. He didn't even text last night to say he missed her. She may not address his texts, but something in her fluttered at seeing that every night before bed.

Who was she kidding? She missed him, too. In so many

ways, but her heart ached every time she thought about reaching out. If seeing him with another woman had hurt this bad now, how would it feel when he actually cheated on her?

She sipped her coffee.

"Claire!"

Her head snapped up at Logan's voice. Leaving her coffee on the table, she left the break room. Logan stood in the middle of the office. Drew and Morgan were in their office doorway while Aiden and Phoebe stood in his. Lacy smiled while leaning into Jonah. Emily stood at the end of her desk so she could see.

Finally she let her gaze fall back on Logan. From his freshly cut dark hair to his clean shaven jaw, he looked good enough to rub against. He wore an actual grey suit instead of his button down and ties. The cut followed his trim figure perfectly.

She took in a deep breath and finally focused on his golden brown eyes. They looked at her with so much love, her heart got stuck in her throat.

"Sorry to interrupt everyone's day." Logan glanced around with a smile. "But you guys weren't working that hard anyway."

As a few chuckles sounded, he stepped forward. He took her hand in his and she almost jerked it back. His touch was so warm and she wanted it, but she couldn't have it. But for now, she didn't take her hand from his and let his warmth curl up her arm.

"I need to tell you something, Claire."

"Shouldn't we talk in private?"

"No. Fuck that. I want everyone here to know what the hell you do to me." Logan grinned and winked at her. "I'm not a poet and I'm not quite as dramatic as Jonah, but I knew from the moment I saw you that I needed you in my life."

She started to slip her hand from his, but he caught it and stepped forward bringing his warmth closer to her.

"I thought we were meant to be friends. After all, you're so cool and smart and an actual football fan. You have a mouth that frankly I'm in awe of most days. You make work fun. And pretty soon I told everyone you were my best friend. And you are."

Claire glanced at Phoebe who smiled at her. "Logan, I don't understand—"

"That's what I'm trying to do here. I want to clarify some things." Logan waited until her gaze found his again. "I have never had a girlfriend before in my life. I have never had anyone I called my best friend before. I thought being your best friend would be enough. The attraction was always there for me. I always wanted you but couldn't have you. But when you kissed me at your lake house, something new formed between us. Pretending to be your boyfriend wasn't an act. I just had to do what I always wanted to do but was too afraid to do.

"I fucked things up though." Logan squeezed her hand. "I thought the label would be too much. That calling you my actual girlfriend would be inviting rejection. To me, you will always be my best friend."

Claire pressed her lips together and pulled back her hand, pressing them against her pounding heart. "I can't do this, Logan. I can't wait around until someone else tries to take you from me or you go willingly into someone else's arms."

"Then stay in mine." Logan dropped to one knee and pulled out a box from his pocket.

Her brain couldn't make sense of what it was seeing.

"Claire Elizabeth Lake, I want you to be my best friend for life. Will you marry me so we can be together without worrying about other people?"

"Are you insane?" Claire asked, taking a step back. Her heart thumped. "What the fuck, Logan?"

He raised his eyebrow, but scooted forward on his knee to get closer to her and opened the box. What the hell was he thinking? A princess cut shaped diamond sparkled in the office light. It was beautiful. It was perfect, but he was insane.

"You and I will never be ordinary, Claire Bear. We can't just date. I don't want to waste another minute of you wondering when I'll sleep with someone else. It's not fair to you to fend off other women. I don't want to spend nights fending off other men. I've known for a year the only person I could ever see me spending the rest of my life with is you.

"So, fuck it, let's get married."

Her heart had pounded harder with each of his words, but his last statement. . . . Claire narrowed her eyes at him. "Fuck it?"

He stood and placed the ring box in her hand. "I want you with me always. I don't want to share my time with anyone else but you. I love you. Probably from the moment I met you. There's no one more perfect for me for the rest of my life than you. So yeah, I want to lock that down and put a ring on it. I want a ring on my finger that will discourage the ladies. Probably not all of them—because I'm gorgeous, but instead of saying I have a girlfriend, I want to say I'm in love with my wife."

Claire turned the ring box over in her hand. Her heart beat so hard she was afraid something might rupture. This was too soon. She wanted commitment, but this was over the top. "Logan—"

"That doesn't sound like a yes voice." Logan closed the distance between them. His hand wrapped around the nape of her neck and tipped her head up toward his. She could see the love in his eyes. "No one has ever made me feel the way I feel when I'm with you. I would be an idiot to let you go. I know it seems fast, but we have the rest of our lives to take it slow. Together."

Her insides melted. Claire cupped her hand against his jaw. "You know you kind of trapped me in a corner here."

"Did I?" He gave her a cocky grin. He knew exactly what he did.

"Asking in front of the office isn't very professional." She raised an eyebrow at him, even as a small smile tugged at her lips.

"We all know everyone else in this office bones on the regular." He leaned in close to her ear and whispered loud enough for everyone to hear. "The copy room has a lock for a reason."

Claire laughed.

"What's it going to be, best friend?" Logan held up his pinkie with a smirk. "Best friends forever?"

She went up on her toes and pressed her lips against his. His arms wrapped around her as his lips claimed hers like he didn't care if everyone watched. She pulled away and took in a deep breath.

"I love you, Logan, but if I marry you. . . ."

He opened his mouth, but she pressed a finger over it.

"*If* I marry you, you have to stop calling me Claire Bear."

"Deal, no take backs." Logan looked around the room. "You heard her as long as I stop calling her Claire Bear, she's my wife. That's completely legally binding. You're all witnesses."

"Logan!" Claire grabbed his chin and turned his smiling face to hers.

"Let's go to the copy room." Logan winked.

She shook her head. "I didn't even say yes."

"But you will." His tone was confident and his eyes danced.

"This is crazy." She smiled and traced his lower lip with her thumb.

"I brought champagne. Hope you don't mind not working for the rest of the day. I feel like celebrating." His eyes focused in on hers. "I love you, Claire Bear."

She rolled her eyes. "I love you, Wolverine."

He lowered his lips to hover over hers. "Say it."

She grinned against his lips and then whispered, "Yes."

EPILOGUE

"Get your fucking head out of your ass, ref!" Claire looked around the table for something to throw, but Logan had already snatched the towel off the table.

Her dark eyes lifted to him and narrowed. He held out a napkin. She sighed and wadded it up and threw it at the TV.

"It's just not as satisfying." Claire slumped in her seat at the bar table.

Brick nodded at Logan. Logan just smiled and shrugged his shoulders.

"Why do they always play like a bunch of prissy-ass babies in the preseason?" Claire said around a bite of wing. "It's like they aren't even trying."

The server stopped by with two new beers. Claire grinned at the server before downing half the beer. Her ring glinted in the light. She put down her mug and belched twice.

"My wife, everyone," Logan said to no one in particular.

Claire stuck her tongue out at him. "You didn't have to

actually put a ring on it. That was your idea. I was good with living in sin."

Logan smiled at her. They'd gotten married four months ago. Even though he'd been willing to fly to Vegas the next day, Claire and both of their mothers had insisted on having time to actually plan a wedding. "I prefer living with my wife. Do you want the last wing on your plate?"

"Do you want to keep your fingers?" Claire asked while practically hovering over her plate of food like a wild dog over a carcass. Logan was tempted to try to snatch something off her plate just to see if she'd bite him.

Logan shook his head as the game came back on. He wrapped his arms around Claire's waist and drew her back on her bar stool to rest against him. Still focused on the game, she leaned into him. He inhaled her rosemary and mint scent and held his breath for a moment.

Her hands came up to weave into his and her head propped against his shoulder. He could just see her smile from this angle. He exhaled. Nothing better than a good game, good food, and the love of his life in his arms.

"I love you," he said into her ear.

"I love you, too." She settled more firmly against him. "Order me another beer and I'll belch you the National Anthem."

Logan laughed. "You do that and I'll have to use one of my chits here at Legend's."

"I still think you cheated."

"I'd never cheat at minigolf." Logan squeezed her.

"To get extra chits you would," she grumbled.

"You're probably right. But I didn't. Now shush, I'm trying to watch the game."

She pinched his arm at being shushed, but she settled in. Fuck, he loved this woman.

ALSO BY AMY LARK

Just Ad Love Series

Not Quite Enemies

Not Quite Roommates

Not Quite Faking It

ALSO BY AMANDA BERRY

L.A. Cinderella PUBLISHED BY HARLEQUIN

Fox Creek Series

Yours at Last

One Night with the Best Man PUBLISHED BY HARLEQUIN

More Than Friends

ACKNOWLEDGMENTS

These two almost wrote themselves. Logan's and Claire's evolving relationship was so much fun to write. I hope you enjoyed reading it.

Thank you to Bria Quinlan for editing this book and helping me make Logan a hero to root for, while maintaining the sexy fun of the story. MK Book Editing for providing copy edits even if I don't like copy edits. Amanda Bonilla for proofreading and catching the things my eyes just can't find at this stage. And for the wonderful covers, thank you Sarah Kil Creative Studio.

My writing life wouldn't happen without Jeannie, Shawntelle, and Sela. We've been together since the start of this crazy journey for all of us. The encouragement and help we provide each other is necessary to keep me sane in this career.

To the Hermits! Our beach retreat helped me get back on task and a lot of the words in this series were made during our time together.

To the friends I've made during the pandemic and who kept me accountable for every word written. Who knew video sprints were what I was always looking for? To Carrie, Sarah, Holly, Selena, Danielle, Ivy, and a whole host of others: Thank you for being my daily push I need to stop procrastinating and do!

ABOUT THE AUTHOR

Amy Lark is a contemporary romance author. A Midwest girl stuck in the swamps of the South, she lives with her husband, her dog, and two cats. When not writing steamy romance, she's doling out advice to her children and bowing to her pets many demands. Find out more about upcoming books at amylark.com.